SWITCHBACK

SWITCHBACK

a novel

Clair M. Poulson

Covenant Communications, Inc.

To Ruth, who is there for me in both good times and bad.
I would find no success in life without her constant support and love.

Chapter One

"Ah, this is the ticket," I breathed aloud, plunging my bare feet into the roiling water of my hotel's outdoor Jacuzzi and taking a strawberry smoothie in hand. This was precisely the way a vacation should be—full of rest, relaxation, good food, and, most of all, peace. I opened my eyes just long enough to take in the ocean horizon stretching in front of me, then closed them and sunk up to my chest into the massaging jets. Two weeks in sunny San Diego had been a good idea, and I had come at just the right time. April meant no students, few families—I practically had the hotel to myself during the day—and of course, great weather.

A musical ring sounded from a nearby pool chair. I had an incoming phone call. *Leave it, Rocky. Leave it.* I squeezed my eyes tighter, convincing myself to ignore my phone and focus on my emotional well-being—the stress of the past year had really taken its toll on me. But habit is strong. By the time I had grabbed a towel and picked up my pants from the chair, the ringtone had started its merry tune again.

I pulled the phone out of a front pocket and, without checking who was calling, said, "Hello, this is Rocky."

"Rocky, I need a favor." I recognized that commanding voice almost immediately. Glenn Gridley, wealthy cattle rancher, professional rodeo calf roper, and ill-tempered old man.

"Hello, Glenn. I'm out of town right now," I said shortly. Glenn and I went way back. I had worked on his ranch for a year before his mission and had done a series of investigations for him over the years. But our last meeting hadn't ended well at all, and I was not in the mood to take up another of his projects.

"Don't give me that, Rocky," he growled. It was hard to forget that deep voice when it was raging. It was on the brink of rage now. "Someone stole my best roping horse!"

"What?" I paused as I processed this information. I was familiar with the horse in question: a solid brown quarter horse that had brought fame and fortune to his owner throughout the rodeo circuit. A horseman myself, and a fan of rodeos, I had watched from the stands numerous times as Glenn and Badger won competition after competition over the past three years. Badger, a six-year-old stallion, was said to be valued at somewhere in the neighborhood of a quarter of a million dollars. Besides winning a lot of money in the rodeo arena, he brought his owner five thousand dollars every time he stood at stud, and he was in high demand. If Badger was, indeed, missing, this was a real tragedy.

"I'm sorry to hear that," I said sincerely. "What are the police doing about it?"

"I haven't reported it," he said, the anger in his voice so strong now that it made me wonder how a guy could be so cantankerous when asking for help.

"Why—"

"I have my reasons, Rocky. Don't push me on this. I want Badger back. After you find him, then we'll talk about going to the cops."

I sat on the pool chair next to my pile of clothes and looked out over the blue Pacific while I thought about what to say next. I was not about to give up my vacation to Glenn Gridley. Although I knew him to be a decent man—and he clearly loved his family, as I'd seen firsthand—he and I were not exactly friends. He had a volatile temper that could erupt without warning, and that kind of personality gets tedious after a while. I found myself regretting not changing my cell phone number when I had the chance, but I hadn't expected to hear from him again after his tirade six months ago.

I heard a faint "You there, Rocky?" from my phone as I thought back on that day years ago. It was late October, and I was representing a client who I later discovered was married to Glenn's youngest sister. They were in a nasty divorce battle, and Glenn's brother-in-law had retained me to look into certain activities he claimed his wife was involved in. The moment I learned that the

Gridleys were involved, I was ready to back out, but then I uncovered evidence that my client was lying both to me and to his soon-to-be ex-wife. I had not yet finished my report when I got a visit at my office from Glenn and his three daughters. That was a memorable day in more ways than one.

"Rocky!"

I guess I'd stalled long enough. I wasn't at all sure that I would like to have Glenn Gridley for a client again. I could envision us butting heads. "Mr. Gridley," I began. I could hear his breathing quicken at my formal address. "I am unavailable at the moment. I am out of state and don't expect to return for a while yet."

"How are you going to find my horse if you aren't even in the area?" the upset rancher demanded.

"I don't recall telling you that I'd take your case," I said mildly. "And after our meeting in my office in October—"

He cut me off. "Forget that," he said, as if his simply giving the order meant that I could easily wipe our previous association from my rather good memory. "I was angry because I thought that you were trying to spread dirt about my little sister. My daughters convinced me that you did, in fact, do her a favor. I was wrong, and I apologized."

Indeed he had. And it was true that I had done him a favor. But I look for truth, not for dirt. Once Glenn had become calm enough to listen to me and his three daughters, he'd told me that he appreciated what I'd done. But I will never forget his angry accusations against me. From that point on, I had promised myself that I'd have nothing to do with Glenn Gridley.

I hadn't completed my thought, so I said, "I don't know why you want me to go after your horse. I got the impression that you didn't care much for me. If you can't trust me, I don't see how we can work together."

"Look," Glenn said, taking a deep breath. I could tell he was trying to keep his tone light but it was a struggle. "I know things haven't been that great between us for a long time, but I need your help today. I want my horse back, *pronto*. You know what his disappearance means to me."

There was a long pause. Then he said, "This has nothing to do with personal feelings. It was my brother-in-law who I didn't like, not you. I admit that you were fair. And I believe you can accomplish what I don't want to ask the cops to do—I don't want or need that kind of publicity. Also, they probably wouldn't work as hard at solving it as I think you would. You know our family better than any cop." That almost sounded like a compliment.

"Glenn," I tried again as I strolled toward the salty water of the Pacific. "I am far away on vacation. Let me suggest a couple of other investigators you might try."

That wasn't the answer he was after. "You do investigations!" he exploded. "My money is as good as the next guy's. Name your fee, and I'll have a check ready as quick as you can get back."

This wasn't going well. I heard a female voice in the background, a gentle, calming voice that I recognized. My heart did a small flip as I listened to her say, "Dad, shouting at him isn't going to help. You know he can do the job. Why don't you let me talk to him?"

I could picture the proprietor of that voice as though she were standing in front of me. Shanice Gridley was a special person to me. Even though she was four years my junior, being with her had always felt comfortable, and we'd spent a lot of time together when I worked for Glenn. I will always remember her long, brown hair flying in the wind as we rode through the fields of her father's ranch, inspecting fences, checking cattle, and laughing about her younger sister Cindy's many admirers. The last time I had seen Shanice, Cindy, and their youngest sister, Jena, had been at that October meeting in my office.

Glenn's voice was slightly softer when he spoke again. "Shanice wants to talk to you," he said. "If you won't listen to me, perhaps you'll listen to her." Apparently she still had a calming effect on him. Maybe she would understand that I was on vacation, that I really wasn't in any position to begin an investigation right now—not for Glenn or anyone else.

"That's fine," I said, not bothering to tell him that I'd listened to every word Shanice had just said. What I'd done was reject his request for help. If he interpreted that as my not listening, then I supposed that I'd be accused of not listening to his daughter as well.

"Hi, Rocky. How are you?" Shanice asked. Her voice seemed slightly deeper than I remembered. Sadder, even?

"Hi, Shanice. I'm great. How are you doing?" The conversation had just begun, and yet suddenly, I didn't want it to end. I missed talking to Shanice Gridley.

"I'm fine. I'm sorry to ask you to take this case, but it's really important to us. We love Badger, and the ranch just won't be the same without him. I don't know what we'll do if we don't get him back."

I could already feel my resolve wavering, but I tried to remind myself of the importance of my time in California. I hadn't taken a vacation for years. Who knows when I'd do it again?

"It's great to talk to you, Shanice, but I'm on vacation right now," I said. "The past six months have been crazy. It took a lot to get away, and I just don't think I can take the case. You understand, right?"

"Of course I understand, but I'm sure you also realize how much we need you. No one knows our family, or our horses, better than you. Our horses are our life—we love them like family. And you really are the best private investigator Dad's ever seen." I could hear Shanice's emotion through her words. She was desperate.

But her approach wasn't fair. Glenn was concerned about the value of the horse both now and in the future. Shanice, on the other hand, cared about the horse as an individual, much as I felt about my two horses. She made Badger's theft a personal rather than a financial matter. As I walked along the beach in front of the hotel, I finally squared my shoulders and focused on what was in front of me. The cool Pacific Ocean rolled over my feet as a large wave pushed ashore, and I made my decision.

"Shanice," I began. "As I explained to your father, I am on vacation and won't be back in Utah for several days. You need someone who can go to work right now. I can give you names of several great investigators who might be willing to help you."

There was no angry outburst, just a pleading request as she said, "I remember how smart and persistent you are. I know you probably thought you'd never hear from us again, but we need you. I convinced Dad of this, and he agreed to call you. Please, we need your help, Rocky. You understand our love for horses. Most of all, you know us, so I think you would be more likely to work harder for us than someone who doesn't. I hate to think what some awful person might be doing to that wonderful horse."

I took a deep breath. This sort of case needed immediate action, and I was enjoying my time alone on the beach. I was looking forward to another week away from the pressures of my work. "I'm sorry, Shanice," I said. "I'm simply not available now. I'll be back in a week. When I get there, if you haven't found Badger, then I'd be glad to help. In the meantime, you might consider trying someone else."

The phone was silent for a long moment. I could hear Shanice breathing into it. When she spoke again, there was resignation in her voice. "I'm sorry we bothered you. And I understand the fact that you don't have time to help us right now. I should have known better than to try to persuade you to return home and go back to work. One of the things I've learned about you over the years is that you don't let emotions persuade you. You work on facts, no matter which way they lead."

"Thank you," I said. "Let me refer a couple of other investigators." I gave her their names and told her where to find their numbers. "If I were your father, I'd also make a call to the Box Elder County Sheriff," I added. "I don't know him well, but I know him by reputation. I hear he's a very good lawman." Then I said something I probably shouldn't have, considering that I was on vacation. "If neither of the men I mentioned work out, call me back."

I'd no sooner broken the connection than I regretted saying that. I could only hope that one of my colleagues would take the job. If not, I had almost made a commitment. But I consoled myself with the hope that one of them would take the case. If so, it was probably the last time that this family would call me.

The surf was much higher now, and I decided to hit the water for a little while. I returned to the pool area to grab my clothes, then walked back to the beach and left the items on top of my towel a short distance from the water. Then I waded into the ocean, pulled on a pair of goggles, and backstroked between a nearby buoy and the shore for the next thirty minutes, frequently checking to make sure no one messed with my stuff on shore.

At around four p.m., I dried myself off, flashed a weak smile at a couple of young women who walked by, and then picked up a book in my room before heading for the pool area. Reading proved futile, however; I couldn't get the call from Glenn and Shanice Gridley out of my head.

Back in my hotel room, I showered and then sat down to plan the evening and the next day. There were a number of places I'd considered visiting when I first decided to take a vacation, but strangely, none of them held as much appeal now as they had done then. I had already visited a couple of temples in the area, attending a session in each one. I'd also gone to church in a singles ward in Los Angeles on Sunday. In the back of my head, I'd hoped that I'd find a pretty, single woman who might agree to spend an evening or two with me and guide me to the most interesting places in the city.

I'd dated some in my life, but at thirty-two, I'd never even come close to marriage. I'd thought that maybe I'd find a prospect in a singles ward in LA. That had been a stupid idea. I didn't meet anyone that sparked much interest in me, and if I had, I don't know that I'd have worked up the courage to ask her out. Part of my problem, I now realized, was that I was looking for the perfect girl. In fact, if I were honest with myself, there was no question that I compared every girl I met with Shanice Gridley. We'd been very close before my mission, and I had secret hopes of dating her when I returned. But it wasn't meant to be. She'd been married for six months by the time my mission was complete.

I had to admit that I wasn't exactly secure when it came to dating. I knew my failings, and I had always been afraid that the women I met could readily see them as well. I wanted a wife who I could connect with on a deeper level, and yet I don't think I'd ever given another girl a chance. I had been fooling myself all these years, and because of that, I was quite lonely. Maybe I'd always be lonely.

I lounged around for a few hours in my hotel room and then ate dinner at a restaurant on the top floor, alone. That was my life: alone. After dinner, I wondered what to do with myself. I realized with a start that my vacation wasn't all I had been telling myself it was; I was bored stiff. I pulled out my cell phone and made a call.

"Hello, this is Glenn Gridley," I heard a crusty voice answer. He was clearly still upset over the loss of his horse. Well, I'd called him this time, so I guessed I'd get to the point.

"Glenn, this is Rocky Revada."

"Your friends are no more agreeable than you are," Mr. Gridley growled.

"They aren't exactly my friends; they are my competition," I corrected the rancher.

"Then why did you refer me to them?" he asked accusingly.

"Because I'm on vacation," I admitted.

"So what is this call about?" he asked. "Have you thought of someone else you might refer me to?"

I took a couple of breaths before speaking. This guy could prove to be a difficult client. But since his call earlier, and especially after talking to his daughter, I had lost interest in my vacation. I let out the second deep breath and said, "I think I can be back by morning, if that's not too late."

Glenn Gridley might be a short-tempered guy, but he was also a decisive one. "You're hired," he said with finality. "Call me as soon as you're back. We'll meet you at your office first thing." I assumed that meant him and Shanice, and maybe a son-in-law and other daughters as well.

I was lucky and got a flight that would have me back in Salt Lake City by eleven that night. That meant that I could be in my house on my small farm outside Logan before one in the morning. I'd call Glenn at eight and be at the office shortly after that.

Chapter Two

I OPENED THE BLINDS ON the large window of my office, letting the early spring sunlight flood my small building in Logan, Utah. The clock on my wall announced that it was eight-fifteen in the morning. I sat down behind my desk and ruffled a few papers, an inadequate attempt at tidying up an office that clearly showed the lack of a feminine touch. It was usually a mess.

I had just finished shoveling most of the mess out of sight by the time my door opened and Glenn stepped in, followed by Shanice. There wasn't much change to the old man—he still wore the same worn, black cowboy hat, and his tall frame and tanned skin mirrored the hard life and temperament he was so known for. Shanice, on the other hand, had been transformed. I remembered her as thin when she'd come to my office in October, but she seemed tiny now. Her blue, Western-cut shirt hung loosely off her frame, as if it were two sizes too big. And her eyes had a haunted look, as though the life and energy I remembered had been drained long ago. *Had she had that look in October?* I wondered. I suddenly felt sick.

Trying not to show my reaction to Shanice's changed appearance, I offered them chairs in front of my desk and sat down, picking up a pen, which I poised over a yellow legal pad. At the same time, Glenn also pulled a pen from his pocket and pointed it toward his checkbook.

It was time to be professional. "I'll need some details," I said.

"Of course. Where should we start?" Shanice asked, her dark brown eyes concentrating on . . . my pen.

"Well, how about where your father's horse was last seen," I said, making a notation on the legal pad.

"That would be in his stall in our barn at the ranch," Glenn said with a stony face. "I personally attended to him at eight the night before last."

"And he was still there at ten when Cindy and I walked through the barn just before retiring for the night," Shanice added.

"I didn't notice anything out of the ordinary that night, but when I went back out at seven yesterday morning, Badger's stall door was hanging open, and he was gone," Glenn said.

"Do you still keep the barn doors unlocked?" I asked.

"Yeah. Up to this point, there hasn't been a need to lock them," the rancher answered. As I wrote on my pad, I pictured the enormous tan-colored metal barn in my mind. It was a short distance beyond the ranch house on the same private lane. Glenn continued. "Anyone stealing a horse would have had to pass the house, take him from the barn, and then either lead or haul him past it again."

"That isn't impossible, though, right?" I said, coming back to our conversation. Knowing his ranch as well as I did, I knew there were more ways than one to steal a horse from his place.

"Not impossible, but I can't imagine anyone trying it. There's no way anyone could take a truck and trailer to the barn without waking me up. I am a light sleeper," Glenn said. "They had to have led him out on foot."

"Could someone have led or ridden him across your ranch and out some back way?" I asked.

Glenn rubbed his chin. "Yes, of course that's possible. But you'll remember, my ranch is big. It's actually bigger now than it was when you were there. It would be a long walk in order to reach a gate somewhere."

"I'll want to have a look at your place," I suggested. "It will be a nice refresher, and I'll get a feel for the new changes. Now, let's talk about who you think might have stolen Badger."

"If I knew that, I'd have him back by now," Glenn growled.

My question had nothing to do with who he *knew* had stolen his horse. I rephrased the question. "I'm sorry," I said, trying not to sound too defensive. "What I meant to ask is if you know of any people who might want him and are dishonest enough to take him."

Glenn and Shanice glanced at one another. It was Shanice who spoke. "Not really. You've seen us in rodeo competitions before, and you've seen Badger in action." I thought back on the many times I'd watched Shanice and Glenn. Glenn was a very impressive roper, but the two of them together were stars. They'd received several honors as a team roping partnership. "Badger is one of the best roping horses, both for team roping as well as individual roping, in the western states. I'm sure lots of ropers would love to have him, and we've received offers for Badger numerous times, but I can't think of anyone who might want him bad enough to steal him," Shanice said, her brow furrowed.

"I can't either," her father added. "Anyway, if a roper took him, they'd never be able to use him. He would be recognized."

"Could you recognize him if you saw him? I remember Badger to be solid brown. Are you saying that he has distinctive markings unlike any other horse of similar size or body structure?" I asked.

"No, you're remembering right. He is solid dark brown—he has no white on him," Shanice said.

"Is he branded?" I asked.

Glenn's face darkened at that question. "No, I don't brand my horses. You should know that."

"True. What about tattoos, you know, inside his lip?"

"Nope, never done that either. But all of my horses are properly papered," he said gruffly. I could tell Glenn was not enjoying the turn of our conversation. "And their DNA is on file at the American Quarter Horse Association. When you find him we can prove he's mine."

"So it is possible that someone else could, after, say, a year or so, use him, and you couldn't be sure he was yours without pulling hair samples and having the DNA tested?"

Apparently that thought hadn't occurred to either of them before. Their eyes locked for a moment. Glenn slowly began to nod, and Shanice took a deep breath. This time it was Glenn who said, "Well, maybe from a distance, Badger would be like any other horse. But I would know him if I rode him—and possibly if I saw someone else ride him."

"Okay, that's something," I said. I had finished with my initial questions, so I said no more, but I could tell what I'd already asked had them worried. Glenn's brow was furrowed, and Shanice was staring unblinking at the floor.

"Listen, I think I have enough information to get started. I'll give it my best effort," I said, giving them a reassuring smile. "If you still want me to, that is."

"That's why we're here," Glenn said brusquely. He was still holding his pen and checkbook. We discussed my fees and what I would require as a retainer. He wrote a check, tore it out of the checkbook, and handed it to me.

"Sounds good," I said. I put the check in my desk, locked the drawer, and got to my feet. "Let's go over to your place, then." Shanice didn't get up when I did, and I realized that she hadn't said a word for some time. All she did was shift nervously in her chair, wringing her hands together. I caught her eye before walking around my desk.

"Is there something else?" I asked her, moving back behind the desk.

Her eyes grew slightly misty, and she fiddled with the top snap on her shirt. I sat down again and leaned toward her across my desk. Her father also sat down. "What is it, Shanice?" he asked, his typically gruff voice now soft as he placed a hand on Shanice's knee. Even his gaze was gentle as he waited for her to speak.

Her eyes looked up at her father, then finally met mine. She brushed a tear away and then said, "Alden Overton, my ex-husband, isn't exactly a great guy." I felt like I had just been punched in the gut. *Ex-husband?*

I shifted my eyes just long enough to see the rancher's face darken and his eyes narrow. I tried not to let the surprise show on my face as I said, "Ex-husband? I'm sorry, I hadn't realized you were divorced."

Shanice shrugged and sighed out a short laugh.

"Yeah," she replied. "It didn't work out. He turned out to be the exact opposite of the person I thought he was." She looked at the floor again as her shoulders slumped, then she leaned over and put her head in her hands. I had to change the subject. I figured I'd learn more about her failed marriage in due time.

"Are you suggesting that he might know something about Badger?" I asked.

She raised her head, nodded ever so slightly, and lowered her eyes. I waited, thinking that Glenn would say something, since the mention of his former son-in-law had seemed to negatively affect him. He waited for Shanice to continue, his concerned eyes on her profile. She finally looked up at me again and said, "I married stupidly. We divorced several years ago. My daughter was only two at the time." Again, another invisible punch in the gut. So Shanice was not only divorced but a mother. I kicked myself for being so surprised. She had been married for several years; it made sense that she should have a child. I'd never known her married name—to me she was Shanice Gridley, which is how I had always remembered her. I guess she was actually Shanice Overton.

She again grew silent, and her eyes shifted until they were looking past me at the painting of a band of wild horses on my wall. No wonder the life in her eyes was missing. She had been through a terrible situation and was clearly still in turmoil.

Her eyes shifted again to me, and she said, "I wouldn't put it past Alden, even though we've been divorced for four years. He calls me every so often and threatens to take me back to court and take my daughter."

"Is that a viable threat?" I asked, lifting an eyebrow.

"It darn sure isn't!" Shanice's father thundered so loudly that she jumped. "Shanice is a great mother, and she dotes on little Tyra." His face softened as he spoke his granddaughter's name.

Shanice said, "He remarried. I'm single, and his argument is that Tyra would be better off growing up in a family with two parents rather than a single parent—one whose whole life is wrapped up in the ranch."

"That's not true, and Alden knows it," Glenn said, his face again dark and angry. Those flashing eyes looked at me. "He just wants to quit paying child support. Not that he keeps up on it like the court has ordered him to. I agree with Shanice, Rocky. Alden *would* be capable of such a thing."

I looked over at Shanice. Her eyes were still misty. I would ask more about Alden later, I decided. So I shifted the focus of our conversation. "Are there any others you can think of who might do something like this?" I asked.

She shook her head, and again I stood. "Then let's go out to your ranch."

* * *

I drove my Chevy pickup into the Gridley ranch yard behind Glenn's black Ford. They stopped just past the large, rambling ranch house in front of the huge barn. I parked behind them and got out. Shanice shut her door and walked toward me, past her father's pickup, but only partway to me, and said, "Let's go inside the barn first, Rocky."

"Whatever you say," I answered. It felt great to be back on the Gridley ranch.

Shanice reached up and smoothed out her hair, waiting until I'd walked to where she stood. Then, side by side, we followed her father, who was already walking rapidly through the large, open barn door. I looked closer at the barn, and the surrounding ranch landscape, as we approached it. Just as Glenn had suggested, many things had been added or removed since the last time I had visited the ranch years ago. As I walked through the barn door, I noticed large skylights in the roof, which made the barn as bright inside as if the long banks of lights had been turned on. The barn still smelled of horses and hay, moisture, and faint ammonia, odors that brought back fond memories of my time on the ranch.

A row of stalls ran down two-thirds of the north wall. The other side of the barn was filled with a variety of farm equipment—tractors and so forth. There was also a small stack of hay near the center, and at the far end, there was a large round corral, one the Gridleys used to train their roping horses. There were also enclosed areas that I assumed still held tack, grain, and the ranch office.

Glenn had already stopped about sixty or seventy feet inside the barn. He opened a stall door, and as soon as Shanice and I reached him, he said, "This is Badger's stall." This was news to me. The stall had been used by a different roping horse when I had been there last. I studied the door and then the interior of the stall. It was much bigger than I remembered—approximately twenty by twenty feet. The Gridleys must have knocked down the old stalls and replaced them with a few larger ones. Beyond this observation, there was nothing noteworthy to see.

"These stalls are a lot bigger than I remember," I said.

"Yes," Shanice replied. "We had a section of the old stalls replaced with these large ones a few years ago."

"So not all of your stalls are this large?" I asked.

"No, only about half of them are. I like my best horses to have plenty of room when they're in here," Glenn said. I nodded.

"Do you keep Licorice Stick in one this size?" I asked, looking at Shanice as I spoke. Licorice Stick was Shanice's prized roping horse, a solid black gelding with nearly the same monetary value and rodeo credentials as Badger. In fact, he was Badger's half-brother.

Her face began to glow, a sight that warmed my heart. This was a glimpse of the Shanice I remembered. "Come with me," she invited. "He's right down here." She led the way three stalls farther along. It was the last of the large ones, I noted as I followed her. A beautiful black head stuck itself over the stall's half door. "This is Licorice Stick," she said, as a large pair of liquid eyes gazed at her and then turned their attention to me.

Shanice reached up and rubbed his forehead, but he pulled back into the stall. Shanice stood there staring at him, a puzzled look on her face. She opened the stall door and spoke to Licorice Stick as she checked the horse's grain and water buckets.

"Is something wrong?" I asked. Her confused reaction hadn't been lost on me.

"I don't know," she said a bit nervously. I said nothing, just waiting and thinking as I looked about the huge barn. Shanice disappeared into the stall and shut the door behind her. I noticed the large doors on the far end, past the round corral. I looked at Glenn, who was now standing next to me and fidgeting impatiently with his large hat. "I assume those doors on the west end of the barn are still in working order," I said.

"Of course they are, but we don't use them much," he responded.

"But is it possible that Badger could have been taken out that way?" I suggested.

"Yes, it's possible," he said gruffly. "But we always use this east end."

"But you are not the thief," I said blandly.

He slammed one fist into the stall door behind him, startling the stall occupant, and said, "By golly, Rocky, it never occurred to me that someone might use that end." He seemed more upset that he hadn't thought of it before me than he was that the thief might have used that entrance, but I let it pass. I had been prepared for Glenn's stubborn resistance to new ideas and information.

"That's understandable," I said, momentarily focusing my attention on Shanice's voice as she spoke to Licorice Stick from inside the stall. "If there are hoof prints going through that door, it would be safe to assume that the thief, or thieves, took your horse out that way." The remark had been casual, but Glenn seemed to agree.

"Let's go look," he said with a nod, striding purposely toward the west end of the barn. He slowed down after we'd passed the round corral. He was studying the ground carefully, as was I. When he looked up, there was anger in his eyes. "They went this way," he said conclusively. He took another step toward the door.

"Wait," I said, studying the dirt closely. "There are two sets of horse tracks going out and another coming in."

"So, maybe they led him around a bit before getting the door open," he said impatiently.

"Maybe," I said, still studying the dirt floor. "But look closely. There are clearly two sets of tracks here." That got Glenn's attention, and he bent over to where my finger was pointing out one set of tracks followed by a second, smaller set. "And look at this. Whoever took him was not wearing boots." I pointed to one set of tracks as I spoke. "Tennis shoes of some kind. Wait. The other tracks are boot prints. There must have been two people," I concluded, pointing to the second set of tracks.

"I see that," he agreed, shaking his fists. "I would sure like to get my hands on these horse thieves."

I ignored his comment and instead asked, "Can this door be opened from out there without coming inside first?"

"Yes, it has a hasp, but we never lock it," he said in disgust. He seemed upset enough that I wondered if he would be locking the barn doors from this day forward.

"Dad!" Shanice suddenly screamed, her voice filled with horror. "Come here."

Glenn spun on his heel and started running. I did the same. Shanice was shaking when we reached her. She was standing just outside Licorice Stick's stall. The horse had been haltered and was standing behind her. "What's the matter?" Glenn asked when we reached her.

"Something's not right with him, Dad," she said in a trembling voice.

"Then call the vet," he responded irritably.

"He's not sick. I've felt him all over. Physically, I think he's okay. He's just acting . . . I don't know . . . different." As she spoke, I watched her closely. That same puzzled look she'd had when she first attempted to rub the horse's head was still on her face, only it was more pronounced now, and her face was pale. Shanice never struck me as someone who would invent a situation. Her reaction was worrisome to me. Something didn't seem right.

A disturbing thought occurred to me at that moment. "Shanice," I asked as her father stepped to the horse and began examining Licorice Stick himself, "what's different about him?"

Shanice glared at her dad, then looked at me and let out a deep breath. "He isn't as friendly with me as he usually is," she said. "From the time he was a colt, Rocky, Licorice Stick liked to give hugs. You know, I'd put my arms around his neck and he'd nestle his nose in my back, almost like he was returning the hug. I tried that, and he didn't respond."

"Yeah, one of my horses does that," I said.

"And frankly, he doesn't look quite right, at least his face doesn't. You know how horses are. They all look slightly different, like people."

"To people who know horses," I added. "If you saddled him, would you be able to tell if he was acting the same as usual?"

"Yes. Licorice Stick has a certain feel to him. Every horse has. Are you suggesting that I ride him to make sure?"

"Saddle him," I said in response.

"What's the need for that?" Glenn asked, clearly getting angry. "I didn't hire you to play vet. Let's go back down to that end and make sure they took my horse out that way."

"Humor me," I said, returning the glare he was giving me. "If you want me to find your horse, I need as much information as I can get."

"But not about Licorice Stick!"

"When I asked you if you'd know Badger when you saw him, you told me you could be sure if you rode him," I reminded him.

Shanice had moved away, leading the horse over to what I remembered as a tack room. The rancher shook his head in frustration, but he followed me as I started across the barn to join Shanice.

She saddled her gelding in short order, and then she climbed on, right there in the barn. She directed him toward the open door at the east end. Her father and I followed wordlessly. Once outside, she rode around the side of the barn to the south side, where the road was dirt rather than gravel. Then she kicked him, and he took off at a lope. A hundred feet or so later, she pulled on the reins, and he came to a stop, throwing his head like he wanted to keep running.

Glenn snorted beside me, then he said, "My girl's right. That horse is definitely not acting normal."

"In what way?" I asked, my suspicions growing.

"Licorice Stick has a great sliding stop. He lowers his back end and slides. You know what I mean." I did. This was how Glenn and Shanice trained their roping horses. "He never stops roughly like that," Glenn continued, throwing a hand in the direction of his daughter. "He's acting like he doesn't know what he's doing."

Horse and rider loped back to us, and Shanice jumped off the horse. "Did you see that, Dad?" she asked.

"I sure did. He's not himself."

"Are you sure that's your horse?" I asked.

Both of them looked at me like I was nuts. "Of course it's her horse," Glenn said. "What are you suggesting, Rocky? We are not horse thieves."

"But someone is," I said. "Are you sure that's Licorice Stick?"

"He looks a bit off, but—" Shanice said, her voice trailing off. I watched as understanding began to dawn in her eyes. She looked abruptly at me, her eyes wide.

"Let me ask the same question that I asked about Badger," I said. "Does he have any identifying marks?"

"No, he's solid, just like the other one," Glenn said.

Shanice studied the horse for a moment, and then she said, "His face isn't quite right. But to be sure, he does have one identifying feature. There's a tiny patch of white under his tail. It can't be seen except when you lift his tail."

"Why didn't you think of this idea in the stall, when you first had concerns?" I wondered aloud to no one in particular. Shanice stuck her tongue out at me, and I suppressed a smile.

"Maybe I didn't think of it then, Rocky." She elongated the *r* in my name. "We're not all geniuses like you." I could tell she was frustrated but just teasing me. The lines of her mouth formed a smirk as she stepped around the back of her horse. As Glenn and I followed, I could just make out the words, "What normal person would think their horse had been stolen, when there's a horse standing right where he should be?" I smiled broadly then. Shanice's back was to me.

She lifted his tail and let out a soft shriek, her eyes growing big. "This is not my horse!" she said. As she turned toward us, her face went pale, and she began to tremble.

Her father also looked deeply affected by this news. His eyes glazed over a moment, and I wondered if he was calculating numbers in his head. Even as a gelding, Licorice Stick was worth nearly as much as Badger in the roping arena. After a few minutes, he seemed to accept the inevitable and looked at me with respect in his eyes. "How did you figure it out?" he asked.

"Remember when I pointed out two sets of horse tracks coming in from the back way and only one going out?" I asked. "But there were two sets of human tracks; one was made by someone wearing boots and the other by someone wearing tennis shoes. Both of those sets came in and went out."

"Rocky," Shanice said in alarm, "are you suggesting that someone took both my horse and Dad's but left this one in place of mine?"

"That's exactly what I'm saying, if you're sure this is not Licorice Stick," I said.

"Oh, I'm sure now. But DNA will prove it if we need to go that far."

"We don't need to do that at this point," I said. "Let's have a look at the far end of the barn again."

"Don't say a word about this to anyone," I cautioned a few minutes later as we again studied the area around the west door. "We don't want the thieves to know that we have any idea what they've done here."

"It's probably that worthless ex of yours," Glenn said fiercely.

Shanice nodded. "Could be," she agreed, hanging her head slightly. I put my hand on her shoulder, smiled, and whispered, "It's okay. Don't beat yourself up over something that happened four years ago."

"Thanks," she said, nodding. I wasn't sure if she believed what I said, but I wanted her to know that I still believed in her.

I had a lot more to do today, and I was anxious to get going, but there was one more thing I needed to know before I left. "Glenn,"

I began. He looked at me inquiringly, and I continued. "Have you changed the use of your land much since I was here? You have corrals here and fields back there. Is that just dry pasture?" I waved toward the many acres that could be pasture or hay ground or both. It was hard to tell this time of year since it was still early spring and nothing was growing. "And beyond that you must have a lot of undeveloped ground."

"That's right," Glenn agreed, "on both counts."

"How many ways are there to get onto your property back there?" I asked, waving to the west.

"There are several gates. And of course, a thief probably wouldn't hesitate to cut a fence. But like I told you earlier, it's quite some distance across my property, both to the west, the north, and the south. It would take time, but they could have led the horses all the way through the corrals and those fields and never have to go through our yard or past the house."

"Who would know that besides your former son-in-law?" I asked.

"Lots of people," he said thoughtfully. He looked at Shanice, who seemed lost in thought. She finally shook her head, and he said, "None that I can think of who might steal my horse . . . I mean, our horses."

That didn't answer my question, but I let it go for now.

Chapter Three

IT TOOK ME SEVERAL HOURS to check the gates around the Gridley ranch. There were signs of a truck and horse trailer having been parked near a seldom-used gate on the north side. It was well over two miles from the ranch house. Even a novice would have concluded that horses had been led fairly recently through that gate and loaded on a trailer. But I noticed something a novice might have missed. The horse trailer was a small one, probably an old two-horse trailer. The horses had milled around some. Tracks led back and forth through the gate, and it seemed that at least one horse had not wanted to get into the small trailer.

When I brought my conclusions to the attention of Glenn, he listened but seemed distracted, so I said no more about it. I thought maybe he'd have more interest after I'd gathered more solid evidence. After I'd taken a few photographs and made myself some notes, I left the ranch to begin trying to sort out the case I'd been hired to solve. Unfortunately, I didn't have much to go on yet. The name of Alden Overton, Shanice's ex-husband, was on my mind as I drove away from the ranch.

My first stop the next day was the home of Alden and his current wife, Pam, in Brigham City. Pam was home and told me that her husband had left earlier for his office in Ogden, where he worked as a financial consultant. When I arrived at that office, I learned that he had not shown up to work that morning. No one had any idea where he was or why he was several hours late.

I left there, wondering what to do next. I really needed to talk to Alden so I could try to get a sense of whether or not he was in any way involved in the disappearance of the two valuable horses. His failure to come to work was suspicious. I sat in my truck for a few minutes after leaving Alden's office. I may have looked idle to pass-ersby on the sidewalk, but I was actually very busy. I was thinking.

I eventually came to a conclusion: most major crimes like this one were motivated by one of two things, if not both. The first is money. The second is love gone sour. I wanted to talk to Alden about the failed love motive as well as the money motive. *Where else could I find him?* I wondered. After mulling that over in my mind for a few minutes, an idea formed, and I started my truck, intent on following up. I was on I-15 headed north when my vibrating cell phone announced an incoming call.

I glanced at the screen, and when I saw who the caller was, I pulled over to the side of the freeway and took the call. "One of my men just called me," Glenn reported. He sounded very upbeat. "My horse has been found. He was way out on the southwest corner of the ranch, just wandering around."

"How did he get there?" I asked.

"I don't know, and frankly, I don't care. I got what I wanted—I have Badger back."

"I'm assuming that Licorice Stick isn't with him," I said as my mind digested what he'd just told me. A thought nagged at my mind, but I knew better than to share it with Glenn until I was sure.

"There's a lot of country over there. We'll check it out, but so far, he hasn't been seen."

"What do you want me to do at this point?" I asked.

"Come back to the house, and let's talk about it. Licorice Stick is a very good horse, but he's not in the same category as Badger," Glenn said.

"So you aren't willing to spend as much money getting him back as you were willing to for Badger?" I asked, wondering how his daughter would feel about that if my suspicion proved to be correct.

"That's right," he responded. "Licorice Stick can't stand at stud, which makes him less valuable to me."

I understood that. "I'll head up there right now," I told him.

* * *

The day had turned cloudy and was threatening some heavy April showers by the time I arrived at the Gridley ranch. Sure enough, Glenn was in front of the barn with a solid brown horse. I didn't see any sign of Shanice and found that I was disappointed—Badger's return most likely meant the end of the case. Who knew when I'd see her again. However, the two younger Gridley daughters were with Glenn.

As I approached the small group, I was amazed at how much Cindy and Jena had changed. Like their older sister, they were very attractive women. Cindy was the older of the two—if Shanice was twenty-eight, that would make Cindy twenty-two—and she was a happy, fun-loving girl. Her long, dark blonde hair was in a ponytail that hung beneath the back of her pink felt Western hat. Jena was twenty, the most reserved of the three Gridley women—and now clearly the tallest. Standing next to her now, I could see she was almost as tall as I was. Her light blonde hair was cut quite short, and she was hatless but, like her sister, was dressed in a Western-cut blouse and jeans.

"Hi, Rocky!" Cindy exclaimed as I approached them. "It's great to have you back with us." She gave me a broad smile, which made me feel surprisingly uncomfortable. It had been a long time since I'd seen these girls. I didn't know them quite as well as Shanice—they'd been quite young when I'd worked on the ranch before my mission—and seeing them all grown up made me a bit tongue-tied.

"Can you believe Badger is back already?" Cindy asked, so happy she was almost bouncing.

"That's great news," I said as I turned my attention to their father and waited for a report.

"He seems to be in good shape," he said without looking up as he ran a hand down one of the horse's front legs.

"You're sure that's Badger?" I asked nonchalantly.

Glenn looked up sharply and then rose to his full height, which had to be five feet ten inches because he and I stood eyeball-to-eyeball. He looked at me for a moment, a thoughtful look, and then he turned back to the horse. There was a loud crack of thunder. He glanced up at the darkening sky but didn't say a thing. I was pretty sure he was mulling over my question because his brow became furrowed.

"Of course he is," Jena said after the thunder had died away. She was almost as tall as I was, and her blue eyes looked directly into mine when I turned her way.

"Good," I said. "I was just thinking about Shanice's horse."

"Badger was found on our ranch," Cindy said, as if that settled the question. Some of the bounce had vanished, however.

It completely vanished when I said, "So was the horse that Shanice found in Licorice Stick's stall."

Another loud crack of thunder was followed by a sudden, heavy downpour, and we all hurried into the barn to get out of the rain. Once inside, Glenn, whose face had turned pasty, said, "He sure looks right, and he is as friendly as ever. He must have gotten away from them before they got him loaded." Despite what he was saying, there was reservation in his voice.

"As long as you're sure," I said. "So what would you like me to do?"

Glenn's face turned hard. His eyes met mine as he said, "I'd like you to wait while I saddle this horse and work him out a bit. Then I'll know for sure that it's Badger."

I suppressed a smile and very quietly countered Glenn's statement with an "Or not." *Look at that. Glenn Gridley's taking my advice,* I thought as I watched him enter the tack room. If only Shanice were here.

Cindy stepped close to me and quietly asked, "You think it's not Dad's horse?"

I turned toward her and said, "I don't think anything. I just thought you folks would like to be sure."

"Sure we would," she said, giggling and laying her hand on my arm. Shanice always said Cindy was a bit of a flirt, and I could see she hadn't lost this side of herself over the years. I smiled, not moving until she removed her hand and walked to the tack room entrance.

"I think you might be right," Jena said. Her short hair was slightly damp from the rain, and concern filled her blue eyes. "Dad will be devastated."

"Maybe not," I said. "I hope it is Badger."

"I do too," Jena agreed. "But I have a feeling . . ."

She didn't say what that feeling was, but I could tell from the look on her face that she didn't expect her father to make the conclusion he hoped for when he mounted the stallion.

"Let's wait and see," I said as we passed the stall where Licorice Stick was supposed to be. The stall was empty, and the door stood open. "By the way, where is Shanice? I thought she'd be here."

"She took Licorice Stick's replacement out to the area where our guys found Badger—or whoever that horse is," she said. "She's looking for the real Licorice Stick. I imagine she's soaked by now."

"I take it she didn't bring a jacket with her?" I asked.

"You know Shanice. I do hope she's okay out there, though. It's been pretty stormy."

"I'm sure she's fine," I said. "She's just like your dad in that regard. She won't let a little storm stop her."

A moment later, Cindy fell in beside Jena and me, and the three of us followed Glenn and the horse to the east door. From inside the barn, I could see the rain falling in sheets. Glenn ignored it and got on the horse. But he didn't go out into the deluge. Instead, he turned him and spurred. The horse reacted and bolted for the round corral at the far end of the barn. Glenn rode him straight through the gate and circled the corral. He stopped him suddenly and sprang from the saddle. Then he was back in it, and he raced the horse back to where the three of us were standing. He repeated the entire exercise before riding back to us, his face a study in fury. I didn't need to ask, but for the sake of formality, I did it anyway.

"So, is this your horse?" I asked.

"You know it's not," he growled. "He's not even a good imitation."

It looks like I still have a job, I thought as I heard a cell phone ring. Cindy pulled a tiny pink phone from a front pocket of her tight-fitting jeans and answered.

"Shanice, where are you?" Cindy asked. As she listened, her face turned pasty white and she began to tremble. Her father let go of the reins of the horse and grabbed hold of her. The fury on his face was replaced with worry. "What's the matter, Cindy?" he asked. "Is Shanice hurt? Did that . . . that . . . horse do something to her?"

"Dad, Alden's dead," Cindy whispered, then she slowly sank to the floor. Her father squeezed her shoulders, and Jena knelt beside her. I could only guess that the shock on their faces mirrored my own.

"What are you talking about?" Glenn asked urgently.

"He's in a ditch about a half mile from where they found Badger," she said.

"What was he doing on our ranch?" he asked no one in particular. I was wondering the same thing, but I didn't see that as the pressing question for the moment.

"What about Shanice?" I asked. "Is she out there too?"

"She. . . she. . . found him," Cindy stammered.

I pulled out my phone and punched in the number of the Box Elder County Sheriff's Department. After speaking to a deputy for a moment, I touched Cindy's shoulder. She looked up at me. "Cindy, take my phone and tell this man what you know," I said sternly.

Her hand was trembling so terribly that she almost dropped my phone when I handed it to her, but she did as I asked. "My sister says she thinks he was shot in the back," Cindy said a moment later.

Murder! So much for keeping the switching of a pair of roping horses a secret, I thought. My mind turned to Shanice. It sounded like she was alone in a storm with the dead body of her ex-husband. I wanted to get there as quickly as possible to make sure she was all right.

Glenn quickly pulled the saddle off of the dark brown stallion and put him in a stall. Then he said to Jena and Cindy, "Let's go girls." By the time he glanced at me and added, "You better come too, Rocky," my keys were already in my hands. By then, the deluge was over.

Jena jumped in Glenn's truck with him, and Cindy jumped in with me. We followed her father deep into the large ranch. We arrived well in advance of the sheriff's department and found Shanice sitting on a fallen cottonwood tree, her head in her hands and her clothes thoroughly soaked from the rain. We stopped near her and got out of our trucks.

When her father ran over to her, she pointed and said in a strained voice, "He's over there."

I followed the direction of her finger and discovered what she had already found. A man's body was lying facedown in an old ditch about thirty yards away. Glenn put his arm around Shanice's shoulder as he sank down beside her on the tree trunk and spoke softly to her. It was raining lightly again, but neither Glenn nor Shanice seemed to notice.

I approached the body. The cause of Alden's death was not hard to discern—he'd been shot in the back all right. Not once but twice. His face was lying in a puddle of newly gathered water.

After a couple of minutes, Glenn rose from the tree trunk, patted his daughter on the shoulder, and walked over to where I was standing a few feet back from the body. His younger daughters also came over.

Cindy grabbed her mouth after a very short look and stumbled away from the ditch, where she threw up. Jena had stepped beside me, and as she looked, she became faint, and I literally had to catch her to keep her from falling. I assisted Jena across the rough terrain back to her father's truck and helped her in. She dropped her head in her hands and began to sob.

Cindy recovered quickly, but she didn't go near the body again or even look in that direction. Instead she sat beside Shanice on the fallen tree and put her arm around her sister's shoulders. Glenn remained frozen to the spot where he'd first caught sight of the dead man. I walked over to him and said, "Are you sure it's Alden?"

He shook his head. "It could be him, but I couldn't say for sure, the way that body is laying. But Shanice says it's him. She'd know."

We heard sirens in the distance. "Would you like me to go out and escort the cops back here?" I asked.

"No, you stay, if you don't mind. Would you see if Shanice will get in your truck? She's going to catch a cold. She's soaked, frozen, and probably in shock." Glenn's gruff side seemed to have vanished somewhere between the barn and our current location. His voice was tender and filled with emotion.

"Sure thing," I said and turned toward the fallen tree. "Shanice, Cindy, let's get you two out of the rain. Your dad and Jena are going to go meet the officers."

Shanice looked up at me. Water was dripping from the brim of her white felt hat. I held my hand out to her, and she took it. I pulled while Cindy took hold of her other arm and steadied her. As soon as she was seated in the front seat of my truck, I pulled a blanket from under the back seat. Cindy helped me put it around her and then climbed into the back seat. I got in behind the wheel and started the engine. I reached across her and punched on the seat warmer. "We'll get you warm," I said. I turned the heater up full blast.

"Thanks, Rocky," Shanice said, giving me a short glance. She was shivering, and I reached over and tucked the blanket tighter around her shoulders and legs.

A couple of minutes passed in silence. Finally, Shanice spoke. "He cheated on me," she said, her voice subdued, almost like she was talking to herself. She looked over at me, and I nodded when I saw the pain in her eyes. "I didn't see it coming. He hurt me badly, Rocky, but I never would have wished him dead." She was silent for a moment, still shivering even though it was getting quite warm in my truck. "Who would do such a horrible thing?"

I shook my head; clearly I had no idea. I asked her an unrelated question. "Where's the horse you were riding, Shanice?"

She glanced out of the window, where the rain had almost stopped. "I . . . I don't know. He was right there." She pointed to the fallen tree she'd been sitting on. "I forgot about him."

"I'll see if I can find him. I don't think he has gone too far, with bridle reins dragging and a saddle on," I said.

"Don't leave us, Rocky. I mean, can you wait until Dad gets back here with the police?" she asked, her eyes pleading.

"Of course, then I'll go have a look."

Her vacant eyes suddenly looked past me, out the window, as if she were searching for something. "It's a good saddle on him," she said, her forehead creased. "I mean, it is fairly new. I wouldn't want him to ruin it."

"I understand," I told her, and I truly did.

"I really hoped I'd find that my horse had been returned—or never truly taken—like Badger was," she said as she hugged my blanket more tightly around her.

Cindy leaned up over the seat and said gently, "It's not Badger. He looks just like him, but Dad rode him and said he's a fake. And I could see that just from the rough way he stopped. There was no slide at all. You know that Dad has never trained a roping horse that doesn't slide to a stop. No good trainer does."

"That's right. You taught me that, Shanice," I said, trying to offer my support while directing the conversation away from the murder and stolen horses.

Shanice smiled weakly at me then shuddered. "So somebody traded horses with us," she said flatly. "And we got the short end of the trade."

"Yeah, I'm afraid that's what it looks like," I told her. "Actually, I wouldn't exactly say they traded you." Her eyes met mine, and I finished with, "They switched with you, Shanice. And now I've got to find them so we can switch back."

"Why did they leave that brown horse out here but put the black one they switched for Licorice Stick in the barn?" Cindy asked.

"Did the brown one have a halter on?" I asked.

"Yes," Cindy answered. "And it still had the lead rope, although it was about torn in two."

"It must have gotten away from the thieves when they were headed for the barn," I said. Cindy and Shanice both looked at me, so I explained what I had found at the north gate. "They probably planned to leave both horses in the stalls but Badger's replacement wouldn't cooperate. If they had, it might have been longer before you noticed you had the wrong ones."

When the sheriff's deputies arrived, I spotted someone I had no intention of working with anytime soon. Blaine Springer was a seasoned officer in his mid-forties. He'd been a uniformed officer for years and was now a detective. Unfortunately, he and I had crossed paths a couple of times on cases I'd worked that had brought me from Logan over into Box Elder County. His dislike for me was no secret. I groaned loudly when I saw Blaine, which made Shanice jump.

"What's the matter?" Shanice asked, giving me a worried look.

"It's nothing," I told her, pointing to Blaine as he made his way over to the ditch. "That's Blaine Springer, a Box Elder County detective. We're just not the best of friends, that's all." As I was talking, I could see Blaine turn around and take notice of my truck—and me inside.

"It doesn't appear that he likes you much, either," Cindy said, giggling softly. Blaine eyed me with suspicion as he walked toward my truck. The closer he got, the louder his strings of profanity became, and I finally decided to meet him halfway to spare Shanice and Cindy. Unfortunately, Shanice and Cindy got out of the truck and followed me. Even from where I stood, I could see how tightly he clenched his fists against his sides. This was not going to be pleasant.

"What are you doing here, Revada?" Blaine demanded when we reached him. A small man with very little hair on a mostly shiny head, he peered at the world down a long, skinny nose through deep-set, narrow eyes that were somewhere between green and brown. Seeing those eyes made me feel a bit guilty about a comparison I had once made. In my line of business, Blaine was pretty well known for his lack of thoroughness in cases. Those who worked with him could typically expect to do most of the work. Blaine was more interested in criticizing every detail and flying under the radar of his boss. I guess I shared this lack of respect for him because I had called his eyes the color of old manure during a talk with one of his colleagues. My description was accurate, but I had immediately regretted saying it, and as I'd feared, my unkind remarks had made their way back to him. After that, our civil working relationship went sour. He now went out of his way to remind me of the incident and his hatred toward me. The man's ego was clearly too fragile to mess with, which only deepened my dislike for him.

"Hello to you too, Detective Springer," I said, keeping my tone light. He glared up at me as I caught Glenn's eye. Glenn made his way over to where we stood next to a clump of willow trees.

"I think your playtime is over. You can run along back to Logan now. We can take it from here." Even from Blaine, this comment was below the belt. I had every right to be there—whether I was working on a case or not. Shanice's eyes popped, Cindy's mouth dropped open as she looked at me, and Glenn went red. I was offended, but not too badly, since I had expected no less from Blaine. I had to choose my response carefully. It was not my place to explain that I was investigating stolen horses, particularly since the case could, possibly, have belonged to Blaine had Glenn chosen to report the crime.

I finally said with a forced smile, "I'll just be looking around for the horse that Shanice was riding. It seems to have run off on her after she found this body." I pointed toward the current resident of the ditch.

"What do you think you're doing here in the first place?" Blaine demanded again, his already small eyes constricting in anger.

"He's a friend of the family," Glenn said before I had to make something up. "We asked him to come out."

"Well, I'm in charge here now, and I'm asking him to leave," Blaine growled. I smiled more naturally this time, an act that only served to make the detective angrier.

"I'll be looking for the horse," I said. "You go ahead and see if you can solve a killing."

Blaine trembled with anger, but I intended to do just what I'd said I would. So I turned to Shanice, who was looking totally baffled by the scene she'd just observed. "I'll see what I can do about your horse. Maybe I'll catch up with you back at the house later."

Before I could turn to leave, however, Blaine looked at Shanice and said abruptly, "You would do well, Mrs. Overton, to avoid this man's romantic overtures. He's even worse than that last man you married."

Shanice turned red, Glenn turned purple, and I turned away. I was rummaging in my truck searching for a halter and lead rope when Glenn responded, "He is not dating any of my daughters, but he is a much better man than that one lying there with bullets in his back."

"What are you talking about?" Blaine asked from behind me.

"You are speaking ill of the dead," Glenn said. "It's my former son-in-law who has been shot. And I expect you to find out who killed him."

Chapter Four

I FOUND THE BLACK GELDING about a mile from the murder scene. The bridle reins had been stepped on and broken but the saddle was okay—he had not rolled on it or scraped it against a tree. I replaced the broken bridle with my halter and lead rope. Horse in tow, I returned to my truck sometime after Detective Springer and his colleagues had left and Alden's body had, presumably, been taken away to be delivered to the state medical examiner. Glenn and his daughters were also gone, so I decided to lead the horse back to the barn.

The horse himself, pretty, black, and gentle, was as worthless as ever—except in one regard. I suspected that he was a registered quarter horse and someone had papers on him. As closely as the two horses were in appearance, it was conceivable that whoever had stolen the real Licorice Stick could use this horse's papers to sell him to an unsuspecting buyer. It would be difficult for a buyer, or even a state brand inspector, to determine that the stolen horse was not the one identified on the papers. The same would be true of Badger and the horse that was now in Glenn's barn. Someone had switched the horses, and I wondered if they had done it for more than spite—that they'd done it for profit. I felt that it was important to keep that angle in mind.

I was quite certain that Alden Overton's death and the theft of the roping horses were somehow tied together. It might have been proper to let the officers know about the theft of the horses at this time, but my client didn't want that. And as I thought about it, I felt the same way. If Blaine knew about it and included it in his investigation, widespread knowledge of the theft might have made things more difficult for me to conduct my own investigation. The more people who knew that the theft had been detected, the more likely it would be that the thieves would have their guard up.

My left arm dangled out of the window, holding tightly to my lead rope and coaxing the black horse, which I'd come to think of as Switch Two, along as I drove back toward the ranch yard. I'd tossed the bridle and broken reins into the bed of my truck. The sun was shining now, and the ground was steaming as I made my way around large pools of water and muddy bogs. The horse occasionally tried to jerk away, but I kept a firm grip on the rope. I wasn't about to go slogging around looking for him again, as I'd done the past two hours. My clothes and boots—socks and all—were soaked through, and I was chilly despite the truck's blowing heater and the warmed seat beneath me. When I finally drove into the yard and stopped in front of the barn, I had formed a plan for the rest of the day. My first visit would be an uncomfortable one, for sure, but I had to return to Pam Overton's house in Brigham City. I would probably be behind the police in that visit, but my questions would be different than theirs. I wanted to see if Pam knew whether Alden had mentioned anything about the missing horses.

I had already stripped the saddle off of Switch Two and was leading him towards Licorice Stick's empty stall when I heard my name called out. I looked over my shoulder to see Cindy walking into the barn, holding the hand of a pretty little girl with long dark hair. "We came to help you," Cindy called out.

"Great!" I said. I waited as they walked to where I was holding the horse. "Is this Shanice's daughter?" I asked Cindy, bending down to shake hands with the girl.

"I'm Tyra," the girl said. She had the bright eyes and confidence of her mother, and I couldn't help but grin at her.

"Nice to meet you, Tyra. I'm Rocky."

"I know you," she said in a silly voice. "Mom told me." Surprised, I looked up at Cindy, who just shrugged her shoulders and reached out to brush her fingers through Switch Two's forelock.

"Well, that's great," I replied lightly, standing up. To Cindy, I said, "I think I've about got it here. I left the saddle and bridle there in front of the tack room. I'll put them away as soon as I put Switch Two in his stall."

"Who?" she asked.

"Sorry, I needed some way to refer to this horse and the one now back in Badger's stall," I said.

She grinned. "So that one," she said, pointing toward Badger's stall, "is Switch One and this one is Switch Two?"

"Not very original," I said. "But at least I can keep things straight in my head and in my case notes. You guys should probably refer to them as if no switch has been made, though, at least to anyone but me and each other."

"Why would we do that?" she asked as the little girl slipped past me and began to stroke the head of Switch One. She got a strange look on her face when the horse pulled back from her touch.

"I don't want whoever did it to know we've already figured out that you have the wrong horses," I said.

"Why?" she asked with knit brows.

"They will be less careful if they think they've gotten away with what they did," I explained.

"Ah," she said, nodding her head. "Shanice said you were smart. She's right."

"Shanice hadn't seen me in a long time before I took this case. She could be wrong, you know."

Cindy grinned again. "I don't think so. Alden was a dud, which has made Shanice more careful. She is a much better judge of men now." She looked at me directly, without any kind of reserve, and I suddenly felt warmth in my face.

"I hope I don't let her down—or your dad," I said, feeling awkward. Cindy must have sensed my struggle because she put her hand on my arm, and I felt myself flinch slightly. The warmth in my face turned hot.

"What about me and Jena?" she asked. "We're all part of this. We're a close family, in case you've forgotten."

"I haven't, and I don't want to let any of you down," I said, embarrassed, only too aware of my inadequacies when it came to women. I smiled sheepishly as I led Switch Two past Cindy and Tyra. I turned him loose in the stall and shut the door.

"This is my halter. The bridle reins were broken, but the bridle itself is fine. I'll put the saddle and bridle away for you." I started toward the tack room as I spoke. "I would appreciate it if you folks would lock the barn at night until I get to the bottom of this. I don't want Switch One and Switch Two to disappear."

"They aren't Switch One and Switch Two, Rocky," a little voice said.

I stopped and looked down. Tyra was looking up at me with an accusing look in her big, brown eyes. I knelt down so I could be at her level and asked, "Then who are they?"

She put her little hands on her hips and said, "The black one is Licorice Stick. He's my mom's horse. And Grandpa's horse is Badger."

"Well, aren't you smart! Thanks for clearing that up," I said, smiling at her. Suddenly, she leaned in and wrapped her arms around my neck. She was so sweet, I couldn't help but hug her back.

"What was that for?" I asked gently, after I'd let Tyra go. She just shrugged, grabbed a small bucket of oats from a nearby shelf, and walked to Switch Two's stall. The horse stuck his head out the stall door, and his nose disappeared into the bucket as Tyra held it out to him. I looked up at Cindy and grinned.

"She likes to give hugs," Cindy said quietly, her voice full of awe. "But she usually reserves them just for us. I've never seen her do it with someone she hardly knows before. She must really like you."

I stood up, and Tyra's eyes followed me. "My mom's sad," she told me from her spot next to Switch Two's stall. "She's been crying."

"I know your Mom's sad," I said as I looked at Cindy. "Does Tyra know why Shanice is sad?" I asked very softly.

"Not yet," Cindy said with a warning note in her voice. "Shanice will tell her when the time is right."

"I won't say a word I shouldn't," I promised. I walked over to Tyra, knelt down, and looked into her eyes. For some reason, I wanted to make things better for this sweet little girl and her wonderful mom. "I'll see if I can help make her happy again," I told her.

Cindy smiled and touched my arm when I stood up. "Thanks, Rocky," she said. "I'm glad we have you here to help us."

"I just hope I can," I said. "I'll put the saddle and bridle away now." I started to reach down.

"I can do that," Cindy said, taking hold of my arm. "Shanice and Dad want you to come in the house for a few minutes before you leave."

"Sure," I said. "I'll do that, but I can—"

"You go now. Tyra and I can take care of things here," she said firmly. "I made some hot chocolate, and they are saving some for you."

"Thanks," I said. "Then I'll see you two later."

"We'll be in shortly," Cindy said. "And again, thanks for being here."

As I headed for the barn door, I was feeling kind of stupid. The only thing that I'd done so far that had actually helped them was finding Switch Two. I was also feeling pressured. These people were counting on me to deliver. And that might not be easy, if it was even possible. I had to face the fact that the stolen horses might have been moved out of state, or even clear across the country. I had to get busy and work quickly.

I had never before seen the woman who answered the door. She appeared to be in her fifties with short brown, but graying, hair, tied up in a severe bun. She was about five feet four inches and quite round. My first thought was that of Mrs. Gridley, but I remembered her being taller and thinner with lighter hair. No one had mentioned Glenn's wife since I'd started the case, and I was beginning to wonder why.

"Hello," I said as I stepped into the house. "I'm Rocky Revada."

"It's nice to meet you, Rocky," she said in a friendly voice as she looked at me with an appraising eye. "My name is Rose Critchfield. I'm Glenn's sister—his other sister," she said with a knowing eye. There was very little resemblance between her and the younger sister whose husband I had represented.

"Please come this way," she said, motioning down the hall. "Glenn and the girls are waiting for you in the family room. Cindy made some hot chocolate. I'll get you a cup. You look like you need some warming up."

I reached down, pulled my muddy boots off, and set them by several others on a rug near the door. My socks were damp, but at least they were clean. I didn't want to make a mess of the house, but I also didn't want to parade around barefoot.

Glenn was sitting on a high-backed wooden chair next to a piano in the corner of the room. Jena sat on a matching chair next to him. Shanice was on a sofa made of off-white fabric. "Please, sit down, Rocky," Rose said, pointing to the sofa.

"I'll stand," I said. "I'm wet and muddy. I'd ruin your sofa."

No one seemed to disagree. Rose even looked relieved. Then Jena stood and said, "You can't ruin this chair. I'll sit by Shanice."

As I stepped toward the chair Jena was vacating, I looked at two pictures that were hanging above the piano. They were side by side in matching frames. One was of the Logan Temple. The other was of a smiling couple who looked to be in their thirties. It was Glenn and a beautiful woman with hair about the color of Jena's. I remembered her more clearly now. That was the wife and mother I'd wondered about.

"Did you have any luck?" Shanice asked as soon as I'd taken my seat.

"I found Switch Two," I said, taking a moment to explain the nickname. They all nodded in agreement at my reasoning. I also admonished them to refer to the two horses, when in the presence of others, as Licorice Stick and Badger. "Switch Two is in Licorice Stick's stall," I finished.

"Is my saddle ruined?" Shanice asked. Her eyes were red from crying, and she looked drained. "I'm worried that he might have rolled with it on."

"There's nothing a little oil won't put right," I said. "And all the bridle needs is a pair of new reins."

"Thanks for doing that for me," Shanice said.

"No problem. And I met Tyra out in the barn. She gave me a big hug out of the blue. And she's beautiful," I said. "She looks just like you, Shanice."

"Thank you," she said, a faint pink rouging her cheeks. "She will be devastated when she learns what happened. She loved her dad, and that's what makes me the saddest of all. She didn't know what a jerk he was," she said as her eyes narrowed. "Now that he's dead, I can't think of any reason why she ever should."

"What if it turns out he was the one who stole your horses?" I asked bluntly.

Shanice slowly shook her head.

"You don't think he did it?" I asked.

"I don't know, but I've been thinking about it. If he didn't do it, he probably knew who did—he had some strange friends. But I hope he had nothing to do with the theft. At this point, I'm most concerned about Tyra. I would rather she never know the kind of man her father really was. He was my mistake, not hers."

I gave her a look that I hoped reminded her of what I told her earlier, and she held my gaze for a moment before turning away. I turned to her father. "Cindy said you wanted to see me?"

"Yes, I just wondered what you plan to do now," he said. He also looked drained, but he still had his customary gruffness.

"I plan to go visit with the current Mrs. Overton," I responded.

"That sounds good. Keep me posted."

"I'll do that," I said as Rose came into the room with the mug of hot chocolate and handed it to me. I took a sip. It felt good as the warmth of the liquid journeyed to my stomach.

"You've met my older sister," Glenn said, gesturing toward the open doorway. Rose had quietly left the room right after giving me the hot chocolate and had not reappeared since. He gave me a knowing look that made me wonder if he was thinking about my case involving his younger sister.

I cleared my throat before saying, "Yes, she's a nice woman."

"She lives here with us. She's part of the family," he said.

"Aunt Rose helps us take care of the house and yard," Jena added. "She also helps with Tyra. We love Aunt Rose a lot. She's more of a mother to my sisters and me than an aunt."

"I'm glad she came to stay with you. I was wondering why I hadn't met her before," I offered. "I hope you don't mind my asking, but what happened to Mrs. Gridley? I always appreciated her kindness and generosity."

Shanice spoke up then. "Mom died of cancer about a year ago. That's the main reason Rose came to stay here on the ranch. Her husband was killed in a car wreck about a year before Mom died. They never had children. And Mom was so sick with cancer that Aunt Rose offered to move in with us and take care of her."

"We love her a lot," Jena said, dabbing at her eyes with a tissue. "She's never left."

"And we don't want her to," Glenn added. "I don't know what we'd have ever done without her." There was a touch of emotion in his voice, and he glanced at the pictures above the piano, but he cleared his throat as if he were embarrassed.

I was flattered by this glimpse into this wonderful family's secrets. I felt for them over the loss of their wife and mother. I remembered her as a vibrant woman, very similar to Shanice.

After several minutes of silence, Glen asked, "Well, Rocky, do you have any other questions before you get back to work?"

"I think I'm pretty clear on what needs to happen next. Is there anything else you'd like me to do?" I asked.

"There is," Glenn said. "I'm afraid that I don't have a lot of confidence in Detective Springer. He botched the investigation into the theft of Hal Cramer's cattle a couple of years ago, and they weren't nearly as valuable as Badger." His eyes met mine but his eyebrow was cocked. "From the interaction the two of you had earlier today, I came to the conclusion that you share my feelings."

"He's not someone who inspires confidence," I agreed.

"So you can see why I didn't want to report the horses stolen?"

"I understand completely."

"If he does find the person that killed Alden, it will only be because he got lucky—real lucky."

"I wish you weren't right," I said. "But I've also seen the kind of work he does. He's lazy, sloppy, and prone to jumping to conclusions and then clinging to them regardless of evidence to the contrary. However, I think that if he were properly motivated, he could do good work. He's smart enough, he just prefers to take the path of least resistance."

"Which is why I would like you to try to find out for us who killed Alden," Glenn said.

"Whoa! That's something altogether different. I don't know if I should do that," I said, standing up and nearly spilling hot chocolate on the floor. Embarrassed at my outburst, I settled myself back in my chair, drank some hot chocolate, and then looked up again. "As you already saw, my relationship with Blaine is shaky at best. He'd object strenuously, to say the least."

"Let him object, Rocky. I trust that you can work around him. I don't want Alden's killer going free. Anyway, I think it is very likely that his death and the loss of our horses are closely related, particularly since Alden's body was found on our property."

I couldn't disagree with that, so I nodded and said, "I'll give it a shot."

"Thanks, Rocky." He glanced over at Shanice.

"You bet," I said. "So unless there's something else, I'll get to work. And if you don't mind, I think maybe I'll run back out to where his body was found. I'd like to have a look around myself. I really haven't done that."

"You do that," Glenn agreed. "Although I'm afraid the rain washed tracks and the like away. I heard Springer say that."

"It's possible," I said, "but you never know what else might be there. I'll see what I can find." I stood up, took one long last drink of my hot chocolate, and then turned to leave the room.

"Wait, Rocky," Shanice said suddenly. I looked at her, and she smiled. Despite her sadness and fatigue, the smile made her face look radiant. I wondered why Alden let a woman like her get away.

"What are you thinking?" I asked as she looked quizzically at me.

"I'm thinking you need to go to Logan and get some dry clothes. I don't want you to get pneumonia on account of me," she said with a fading smile.

"Good advice," I promised. *For later,* I added silently to myself.

I took the next full minute of silence as a dismissal and started for the doorway. Shanice also stood, and she took the cup from my hand. "I'll walk Rocky out," she said.

Her father nodded, and I followed Shanice. "Let me put this in the kitchen," she said, "and then I'll meet you at the door. I see you need to put your boots back on. I already have dry ones." She hurried away.

Chapter Five

I WAS STILL STRUGGLING TO pull the first of my two soaked boots over my damp socks when Shanice joined me at the front door. As I finally succeeded in forcing my foot into the boot, the door opened and Cindy and Tyra came in. "Hi, Mom," Tyra said, looking at her mother with searching eyes. "Rocky said he's going to make you happy again. Are you happy now?"

I began tugging at the second boot, suddenly feeling very self-conscious. I looked up sheepishly at Shanice as she knelt and said, "I'm a little better, sweetie. How are you?"

"I'm good. I fed oats to Licorice Stick all by myself!" Shanice laughed at Tyra's excitement and gave her a quick hug before standing up again.

"But later, after I talk to Rocky alone for a minute, there is something I need to tell you."

"Will you tell me why you were sad?" she asked.

"Yes, I'll tell you that," Shanice promised, looking away from her daughter.

"You're *still* sad, Mom," Tyra said. She turned her eyes to me, and they narrowed as I pulled my pants over the top of my boots. Shanice excused herself briefly, and I watched her walk down the hall. "You didn't make her happy yet," Tyra accused me. "You promised."

"I'm sorry, Tyra. I'll try to do better." Then I knelt down and put my large, calloused hands on her little shoulders. "I'm afraid I can't do it alone. I'll need your help. Will you help me make her happy?"

"I don't know how," Tyra said, her eyes downcast.

"You'll figure it out, but to start with, you make sure she knows how much you love her. Will you do that?"

She looked up until I was staring directly into those dark brown eyes that looked so much like her mother's, and she gazed right back and said, "Yes, I will."

"Good." I stood up and smoothed her hair. She smiled up at me, and I felt an affection for her that I had never felt for any children except my own nieces and nephews. I suspected that Shanice, despite having to raise this little girl on her own, was a very good mother.

To my surprise, Tyra again stepped impulsively to me, threw her arms around my thigh, and laid her head against my leg. She never said a word, and I felt a catch in my throat as I looked at Cindy. Her eyes were misty. I patted Tyra's back, feeling more determined than ever to find out who killed her father and bring him to justice.

A minute later Shanice returned, two wet tissues in hand, and said, "Tyra, I need to talk to Rocky outside for a minute. You go with Aunt Cindy and have some more hot chocolate. You and I will talk in a minute, okay, sweetie?"

Once outside, Shanice said, "My heart breaks for her. My mistakes have hurt her so much. I wish I could change the past. And yet, I would never want to be without her. She is my life." She brought the tissues to her face again, but they were so wet, they crumbled into pieces and stuck to her skin. I casually reached up and brushed the tissue off, and Shanice blinked rapidly and then looked at me in surprise.

"I wish you would stop blaming yourself for everything. I know you, Shanice. You would never knowingly marry someone like the man he turned out to be." Shanice sniffed and nodded, so I continued. "I'm really impressed with Tyra. You are doing a great job, even though I'm sure it has been hard. And she loves you with all her heart. That's why she is so worried about you. We all wish we could do things over at times. Take me, for instance." I stepped back and swept my arms along my body as though I were displaying a prize in *Wheel of Fortune*.

My attempt at silliness worked. Shanice looked me over and started to giggle. She shoved me lightly with her hand and said, "You're ridiculous."

"No, I'm totally serious. Look at me. I'm thirty-two and don't have a thing to show for it."

She did look at me then, her eyes narrowing.

"No, Rocky. You are a smart and successful man," she said with a smile. "And you haven't made the kind of serious mistakes I have."

I found myself wanting to kiss her then, so I looked away from her, determined to shake off the attraction and pay attention to my job.

"I better get going," I said, turning and walking to my truck. But Shanice kept pace with me. When I put my hand up to open the door, she laid hers on it, and I felt a jolt go through me.

"There is something else I need to talk to you about," she said. "Can we step in the barn for a minute where no one will see us talking?"

"Sure," I said, thinking that might not be wise at the moment. But then I wasn't always wise. I let go of the door handle, and her hand, regrettably, left mine. Together we entered the barn.

Once inside, she turned and her eyes searched mine for a moment. "Can you keep what I am about to tell you in confidence?" she asked.

"That goes with the business I'm in," I told her.

She nodded. "Dad would never tell you this, but our ranch is in a bit of trouble."

"You mean because of losing your best horses?" I asked.

"That only makes it worse," she said. I said nothing as she took a deep breath and seemed to be thinking, her eyes staring into the cavernous interior of the large barn. Finally, she shifted her feet and looked at my face again. "We are in serious financial trouble," she said. "We could never afford to replace Badger and Licorice Stick. And without them, we will not get the winnings we'd planned on this summer in the rodeos, nor will we get Badger's stud money. We had big plans, plans that Dad has been counting on to help get us back on our feet. More than ever, we need to work the rodeo circuit this coming summer."

"Then I guess I better get busy and find those two horses for you," I said, trying to sound light-hearted.

"That will help," she agreed with a solemn face. She looked away from me. "We don't know why our finances are so tight. The girls and I have talked about it, and we wonder about our accountant—whether or not he is doing his best for us. But Dad trusts him implicitly, and he won't hear a word of it. He says it's just that the price of cattle has been down, that fuel is getting expensive, that our machinery is getting old and requiring too much maintenance, and that our hired men are costing us too much."

"Is all that true?" I asked.

"Well, yes, but it's not all that different from how it's been in the past when we were not in any kind of financial trouble. Dad let Vance Winskey, one of our ranch hands, go. We hated to do that, and he was not very happy at the news. Anyway, we only have two now, and unless things change, they might have to go too. The girls and I do a lot of the work, and we enjoy it, but I swear, Rocky, the money is being bled away from us."

"Would you like me to look into that?" I asked. "I do understand accounting quite well. That was my major at Utah State, and I have some experience in those kinds of cases."

Her face brightened. "Really? That's great. But Rocky, I don't mean to sound like I'm accusing our accountant of anything. He's a really nice man. Dad trusts him, and I don't have a reason not to, except that the money is disappearing, and he doesn't seem to have any answers for us."

"What's your accountant's name?" I asked.

"Hal Rodgers," she said. "He works for an accounting firm down in Ogden. He's actually one of the supervisors there." She shifted nervously, started to say something else, and then stopped.

"What is it, Shanice?" I asked.

"Oh, nothing," she said with a shake of her head

I could tell there was something, so I said firmly, "Shanice, if I am to succeed in this investigation—which seems to get more complicated by the minute—I need to know everything you can tell me about anyone in any way connected to your family or the ranch."

"Dad doesn't know this," she said.

"And you don't want him to," I guessed.

She nodded and rubbed her eyes. "Hal introduced me to Alden. He told me what a great guy he was. I think he knew different, and I should have too, but I was just a girl, and Alden seemed nice. I was a little wild at the time. I'd quit going to church. I was breaking my folks' hearts," she admitted.

I hadn't known all those details, but I didn't think they mattered now. Whatever wild streak Shanice had experienced seemed to have mellowed out. "We all make mistakes," I reminded her. "But why would this make a difference now? The truth about Alden came out, and you moved on."

"*Trying* to move on, sure. But Dad doesn't know that Alden worked for Hal for a while, and that would make him angry."

"Why?" I asked.

"Because Dad complained about Alden to Hal several times, and Hal never once let on that he'd ever known Alden before we eloped to Las Vegas." I must have looked surprised at this news of their elopement because she said, "I know. Not many people knew. My parents did a pretty good job spreading the word that we'd gotten married—without sharing details. Anyway, Hal did know Alden. Alden was a financial consultant when I met him. But it was only shortly before that when he worked for Hal. And that isn't the worst part of it," Shanice told me.

"So let's have the rest," I suggested.

"Hal made me promise to never tell Dad that he and Alden were friends. Why did Hal want to hide that?" she asked earnestly. "I don't understand it."

"You have a point, Shanice," I told her. "I'll look into it. But I will need your help."

"I don't know what I can do," she said grimly.

"Somehow, I need to get access to your family accounts," I said. "Is there any way that you can—"

She cut me off with a wave of her hand. "I don't have any access to them," she said. "I can't do that."

"Do your sisters know about Hal and Alden?" I asked.

"No, nobody in the family does." Shanice began wringing her hands, and beads of sweat appeared on her forehead.

"Okay, how about this?" I asked after a long, thoughtful pause. "I'll go talk to him and tell him I'm doing some work for your father and that I need to look at the books."

"He'll call Dad," she said with a note of panic in her voice.

"Unless I tell him that I know some things about him and Alden," I said. "I can bluff if I have to. I can tell him that I'm taking an independent look at Alden's murder and that if he doesn't help me, I'll have to talk to you and your father about their business relationship."

"Oh, Rocky!" she exclaimed. "You can't do that."

"Shanice," I said firmly, raising one hand and shaking a finger at her. "If you want your horses back, and if you want me to help find out who killed your ex-husband, I will need some latitude."

She turned away from me. I watched her profile as she stared at the ceiling of the barn for a minute or so. She finally turned back to me. "Okay, Rocky. I trusted you in the past. Now I've just got to do it again."

"I understand your hesitation. We hardly know each other anymore. A lot has happened over the years. In truth, you don't really know me," I said seriously.

"Stop putting doubts in my mind. I do know about you. You have the same feeling about you that you had when we were younger. I feel comfortable around you, Rocky. Being with you feels safe." She paused for a few moments before looking at me sheepishly. "If you really must know, I did a little checking on you before I had my dad call you."

"You wouldn't!" I said with mock exaggeration, but I was surprised that Shanice felt the need to do that. "Well, I did. It's just like you said. It had been a long time, and a lot can happen to a person. I just had to be sure. I didn't want to hurt my family."

"All right," I said. "And what did you learn?"

"That you served a mission in Spain, that you graduated from Utah State, that you got into PI work a year or so after that, and that you are still active in the church," she said. "And I also learned from the way you handled the case with Aunt Agnes and that creep she was married to that you were totally honest. So there you go," she concluded, tapping her finger on my nose. "You do what you have to do, and I'll live with whatever happens." She leaned back against the side of the barn door, folded her arms across her chest, and looked at me.

"Well, thank you for the confession," I said, stepping over to the wall next to her and copying her body position. "Is there anything else I should know, or can I get to work now?"

She shook her head and said, "If I think of anything, I'll call you. I have your number now, after all." She closed her eyes and breathed deeply. When she opened her eyes again, they were shining with fresh tears. "Now I better go break my little girl's heart."

"I wish I could help you," I said.

She forced a smile as she wiped at her eyes, then leaned sideways so her head was resting on my shoulder. "Just find the horses and Alden's killer, and I'll be happy. I promise. And you go get dry clothes on."

"They're nearly dry now," I said lightly as we stood up and headed back into the late afternoon sunshine. "I need to go back out to where you found Alden before I go back to Logan. The deputies might have missed something."

"I suppose that's possible. No one is as thorough as our very own PI, after all." She was teasing me again, so I turned to her and smiled wickedly. "Thanks, Rocky. And good luck."

I got in my pickup as she returned to the ranch house. I watched her until she'd disappeared inside, then I started the truck and drove back to their large fields and beyond. A lot of things had entered my mind as Shanice and I had talked. With new knowledge about the possible embezzlement from Gridley funds, I couldn't help but wonder if everything—the Gridley's financial troubles, the murder, and the theft of the valuable horses—were somehow related. Would it be too much of a coincidence? I didn't think so.

Once I got back to where Alden's body had been found, I got out and examined the area carefully. The deputies had stomped around a lot, and even before they'd ever been summoned, the rain had done a lot of damage to the crime scene. But I had learned long ago that it never hurts to look closely, no matter how many people had contaminated the scene.

I soon concluded that Alden's body had been dragged to the ditch. Despite so many footprints and the rain that had fallen so hard, I could see where some of the old, dead grass was bent in the direction that a body would have been dragged had it been coming toward the ditch from the northwest. I also found where a row of small rocks had been displaced, and in spite of the rain, I could see small troughs where they'd dug up the ground.

I stood for a moment, considering what I had observed earlier about the body. He had been lying facedown in the ditch. The back of his pants and shirt were not as dirty or torn as they would have been had he been dragged without something between him and the ground. I couldn't be sure he wasn't dragged facedown, but I doubted that. It was easier to drag someone from behind. All of these thoughts led me to conclude that Alden had not been killed where his body was found, so I doubted that the deputies had found any bullet casings near the body. Despite knowing that it was getting late and that further investigation would make it difficult for me to get home and then back to Brigham City at a decent hour, I went back to my truck, got my small digital camera, gloves, and a handful of evidence bags, then continued following the indistinct signs where the body had been dragged.

What few tracks I located were very faint, having mostly been destroyed by the pounding rain, but I still managed to follow a subtle trail of bent grass, broken branches, and grooves in the dirt for over a mile. It was especially obvious that Blaine and the others hadn't come this way at all; their tracks in the muddy ground would have been as clear as mine were following the storm.

As I proceeded through an area filled with stubby brush, I found several small pieces of cloth. Some of the cloth fragments were brown and others were red with a small amounts of green. The red cloth was a softer fabric than the brown. I considered that and wondered if the body had been dragged in something, a sleeping bag perhaps. I felt a chill go through me. It was always exciting when something works out on a case. I put on my gloves and stuffed several small, ragged samples into small evidence bags.

I had come through an area filled with juniper trees and now stood below the crest of a small hill that I had yet to climb. I stopped, looked around, and then approached the hill, working my way to the top. I looked around carefully but could see no signs—even subtle ones—that anything had been dragged down the hill. From the top of the hill, I could see a fence a quarter mile or more to the north. I wondered if it had a gate and if a road was close by. I didn't remember a gate being in that area. I decided to check that out later.

I backtracked to where I was able to see the first signs of Alden's body being dragged. There I discovered that the dead grass had been trampled quite a bit. Despite the rain, the evidence had not been completely washed away. This spot was very secluded. I considered what could have happened here then spent the next ten minutes searching every square foot of ground for several yards in each direction. I eventually found what I was looking for—an empty bullet casing. I took a couple of pictures before I slipped my gloves back on and picked the casing up. It was .38 caliber and didn't appear to have been on the ground for a prolonged period of time. I dropped it in a fresh evidence bag.

I looked around a little longer for whatever I might find, but there was nothing that piqued my interest. I then climbed the hill again, convinced that Alden and his killer had come this way together. And I suspected that the killers had returned this same way after depositing his body in the ditch. When I reached the fence, I didn't see a gate anywhere, but a small fragment of cloth, nothing but a few fibers, was caught on the barbed wire atop the fence. I photographed it exactly as I found the sample, then loosened it from the barb, and put it in another evidence bag.

On the far side of the fence was a road, or at least a slightly worn vehicle path, that had been driven on occasionally over the years. I crossed the fence, making sure that my pants didn't meet the same fate as someone else's had earlier. It looked like a vehicle might have been turned around here. I followed the fence line for a short distance and only stopped when I spotted a brown cardboard box lying against the fence.

It was about two feet square and eight inches deep. It was soft from the rain, but still intact. I supposed it could have blown here from about anywhere. I knelt down and looked at it anyway. On the underside was an address label. The box had been sent by UPS to Alden Overton from Amazon.com.

"What in the world?" I said aloud, then chuckled quietly to myself. This case just got stranger and stranger. The bottom of the box had been well-taped and the sun had dried out the box enough that it didn't fall apart when I picked it up. It still contained a few papers, including a packing slip indicating that the box had contained a sleeping bag. I felt that same chill sweep through me again. Apparently, I was on the right track. I wondered if the box could have been in the back of Alden's truck—if he had a truck; most people in this area did—and if it had possibly blown out either as he and his killers had driven this way or after he had been murdered and the truck was returning to the nearest road. The fabric pieces of the sleeping bag I'd found were of an extremely lightweight material. So the entire box—sleeping bag and cardboard—couldn't have been more than a few pounds.

Then I realized that it probably had the sleeping bag in it coming out here, but that the bag had been used to transport Alden's body away from the place of his murder. If so, the box had been discarded in the back of the truck and had blown out as the killer returned from disposing of the body in the ditch—a ditch in such a remote part of the ranch that it seemed unlikely that anyone would find it anytime soon.

I looked at the sinking sun and then at my watch. It was getting late. I started back the way I had come, carrying the box. Thirty minutes later I arrived back at my truck. My clothes had nearly dried out, and even my boots weren't as wet as they had been. I put the box in my back seat, pulled out the filled evidence bags and labeled them, then headed for the Overtons' house.

Chapter Six

THE DAY HAD SLIPPED AWAY from me. If I was going to talk to Alden's widow, I didn't have time to go all the way to Logan and change like I'd told Shanice I would. It was already early evening by the time I headed south from Tremonton. I hoped that I would find Pam Overton alone but feared that I wouldn't. News of Alden's death had most likely spread quickly. My fears were validated when I turned on the street where she lived. There were several cars in the driveway and others parked on the street in front of the house.

This wouldn't do—I couldn't interview her with a crowd around. So I changed my plans and headed for Logan after all. As I drove, I worried about the evidence I had collected. I should let the sheriff's department know about it, but I knew that Detective Springer would try to make something out of my having interfered in his investigation, even though he could have done what I did and found the same evidence if he'd made the effort. And he'd probably ignore my discoveries and the conclusions I'd drawn anyway.

I was torn over what to do. Finally, I drove up Sardine Canyon and went home. After I'd cleaned up, put on fresh clothes and dry boots, and grabbed a tuna sandwich, I got in my truck and headed toward Brigham City again. By the time I returned to Alden's home, things had changed. There were only a couple of cars parked out front: a shining silver Lexus on the street and a bright yellow VW in the driveway.

I parked across the street and got out of my truck. I stood for a moment and studied the house. Even though I'd visited with her briefly earlier in the investigation, I didn't know a lot about Pam Overton. I'd gathered that she was twenty-six, that she had been married before, and that she had a little boy, who was Alden's son. This visit would be different than my previous visits, however; this time, Pam would be grieving. I crossed the street, walked up to the door, and rang the doorbell. A very thin, gray-haired woman, who appeared to be in her late fifties, answered the door. "Hello," I said. "Is Pam at home?"

"Where else would she be?" the little woman growled as she ran a hand through her short, grizzled hair. "Pam has suffered a terrible loss today. She isn't up to more company."

The woman started to shut the door in my face. I stuck my foot out, stopping it from closing all the way. "I very much need to talk to her," I said as I pulled my ID out and held it near her face. "I'm a private investigator, and I'm looking into Mr. Overton's death."

"The police were already here," she said. "They asked her all the questions they had."

"Unfortunately, there were some things they didn't know to ask. That's why I'm here," I said. "With my help, they will get to the bottom of this terrible crime. Are you related to Mrs. Overton?" I asked.

"I'm her mother."

"It's nice to meet you. Your name is . . ."

"I'm Denise Page," she said, and I could see that she was wavering in her resolve to keep me from talking to her daughter.

Pressing my small advantage, I said, "I won't take long, and I'll try not to upset her worse than she already is. It's important. Every hour that passes makes it harder to solve murders like this."

Finally, Mrs. Page opened the door, and I stepped in. She pointed to a chair in the living room that opened right off the doorway. She disappeared, and a moment later, she came back in with Pam, a short, slender woman with short brown hair. Judging by her puffy red eyes and unfocused gaze, she was in great distress. Pam was followed by a well-dressed man of about forty. I didn't have a clue as to his identity. I stood, held out my hand, and said to the young woman, "Hi, Pam. I'm sorry to disturb you again, and during such a difficult time, but I think you can help me assist the police in finding whoever did this horrible thing."

She nodded, sniffled, and wiped at her eyes. The man beside her sidled close to her and took her arm. He seemed very protective. I really had planned to speak to her alone, but I wasn't sure I could get rid of him. "Mrs. Overton, I'm so very sorry for your loss," I said. "I won't take long, but I do need to have a moment or two with you in private."

She glanced at the man, pulling her arm free. "It's okay," she said to him. "We'll only be a moment."

Her voice was soft, but even though the man hesitated, I knew he'd heard her as clearly as I had. "Honest, it won't take me long," I said.

He still didn't move, and the young widow's face suddenly looked determined, but the fellow stayed put and she turned to me. "This is a friend of Alden's," she said. "His name is Mace Healey. He's a banker that Alden has worked with for years. I've known him since before we were married. I worked for a short while at the bank he manages."

"I see," I said, thinking that the man looked more like a weasel than a banker. He was of medium height and build, with short black hair, bushy black eyebrows, and a narrow face. His eyes were so dark, they looked black. He was not someone I'd entrust my money with—if I had enough to entrust it to anyone. "It's nice to meet you, Mr. Healey," I said blandly. Then I put more force into my voice. "This is a private conversation. I'll make it short so you can continue consoling Mrs. Overton in just a few minutes."

"Do I know you?" he asked.

"I doubt it very much," I said. "I don't know a lot of bankers. I don't have much need for people of your profession."

"I'll just sit quietly while you speak with Pam," he said, still refusing to budge an inch from his protective position.

"That will be fine," I said, "but you will have to do your quiet sitting in another room. I am on official business, and you are not part of it. I'm sorry, but that's how it is."

His face darkened, but Pam said in her soft voice, "It's okay, Mace. If I need you, I'll let you know. I think I would like to speak with Mr. Revada."

Mace gave me a withering look before he finally left the room.

"Please, call me Rocky," I said, and she nodded in response. I led her by the arm over to the far end of the living room, suspecting that Mr. Healey wouldn't be any farther from the door he'd just gone through than he had to. He appeared to be the sort who would eavesdrop if he could.

We both sat down, and I said, "Thank you for agreeing to speak with me again. I truly am sorry about your husband." I spoke very low, and I had my back to the door. The banker would have a hard time hearing me in this position, and as soft as Pam's voice was, I doubted that he'd be able to hear her very well either.

She nodded at me and spoke so softly that I had to concentrate in order to make sure I heard every word she said. "I've been worried about Alden for a few days. I tried to tell that police detective, but he seemed distracted. That's why I agreed to talk to you. I want someone to know that Alden was upset about something."

"Do you have any idea what was bothering him?" I asked.

"He didn't want to talk about it," she said. "He got angry with me when I asked him what was wrong. So I quit trying, but it wasn't like him. He'd come home late from time to time, and twice he went out very late at night. I asked him what he was going to do, and he just told me it was business, that it wasn't something he could discuss." She shook her head, and her eyes seemed especially sad. "He used to be open with me. That hasn't been the case for quite some time."

"What nights did he leave?" I asked, hoping she could remember.

"Well, this has been happening off and on for a while now, but the most recent was about two days ago."

"Okay," I encouraged. That would have been the same night that the horses came up missing. I waited for a moment for her to continue, but she seemed lost in thought, so I said, "And the second night?"

"The second was last night." She looked up at me as her lip began to tremble and fresh tears slipped down each cheek. "He was gone for two or three hours, then he came home and went to bed. But he was up again before daylight, and shortly after he got up, his cell phone rang. I asked him who would be calling him so early, but he gave me a look that scared me, and I didn't say anything more. He answered the phone as he left the bedroom so I have no idea who called him. He poked his head in and told me that he had to go again. I asked him why, but he just ignored me, got dressed, and left. That was the last time I saw him."

"Do you know where his body was found?" I asked.

"Not exactly. All Detective Springer said was that they found him on some ranch in the Tremonton area," she said with a puzzled look on her face. "I can't imagine what he was doing on someone's ranch."

I took a deep breath and asked, "Do you know a rancher by the name of Glenn Gridley?"

She looked startled, her eyes widening. "That's Alden's former father-in-law." She pressed on her eyes with closed fists for a moment and then she asked, "Are you telling me it was on his place?"

I nodded.

"That's strange," she said.

"Why do you say that?" I asked.

"Alden hated that man. He blamed him for his first marriage breaking up," she revealed.

I was surprised to hear that. "Did he ever tell you what Mr. Gridley did to break up the marriage?" I asked.

She shook her head. "Not really. He made no secret of his dislike for him. But I don't blame Mr. Gridley for the marriage ending when it did."

I was surprised again. "Why do you say that?" I asked.

"He might have figured out about me and Alden," she said, so quietly this time that I could barely hear her. She looked at her hands, which she was holding folded in her lap.

I leaned closer and asked, "What about you and Alden?"

"We were going out for several months before he and Shanice separated," she admitted without moving her eyes. I didn't say anything, giving her time to say more if she wanted to. She wanted to. "I thought he was single. I had no idea he was married—he never wore a ring when he was with me. I had been divorced for over a year before I met him. He told me he was divorced too."

She left it there, so I prodded, asking, "How did you meet Alden?" She looked past me at the doorway that Alden's banker friend had gone through. I figured it out by the look on her face, but she confirmed my suspicions when she said, "Mace introduced us."

"Did he know that Alden was married at the time?" I asked her.

She sat up then, looking surprised. "I . . . I never asked him. The whole situation was such a shock, I'm sure I didn't want to know. If Mace did, he didn't tell me."

"But you think he might have known?" I asked.

She began to shake her head sadly. "I can't imagine that he wouldn't know. Mace and Alden were great friends. The thing is, after

I fell in love with Alden, I kind of figured out on my own that he was married."

"Did you?" I asked, doing a poor job of hiding my surprise. "How did that happen?"

"Well, after Mace introduced us, Alden and I went out a lot—dancing and things. He was so smart and sweet—particularly since I hadn't dated a soul after my divorce. I was a mess. Within just a few weeks, I knew I'd fallen in love with him. We were in this nice Italian restaurant one evening, and I broke the news that I loved him."

"How did that go over?" I asked.

"Not well at all. His face went pale, and he changed the subject. Not exactly the reaction you'd expect, right? I was suspicious, particularly because he started avoiding me. So I did some digging and figured out he was married."

"You hadn't expected that? There had been no signs up to that point?"

"It had never crossed my mind. I would never do anything like that to someone, so I didn't think anyone else capable of it. I was naïve. I guess I know better now. Anyway, I tried to break the relationship off completely at one point—I think it was about a month later—but Alden had changed his tune by then. He told me he was sorry, that he loved me too, that his marriage was over because of Mr. Gridley, and that he was seeking a divorce. I was pretty forgiving. Maybe I was selfish too. I was comfortable with him; I didn't want to be with anyone else, so we made a deal: we wouldn't go out again until he was officially divorced. We got married six months later." She stopped and was thoughtful for a moment. She rubbed her forehead and then she said, "I can't believe I didn't even think about Mace before now. I can't believe he never said something. I'm convinced he would have known Alden was married."

Just then the man in question popped into the room. "I suppose you two are finished now," he said sharply. He glowered fiercely at me. Then I was aware of Pam getting to her feet. I was surprised to see genuine anger on her face as she shook a finger at him.

"You knew, didn't you?" she asked him, her voice cracking.

Mace smiled at her but I watched as his eyes grew big. Then he asked in an exasperated tone, "Knew what, sweetheart?"

"Why didn't you ever tell me you knew that Alden was married when he and I first began dating? Why did you make me figure it out on my own?"

His eyes narrowed then. "Well, I don't see what the big deal is. You figured it out, didn't you? You didn't need my help."

"But I would never have gotten involved with him if it hadn't been for you!"

"And yet you fell in love with him, tied the knot, and here we are." I tried to wipe the shock from my face while Pam let out a frustrated sigh and fell back onto the couch, her head in her hands.

His eyes darted from Pam to me and back again. Then they narrowed and he said, "I didn't know." I knew he was lying, but Pam didn't respond. Mace looked at me again and added darkly, "So I'll stay until this man is gone."

"I have a better idea," Pam's muffled voice said through her hands. "I'll call you tomorrow. You need to go home now." Did that mean Pam suspected him of lying as well?

"But we aren't finished for the evening. I still need to help you plan—" A flash of panic crossed Mace's face. I could tell he didn't want her to speak with me. What is he hiding? I wondered.

"Well, that's what moms are for, Mace. Mr. Revada and I aren't finished, and I would like you to leave now."

Suddenly, Mace pumped his fist. "I know who you are," he said. Then with triumph on his face, his eyes again darted to Pam. "Do you know who this man is?"

"Yes," she said. "He's a private investigator."

"Not just any private investigator," he said. "This man worked for Alden's former father-in-law. He worked on Mr. Gridley's sister's divorce. He is connected closely to the Gridley family."

I shook my head, caught Pam's eye for a moment, and then said, "I think you need to get your facts straight, Mr. Healy. I worked that case for the man to whom Gridley's sister was married, not for the Gridleys."

He looked slightly shaken. I wondered then if he actually thought what he'd said was true. He frowned at me and then appealed to Pam. "Make him leave," he said. "He's a fraud."

The young woman surprised me further when she squared her shoulders, looked the banker in those small black eyes of his, and said, "Mace, I've already told you he's not finished here. But you are. Please leave now before I ask Mr. Revada to throw you out. I don't like being lied to, and you've done it twice in the past two minutes."

He hesitated, and I learned that this young widow did have some volume in her voice. She shouted at Mace, "Get out! Now! And don't come back."

He finally left, but it was without grace. After the door slammed behind him, I said, "Thank you, Pam. Are you all right?"

She nodded. Her eyes were still shooting fire at the door where the banker had just made his inglorious exit. Her diminutive mother came rushing in. "Is that man bothering you?" she asked, glaring at me.

"Mom, Mr. Revada's not the problem," she said. Her face softened as she looked at me. "Mace was the problem. Rocky—" She looked at me. "May I call you Rocky?" I nodded. "Great. Rocky is being very helpful."

The older woman looked relieved and said, "Then I'll go back to getting little Alden Junior ready for bed." As she spoke, I saw a little boy, about two years old with shaggy brown hair, run down the hall and into the room, where he took a flying leap into his mother's arms. Pam shrieked softly as she caught him, then leaned over him and tickled his little sides. The boy giggled and giggled until he wriggled free and stood in front of her, a huge grin on his face.

"You can't get me, Mama. I'm too fast," he said, his chest puffing and his eyes full of mischief.

"Are you sure about that, mister?" she asked, reaching out and grabbing him. Instead of tickling him, though, she pulled him gently onto the couch with her. The boy calmed instantly.

"Are you sad?" Alden Junior asked, and I remembered little Tyra and Shanice back in Tremonton. My heart went out to these darling kids who now had to deal with their father's death.

"Have you met Rocky?" Pam said instead.

"Hi there, Alden," I said, reaching out and taking the boy's little hand. He just nodded, then pulled his hand back into the safety of his mother's arms and looked up into her face.

"Grandma is going to put you to bed now. You can go choose your story." I could see little Alden's excitement at the prospect of a bedtime story. He leaped off Pam's lap and ran to his grandma, who took his hand and led him out of the room.

"Thanks, Mom," Pam said quietly, and she leaned back against the couch again. I also took my seat. Her soft voice resumed again as she said, "What other questions can I answer for you?"

"Well, first, I'd like to know what bank Mace manages," I said.

She mentioned the name of the bank and then added, "I think I'll close my accounts there. It's down in Ogden. I started banking there when I first went to college and lived in Ogden. And like I mentioned, I actually worked there for a short time." I made a mental note to find out which bank Glenn Gridley used.

"Pam, there are some things that I need to get clear in my mind," I said. "First, and this is going to be a weird question, but did your husband recently purchase a new sleeping bag?"

She looked surprised. "Uh, yes, actually. We were going to take Alden Junior camping in a few weeks. How did you know that?"

"I didn't—that's why I asked."

"But you had to have some idea. No one just asks a question like that out of the blue unless they have a reason," she said, her hazel eyes narrowing suspiciously.

I smiled at her, trying to set her at ease. "Yes, you're right. I already told you that Alden's body was found on the Gridley ranch. I found the box that the sleeping bag was shipped in near the ranch as well."

She nodded, seeming to shrink a little. "Okay. But why the sleeping bag? I don't understand the connection." she asked.

"I'm trying to work that out myself. Next random question: Does Alden own a truck?"

"Yes."

"Do you know where it is?"

She seemed to shrink further. "No," she said, so softly it was barely a whisper. "Do you?"

I shook my head. "But if I find out, I'll let you know."

"Thank you," she said.

"I'm sorry to be such a pest, but there is something else I'd like you to tell me, if you can," I said. "I know this may be hard for you, but please think about the question I'm about to ask." She nodded, so

I forged ahead. "Where do you think Alden was going, and what do you think he was doing the two nights he left late?"

Tears wet her eyes. She rubbed them, and then, without looking up, she said, "I am so ashamed." Then she was silent. Finally, she said in the whisper that I had to strain to hear, "I think he was with another woman."

That was not what I'd expected to hear. I was hoping that she at least suspected something about horses and that she would mention it. "I'm so sorry," I said, and I truly was. I hadn't intended to bring that kind of hurt to her.

Before I said more, she dragged her eyes up, looked at me, and spoke again, a little louder this time. "I've feared for several months that our marriage wasn't going to last. First he tried to steal his little girl away from her mother—he was trying to get custody. I didn't think that was right, and it made him angry when I told him that. Then he gradually became quite cool toward me. Like I told you a minute ago, he and I haven't communicated well for a while. I've worried for some time that he was doing to me what he did to his ex-wife. Then when he left during the first night, I had to know for sure. That morning, when he returned, I checked the voicemail, e-mails, and calendar on his phone when he was in the shower. Both his calendar and his emails indicated that he'd had a meeting with another woman. I was crushed."

"He wasn't being very careful about it, then. I'm sorry," I said.

Pam dropped her head into her hands and began to sob. I sat awkwardly, not sure how to comfort her. So I simply waited.

Finally, I spoke again. "I hate to ask this, but do you have an alibi for the night of Alden's murder?" Pam looked at me with shock in her eyes, then her body sagged slightly.

"The police asked me that earlier today. They thought I might be a suspect in the case, but I assured them that I was home. My mom had just flown in two days before for a visit, so she can vouch for me. She, Alden Junior, and I made popcorn and watched a movie, then went to bed around eight." After a brief pause, she lifted her head, wiped her eyes, and said, "I was thinking about divorcing him, you know. I never quit loving him, but Alden was clearly not the kind of man I thought he was when I first met and fell in love with him.

After learning that he was married, and particularly after we got back together, I felt really guilty. It was so easy for me to believe that I had been the cause of the breakup, even though Alden blamed Mr. Gridley. To feel better, I tried to justify our relationship by blaming his ex-wife and her father. But I don't blame them anymore."

She sobbed again, and I let her. Once more, she lifted her head. "I'll miss him, you know."

I nodded. "Of course you will," I said. Even with the story of her whereabouts the night of Alden's murder, she really didn't seem to be a very likely suspect to me. But I knew that I should keep an open mind.

She wiped at her eyes once more and took a deep breath.

"Pam," I said, sorry to have to ask her more questions in the midst of her heartbreak. But I needed answers. She looked wordlessly at me. "Does your husband own a .38 caliber revolver?"

"Well, you already know that, don't you?" she said.

I shook my head. "No, but I wondered. Do you know where he keeps it?"

She nodded. "It's in the basement in his gun cabinet with his rifles."

"Do you mind if I take a look at it?"

"Of course not," she said, and getting to her feet, she signaled with a slender finger for me to follow her. "It's not here," she breathed after opening the cabinet. She looked suspiciously at me. "You knew it wouldn't be." It wasn't a question this time.

"Is his ammo here?" I asked.

It turned out that he had several boxes of .38 shells, all the same brand. She had no way, she told me, of knowing if any were missing. "May I take one of those bullets?" I asked, planning to compare it with the casing I'd found earlier that day.

"Of course," she said. Then she asked in a shaky voice, "Was he murdered with his own gun?"

She surprised me with that question. Pam was not a dumb person. I hoped she was not a guilty person. "I honestly don't know," I said, "but I think it is a possibility."

I followed her back upstairs and walked to the front door of her home. I had one more question to ask before I left, so I turned to her. "Pam, has your husband said anything about horses lately?"

Her eyes got big. "I won't ask this time," she said.

"I take that as a yes?" I asked.

She nodded. "He said he was going to get a roping horse."

"A roping horse," I repeated as my pulse began to pound.

"That's what he said. It seemed a little bit random to me, but he initially seemed pretty excited about it. The thing is, we couldn't afford a horse and wouldn't have a place to keep it if we'd gotten one. I told him all that, and he didn't say anything more about it."

Pam stepped close to me and laid a hand on my arm just as her mother joined us.

"Oh, you're still here," Denise said.

"I'm just leaving," I told her.

Pam looked up at me, her eyes pleading. She squeezed my arm and then asked, "Rocky, did he steal a horse?"

"I don't know that, Pam," I said. Then I asked, "Do you know of anyone who was angry with him over anything?"

Pam removed her arm as, to my surprise, her mother came storming over. "Alden was a good man," she said fiercely. "He would never steal anything. Has this man been trying to tear down your husband now that he's dead and can't defend himself?"

Pam turned to her mother. "No, he has not. After he leaves, there are some things you need to know."

Her mother's eyes opened wide. "Pam, what is he—"

"Mom, Rocky is trying to help. Please, I'll explain in a minute," she said. Then she turned back to me and asked, "Are you working for the Gridleys?"

"I can't tell you who I'm working for," I said, impressed by her line of thinking.

"I respect that," she said. "But can you at least tell me this?" I waited as she looked me directly in the eye and seemed to think for a moment. "Did someone steal a horse from Glenn Gridley?"

"Why do you ask that?" I asked her, trying to sound like I was puzzled by her inquiry. "Did someone say that to you?"

"No," she answered.

"I see," I responded, trying to maintain an emotionless expression. Then I turned toward the door. "I need to go now. But I will do my best to find out who did this to Alden."

"Thank you," she said. "Please do." Her eyes again filled with tears.

Her mother stepped close to Pam and put her arms around her. "Come, dear. You've had an unbelievably stressful day today." When Denise shut the door, I could see Pam sobbing quietly through the front door's window. She lifted a few fingers in a goodbye signal to me.

As I drove up Sardine Canyon, I couldn't get my mind off Pam Overton. I couldn't see her as anything more than a victim, just like Shanice had been a victim or countless other innocent women who were victims of men like Alden Overton. No man deserved to be murdered, but on the other hand, some people invited such evil fates with their own immoral and dishonest actions. *Could he have prompted Pam to commit such a terrible thing as murder?* I shook my head. It just didn't seem likely.

Chapter Seven

My cell phone vibrated just as I was pulling into my garage. When I accepted the call, I was surprised to hear silence on the other end of the line. I was about to hang up when a harsh, muffled voice spoke. "Rocky Revada, you are in deep water," the voice said. My eyes went wide, and I quickly collected a very small but powerful digital recording device from under my seat and plugged it into my phone. No one said a word, so I decided to break the silence.

"Who is this?" I growled in as deep a voice as I could. I wanted the caller to feel intimidated.

"If you don't quit interfering in the matter of Alden Overton's death, you better believe you'll end up in a ditch somewhere with a bullet in your head." A cold shiver covered me from head to foot. I had expected something important, but I hadn't expected a death threat. I felt grateful I was recording the call.

"How do you know Alden?" I said, trying to keep my voice calm. I hadn't had a threat on my life for a long time. There was no way to be prepared for something like this. I heard nothing but static for several seconds, but I could hear the caller's quiet breathing. So after a full ten seconds, I tried a different approach.

"You're messing with the wrong guy. I've got a perfect track record for hunting down scumbags like you. You'll be rotting in jail before you even know what hit you," I said. I was hoping to get under the guy's ego. Often, callers like this weren't too bright and they'd give themselves away if provoked.

After a moment, the voice said, "Consider yourself warned." The final statement had seemed higher-pitched to me. Was he smiling?

I could picture some crook holding a cloth over a payphone as he spoke. Before I could say another word, I heard a click and the line went dead.

"Well, this is a bad sign," I said aloud. My heart was racing. When death threats start coming, it was usually a good time to hand everything over to the police. I truly didn't want to end up like Alden Overton.

I turned off my recording device, exited my truck, entered my kitchen, and located a can of stew in the pantry. As I watched the bowl turn around and around in the microwave, I had a new thought about this turn of events. Sure, threats were dangerous, but they also meant that I was getting closer to finding what I was after. Whatever digging I'd been doing had made someone nervous. I decided to keep the call to myself for a time—at least until I could uncover more clues—but as the stew was being reheated, my phone vibrated again and Pam's number flashed across the screen. I answered it reluctantly. Her soft voice was very difficult to hear on the phone, so I had to concentrate as she spoke. "Rocky," she whispered, "I'm scared."

"What's happened?" I asked urgently.

"Somebody called me. I don't know who it was. He told me, 'If you want to see your friend Rocky live, keep him away from you and Alden's murder case.'" I was stunned at that news. I guessed the caller was trying to enforce what he'd told me by getting Pam involved as well. I hated to admit it was working.

"Did he say anything else?" I asked quickly.

"He said to call you and tell you that if you didn't listen, he'd make you pay with a bullet to the back of your head. Rocky, I have no idea what he was talking about or why he would call me."

"Well, I'm a little surprised myself," I admitted. "I'm assuming the caller didn't identify himself." I was trying hard to keep my voice calm.

"No, and I didn't recognize the voice, but it was sort of muffled, you know, like he was holding a cloth over his phone," she said.

"What did you say to him?" I asked.

"I told him that I didn't know what he was talking about. I didn't know what else to say. Then he said something about my having been warned and he hung up."

I told her that she should report the call to the police there in Brigham City. She readily agreed to that. I didn't mention the direct threat I'd received, so there was nothing more I could tell her. I was going to continue looking for Alden's killers—cautiously but in earnest.

I had scarcely begun to eat when my phone again summoned my attention.

"Rocky," Glenn Gridley's voice boomed into my ear, "I'm calling for a report. What have you learned since we spoke?"

"Several things," I said, wondering just how much I wanted to tell him at this point in my investigation. "For starters, someone out there may want to put me where Alden is if I continue my investigation," I said, wanting him to understand that this had become a dangerous case.

"Good!" Glenn said. But before I could give him an angry retort, he clarified. "I don't mean I'm glad you are in danger but rather that it sounds like you have rattled someone's chain. Apparently you have done some good." I was impressed that Glenn had come to that conclusion so quickly, but I didn't let on how I felt.

"I don't know if that's the case or not," I said. "But someone would be happier if I left the matter in Detective Springer's hands."

Glenn snorted. "Look, Rocky, I hope you'll be cautious of Springer. There was a huge spree of cattle shootings a few years back, and he handled the case. A bunch of ranchers I know lost money thanks to his sloppy investigation skills—the case went on for months. He also fouled up a cattle theft case."

"This information makes sense to me. I thought as much when I saw your reaction to Springer when he first showed up on your property after we'd found Alden's body. You mentioned the theft case then, but not this other case. I'm glad you told me."

"Well, the guy won't get much done. But you clearly are. Tell me about it."

I told him what I had done after revisiting the murder scene on his ranch. He was irritated that Detective Springer hadn't even bothered to look for the evidence I found.

"It's easy to accept the first theory that is presented and not look further," I said with disgust. "I suspect that that's the way Springer typically works."

"I'm thinking that now isn't a good time, but when this matter is closed, I'll be spending some time with the sheriff. He's a good man, and I don't believe he'd tolerate sloppy work if he realized it was going on," Glenn said.

I didn't know the sheriff all that well, and so I had no opinion. I changed the subject. "I interviewed Alden's widow again," I said.

"Great. Did she give you anything to go on?" Glenn asked.

"A little." I'd come to the point where I couldn't report everything I'd learned or share all my suspicions. But I gave him some of it. "Alden wanted to buy a roping horse, for some odd reason, but it seems he knew he couldn't afford one."

"So maybe he *was* involved in the theft," Glenn said, his voice hard.

"It's too early to tell," I cautioned him. I thought for a moment, and then I decided to tell him a little more. "Alden owns a .38 revolver, the same caliber as the casing I found. But it's missing. His wife doesn't know where it is. His truck is also missing." I let my voice trail off. I'd told him all I felt comfortable with at the moment. The badly marred marriage, the shifty banker, the accountant who didn't want Glenn to know he'd known Alden, the widow's suspicions, and my weak suspicions of his widow—I kept all of that to myself. However, I did have a question for him. "Do you know a banker by the name of Mace Healy from down in Ogden?"

"Of course I do. He manages the bank that handles most of my banking needs," Glenn said suspiciously. "I've been with that bank for years. My association with it goes back to well before Healy went to work there. Why do you ask?"

"His name came up in my interview with Pam Overton. I assume that he's trustworthy," I said, not yet wanting to disclose that Mace had been in the house during my interview with Pam. I'd learned what I needed to know. I didn't want to raise any suspicions in Glenn's mind just yet.

"I've never had any reason not to trust him," Glenn said, but due to the tone of his voice, I thought his answer wasn't as convincing as it might have been. I tried not to feel frustrated at this remark. Glenn seemed to withhold information from me on occasion, even though he was paying me to solve his case. I suspected that his behavior had something to do with his stubborn pride. He didn't want me to think that his life was in total chaos.

Without dwelling further on Mace, I said, "I suppose that I'm going to have to let Detective Springer know what I found on the ranch."

"He'll do nothing with it," Glenn said, his anger rekindled.

That was the reaction I had expected, and I shifted my approach. "I don't want to cross the sheriff," I said. "I guess I'll have to sleep on it."

"You do that, and you be careful," Glenn told me a moment later. "You better get some sleep now. I know you've had a long day."

I lay down in bed a few minutes later, exhausted but unable to sleep. I thought about Alden Overton and the two women who had loved him. Both of them were attractive, bright, sensitive women. And he'd hurt them both terribly. And if Pam's suspicions were correct, there was another woman out there somewhere who, if she'd heard of the death of Alden, was probably also grieving tonight. One of the things I needed to do was locate that woman—if she existed.

The first thing I thought about when I awoke the following morning was that I had stirred up a hornet's nest and that someone from that nest wouldn't mind doing me harm if I kept stirring. And that was exactly what I was going to do. Not a comforting thought, but a necessary one.

I began my stirring at the office of accountant Hal Rodgers. It turned out that his office was only three blocks from the place where Alden Overton had worked in downtown Ogden and not very far from the bank that Mace Healy managed. Hal had arrived at his office only minutes before I did, or at least that's what he told me.

Hal seemed friendly enough, even though he wasn't happy about my interruption of his morning. A man of about thirty-four, he was halfway between five and six feet tall. He was overweight, with a slightly protruding stomach. His hand, when he shook mine, was as smooth and soft as a baby's. His blue eyes were intelligent and looked at me in an appraising way when I showed him my ID and explained that the Gridleys had asked me to take a look at their accounts.

"I can't imagine that anything would be wrong with the accounts," he said confidently. "If they have a problem, they can talk to me directly. But frankly, I'm very busy right now. Could we make an appointment for another time?" Hal had thick blond hair, cut just above his collar and slightly over his ears. Although Hal appeared calm and casual in just about every way, I didn't miss the way his chubby fingers pulled nervously through his hair as he spoke to me.

"It's won't take long," I replied. His eyes narrowed as he watched me take the chair across from him, but he didn't object.

It didn't take a lot of effort on my part to get Hal talking about the Gridleys. He seemed particularly interested in Cindy. The way he spoke of her made me glance at his left hand. Like me, he wore no wedding ring. Unless I missed my guess, he was either in love with Cindy or, at the least, infatuated with her. I suspected that she didn't return those feelings; Cindy's type was more cowboy than soft-handed office professional. I made a mental note to talk to Shanice about Hal's relationship with Cindy, just in case. In the meantime, I decided to see if I could milk Hal for additional information using Cindy as a focal point. He seemed to open up like a steamed clam when he talked about her.

"What about Cindy's dad, Glenn? Do you have a good working relationship with him?"

Hal didn't have a bad word to say about Glenn, but he did finally mention that he was worried about the ranch's finances.

"Do you do all their financial work yourself?" I asked him.

"No, I oversee the work of other people in our company," he replied. "But I do perform the bulk of the accounting for the Gridleys. One of the men I supervise takes care of the day-to-day finances."

"You mean like paying the bills and that kind of thing?" I asked, surprised. "I would have thought Glenn or one of his daughters would do that."

"Cindy collects the bills and sorts the mail, but she delivers it to us. And Conrad actually pays the bills, processes their payroll—which is getting smaller, I'm afraid—and balances the checkbook."

"Don't the Gridleys even have their own checkbook?" I asked. Of course I knew that they did. I had a check in my office that Glenn had written as a retainer for my services.

"Oh, yes, and they can access their account online or by debit card. They use those services for all purchases that aren't made on credit. Of course, Conrad has access to all of that online, and he keeps things balanced for them on a regular basis," Hal explained.

"I'd think someone like Cindy could do that and save them some money," I said. "Accountants doing that kind of work can't be cheap."

"Oh, no, Conrad's not an accountant," he said. "He's just a book-keeper."

"But anything Glenn spends in fees, if their finances are tight, could be a problem, couldn't it?" I asked.

"Yes, but I guess they choose not to do it themselves, and I try to be reasonable with them on what I charge," he said. But then he added hastily, "Like I do with all of my clients."

"Whatever works, I guess. But if I were Glenn, I'd have Cindy do it and have her work directly with you," I said. While Hal chewed on that idea, I added, "She seems smart as a whip to me, and she's sure an attractive gal, wouldn't you say?"

He didn't have to say, and he chose not to. But his round, pale face turned a dark shade of pink. My earlier guess had been right; there was definitely an attraction there. It might mean nothing, but it was something that I needed to keep in mind.

"Tell me a little about Conrad," I said.

"Like what?" he asked.

"Oh, you know, what kind of education he has, what his interests are outside work—that kind of thing,"

"Why do you need to know that?" Hal said as the pink faded and he gave me a searching, somewhat worried, look.

"Hey, in my work, you look at everything and everyone," I said, being careful not to make any statements that could be taken as an accusation or even an insinuation against either Hal or the firm he worked for.

"I see," Hal said as his eyes continued to watch me suspiciously. I waited while he thought for a moment. "Well, Conrad doesn't have a college degree, but he's good with figures. In fact, I'd say he's exceptionally good with figures. I don't have to worry about him messing anything up," Hal told me. "I keep telling him that he needs to go back to school part-time and get a degree in accounting. He'd be a bigger help to our firm if he'd do that, and he'd make more money."

"What interests does he have?" I pressed.

"I don't know all his interests. I do know he works on cars some—not other people's, just his own. And he likes horses. In fact, that's one of the reasons that I originally had him take over the book-keeping for the Gridleys. They have a huge interest in horses, and that gives him a common bond with them," Hal explained as he nodded proudly at his own reasoning.

"Does he own any horses?" I asked.

"I think he has a couple. But I'm not sure where he keeps them. He doesn't have any land that I'm aware of."

"I presume you've heard about Alden Overton's death," I said. Hal nodded. He didn't seem surprised that I was aware he knew Alden.

"Yeah, of course I heard."

"How did you know him, again?" I remembered what Shanice had said about Hal and Alden being such great friends and intro-ducing her to Alden, but I wanted to hear it from him.

"Alden and I used to be good friends. He worked here for several years before he became a financial consultant. Back then, I didn't have an accounting degree, so he and I did the same kind of work."

"Bookkeeping, right?" He nodded.

"And you say you used to be good friends?" I asked. That was an interesting choice of words.

"No, it's nothing like that. We hung out when he worked here—you know, golfing and going dancing with girls and that kind of thing. When he changed jobs, that's kind of where things ended. No reason, really. We were just busy with other things. I haven't seen or heard from him for years."

"Okay. And how well does Conrad know Alden?" I asked.

"I don't know for sure. He knows him—knew him," he amended awkwardly. "It's too bad about Alden. I can't imagine why anyone would want to kill him."

"Someone not only wanted to, someone did," I said bluntly, looking directly at Hal as I spoke.

He didn't flinch as he answered quickly, "It wouldn't have been Conrad." The comment was sporadic, and he offered no explanation as to why he felt that way.

I got to my feet. "If you'd direct me to Conrad's office, I'd like to speak to him for a moment while I'm here."

"Oh, his office isn't in this building," Hal said as he also rose to his feet.

"It's not?" I was surprised.

"No, he works out of our small satellite office in Brigham City. I work up there occasionally myself, but Conrad does all of his work from there. The Gridleys aren't the only clients I have up there that Conrad assists me with."

I got the address of the office. And as I approached the exit to Hal's office, I added, "I would appreciate it if you don't tell Conrad that I'm coming."

"Of course, whatever you say, Mr. Revada."

As I walked back to my truck, I reflected on my visit with Hal Rodgers. I had learned very little, but what I learned could be important. Hal seemed to genuinely like Glenn Gridley and his family, especially Cindy. I had also learned that there were in fact financial problems, but Hal either believed that it was simply misfortune and the economic downturn, or else he wanted me to think he believed that. I also had learned that he employed a man who didn't make a lot of money, who had total access to the Gridley accounts, and who liked horses. And that man might already, or soon would, know that Glenn had dipped into his apparently dwindling funds to pay me a substantial retainer. He would no doubt wonder why.

I wondered if I should call Shanice and see if she could tell me anything that I should know about Conrad before I talked to him. My cell phone began to vibrate. "Good morning, Rocky," said a voice that I found I was glad to hear. She didn't sound very cheerful—not that I would expect her to under the circumstances.

"Hi, Shanice," I said. "I was just thinking about you."

"Really?" she said. "I hope it was a good thought."

"Of course it was," I said with a light chuckle. "I was just about to call you. I have a couple of questions." I had reached my truck and noticed a paper beneath my windshield wiper. "But why don't you tell me what you need first."

"Alden's wife called me," she said as I reached and pulled the paper from beneath my wiper blade, expecting to see an advertisement of some sort. "I know you're busy, but I need to talk to you in person." Her voice had begun to tremble.

"Of course," I said as I awkwardly shook the folded paper open with one hand. "Where would you like to meet?"

I didn't hear her response because my mind had focused entirely on the message that was scribbled on the paper I was holding. It read: *Mr. Revada, apparently you don't value your life. I would advise you to back off if you want to avoid serious trouble.*

"Rocky, are you still there?"

"Oh, uh yes, I was distracted for a moment," I said as I tried to stop my mind from whirling while I gathered my thoughts. "Um . . . where did you want to meet?"

"I just told you," she said with a puzzled tone in her voice. "Didn't you hear me?"

"I'm sorry. I missed it."

"Why are you acting so distracted?" she asked. She did not sound angry with me, just worried.

"I found a note on my truck just now," I said. "I was reading it, that's all."

"Rocky, are you okay?" she asked.

The worry in her voice was somehow comforting to me. "I'm fine. I'm in Ogden, but I was going to head north now," I told her.

"How far north were you planning to go?" she asked.

"I need to talk to Conrad Patel, your bookkeeper," I said. "But I would like to talk to you about him first."

"I'll meet you in Brigham City, then," she said. She named a location.

"Great, I'm headed that way," I said, which was not entirely true. I was actually walking back toward Hal's building. I walked in and went directly to his private office. He looked up in surprise as I stopped in his doorway. "Are you sure Conrad's at work?" I asked.

"He should be. Why do you ask?"

"I don't want to drive all the way to Brigham City to talk to him if he isn't, that's all," I said, trying to keep my voice level.

"You said not to mention that you were coming," he countered. The look I gave him must have scared him a bit, though, because he finished with, "I'll call his cell phone." He picked up the phone off his desk.

"No, call his office number," I said, a little more curtly than I had intended.

"Fine," Hal said, giving me a look that said it wasn't fine but he'd do it anyway.

He dialed and I waited. He also waited. He finally put his phone down. "He's not answering. Would you like me to call his cell number after all?"

"No, that's okay," I said. I'd learned what I wanted to know. Conrad was not where he was supposed to be. Now what I would like to see was a sample of his handwriting, but I decided to wait on that. I didn't want to raise any more questions in Hal's mind than I already had.

I didn't leave for Brigham City when I again arrived at my truck. I looked the truck over very thoroughly instead. I even knelt and looked beneath it. I didn't want it blowing up with me in it. When I convinced myself it was safe, I got in, started it, and drove toward my meeting place with Shanice.

Chapter Eight

SHANICE WAS NOT ALONE WHEN I got to our rendezvous point at a small café in Brigham City. Pam was with her. Those two were the last ones I'd have expected to see together. Pam looked like she hadn't slept at all. Her face was drawn, and dark circles showed clearly beneath her eyes. Shanice also looked tired, but the first thing I noticed about her was the worry on her face.

Both women gave me a brief hug, and then we went inside and found a booth in the corner. I sat on one side, and Pam and Shanice sat on the other, facing me. "You ladies have something on your minds," I said after a waitress had placed glasses of water in front of us.

"We're worried about you," Shanice said. "Pam called me this morning and told me about the threat."

I turned to Pam with what I only hoped was a stern look on my face, but she just smiled and said, "I'm sorry, Rocky, but Shanice has a right to know the kind of danger you're in. I'm not sure you are looking out for your own welfare." I swallowed a groan and changed the subject.

"I didn't know you guys were friends," I said as I looked from one to the other.

Shanice glanced at Pam for a moment, and then she said, "We don't really know each other very well. I would be a liar if I said that I hadn't held bitter feelings against Pam after she took my husband, but I learned later that she hadn't known he was married until it was basically over between us. So I have long since gotten over my anger.

"We were both lied to and mistreated by Alden. And Pam told me that she suspected he was doing to her what he did to me. But despite that, we are both heartbroken that he was murdered, and we want you to catch whoever did it."

"But not at the expense of your life," Pam said softly, brushing absently at her hair with her fingers. I leaned forward so I could hear her better. "I'm worried about you, Rocky. Whoever killed Alden would do the same thing to you to keep from being caught."

"And I'm worried too," Shanice agreed. "It's not worth the danger it's put you in."

I straightened up and said, "Let's get one thing straight. I agreed to do a job, and unless Glenn fires me, I intend to do it. I admit that things have gotten pretty tense in the case, but I'm used to this kind of thing. Threats like this come with the territory. I know how to handle myself. And besides, I'm really only assisting the cops. Whatever I learn will have to be turned over to them."

"So you're saying you're being careful," Shanice said, looking at me flatly. She didn't seem convinced. The worry on her face mirrored that of my mother the day I came home and told her that I was going to ride a bull in the rodeo. I can't say I wasn't flattered to have Shanice fuss about me.

"Of course I am," I said, trying to sound convincing. "And I will continue to watch my back."

"Do you . . . do you have a gun?" Pam asked hesitantly.

"Yes, Pam. I have a gun."

"But do you have it on you?" She looked under the table at my waist, searching for, I could only assume, my gun. I tried to keep the exasperation from my face. She sat up again and looked me square in the face.

"Rocky, I don't see it. You need a gun on you at all times now!" Shanice said forcefully. "Please, go get it. Don't you keep one in your truck?"

"If it makes you ladies feel better, I'll put it on in a little while," I said mildly.

We ordered soft drinks and sipped at them when the waitress placed them before us. Talking about my safety wasn't my favorite topic at the moment, so I turned the conversation to Alden instead. "Do you have any idea who your husband might have been seeing?" I asked, looking at Pam.

She shook her head and rubbed her eyes.

"I need to figure that out," I said. Both girls nodded, and then I said, "Shanice, what can you tell me about Conrad Patel?"

"Not a lot about his personal life," she said. "He's our bookkeeper. He works for Hal Rodgers, our accountant."

"That's who told me about him," I said. It sounded like we'd already reached a dead end with Conrad, so I switched gears. "What about your accountant? I'm curious about something. Does he have a thing for your sister, Cindy?"

"Oh, yes," Shanice said, rolling her eyes as a grin crossed her face. "But believe me, it's all one-sided."

I looked at her for a moment, and she squirmed under my gaze. "There's more, isn't there?" I pressed.

The smile was gone, and while shaking her head, she said, "You know Cindy. She can be a flirt, and guys usually pick up on that because she's very pretty. She used to flirt with Hal, like she does with lots of guys, but he took it as something more serious than it was. She doesn't flirt with him at all anymore, but he has asked her out several times. He doesn't take no for an answer. He makes her nervous now, and she doesn't like to be around him."

I digested that bit of information before I said, "So he could be angry with her."

"Maybe, although I don't think it's reached that point. I'd say he's still crazy over her and still hopes that things will change," Shanice told me.

"But you don't think they will."

"Absolutely not," she said.

"Could he be dangerous?" I asked.

Shanice shook her head. "I can't place Hal in the middle of the things that have happened to us over the past few weeks. I can't imagine a little crush on Cindy escalating that far. Besides, I don't think he's asked her out for quite a while."

"Okay. Can either of you think of anything else I should know?" I asked.

"There is one more thing," Pam said. I looked at her and waited until she went on. "Alden's truck is home now."

"Whoa, you don't say!" I was shocked at that. "Do you have any idea how it got there?"

"No, it wasn't there when you left last night, but when I got up this morning, it was parked in my driveway."

"Have you told anyone but me?" I asked.

"My mother knows, and I told Shanice," she said with a quick glance to her side.

"But not the cops?"

"No. I haven't spoken to them since they stopped by that first night," she said.

"They probably need to be told. Let me give you a number for Detective Springer, the case officer," I offered.

But she gave me a small wave of one hand as she shook her head and said, "I have his number, but I'd rather not call him. He was pretty rude to me when he and the other deputies talked to me earlier. Would you do it for me?"

I didn't exactly look forward to talking to Springer, but I could understand why the idea of calling him was not appealing to her either. So I said, "Of course. But I'd like to swing by your place now and take a look at the truck before he gets there. Would that be all right?"

Pam had driven to the café in her own car, the Volkswagen I'd seen in her driveway. She left as soon as we all got to the parking lot. When she'd pulled out of sight, I turned to Shanice, "I better go over to Pam's now. I'll call the detective after I get there."

"Do you mind if I follow you?" she asked.

"Of course not," I responded, wondering what she had in mind. "See you there in a few minutes."

After I'd looked over the truck briefly, disappointed with what I saw, I called Detective Springer. He was not happy to hear from me if his tone of voice was any indication.

"Pam Overton asked me to tell you that her husband's pickup appeared in her driveway this morning," I said.

"Of course *she* couldn't call me directly. And I suppose *you* are already there?" he asked scornfully. I could imagine his lips curled and his left hand rubbing his shiny head.

"That's right. She asked me to come over, and I did. But I haven't touched a thing, and I'll make sure no one else does either."

Shanice and Pam went inside, but Shanice came out a moment later. "She's lying down, but I suspect that when Detective Springer gets here, he'll want to talk to her," she said.

I nodded. "Shanice, is there anything else you can tell me about Conrad Patel, your bookkeeper?"

"Like I told you at the café, I don't know much about him. But if I think of anything that will help, I'll let you know," she said.

"I know you guys trust him with your money," I said, "but would you trust him with your lives?"

She jerked her head back and stared at me. "What do you mean by that?"

"I mean, do you totally trust the man, or is there a chance that he might not be all that he's tried to make you and your family believe he is?" I clarified.

She was thoughtful for a moment. Finally, she answered. "I can't give you a reason, but I don't personally care for him all that much. But Dad seems okay with him, and Hal gives him high marks."

"And you trust whatever Hal says," I stated.

She took it as a question and said, "On a professional basis, pretty much, yes. What about you?" she asked. "You seem to have a lot of questions about him. Do you think he's okay?"

"Honestly, at this point, I can't see anything wrong with him," I told her, "but until I learn more, I will treat him as though I don't trust him. I've got to keep an open mind."

Detective Springer must have burned up the freeway between Tremonton and Brigham City because he was there in record time. The chip was still sitting tenaciously on his shoulder when he got out of his car. With only a passing glance at the truck, he turned on me and said with a growl, "I'm warning you to stay away from my investigation. If I hear that you've been investigating Overton's murder, I'll make you wish you'd never met me."

I already wished that. I'd wished it for a long time. When I didn't respond to his outburst, he asked, "Is that clear?"

It was clear, and I admitted as much, but I didn't for one second intend to follow his instructions. Instead, I pointed at the truck, a late-model Ford F150 and said, "Unless I miss my guess, I'd say this truck has been washed. It's sparkling clean."

"I can see that," he said dismissively.

"I hope it hasn't also been wiped clean of prints inside the cab."

"I'm not sure I care what you think, Revada," Blaine said, heading back to his car and getting in the driver's seat, where he began talking on his cell phone.

I watched him go. I had been prepared to tell him about the bullet and what I'd learned at the Gridley ranch, but after that remark, I decided against it. So I said, to no one in particular, "I'll be going then."

I caught Shanice's eye, and she followed me to my truck, which was parked right behind hers on the street. There she stopped and said, "Well, he's making great progress on the case, from the looks of it."

I chuckled. "It appears not, but I'll keep on it," I assured her.

"But he warned you not to," she exclaimed, a look of horror on her face but a hint of a smile in her eyes.

"And I didn't listen."

"Are you sure you want to keep working this case for us?" she asked, her eyes suddenly full of worry.

"Yes, I'm sure. You can stop asking." She stuck her tongue out at me briefly, then leaned against her car. I paused and gazed at her for a moment, wondering if this was a good time to ask a question that had been on my mind since my short, contentious encounter with Mace Healy. I decided it was as good as any—or as poor as any. I forged forward. "Shanice, Mace Healy was here at Pam's house when I came to talk to her last night. You know him, right?"

"Sure, that's my dad's banker. I've met him a few times. What was he doing here?" she asked as surprise registered in her face and she glanced at the house.

"Apparently Pam knows him, too—through Alden. I'm not sure what brought him here besides comforting a newly grieving widow, but he didn't want me talking to her and did his best to get me out of there. Fortunately, she sided with me, and he ended up leaving in anger," I told her.

"He can be abrasive," she said.

"That's for sure," I agreed. Then I took the plunge. "He talked about you and Alden. He says your dad caused your divorce."

She threw her arms up in surprise. "You've got to be kidding me. Why would he say that?"

"I was hoping you could tell me, Shanice."

"Well, I can't. It's not true. Alden broke up our marriage all by himself. Dad had nothing to do with it. As you saw a little while ago, I don't even blame Pam anymore."

"If Mace lied about that, can I assume that he might lie about other things as well?" I asked.

She took a deep breath, dropped her hands to her side, and said, "Probably, although I can't imagine why he would."

"I intend to figure that out," I told her intently as my eyes locked with hers. "I'm sorry if I upset you."

Just then I noticed Detective Springer over her shoulder. He was standing beside Alden's truck, glaring at me.

"I think our detective friend wants me to leave," I said.

She turned her head, but then she turned it back sharply. "I wish he'd just go to work," she commented angrily.

"I better go. I'm going to see if I can find your bookkeeper now. I'll see you later."

She touched my arm, sending a pleasant shiver through me. Her eyes searched mine for a moment, and then she said, "You won't let yourself get hurt will you?"

I playfully exaggerated a groan, then smiled at her. "I'll be careful, I promise."

Conrad was in his office when I got there a few minutes later. "So you're the man who's taking Glenn's money" was the way he greeted me after I'd introduced myself. I took an instant dislike to the man and instinctively felt that I needed to watch myself with him. I kept my interview short, which was really my only choice, because he made it clear that he had nothing of substance to tell me.

He even brought up the horse switch, claiming that Glenn himself had informed him. But he also claimed to have no idea how that could have happened or who might have done it. I formed my opinion of him, one which differed from the Gridley family's. That opinion was reinforced by something I observed on his desk. It was not a simple notepad. I really wanted one sheet of paper from that pad. I could see a watermark that I wanted to compare with the one on the threatening note I had found on my windshield while I was at Hal's office.

"Could I borrow a piece of paper?" I asked, pointing to the pad as I did so. "I need to make myself a note before I leave."

He seemed to focus on my intent to leave and gave me the paper without a hint of suspicion. He then stood up behind his desk. I folded the paper in quarters and stood myself. He didn't say a word about me not writing on the paper. He didn't even say good-bye as I left his office, but I was determined to learn more about this uncooperative young man who had such critical access to Glenn Gridley's money.

Back in my truck, I waited until I was a block from Conrad Patel's office before pulling over and comparing the two pieces of paper. The watermark on both was identical, as was the off-white tint and the size. It would take an expert to testify in court that the threatening note was written on paper from the same or a similar pad, but I was convinced. Then a thought occurred to me, and I held the paper I'd taken from his desk and let the sun shine through. What I saw made my heart pound. The paper from the bookkeeper's desk had faint but discernible marks from a pen that had been used to write a message on a previous page. That pen had been pressed hard enough to cause indentations on the clean paper that matched every letter in the written threat.

I put the two papers down, intending to protect them by putting them in my office safe when I got back to Logan later. I also reached into my consul and pulled out my .9mm pistol in its concealable holster and put it inside my waistband. I recognized my action for what it was; I was in danger and needed to be prepared to defend myself.

I stowed the two papers in a small case beneath my seat before putting my truck back in gear and pulling onto the street again. But I didn't continue in the direction I had planned. Instead, I circled around and stopped where I could see the building where Conrad's office was housed. I only had to sit there for ten minutes before Conrad emerged, looked around, and headed for the parking lot beside the building. When he pulled onto the street, I waited until he had gone a short distance. Then I followed him. He made a left turn, continued several blocks, and then made a right turn. Several blocks later, he turned onto SR 89 and headed north—toward Logan.

This was too much. Keeping a reasonable distance between us, I followed him up Sardine Canyon. I didn't like what I learned when we entered Cache Valley. He drove directly to and then past my house first before pulling to a stop as he circled back. I grabbed a powerful set of binoculars and watched as he stuck his hands out of the window of his truck. He was holding a small camera. A moment later he pulled it back in and drove away. His next stop was across the street from my office. He took more pictures and then headed back toward Brigham City. I followed him all the way to his office and watched him until he disappeared inside.

My next stop was the Gridley ranch outside Tremonton. Glenn's sister Rose answered the door. "Is Glenn here?" I asked.

"No, he's out on the ranch somewhere checking some cattle. Can I help you?" she asked.

"What about Shanice? Is she around?" I asked as I looked over Rose's shoulder. Tyra was standing in the hallway watching us. "Hi, Tyra," I called out.

She then began to skip toward us. Rose stepped aside, and Tyra hugged my legs. "Mom's in the barn with the horses," she said. "I'll take you there."

"Tyra, remember, you haven't finished your homework yet. Mr. Revada can find your mother by himself," Rose said firmly.

"I'll do it in a few minutes," she argued. "Please, let me go with him to see Mom."

"You know the rule, young lady. 'Finish your homework the first hour after you get home from school.'" Rose was poking a harmless and yet threatening finger at the little girl.

"But today was our short day," Tyra argued. She put her little hands on her hips. I smiled as I watched her. She moved her argument forward. "I always have it finished by four-thirty. I'll have it done by then, easy. I don't have much today. I promise, Aunt Rose." She still stood the same, but her lower lip began to quiver.

Rose's stern face broke into a smile. "Oh, fine," she said with a sigh. She patted Tyra's head. "Go with Mr. Revada then, but don't be too long."

"I'll see that she's back in time to finish her homework," I said.

With a squeal, Tyra grabbed my hand and said, "Come on. Let's find Mom."

Chapter Nine

TYRA CHATTERED NONSTOP ALL THE way to the barn, skipping beside me as I walked and holding tightly to my hand. I found myself thinking that I could get used to having little kids around more often.

We entered the barn, still hand in hand. Shanice was in front of the tack room rubbing oil on her saddle. Her back was to us, and she was so intent on her work that she didn't hear us approaching—until Tyra called out, "Mom, Rocky came to see us." It made me smile.

Shanice looked over her shoulder. She smiled at us and stood up, dropping the oily cloth beside the saddle. "Hi Tyra," she said with fondness in her voice. She picked up a clean rag and rubbed her hands. Then she turned to me with a furrowed brow. "I had hoped you'd come by today, Rocky," she said.

"Oh yeah?" I said, looking at her quizzically. "Any particular reason?"

"Not really. I just like to see ya. That's all."

"And I do too!" Tyra said, slipping her hand back in mine. Shanice beamed at her, then looked back at me.

"Well, I came to talk to your dad," I said to Shanice, "but he's out on the ranch somewhere."

"What's happened?" she asked. "Or can't you tell me?"

"Of course I can tell you," I said with a smile. "In fact, you can help me with something, if you want."

She smiled back, a smile that had a serious effect on me.

"Come to my truck," I said. "There's something I'd like you to see."

Tyra, still holding my hand, grabbed her mom's hand as well, and together the three of us walked back into the bright spring sunshine. It felt good just being with these two, and it hurt me to think that it would all end when the case was solved.

If I lived to solve it.

That thought came out of nowhere, and it disturbed me more than I liked to admit. I had never dealt with anything this dangerous before. I prayed that the Lord would allow me to get out of it alive.

When we reached the truck, I put on some light gloves and then retrieved the papers I had put in the case beneath my seat. "This was on my windshield this morning when I came out of Hal's office."

Shanice began to tremble as I held the paper with the actual note so she could read it. Her face went pale, and she looked at me with horror in her eyes. "Rocky, you can't go on with this case. This guy, whoever he is, is dangerous. Please. I'll talk to Dad."

"Shanice, would you feel better if I told you that I know who wrote this and left it on my windshield?" I asked.

"Are you going to tell me?" she asked, grabbing my arm and clinging to it.

"Mom, what's the matter?" Tyra asked.

She looked down at the stricken face of her little girl. Tyra had no idea what was going on, and yet she could apparently feel the tension and fear that was emanating from her mother. Shanice said, "Sweetheart, everything is fine. You need to run in the house now and have Aunt Rose help you with your homework."

"Mom, not until Rocky leaves," Tyra protested, her lower lip protruding slightly.

"That wasn't a question, young lady," Shanice said firmly, her face still white from the fright the note had given her.

I spoke up then. "When your mother and I have finished with our business, I'll come in and say goodbye."

"Promise?" Tyra asked.

"Yes, I promise. In fact, I'll help you with your homework if you haven't finished with it by the time I come in," I told her on a sudden impulse.

"Rocky, you don't have to—"

I put a finger on her lips and then said, "I want to."

"Okay, then you run inside, Tyra," Shanice said. "We'll both be in soon."

Tyra skipped toward the house and Shanice turned to me. "You are so good to her. She is very fond of you."

"She's a doll," I said. Then I did something that surprised me. I said, "I wish I had someone like her in my life. I suppose I could have. It's nobody's fault but mine."

"What? Could it be that the optimist has a few regrets of his own?" Shanice teased. Then she reached up and took hold of my face with both of her hands. "Someday you will," she said, her eyes looking deeply into mine. I had never wanted to kiss anyone so much in my life, but I resisted.

"I hope so," I said, dragging my eyes from hers and reentering the real world. "Look at this," I said, showing her the second sheet of paper.

"It's blank," she said, cocking her eyebrows. "What is this about?"

I held the other paper up beside the first one and said, "Look closely at both of them." I wanted to see if she would independently come to the conclusion that I had reached.

She looked puzzled at first, and then her eyes narrowed slightly. "It has the same watermark," she said. "Where did you get this?" she pointed to the blank paper.

"I'll tell you in a moment," I said. "First, look at it closer. Here, I'll hold it up and let the light shine through."

After looking closely at the paper, she gasped. "It has impressions of writing on it." I nodded but said nothing. She looked at the threatening note and then back at the blank paper. Then she looked at me, understanding in her eyes. "The blank one was under the other one when it was written," she said with a nod of her head. "Is that right?"

"It think so," I said as I opened my truck door and dropped the papers on the seat. "And now to your question of where I got the blank one—it is from a pad on Conrad's desk."

Shanice recoiled as hard as if I'd slapped her. Her face went white, and for a moment, I thought she was going to faint. I stepped forward and she fell into my arms. For a long time, I held her against me as her body trembled. Finally, she pushed back. "I'm sorry," she said.

"Don't be," I told her. I'd hold her like that any time she wanted me to. *I better quit wanting her to,* I told myself. She was my client, I was in the middle of an investigation for her, and this kind of behavior was distracting and arguably inappropriate. The thing was, after the investigation, who knew if I'd see her again?

"Rocky, in a professional way, he's close to us. We trusted him. Hal trusted him." Her voice was shaky, and there was a mist in her eyes. "Did he kill Alden?"

"I don't know," I said. "All I've proven so far is that a threatening note was written in his office on his notepad. This certainly suggests that he's involved, and maybe he's the main suspect, but I have more work to do." As I said that, I got the nagging feeling that there was something else I needed to do with the notes.

"You need to take that to Detective Springer," she said. "This will wake him up."

"Maybe, but I doubt it. No, for now, this goes no further than us and your father. Are you okay with that?" I asked.

"I trust you, Rocky," she said, "so I guess I have to be okay with it. But I'm worried about your safety. Aren't you?"

"Of course I am, and to be honest, I've never worked such a complicated case as this one before. It's hard to know who I am watching out for or what they are capable of, which makes it extremely dangerous. But just remember, I've been doing this sort of work for years. I know how to take care of myself," I said with more confidence than I was feeling.

"Dad has got to see those papers," she said after looking at me with what I hoped was tenderness. "Let's go find him."

"In a few minutes," I said. "I made a promise to your daughter. I want to go in and help her with her homework."

"You don't have to do that," she said. "Tyra's only six. Her homework is simple."

"That's the only kind I'd be of any help with. Come on, let's go in before she's finished," I said. I reached for her hand without really thinking about it, and she took it as if it were the most natural thing in the world.

We spent an enjoyable ten minutes with Tyra, but we were both anxious to meet with Glenn. Shanice dialed his cell phone. When she discovered that he was on his way in, she told him that I was here and needed to go over something with him. We left the house a few minutes later and met Glenn in front of the barn.

I let Shanice explain what I had discovered. To say that Glenn was angry would be an understatement. "Let's go have a talk with Hal right now," he said sharply. "I don't want Conrad doing anything for us from this point on. In fact, I want him in jail."

"I think we need to move slowly on him," I said, ignoring the anger that was shooting from Glenn's eyes. "He may not be working alone, and I need a little time to see if I can figure out who else is involved."

Glenn said nothing, but he paced back and forth for a couple of minutes. Shanice leaned close to me and said, "He's cooling down. Give him a minute."

The minute worked for both Glenn and me. He calmed down, and I figured out what I was missing—something else I needed to determine about the note. Glenn ceased his pacing. His face had resumed something close to his normal complexion. He faced me, his arms folded across his chest, and asked, "Do you have an idea who is involved besides Conrad?"

"I haven't formed any other conclusions," I said evasively. "For that matter, I don't know for sure what Conrad's involvement is. It appears that he's threatening me, but I have no proof that he killed Alden or that he stole your horses."

"What do you mean when you say it *appears* that he threatened you?" Glenn asked.

"Someone else could have written the note while sitting at Conrad's desk. Do you have something with his handwriting on it?" I asked.

"He's our bookkeeper. Of course we do," Glenn said sharply. "Let's go in the house."

I retrieved the papers with gloved hands and we went into the living room in the house. Five minutes later, after comparing several notes that Conrad had written to Glenn over the years, we all agreed that Conrad was not the author of the note I'd found on my windshield. His hand-writing was much too poor to match the curvy longhand of the note. Despite this, we all agreed that he almost certainly was involved with the note—that he at least knew it had been written and who had done it. I knew that Conrad had been at his desk for at least a short while on the day I received the note—I had spoken with him. And even if someone had broken into Conrad's office and written the note at his desk, it didn't necessarily mean that his actions weren't suspicious or that he wasn't somehow involved.

We walked back outside to my truck. "You're doing a good job, Rocky, and I . . ." Glenn began and then hesitated as he looked at Shanice. "We appreciate it." I was surprised at this comment. Glenn seemed to be directing some of his softness toward me, which I hadn't expected.

A pickup pulled up and parked next to mine, and Jena and Cindy got out. Cindy asked, "Hey, what's happening?"

Their father looked inquiringly at me, and I shrugged. "Your call," I said, thinking that he wanted my opinion on how much to tell them.

Cindy put her hands on her hips and looked at me. "Okay, Rocky, out with it," she said in mock severity. "I can tell from their faces that you have just reported something significant." She smiled at me.

Jena approached me from the opposite side of where Shanice was standing. She took hold of my left arm and said, "Come on, Rocky. What gives here?" She was also smiling.

Shanice took hold of my right arm in what felt like a possessive move. Cindy watched with a sparkle in her eyes. It was hard not to really like this family. Glenn had clearly decided to tell them, because he handed Cindy the two pieces of paper. As he recited, step by step, what I had just finished reporting to him and what we had learned from comparing the handwriting, fear filled their faces and they gasped.

Both girls were shocked that such a note had been written on Conrad's desk. Even though it was almost certain that someone else had written it, clearly their trust in him was severely tarnished. Cindy more or less made this clear when she said, "It's his office. No one else works there but Hal, and he's not there much. I've never seen it unlocked when he wasn't in it. He must know who wrote the note." The others nodded in agreement.

We moved into the barn where we discussed my options at length. The younger sisters thought that it was time to involve the police. Their biggest fear, they said, was for my life. I appreciated that, but I pointed out that Detective Springer didn't take anything I said seriously. They argued that I had something now that would interest him.

Glenn also favored involving the sheriff himself now. I was certain that he was looking out for me, not for his own interests at this point. So I resisted. "Give me another day," I said.

The family exchanged glances. Finally, Glenn said, "Tomorrow we go to the sheriff. Not to Detective Springer, but to the sheriff."

"Good enough," I agreed. "I better get back to work."

"Be careful," Shanice said. "I'll be praying for you."

"We all will," Cindy added.

"Thanks," I said as I opened the door to my truck. "That will help."

I headed south for Brigham City again. I paid another visit to Pam when I got there. What I wanted from her was a list of places that Alden frequented. I needed to find his latest girlfriend. I couldn't help but think that whoever the woman was, she might know something helpful.

I made several stops after that, but I didn't learn anything that was of use to me. Finally, just as dusk was settling over the town, I drove up Sardine Canyon. The next hour was spent tending to my personal safety. I was still wearing my pistol, but the danger called for more extreme measures. Under cover of darkness, I placed wireless cameras, which I kept around for surveillance of my clients and their associates, at my office and my house—something I'd never done before. The cameras were in place both indoors and out when I had finished. Then I rented a hotel room in Logan and set up my monitoring and recording equipment there.

I had dinner after that and finally retired to my room, where I spent the next two hours with my laptop, typing up a comprehensive report of my investigation to date. I copied the report onto a thumb drive. After that, I transferred the two incriminating papers I had kept in my truck to a manila envelope and put them in the hotel safe along with the thumb drive. My intent was to keep them from being stolen or destroyed. I wondered with more than mild interest who had authored the note and what his or her relationship was with Conrad.

After placing my pistol on the nightstand, I finally settled down with some soft music playing and thought about what I needed to do the next day. The hornets' nest had been disturbed. I wanted to destroy it as quickly as I could so that the stinging insects would cease to be a threat to me or to the Gridley family.

It was after ten when my cell phone rang. "Rocky," Shanice said. "I just called to make sure you were okay."

"I'm fine," I said, smiling at her concern.

"Are you sure you're safe in your house tonight, Rocky? Dad says you would be welcome to come here. We have lots of room."

"That won't be necessary. I'll be fine," I assured her. "I'm not staying at home tonight anyway." I didn't tell her where I was, and she didn't ask.

There was relief in her voice when she said, "I'm glad. I am so worried about you."

"Shanice," I said seriously, "I'm worried about you and your family. You need to be careful too. Keep your doors locked and your eyes peeled."

There was silence for a moment before she said, "You're right. I'll talk to Dad, Aunt Rose, and the girls about it."

We talked for a few minutes after that. After we'd finished our phone conversation, I watched my video equipment for a while. I had ten cameras in use, and all of them were set to come on when there was motion. If and when any of them did, the image they were seeing would be displayed on a portion of my screen and recorded for later use.

Every so often, one or the other of the exterior cameras would begin recording briefly as a car passed on the street or a stray cat walked through the backyard between the house and my barn. My system had a built-in alarm that would alert me to activity that kept that camera filming for longer than a preset period of time. The alert could be set to go to my cell phone too, but I didn't need that feature with my laptop right there. I set the alarm for thirty seconds, hoping that was neither too short nor too long of a time, and went to bed after placing my gun within easy reach on the nightstand.

I was sleeping soundly when my camera alarm went off. I awoke and had to take a moment to orient myself. Two cameras had been activated, both of them at my office in downtown Logan. I watched them for a moment. A figure dressed all in black was messing with my door. I picked up my phone and dialed 911. "There is a break-in occurring at the office of Rocky Revada Investigations," I told the dispatcher. "If your officers hurry, they'll catch the intruder in the act."

My relationship with the sheriff's officers in Cache County and Logan in particular was much better than in Box Elder County. An officer called my cell phone moments later and reported that he was on his way. I told him that I would be headed that way as soon as I could get dressed and strap on my gun. I glanced at the luminous clock next to the hotel bed and noted that it was three in the morning.

None of the other cameras came on, and so I headed out. By the time I got to the office, the cops had a young man in custody. I explained briefly to the officers why I had the surveillance equipment operating, about the threats on my life and the danger involved in the case I was working. They didn't ask about the case, but they did want to know if I recognized the young hoodlum who had succeeded in gaining entry to my office before they caught him. I didn't.

The young man was surly and totally uncooperative, so one officer hauled him off to jail while the others and I began to examine my office. We found what appeared to be a small homemade bomb with a triggering device designed to be attached to the door, which upon being opened would set off the bomb. In the suspect's car, which was parked behind the office, we found another bomb exactly like the first. "That was probably for my house," I said calmly while my stomach did acidic somersaults.

At the jail, they were already interrogating the young suspect. His name, the officers informed me, was Victor Rivera. He was about twenty and had a long rap sheet. But this bombing attempt, they said, was far more serious than anything he'd been arrested for before. He had waived his right to an attorney, but he wasn't admitting anything of substance.

I asked if I could try a question or two on him. Permission was granted, and I stepped into the interrogation room. "How much is Conrad Patel paying you to kill me?" I asked without foreword.

The look on his dark face was all I needed to tell me that Conrad had, in fact, hired him. His verbal answer was what I had expected. "I don't know what you're talking about, man," he said.

The officers resumed their questioning. With the opening I had made, it didn't take long for them to get a confession out of him. He wasn't nearly as tough as he thought he was when he heard that he was facing the rest of his life in prison if he didn't come clean. He even admitted to writing the note and leaving it on my windshield—at Conrad's suggestion, as I had suspected.

He was booked in jail on a million-dollar bond, and I went back to my hotel room, arriving there shortly before five. I checked my cameras. There was no activity at my house and no more at my office once the officers left. I went back to bed, convinced that Conrad was our man. The cops said they'd find him.

Chapter Ten

I WAS AWAKENED AGAIN AT seven by my pesky phone. I was groggy from lack of sleep. "Rocky Revada?" the male voice asked.

"This is Rocky," I agreed.

"My name is Detective Burke Christensen of the Brigham City Police Department. I was informed that you had an attempt made on your life a few hours ago, and that you know who was behind it."

"That's right," I said. The detective's name was familiar. I vaguely remembered crossing paths with him on a case about a year ago. If this was the guy I was thinking of, he was a detective that inspired confidence—unlike Detective Springer.

"Would it be possible to talk with you this morning?" the officer asked.

"Of course, but I will need a little time to get ready and drive down there," I said, regretting the sleep I wouldn't be getting.

"Hey, I have a better idea," he suggested. "I'll drive up there. That way maybe you can get dressed and get something to eat before we meet."

"That would be great." I told him where to find me, and then headed for the shower.

We sat in my hotel room forty minutes later. I had retrieved my papers from the hotel safe, and I showed them to Burke, giving him a brief background on the past couple days. "Why didn't you let me know yesterday?" he asked.

"I figured he would try something if he didn't know I was on to him," I said.

Burke nodded his head. "And you were right. Okay, let's take this from the top."

"I would appreciate it if you would keep all this in confidence," I said.

He gave me his word. So I told him who I was working for and why. When I mentioned the sloppy work that Springer had done on the Gridley ranch, he said, "Sounds like Blaine. If it isn't dumped in his lap, he usually doesn't find it. Not that he isn't capable, because he is—he's just lazy at times. I've actually seen him do some very good work."

"I'm glad to hear that, but in this case it's worse than that," I said. "He won't even let me give him any help."

For the next half hour we discussed future strategy. I felt a load lifted off of me. I now had some competent help. We agreed that the first thing we needed to do was visit the accounting firm where Hal Rodgers worked in Ogden.

I was on my way to Ogden, following Burke, when Shanice called me to make sure I was okay.

"I'm not lying in a gutter yet," I joked lightly.

"Ha ha, very funny," she replied, clearly not amused at my attempt at humor. "I mean it, though. Is everything all right?"

With the exception of my mother, I'd never had anyone show so much concern about my safety. I decided not to tell her just yet about the night's activities. "Nothing eventful to report," I said, a smile on my face. "And are you guys okay?"

"Fine, under the circumstances," she said. "What are you doing this morning?"

"I'm headed for Hal Rodgers' office as we speak."

"Why?" she asked. "Are you going to tell him what you found in Conrad's office?"

"Probably," I said. "I'll call you later."

"And Rocky?"

"Yes?"

"Please keep me updated. I know you hate it when I badger you about your safety, but I really am worried. I don't know what I'd do if something happened to you." Her voice caught at the end, and I was surprised when emotion welled up in my chest at her words. If only she knew how much I felt that way about her, too. Instead, I just assured her I was wearing my gun and told her I'd be careful.

Hal was in his office when Burke and I arrived a little before ten that morning. Hal appeared to be genuinely surprised when Burke produced his badge and told him that he was there on official police business. When I presented him with the evidence of Conrad's threats against me and the admission from Victor Rivera, his hands began to shake, and he broke out in a sweat.

"We'll fire him," he said, after nervously clearing his throat.

"I would hope so," Burke said. "We'll be arresting him as soon as we find him, so he won't be available for work unless he can make bond, and that will not be easy since he will be charged with conspiracy to commit murder—among other felonies."

Hal rubbed his face with his soft hands and asked, "What can I do to help you gentlemen?"

"A couple of things," Burke said. "First, Conrad doesn't appear to be at home or at his office. Would you try calling his cell phone? If you reach him, have him come down here to see you. I'll take it from there once you get him on the way. I'll also have an officer from Logan come down. And don't let yourself sound as nervous and upset as you look if you get him on the phone."

"I can do that," Hal said, reaching for his phone.

"Wait just a moment," I said, and Hal paused. "There is something else. I will need to see all your books and files on the Gridley account. And I mean everything. I want tax records, checkbooks, bank statements, deposit slips, bills paid, and everything else. If Conrad needs to provide any portion of that, make sure he brings that with him."

"What will you do with all of that?" he asked, looking quite bewildered.

"I will be going through everything with a fine-toothed comb."

"But you won't know what you're seeing, will you?" he asked doubtfully.

"I have a degree in accounting. I can handle it," I assured him.

"Oh," he said, surprise evident on his face.

"Now you can make the call," Burke told him.

"That's funny," Hal said a minute later. "He always answers his phone if he's not at the office during business hours."

Hal looked both puzzled and worried. He was badly shaken, or at least that's the way it appeared. Of course, he could be a very good actor, I reasoned. Conrad may have had others besides Victor Rivera helping him.

Burke walked to the door and said, "I'm going to attempt to locate our boy Conrad."

I followed him out, promising Hal that I'd be back in a couple of minutes and expected him to have something ready for me to begin going through. From my truck, I pulled out the threatening note and the blank paper I'd obtained from Conrad's desk, then handed them to Burke. "You might need these," I said. "Take good care of them."

"Thanks, Rocky," he said. "I'll put them in the evidence room as soon as I get back to Brigham City."

A few minutes later, I returned to Hal's office and began the tedious process of looking through the financial records of the Gridley ranch. I broke for a quick lunch at noon and then resumed my work. Hal was ready to close the office at five that evening, so I stopped then as well. But I did remove some documents that I felt needed closer examination; I thought I'd do that during the evening at my hotel room.

As I exited the building where Hal's firm was housed, I was confronted by Detective Blaine Springer. I wondered what he was doing in Ogden. He had just exited his car, and when he looked up and saw me, his fists curled into tight balls and his eyes shot fire at me. "Is something the matter, Blaine?" I asked in a matter-of-fact tone.

"You!" he said. His fists were clenched so tightly that his knuckles were turning white. "I've a mind to haul you off to jail right now."

"Really, what have I done?" I asked mildly.

"You are interfering with an ongoing investigation, as you well know," he snarled. "And I'm not allowing any more of it."

I moved past him with the armload of files I was carrying. If he wanted to talk to me, I decided, he'd just have to follow me to my truck. He did just that. I put the files in the backseat of my Silverado and then faced Blaine. "Listen, Detective, if you're here to talk to Hal Rodgers, you might want to hurry. He's about to leave for the day."

"Give me those," he demanded.

"Give you what?" I asked, trying to give the appearance that I didn't understand what he wanted.

"Those files you just put in your truck."

"Those aren't for you," I said. "You can't take them."

"You . . . are . . . interfering!" he hissed.

"Listen, I've heard about enough," I told him mildly. "I have work to do. I don't have time to stand around listening to you stammer."

I didn't think his face could possibly get any darker, but I was wrong. "Now!" he said, stepping closer to me and holding out his hand.

"It's not going to happen. These files have nothing to do with you. They are part of a financial examination I'm conducting for a client," I said.

"Who's the client?" he asked.

"You know better than to ask me that," I said, shaking my head. "Really, I have to go."

He brought his clenched fists to chin level and stammered something I couldn't make out. Then he said more clearly, "Any evidence you stole from me needs to be turned over right now!" he demanded.

"Blaine, slow down here. I didn't steal anything from you. I turned the truck over to you, didn't I? What else is it that you think I have that should be yours?"

"You know full well that there is more," he said, his eyes roving over my truck.

I couldn't help but grin at him. "Detective, I can see straight through you," I told him. "How do you know you want something when you can't even identify what it is you think I have? You are grasping at straws."

"I guess I'm going to have to take you in," he said maliciously.

"I don't think you ought to do that," I suggested, doing my best to keep my temper in check. I was doing pretty well, under the circumstances. I just hoped he wasn't going to push me much further. Like most people, I do have a breaking point.

"Come on, let's go," he said.

I decided that maybe it would be a good idea if I went along with him rather than make a scene here in a public place. "I'll follow you," I said. "I'm not leaving my truck in Ogden while we go all the way back to Brigham City."

He stammered something again, and then said, "No, I'll follow you, but try something and I'll have every cop in Weber and Box Elder Counties after you. And that includes using your cell phone. Don't try to call anyone."

On the way to the office, I used my OnStar phone to call Glenn Gridley. I reached up like I was adjusting my mirror and pushed the phone button. Then I used voice dial to call his house. I had entered his number in the memory like I always did when I had a new client. But the number entered was his home number, not his cell. Rose answered, and I said, "Rose, this is Rocky. I don't suppose that your brother is there."

"He's not, but you can reach him on his cell phone," she said. "Would you like that number?"

"Not right now, but I would appreciate it if you would call him for me and tell him that I've been arrested by Detective Springer. He's taking me in right now. I might need Glenn's help."

"Consider it done, Mr. Revada," she said, her voice filled with indignation. Apparently she was well aware of Blaine's unprofessional behavior.

I was just pulling into the parking area at the sheriff's office in Brigham City when my OnStar phone rang. I touched the button. It was Shanice, and she sounded angry. "Rocky, what's going on?"

"That's what I'd like to know. Detective Springer seems to think that I've broken the law somehow. I can't reason with him. I don't know if his boss is here or not, but if you or your dad would call him, I'd appreciate it. Also, there is a detective with the Brigham City Police by the name of Burke Christensen. I've done some work with him today. He's a reasonable guy, and he won't be happy to hear that Blaine is holding up our investigation. Get a hold of him too, if you don't mind."

"Okay, Rocky. And then I'm coming down there," she said. I spotted Blaine making his way along the sidewalk to my truck.

"I've got to go. Talk to you later," I said quickly. I turned my truck off, slipped my recording device into my front pants pocket, and got out.

"In here," Blaine ordered as he jerked a thumb in the direction of the building.

I didn't say anything, but I did go with him, and as we walked, I reached into my pocket and started the recorder. We ended up in his office, and I sat down after he did, even though I was not invited to do so. Only then did I speak to him. I said, "So Detective, am I under arrest or what?"

"You bet you are," he said. "What did you think?"

"I thought you were smarter than this," I said. "What exactly are you charging me with?"

"I'll disclose that information in a minute, after you and I discuss what you've been up to," he said.

"I can't imagine what we have to talk about," I remarked, trying to sound casual. "If you have some questions that I can answer, I'd be glad to do that, but I doubt that you even know what to ask."

"You seriously underestimate me, Mr. Smartmouth," he said as he placed his hands on his desk and leaned forward, his face in a scowl and his fists clinched again. "I have several questions, and I expect you to answer them truthfully."

"Okay, shoot," I said mildly, smiling inwardly at how seriously he underestimated *me*. He sat back in his chair, pulled out a legal pad, picked up a pen, made a notation that I couldn't make out at the top of the paper, and then, leaning forward again, he asked, "What did you do out on the Gridley ranch?"

"When?"

"You know when. Knock off the smart mouthing and answer my question."

"Detective, I have been there more than once. You'll need to specify exactly when you're talking about."

"The day Alden Overton was found," he said. "What did you do while my men and I processed the crime scene?"

"I hunted for Shanice Overton's horse, the one she was riding when she discovered her ex-husband's body. It had wandered off in the chaos. It took me some time, but I did find it, and I took it back to the barn for her," I said truthfully.

"What else did you do?" he demanded.

"What exactly are you thinking that I did?" I asked mildly.

He slammed his fist down on his desk so hard it shook. "I'm asking the questions here," he hissed. His bald head was so red, I hoped it didn't start a fire. "You messed with the crime scene," he said through clenched teeth. "You destroyed evidence. Why did you do that?"

"What evidence did I destroy?" I asked, fighting hard to keep the exasperation out of my voice.

"That's what I expect you to tell me."

At that remark, I relaxed a little. I had thought at first that Blaine had somehow figured out that I had hiked north from the area where the body had been found, but he obviously hadn't. I said, "Let me make one thing clear, Detective. I didn't do anything around where the body was found except look, and I only did that after you had abandoned the scene. I snapped some pictures, and you are welcome to copies of them if you'd like."

"I have plenty of pictures," he growled. "Tell me what else you did and what evidence you destroyed."

I smiled at him, which only infuriated him further. "Okay, let me tell you what I did," I said as I thought about the fact that this interview was being recorded and that he had failed to read me my rights under Miranda. He should have known better. "I hiked north from the site where Alden's body was found."

"Why did you do that?" he asked.

"Because you clearly didn't bother to, and I was afraid that in your negligence, there might be some evidence that you missed," I said, provoking him but not caring.

"Ha, ha," he said. "And I suppose you actually found something."

"I did, but I didn't destroy it." I then recited what I had done and what I had found. I left him to draw his own conclusions. But when I had finished, he knew about the small fragments of cloth I had found, the .38 caliber pistol shell, the probable location of the actual murder, the drag marks, the footprints, the piece of fabric that I'd taken from the fence, and the sleeping bag box.

"And where is all that evidence now?" he asked.

"I have them in safekeeping," I told him.

"So you admit you didn't turn the evidence you collected over to me?" he asked.

"I do, but I had every intention of doing so the moment I felt confident you would handle them properly. And again, I will share copies of my photographs with you."

"What else did you do?" he asked.

"Nothing that matters," I said.

"I'll decide what matters," he shouted. "Keep talking."

But I didn't have the chance to say another word. In that moment, the door to his office burst open and the sheriff hustled in. For the sheriff's benefit, I stood up and said, "Am I free to go now?"

"No, you are not," Blaine said hotly.

"Either tell me what I'm charged with and book me, or I'm walking out of here," I said firmly.

"Sit down," Blaine ordered. As I disobeyed, he turned to the sheriff. "This man has been interfering in my murder investigation on the Alden Overton case."

"I hope you have some proof," the sheriff said. "There are some highly agitated citizens on their way down from Tremonton. And Detective Burke Christensen from the Brigham City PD is in my office with some very interesting information." He turned to me, "I think we've met before. It's nice to see you, Rocky." We shook hands casually as I said, "It's nice to see you, Sheriff."

Sheriff Andy Perkins and I had crossed paths a few times on cases over the years. From what I'd seen of him, he seemed to be a kind and intelligent man in his early fifties. He was tall and slender with thick brown hair and a broad, square face. His light blue eyes shifted from me until they were focused intently on his deputy. His face wore a frown that clearly showed the sheriff's disapproval. Even Blaine seemed to notice the sheriff's countenance; he adjusted his posture in his chair and looked at the clutter of files on his desk.

When Blaine opened his mouth to speak, however, I realized I was wrong. He'd completely missed the signals from his boss. With unfounded confidence, he turned to the sheriff and said, "I've taken notes of our interview, Sheriff. He admits to collecting and withholding evidence from me." Even I was surprised by this new level of ignorance.

"Is that so?" The sheriff's question lacked conviction, as though he were responding half-heartedly to a tattling child.

I took a chance as I stepped back toward the door and asked, "Sheriff, do you mind if I wait in the lobby with Detective Christensen? I'd like to see if he's found anything more on the guy who tried to have me killed last night." The effect of that statement on Blaine was quite profound. He about popped his bald head off as he whipped his head toward me.

"Go ahead, Mr. Revada," the sheriff said. "We'll talk later."

"Fine," I said. "And when we do, I'd like you to listen to the discussion that Blaine and I have been enjoying."

"It's not recorded," Blaine said with a snap.

"Maybe not by you, but I am more thorough than that," I said, pulling the tiny recorder from my pocket. "Every word spoken is on here, and those you forgot to speak are not. You know, a little recitation known as Miranda."

I left him stammering and joined Burke in the lobby.

Chapter Eleven

By the time the sheriff exited Blaine's office, Glenn and all three of his daughters had joined Burke and me in the lobby. "Why don't you all come back to my office," Sheriff Perkins said.

"Where is Detective Springer?" Glenn asked.

"He's in his office typing a report," he said shortly.

The sheriff waved us all to chairs and then seated himself behind his oversized desk and said, "Rocky, I'm sorry that Blaine was so overbearing with you."

Despite my knowledge of the sheriff's tendency to be fair, I was concerned that he may still charge me for not immediately disclosing the evidence I'd found on the Gridley ranch. "So am I under arrest or not?" I asked bluntly. "Because if I am, I want an attorney down here before we talk about anything."

The sheriff smiled sourly. "Blaine was a little hasty, I'm afraid. You are not under arrest or charged with anything for right now. Do you object to these other folks being here while you play your little recording?"

"Of course not. I'm glad to have them here. They all have an interest in what's happening."

I slipped the recorder from my pocket and explained that I had turned it on as Blaine and I were walking to the building from the parking lot. Then I let it play for my small audience. The sheriff's face remained blank and emotionless during the entire time the recorder was playing. Glenn, on the other hand, was frowning when we began, and by the time we'd finished, he was purple with rage. Shanice kept shaking her head in disbelief, and her sisters kept looking at me with shock on their faces.

When the recorder finished its tattle-tale job, I shut it off and put it back in my pocket. "If I can clarify anything for you, I'd be glad to," I volunteered.

"First, thanks for doing what Blaine and my other deputies should have done," he said. I could tell he was not happy. "Frankly, these things have been happening far too much lately. I've seen too much sloppy work from Blaine, and I've a mind to let him go. This kind of thing just isn't called for." Suddenly, Blaine's job was on the table—something that would mean I wouldn't ever have to work with him again. It was a dream come true, and, yet, I didn't feel right about it. Did I dislike Blaine? Yes? Did I lack respect for him? Absolutely. But did I want to be responsible for the loss of Blaine's job? No way.

"Look, Sheriff," I found myself saying. "Blaine is sloppy, I'll give you that. I'll be the first to admit that I'm not a fan of working with him. But to fire him over this, I just don't know. Perhaps you should give him another chance." The sheriff looked down at his desk for several seconds, deep in thought. Then he focused his eyes on me.

"Well, you may be right. I think I would be justified in such a decision, but I appreciate your comment. It's best to not be overly hasty. I'll speak with him and see what I can do to motivate him to try a little harder. It isn't fair to these folks," his hand swept over the Gridleys, "to deal with such a reckless detective, but I have seen good things from Blaine." I nodded.

After another long pause, the sheriff said, "Okay. Thank you, Rocky. Well, with that said, maybe you could do me a favor. I think this is a good learning moment for Blaine. I would like you to take him out there and show him what you saw. And if you don't mind, I'd like you to bring me the bullet casing, box, pieces of cloth and whatever photos you think might be of value."

"That's not a problem, if Blaine can stand my company," I said, groaning inwardly at the thought of babysitting him and yet feeling lighthearted at the same time. Blaine would keep his job. Perhaps this made up for my rude remark a few years ago.

"He owes you big time," Sheriff Perkins said with a frown. "He may not like it, but he'll cooperate from here on out if he values his job." He then turned to Glenn. "Tell me what's going on with your horses."

Glenn glanced at me and said, "Sorry, Rocky, but I mentioned the horses to Sheriff Perkins on the phone." Then he turned back to the sheriff. "Actually, what we have is a switch."

For the next few minutes, Glenn and the girls brought Andy up to date on the problem, and then Glenn said, "I hired Rocky to see if he could find out where our horses are and help us get them back. And to be honest with you, I asked him to do a little poking around and see if he could come up with anything on Alden's murder. Rocky is a very good investigator. I hope you won't stop him from continuing to poke."

"He's welcome to," the sheriff said. "All I ask is that he keeps me informed of anything he finds that will help us." He turned and looked at me then.

"I'd be glad to, Sheriff," I said. "Let me tell you what I've learned so far."

Detective Christensen broke in. "Rocky's got someone's attention, as I mentioned earlier. I can't find Conrad Patel, the bookkeeper. He seems to have vanished after his failed attempt to blow Rocky up."

"What? Are you joking?" Shanice cried, her eyes throwing daggers at me. "Nothing eventful to report, huh? Weren't those your words? You said you'd be careful."

I looked at her and said, "I was careful, Shanice. If I hadn't been, I'd be scattered in little pieces all over Cache Valley." She scowled at me, and I decided to tone down the joking a bit. She looked genuinely frightened about this new turn of events.

"Rocky outsmarted Conrad, who hired a young villain to do his dirty work for him," Burke said. He gave a condensed but accurate version of my activities during the night.

Shanice dropped her head into her hands after he'd finished. "Rocky, I'm scared," she said without looking up. "I don't want you to get hurt."

"That makes two of us," I agreed with a weak smile aimed at the top of her lowered head.

"It makes a lot more than two," Glenn said. "Believe me, the girls and I don't want anything to happen to you." Once again, I was surprised to find Glenn's softer side directed toward me. I admitted that I liked the guy a lot more in those moments.

"And neither does little Tyra," Cindy said firmly. "I don't know if you realize it, but she idolizes you."

"Yeah," Jena chimed in, "it's Rocky this and Rocky that all the time lately."

I nodded an embarrassed acknowledgment and then, changing the subject back to business, said, "The sheriff is waiting to hear what I've learned, and I suppose you folks are too."

When I'd finished my report, the sheriff said, "It sounds to me like the Gridleys are right. You need to be extremely careful. If you'd like, I'll assign a deputy to work with you until we find Conrad."

"That won't be necessary," I said quickly. I wanted to take no chances of being stuck with Blaine. "I work best alone."

Suddenly, my cell phone vibrated. There was no number displayed on the screen, and when I answered, a familiar, muffled voice responded. I quickly held up my hand for everyone to be silent and put the phone on speaker. The voice said, "When I tell someone not to interfere, I mean it." After a very brief pause, the voice added, "Conrad followed Alden's steps. Keep it up and you'll be doing the same." The phone call ended abruptly.

Everyone around the room looked at one another with wide eyes and hanging mouths. No one said a word for several moments.

"I think we need to go back out to where you found Alden's body," I said as I got to my feet. My movement seemed to wake everyone from their stupor. "And we need to do it now. It'll be dark before long, so we don't have much time."

"What are you thinking, Rocky?" the sheriff asked as he lifted his considerable height from his chair.

"I don't think Conrad is the main player in this whole thing." I waved my cell phone. "Someone else is, and that someone apparently thinks Conrad might have overstepped his bounds, making the guy who just called me very angry," I said. "Get Detective Springer, Sheriff. And Burke, you might want to come too. He's your missing person."

When Blaine joined us a few minutes later, his face was red, and he avoided meeting my eyes when I looked at him. Out in the parking lot, after I had briefed Blaine on the phone call, Shanice announced, "I'm riding with you, Rocky."

I had no argument with that. I was especially glad that I wouldn't be riding with Blaine Springer. Shanice and I climbed in my truck and, with a procession of vehicles, we headed north and then west to the Gridley ranch. Despite the tension and tragedy Shanice was dealing with, I enjoyed her company.

Glenn was in the lead as we pulled into his yard. He proceeded past the barn, then stopped at the first of three gates that we would be passing through before we reached the spot where Alden's body had been dumped. Jena and Cindy took turns opening and closing gates. When we arrived, Glenn stopped well short of the ditch where Alden's body had lain.

I walked past Glenn to where I could see into the ditch. All three girls followed. Cindy screamed, and Jena sat down on the dead tree that Shanice had been sitting on just a couple of days ago and buried her head in her hands. Shanice, trembling violently, grabbed me for support.

Andy shook his head. "You figured that out right," he said glumly. Conrad Patel wouldn't be writing any more checks for Glenn Gridley. He was lying face down in almost the exact spot that Alden had occupied. Surprisingly, it was Detective Springer who approached Conrad first and checked him for any sign of life. I hadn't expected there to be any, considering the bullet hole in the back of the young bookkeeper's head.

The only difference in the way this body was lying and the way Alden's had been was the hands. Alden's had been loose, but Conrad's were tied behind his back with a double strand of blue baling twine. Just inches from one of those hands there was a piece of paper sticking out of Conrad's back pocket. Andy pulled it out with gloved hands and opened it. As he read, he shook his head. "What does it say, Sheriff?" Glenn asked.

"It's addressed to you, Rocky, and it's typed this time. It says: *Conrad tried to handle you himself, a mistake that cost him dearly. Those who disobey my orders are the first to fall. Drop the case or you'll be next.*"

As the sheriff looked up, Shanice collapsed against me. If I hadn't been holding her, she'd have gone clear to the ground. "Oh, Rocky," she moaned, "What are we going to do?"

"We are going to find this guy, whoever he is. And I'd bet a good chunk of change that when we do, we'll find your horses," I finished.

"Rocky," Andy said, "would you mind showing me where you walked the other day? I'd like to see if they followed the same route this time and if it was done in the same way."

"It's almost dark, but we can take flashlights," I suggested.

"Thanks. Blaine," he said, turning to the chastened detective, "get some help here and process this crime scene. And be thorough this time." I saw Blaine nod as he ground his boot into the dirt.

"I'll help if you need me to," Burke volunteered.

"Blaine can use your help," Andy agreed. "We appreciate it."

"The girls and I will go back to the house," Glenn said, his voice wavering slightly.

"I'm going with Rocky and the sheriff," Shanice announced. Glenn looked at her for a moment, and then he shrugged wearily and started back to his truck.

Two minutes later, I'd strapped on my gun, picked up my camera and a handful of evidence bags from my truck, and joined Andy and Shanice on a northbound trek through the fields, sagebrush, and trees. The drag marks were plain despite the fading light. Once again I found several fragments of cloth. As before, some were red and some brown. After we'd collected the fourth piece and had put it in an evidence bag, I said, "It appears they used the same sleeping bag to drag Conrad as they did to drag Alden."

"How do you know that?" Shanice asked.

"I don't know it, but I'm pretty sure. The pieces of cloth we've found are the same color and fabric as the ones from the other day," I explained.

We trudged on. We turned on our flashlights as the sun faded, which helped, but the lack of daylight slowed us down quite a bit. "We'll have to come back in the daytime," the sheriff conceded after a few more minutes, "but let's keep going for now."

When we arrived at the area where Alden was shot, I said, "Let's go slow here. This is about where Alden died."

"Surely they didn't shoot Conrad here too," Shanice said.

"People do strange things, Shanice," I told her. "Do you recall what Pam told you the man who called her said when he threatened me?"

"Not exactly," she answered.

I told her as Andy listened with interest. "He said if I didn't quit investigating, I would end up exactly like Alden did. The guy on the phone earlier said something similar. That's what made me think that Conrad might be where we found him. Then the sleeping bag was used again, and this was where Alden was murdered. I think we'll find a .38 caliber casing here."

It was fully dark by the time my prediction came true. It was Shanice who said, "Rocky, here it is."

The light from the bright halogen bulbs of her flashlight reflected off the brass of a casing. The sheriff carefully retrieved it and examined it closer. It's reasonably fresh," he said. "And it's .38 caliber."

"You knew, Rocky," Shanice said quietly.

"I suspected," I reminded her. "Educated guess, you might say."

"Let's move on," Sheriff Perkins suggested.

We trudged up the hill toward the place where I'd first spotted the cloth snagged in the fence. I hesitated at the edge of the trees as we topped the rise. I thought I saw a brief glint of light in the distance ahead of us.

Suddenly, I saw a muzzle flash and threw myself and Shanice to the side as a bullet literally passed by my right ear—I heard it whistle by. We fell heavily to the ground, and the sheriff also dropped. A second bullet threw up dirt ten or fifteen feet in front of us, and then an engine fired up, headlights came on, and a vehicle roared east along the fence. I could see the distant steel fence posts gleam in the headlights.

"He was waiting for us," Sheriff Perkins observed soberly. "You moved just before I heard the sound of the gun firing, Rocky. How did you know?"

"Muzzle flash," I answered, standing with the sheriff. Shanice didn't move. "Shanice, are you okay?" I asked in alarm. I knelt beside her, my heart in my throat.

She groaned and rolled over. "I'm okay," she said in a raspy voice. "I hit my head when we fell." She put her hand up to her forehead and rubbed at some of the blood that was starting a slow trickle down the side of her face.

I helped her to her feet, and she threw her arms around me. "Oh, Rocky, that was too close," she said as she laid her head against my shoulder. I held her like that for a few moments, even as I questioned the reason behind my thumping heart. Was it because we'd just cheated death, or was it having Shanice in my arms?

I was aware of the sheriff standing near us, talking on his cell phone. He was reporting the incident and ordering officers to look for a vehicle in the area. When he finished, he said, "That's a waste of time. We don't have a clue what the gunman was driving."

I reluctantly pulled back from Shanice and said, "Let's go over to the fence. I don't think we'll get shot at again." She looked panicked at that suggestion, so I said, "Do you want to stay here?"

"Let's see," she said after a moment, putting her finger to her chin and cocking her head to one side. "Do I want to stay by myself in the dark and maybe get shot at, or do I want to come with you and maybe get shot at. I think I'll take my chances with you." I was happy to hear the sarcasm in her voice. She was putting on a courageous face, even though I knew she was terrified.

I would have been surprised at this point if we didn't find some cloth fragments stuck to the barbed wire. But instead of one piece, we located three. "This is nuts," the sheriff said as we started back to join the others.

Blaine and Burke met us at the place where the murders had occurred. "We heard a rifle," Burke said. "We were afraid that you'd been ambushed."

"We were," the sheriff said. "The muzzle flash and Rocky's swift action saved us. Since you men are here, let me explain something. This is where Rocky found the bullet casing that was likely from the gun that killed Alden. We also found one tonight. It appears Conrad was shot here and dragged on something, probably a sleeping bag, back to where we found him, exactly like Alden was."

Both detectives shook their heads, and we all headed back to the vehicles. When we got back, Glenn was there again. He was breathing hard. "I heard shots," he said with furrowed eyebrows. "Is everyone okay?"

We told him the story as the body of Conrad Patel was loaded in an ambulance.

I slept better that night when I finally got back to the hotel in Logan. It wasn't because I was no longer keyed up; it was out of sheer exhaustion. Unfortunately, I didn't get to do the closer examination of the files I'd brought from the accountant's office as I'd planned. But I figured that could wait a few more hours. My body could use some R&R after such a close call.

Chapter Twelve

WHEN I GOT UP LATE the next morning and went to work on the files, I soon found something of significance. "Shanice was right," I said aloud, feeling pride swell in my chest. I called Sheriff Perkins in the early afternoon. He was out of his office, and I had to call his cell phone.

"Good morning, Rocky," he said cheerfully. "Have you had a chance to look at any of the financial records?"

"That's one of the reasons I'm calling," I told him. "Someone has been methodically and expertly bleeding Glenn's ranch dry."

"Embezzlement?" he asked.

"Yes, I think so. It appears that payments have been made to certain vendors that look very legitimate, and had I not done some checking, I would have thought them to be. But it turns out the vendors don't exist. The bills filed in support of the payments are fakes."

"Should Hal, the accountant, have caught it?"

"Possibly, but the bleeding has been very smoothly done. If I hadn't been looking for it, I would have missed it myself. So Hal might have missed it too. After all, Conrad paid the bills. Hal would not very likely have a way of knowing if a bill was legitimate or not. In addition, I think some legitimate bills may have been paid in cash and Conrad made receipts for a larger amount then simply skimmed off the difference. That needs more checking into. It could also be that some payments were received by Conrad, who simply didn't give a receipt to the payee and then kept the money. This will require a lot more investigation. We need to find out exactly who Gridley did business with and then we can take it from there. At any rate, Conrad was a lot smarter than Hal gives him credit for. "

"Okay, what now, Rocky?" the sheriff asked.

"I think I'll have a CPA look it over when I finish, but I know that theft is occurring and has been for some time," I explained.

"How long?" he asked. "Or have you been able to determine that yet?"

"The records I brought with me only go back six months, but it has been going on during that entire time. I suspect that I will find it in earlier months as well when I look for more of what I've found here."

"When you're ready, bring it to me. We'll see what we can do about expanding your investigation and then bringing charges against the responsible party," he said. *If that person is still alive,* I thought.

"Conrad is a main part of it, but I think it goes deeper than just him. I'm not sure he could have set up all the fake accounts by himself. I think there is still someone I have not been able to identify who has profited from what Conrad did. And my guess is that the scheme also includes other victims in addition to Glenn. I'll get back with you on that if I find anything," I promised. "In the meantime, I've been thinking about what happened to us last night. You've probably already considered this, but I thought I'd mention it just in case. It might be helpful to you at some point if you had one of the slugs that were fired at us."

"That would be good," the sheriff agreed. "If we find a suspect, then we could search for a rifle that might match up with the slug. But how easy will it be to find a slug?"

"The one that nearly took my ear off is probably a lost cause, but the one that threw dirt in our faces isn't," I suggested.

"That's right," he said with enthusiasm, "Unless it skipped off a rock and went back over our heads, it may be right there in the ground in front of where we were hunkered down."

"I can take a break from this and go help if you're short of manpower," I offered.

"I know you have a lot to do, Rocky, but I've got my officers spread pretty thin today. Would you mind?" he asked.

"There's a reason I'm an investigator instead of an accountant," I said. "I can only study figures so long before my eyes start getting blurry and my brain starts to sizzle. I'd be glad to take a look. I have a very good metal detector."

"That would be great," the sheriff said. "And by the way, I think Blaine Springer has had a wakeup call. He will probably never be a fan of yours, but I promise that you'll find him a lot easier to work with in the future." I was glad to hear that, because I really didn't enjoy butting heads with anyone in law enforcement.

It took a few minutes before I was able to leave and return to my hotel room to check the images from the cameras that I was still using to monitor my home and office. The equipment showed no activity since the last time I'd checked a few hours ago. Knowing that, I decided to make a visit to each place. My metal detector was at the house, and there was a book on detecting embezzlement at my office. I'd used the book in previous cases and thought it might offer some insight now. I may not have found all the ways that money was being embezzled, and I didn't want to miss anything. I gathered up the files I'd been working on and took them down to the hotel safe as I left.

An hour later, with my pistol still at my waist, I headed for Tremonton. On the way I called Glenn and told him what I was doing and how I also wanted to meet with him sometime to discuss some things I'd discovered that would be of interest to him. He didn't know about the discussion that Shanice and I had had—that I was looking into the finances of the ranch. I was certain he would be interested in what I had learned, but I feared he would also be extremely upset that we'd gone behind his back. Only time would tell.

I was almost to the small town of Fielding on SR-30 when my vehicle phone sounded. It was Shanice; apparently she had saved the number from when I called the ranch the day before. *Good move,* I thought as I answered the call. "Hi, Rocky," she said cheerfully, her voice filling the cab of my truck like a sweet fragrance. "Sleep okay?"

"Better than the night before," I said. "But then I was so exhausted that there was not much choice. My body shut down as soon as I hit the pillow. How about you?"

"I lay awake most of the night," she admitted. "I've never been shot at before. Rocky, I'm really frightened."

"As well you should be," I assured her. "I am too."

"I don't believe that for a moment," she said lightly.

"I hide it well," I admitted, "but I get scared just like the next guy."

"When will you be here?" she asked.

I smiled at the direct question. "I don't recall mentioning that I was coming. It appears you've been doing some investigating of your own, Shanice," I teased. I heard her laugh lightly as I answered, "I'll be there soon. I'm almost to the interstate."

"Hey, it's not my fault that Dad likes to keep me informed of your whereabouts at all hours of the day," she said. I chuckled quietly, trying and failing to picture Glenn in that role. "Well, I'm glad you are coming to see me. I mean, us. Dad says you're going out to where we were shot at. Could you use some company?"

"It depends," I said.

"On what?" she asked, feigning offense. "Do you have someone else in mind?"

"You know I don't," I said casually. "It depends on who wants to go."

She chuckled at that. "What would you do if I said it was Cindy who wanted to go?"

"That would be okay. I like Cindy."

"I think she and Jena would both jump at the chance to go out there with you, but I admit, I'm kind of selfish. I was hoping you'd let me come alone. I can be of more help that way."

I thought about stating the "many hands make light work" line but decided against it. "I'd like that a lot," I said honestly, grinning to myself.

"Oh good. I had a whole list of reasons why only I should come with you, in case you disagreed. I guess I'll never get those hours back again . . ."

I laughed at that. I could never picture Shanice pouring hours into such a list. "I don't believe that for a minute, Shanice. You knew I'd say yes. By the way, you were right in what you told me."

"About what?" she asked.

"About the ranch finances," I told her. "I'll explain when I get to your place."

"We'll be in the barn," she said. "I'm working with a filly and Dad just pulled a tractor in to change the oil."

By the time I got there, Shanice was rubbing down a tall, pretty paint filly. Glenn was near the round corral in the massive barn working on a large John Deere tractor. He rubbed his hands on a rag when he spotted me walking through the barn. Shanice waved one hand and called out a greeting. "I'll put this horse away."

When I'd reached him, Glenn said, "I'd shake hands, but I'm a bit greasy. I used to have one of the ranch hands do this, but since we let Vance go, the other guys are too busy. So I get to do it. Shanice wants to go out there with you. Is that okay?"

"Of course it is. She called me already."

He smiled weakly, then the smile faded away. His face was drawn and his eyes were bloodshot. This business was taking its toll on the sturdy rancher. He looked over to where Shanice was leading the horse, and said, "She's a good girl, Rocky. I'm glad to see you two are still good friends. She hasn't had much to do with men since Alden pulled his rotten stunt on her."

"You know I'd do anything for her, Glenn," I said as I felt heat creeping into my face. I hoped he didn't notice.

He gave me a penetrating look, glanced again toward his oldest daughter, and again looked deeply at me. "She likes you, Rocky. She was hurt once, and I don't want to see that happen again."

I stared at him, trying to control my sudden rapid breathing. "I understand," I finally said. *Did Glenn just suggest that I date his daughter?* I wondered, hoping that I wasn't reading him wrong. I also hoped that he wasn't reading *her* wrong. Since I'd returned to the Gridley ranch, Shanice had acted like, well, Shanice. She and I had always had a good time together. I'd be lying if I admitted that I didn't wish for something more, but it was hard to tell with her. I knew she liked me; the question was, did she like me as anything more than a good friend. Maybe there would be a chance to date her after this case was resolved. Only time would tell.

"You had something you wanted to report," he said, changing the subject.

"Yes, but if you don't mind, I'll wait for Shanice. I'd like her to hear it too."

"She'll be with you for a while after you leave here," he reminded me.

"Right, but this is kind of a, well, nasty bit of news I have. I don't want to have to tell it more than once," I said. "And what I've found was because of something Shanice suggested."

"She's a bright girl," he said with fondness in his voice.

While we waited, he and I discussed the murder of Conrad. He seemed genuinely puzzled over what Conrad had tried to do to me. "I never saw that side of Conrad. He was efficient and kept right up on things. I'll miss him, quite frankly."

"Have you decided what to do as far as replacing him goes?" I asked.

"What do you think I should do?" His question surprised me, but I had an answer for him.

"What about Cindy?" I suggested.

"That's interesting, Rocky," he said, rubbing his chin thoughtfully and leaving a smudge of black grease there. "I was thinking the same thing. The only trouble with that is that it would mean her working more closely with Hal Rodgers, and I don't know if that would be good. He's infatuated with the girl, and as much as I like the guy, he'd never make a good husband for her," he said.

"Who wouldn't make a good husband for whom?" Shanice asked as she walked up behind us.

Glenn turned and smiled at his daughter. "Rocky thinks that we should let Cindy keep the books for us. I was thinking the same thing."

Shanice chuckled. "But you don't want her to be around Hal too much," she said shrewdly, looking from one of us to the other and back again. "And I agree with that. Frankly, so would she. But I still think Cindy would be good with the books. She can deal with Hal if she has to."

"After I finish telling you what I have to report, you might not want anyone working with Hal or that banks," I said. "I spent most of yesterday and much of the morning going over Conrad's records of your finances." I looked directly at Glenn. "I don't like what I've found, and you won't either."

"What are you talking about?" Glenn said, his face growing dark. "I thought you were looking for stolen horses and a rotten killer. I never asked you to look at the books."

"But *I* did, Dad," Shanice said.

"Why would you do that?" he asked angrily. "We can't afford to pay Rocky to do more than I've asked him to do."

I intervened at that point. I didn't want to see an argument between those two. "Glenn, I'm not sure where you think I should be looking for horses, or for killers either, for that matter. But I believe that Shanice was right, and that I'm looking in *exactly* the right place."

Glenn looked puzzled, and his anger faded away. "What have you found?"

"Embezzlement," I said. "You guys are being bled dry." I caught Shanice's eye. She nodded in understanding.

"But how can you tell that?" Glenn asked. "Maybe you're wrong."

"Dad, Rocky has a degree in accounting," Shanice said. "And he's worked embezzlement cases before."

Glenn spread his greasy hands. "I didn't know that," he said.

"Not many people do, but it's true. I'll have a CPA double-check my work when I get through, but I know what I'm seeing, Glenn. Conrad, and possibly others, have been stealing from you. And there may be other victims besides you."

Glenn turned away. Shanice reached out and touched my arm as she shook her head sadly. Neither of us said a word as we waited patiently while Glenn digested the bad news. When he faced us again, he said, "Thanks for finding this out for me, but I still don't see what that has to do with murder and horse theft."

"Most murders occur over one of two things: money and love, or the lack thereof," I said.

Glenn nodded. "Okay, so maybe there is a connection to the money, but what about the horses?"

"In my experience, when people get greedy, they look for more than one way to steal from their victims," I told the two of them. "Now, don't get me wrong. I'm not saying that there is a connection, but it's certainly a lead worth following, don't you agree?"

Glenn shook his head and then contradicted the action when he said, "Yes, I do agree. But Hal and Conrad? I can't see it. And what does Alden have to do with them? There has to be a connection with this to his murder, unless you're wrong, Rocky, and the murders and horse thefts have no connection to one another."

Shanice caught my eye, and she shuddered involuntarily. Her father noticed and instantly asked, "What is it, Shanice? Is there something I don't know?"

Without looking at her father, she said in a very tiny voice, "Yes."

His voice became hard. "What haven't you told me?" he demanded.

"I'm sorry, Dad. I hurt you so much when I married Alden, and I feel like I can never completely make up for it." The emotion was thick in her voice. Glenn reacted by stepping to her and placing his hand on her back.

"It's okay," he said softly. "Despite the mistakes we've all made in this situation, your mother and I have always loved you, and love you still. We just want you to be happy."

She lifted her head, made brief eye contact with me, then turned to her father and met his troubled gaze. She sniffed, then said, "Thanks, Dad."

"So what did you want to tell me?"

"I can't believe I've kept this to myself for so long. I didn't want you to be mad at Hal, so I never told you that it was he who introduced me to Alden."

Glenn's mouth moved wordlessly for a minute, and then his teeth were grinding. Finally, he said, his eyes narrowed, "How did Hal know Alden?"

"Alden used to work with him at the accounting firm. He had a job just like Conrad's."

"Did Hal fire Alden?" the rancher asked his daughter, who was nervously twisting her hands but still holding his gaze.

"No. Back then, Hal wasn't the manager of the business. I think he was actually a bookkeeper as well. Alden quit, but it was on good terms. He took the job he had when I married him," she revealed. "The last I knew, they were still friends."

Glenn turned again, fighting, it seemed, an inward battle. Shanice reached for my hand, and I gave it to her. She gripped tightly. I gripped back, rubbing my thumb over her knuckles. She tried to smile at me, but it fell short. I pulled her close, and she did not resist. She whispered, "Thanks." Her actions, I told myself, might not mean anything more than a need for support in the face of her father's anger, because he *was* angry.

When her father turned back, his eyes drifted to our entangled hands, and then he looked up and into my eyes. "When the Lord gave me Shanice," he began, then he choked, and a few tears wet his eyes. I hadn't seen this much emotion in Glenn for a long time. Maybe never. He struggled for a moment to gain his composure, and then he went on. "When He gave her to me, I think He did it for two reasons. The first was as a test, to see if I could develop patience when she drifted from the teachings of her mother and me—and the Church itself."

My eyes moved to Shanice's face, and she smiled wanly.

Glenn cleared his throat, and we both looked back at him. "And the second," he went on, "was as a blessing. Thank you for pointing Rocky in the right direction on our troubles. I love you, dear. You are so much like your mother."

Big tears wet his eyes and started down his cheeks. He wiped at them, leaving more black smudges on his face. He turned away again, clearly embarrassed at his show of such tender emotion. Shanice let go of my hand, wiped her own wet eyes, and stepped over to him. She touched his shoulder, and when he turned, she threw her arms around him and hugged him fiercely. He returned the hug, streaking her bright yellow, Western shirt with a thin smattering of grease. The two of them stood that way for a couple of minutes. I looked away, not sure what to do with myself. I stepped over to the tractor and looked at it, not really seeing it.

Finally Glenn said, the emotion gone from his voice now, "Keep me posted on the matter of our finances, Rocky," he said. "I'll depend on you to advise me on what action I should take. And I would appreciate it if you would talk to Sheriff Perkins about it. I don't want to be the one to turn Hal in . . . if it comes to that."

I didn't mention the fact that the sheriff was already in the loop. "I'll take care of it," I said.

"Thanks. Thanks to both of you. I better finish up here now. You kids get going, and let me know what you find out there."

We kids did as he said. But as we got going, hand in hand, he called out, "Rocky." We both looked back. He said, "Thanks," and nodded his head, his eyes on Shanice. "Do as I asked, Rocky, and good luck."

I knew exactly what he meant, and I felt a twist in my gut followed by butterflies. "I'll do my best," I answered with some trepidation. I was feeling in over my head. After all, I had never had a lot of luck with relationships. What if I messed something up with Shanice, too? With that thought troubling me, I led Shanice from the barn.

I helped her into the truck, and after we started down the lane past the corrals and to the first gate, she asked, "What was that all about?"

"What was what about?" I asked as the butterflies fluttered faster inside me.

"You know exactly what I mean—that mysterious little exchange with Dad," she said.

"Oh, that," I said, nodding my head as I tried to act nonchalant. "It was about something we were talking about while you were putting that filly in her stall."

"And what was that?"

I smiled at her. "Well, Miss Nosy, you'll just have to wait, now, and see." Before she could respond, I stopped and opened my door. "I'll get the gates," I said, and hopped out. "You drive."

She slid over to the driver's seat as I opened a gate.

Chapter Thirteen

WE WERE NOT ABLE TO drive all the way to the spot where we had been shot at. But we were able to get within about a quarter of a mile from the base of the hill just past where Alden and Conrad were shot. I grabbed the metal detector from my truck, and we started toward the hill. Once at the top, we stopped at about the same spot we had the night before, just before leaving the large stand of juniper trees.

I glanced at Shanice. She was staring ahead, between the trees and toward the fence. She was trembling. "We are close to where the bullet should be," I said.

"How did he shoot so accurately in the dark?" she asked, her eyes still gazing into the distance.

"He must have had a night scope on his rifle," I said.

"Oh, yeah, one of those things that makes everything look green," she said. She turned to me and smiled. "About the color I feel right now."

"I'd say you look more pink than green," I said.

"Well, gee. What a compliment," she said. I reached into the truck and offered her my hand, which she took as she scooted over to the edge of the seat and jumped out. "I still can't believe what a close call that was last night. I really do feel a little woozy just thinking about it."

"Are you wishing you hadn't come?" I asked. "You can go back to the truck if this is bothering you too much."

"No way," she said. "I like being with you."

"And I like having you with me," I said as tension seemed to fill the air between us. Our eyes met, and for a moment our gaze held. She stirred feelings inside me that I hadn't felt in years. I liked those feelings. *I am being paid to work right now,* I reminded myself.

I dragged my eyes away from her and suggested, "Let's see if we can find a bullet."

She stood back while I examined the ground. Finally, I was pretty sure I'd found the place where we had dropped to the ground when the first bullet whizzed past us. I stepped into the position I thought I might have been in when that bullet nearly took my head off. I was pretty sure about where I'd first seen the muzzle flash near the fence. Shanice was watching me, saying nothing. I liked the feel of her eyes on me, but I tried to concentrate on what I was doing. I slowly turned until I was facing the trees behind us. I sighted through them at eye level. I marked the spot where I was standing with the heel of one of my boots and looked toward the fence where I'd seen the flash. Then I walked straight toward a tall, broad juniper tree. I couldn't imagine that I would be lucky enough to find that first bullet, but it was worth a little effort.

The ground sloped away a little, so when I arrived at the tree, I stopped and looked up a couple of feet, judging that there was at least that much slope to the ground. Shanice had followed me and was looking at the tree too. She said, "Could it be a little higher, like up there where the wood seems to be chipped away?"

"Smart-aleck," I said with a grin in her direction. About eighteen inches above where I'd been looking, the tree was still over a foot in width. The trunk was freshly marred at that point. I couldn't quite reach the spot, so I looked for a place to put my foot and hoist myself up. Shanice said, "You could lift me that high, couldn't you?"

"Sure," I said, and locked my hands like I'd done many times when giving someone a boost onto the back of a horse. She placed one foot there, put one hand on my head to steady herself, and I lifted. "Good enough," she called down to me and her hand left my head. "Do you have a knife?" she asked. "I think it's in here."

"I can't reach it while I'm holding you," I said and slowly let her back down. I dug a pocket knife from my pocket, and we repeated the elevator routine. "Good," she said again, and I stopped, trying to hold her steady. "I'll hurry," she said after a minute, about the time my back started to ache and my arms began to shake.

I looked up and watched as she dug with the knife into the wood. "It's going to take me a minute. Do you need a rest?" she asked.

"Keep working. I'll be okay for a little bit. You aren't very heavy." I didn't want to admit that I was tiring.

She apparently took my words as a compliment because she said, "I think you are lying to me, but thanks all the same." I waited while she worked, my back aching in earnest. She shifted a little from time to time. Finally, when I was about ready to admit that I needed a break, she said, "I've got it. You can let me down now."

After she had stepped out of my hand, I straightened up, stretched my back, and worked my arms. She grinned at me, the bullet in her hand. "I'm heavier than you thought," she said.

"No, you are exactly the right weight," I said.

I put the bullet in an evidence bag. "Let's see if we can find the other one now," I said, taking her by the hand and leading the way back to edge of the sagebrush flat.

Within five minutes, my metal detector began to beep. I reached down and felt in the soft, moist ground. The bullet was there, and it was not even blunted badly. I held it up, showing Shanice, then put it with the other bullet. "Now all we need to do is find the gun that fired these."

"We, as in me and you, or we as in you and the sheriff and his deputies?" she asked with a teasing grin.

"I would prefer we as in me and you, but it's going to have to be we as in me and the cops," I said with a smile. "I don't want you to be in another situation where you might feel green around the gills."

"I'm fine now," she said.

"Good, because we aren't through here yet."

"What else is there to do?" she asked. I didn't miss the flash of worry that crossed her face briefly.

"I need to make a diagram so that we can show where the bullets were found, where we were standing when the first shot was fired, and then where we were cowering on the ground when the second one threw dirt on us," I explained. "I also need to take a few pictures."

I plunged a large stick into the ground where we had been standing the night before, then we walked north across the four or five hundred yards to the fence. After crossing the fence, we searched the ground and found tracks, both boot and shoe prints as well as tire tracks.

"That's interesting," I said quietly. Shanice raised an eyebrow at me, so I continued, "If I remember right, these tracks look similar to the ones found in your barn."

"Really?" She walked over and knelt down beside me to take a closer look. "Is it possible?"

"I don't see why not," I said. "I've suspected for a while that the missing horses and murders might be related. This certainly provides positive evidence toward that theory." I took several pictures of the tracks with my little camera. Then I looked the ground over more closely. "Luck is with us today," I said, and I pointed to a rifle casing a few feet from the fence. "There is one of the casings. I don't suppose we can find the other one."

She helped me look, and we found it just a few feet from the first one. "We really are lucky," I said.

"Come on, Rocky. Give yourself some credit," she said seriously. "You are very thorough and persistent. I'm impressed."

I pulled out my camera again and photographed both casings before putting on gloves and relocating them to a second evidence bag. I wrote on both evidence bags at that point, and then I took pictures of the tire tracks. That done, I said, "Now all we have to do is make sure we are lined up with the tree that the bullet was in and with the stick marking where we were standing when the bullets flew."

I looked south, toward the distant stick, and couldn't see it. "Shoot, our stick fell down," I moaned.

"I'll go stand there," she said.

"That'll work," I agreed, and I helped her back across the fence.

As she walked across the flat, I took a small notebook from my pocket and drew a diagram. Once she was there, I sighted down my arm. Everything lined up perfectly. I decided to take one last look around before I crossed the fence. I made a wider circle around the area where the shooter's vehicle had been parked. That's when I found four cigarette butts. My heart leaped at such a huge find. In this day and age, DNA could be taken from the butts and used to identify the person who had smoked them. As I was collecting them, I was surprised when Shanice walked up to me, the fence between us.

"I got a little bored," she said before I had a chance to ask.

"I'm glad you came back. Look what I found," I said, holding the evidence bag across the fence so she could see it.

"Cigarette butts," she said. "So now we know that we are looking for a smoker."

"More than that," I said. "We are looking for two smokers: one who smokes Camels and one who smokes Marlboros."

"Wow, this is like *CSI*," she said.

"More than you think," I suggested, grinning at her. "We are looking for two people whose DNA matches the samples that the sheriff can have a lab take from these butts. It never ceases to amaze me how stupid criminals can be."

She returned my grin and then asked, "Do you need me to cross the fence again? Or are you through here? I usually manage to scratch myself when I cross a fence."

"Hey, that gives me an idea," I said, cutting her off. "Whoever killed Conrad crossed this fence. And I'm guessing it was in the dark. There could be blood on one or more of these barbs. It may be a long shot, but it's worth a try."

"Let's look. I'll stay over here," she said.

We searched up and down the fence for a hundred feet or so in each direction. But we couldn't spot any blood. "We tried," I said as I climbed carefully back over the fence.

I counted off the steps from the fence to where we had been shot at and noted the distances on my little diagram. Then I finished by triangulating the location of the bullets using some distinct and very large junipers. "This is so we can be sure to find this place again if we have to," I said. I finished my diagram, dated it, added my initials, and told Shanice that we could go back now.

We headed south, walking in companionable silence for a few hundred feet. After a while I said, "Shanice, I want to develop a list of likely suspects. Who do you know that smokes?"

"Well, let's see. Ricky doesn't, but Shawn does."

"Who are they?" I asked.

"They're our ranch hands."

I stopped, put my metal detector down, and pulled out my notebook. I turned to a clean page, dated it, and then said, "Give me their full names."

She did, and I wrote *Ricky Snyder* and *Shawn Wheeler*. "Who else?"

"Well, I guess we should include Vance Winskey, even though he doesn't work for us anymore," she said.

I added his name below Shawn's with a notation of how he was connected to the Gridleys. "I'm sure Mace Healy smokes," she continued. "But Hal Rodgers doesn't. He's repeated that fact to Cindy several times." She then listed a few of the men and women they associated with through their rodeo roping. When I prodded, she added a couple of other ranchers who lived within a few miles of their place. Finally, she said, "I'm sure I'll think of others, and so will Dad and my sisters."

I put the notebook back in my pocket, picked up my equipment, and we began to walk again. "By the way, when is Alden's funeral?" I asked. "I was thinking I should go."

"It's tomorrow morning at eleven in Brigham City. I was planning on going for Tyra's sake. After all, he is her daddy. But why would you want to go?" she asked. "You didn't even know him."

"Just to observe," I said.

"I see. Let me guess. You are going to look for someone in particular. Maybe check up on a certain mistress?" she said, rewarding me with a bright smile. I was surprised that she could talk so openly about the situation now. She seemed to be healing.

"Very impressive. I think you have been spying on me," I said.

"Nah, more like a lucky guess," she said, shaking her head slightly at me as we piled into the truck.

"Well, I can't deny that. Pam is convinced that Alden was involved with someone on the sidelines—"

Before I could finish my thought, she asked, "And you really think she might come to the funeral?"

"Yes, it wouldn't surprise me. And if she does, she'll probably be alone. I really need to find her, whoever she is, and I simply haven't had time to look so far. Alden might have told her something that would be helpful in figuring this whole thing out. And then, like I said, I will be observing—watching for anyone who might seem suspicious to me."

"I could help you do that," she said.

"That would be great. And I was also thinking about talking to Pam this afternoon and asking her to do the same," I said. "If you happen to notice any of these people near the ranch," I added, tapping the notebook that was beside me on the seat, "give me a call. And check with your family; see if any of them know anyone besides the people you've given me that I should be aware of. I'll be passing this list on to Sheriff Perkins."

"Would you like to come in and have some lunch?" Shanice asked when I pulled up in front of the ranch house.

I would have loved to, but I needed to keep moving. "I'm sorry, may I have a rain check? I need to get a lot done before the day's over."

"Sure," she said with an inviting smile.

"Great, then I'll see you later," I said, and I drove away feeling very alone. I'd lived by myself since my mission and normally worked by myself, and yet now, after all that practice of flying solo, I was lonely in a way I wasn't familiar with. I wasn't sure quite how to handle this.

My next stop was the sheriff's office. Luckily, he was in, and I turned over the evidence I'd collected along with a copy of my diagram. "This is great," he said. "You do excellent work, Rocky."

I left a few minutes later and drove down to Brigham City. Pam's mother invited me in. She was much friendlier to me now than the first time we'd met. "It's nice to see you again, Mr. Revada," she said. "Please pardon the mess. A lot of family members are here for the funeral tomorrow."

"I just need to speak to Pam for a minute. I won't take long, Mrs. Page," I said as I stepped in and saw that the living room was indeed filled with visitors.

"I'll get her. She's in her bedroom right now. She's resting," Mrs. Page said.

"I'm sorry to disturb her, but this is important," I said.

"She'll be glad to see you. Just a moment and she'll be here." Mrs. Page left the room.

Pam came in and smiled when she saw me. "Thanks for coming by," she said. "What can I do for you?"

"I need to talk to you privately," I said. "Is there some place we can go to speak alone?"

She looked around. "The house is full," she said. "Maybe we could go outside."

I agreed with that, and she said, "First let me introduce you to some of my family." She turned and called to the people in the living room. "This is Rocky Revada," she said, "He's the man I was telling you about. He's helping the police catch whoever killed Alden."

She then named several of them, but the only one that interested me was a man she introduced as Alden's brother, Chase. He was the only one who seemed to be from Alden's side of the family. I had already picked him out; he didn't fit in with the others who were all clean, nicely groomed men and women. Chase had greasy, long, dark blond hair and a long, tangled beard. He was a small man, a good six inches shorter and sixty pounds lighter than his brother had been. He appeared to be somewhere in the age range of thirty. He didn't look at all like Alden, and he didn't look at all like he was glad to make my acquaintance. I noted the package of Camel cigarettes poking out of the top of his faded and soiled shirt.

Once we were outside, Pam said, "Would you mind if we left here for a little while? I can't stand being around Chase, and he doesn't act like he's going to leave for a while yet. I hate to be rude to him. He's the only member of Alden's family here." She looked back at the house. "To be honest with you, I need a break from my family too. I feel smothered."

"It's fine with me. I haven't had lunch. Maybe we could go somewhere and get something. I'll get you some too, if you'd like," I offered.

"That would be so nice, Rocky," she said with a wan smile.

We rode in my truck to a nice restaurant and went in together. We asked for a private table, and the hostess smiled at us. She clearly thought we were a couple, and neither of us told her otherwise. After consulting Pam, I ordered lunch for both of us. While we waited for our food to be prepared, I brought up the subject I had to discuss with her. "I understand the funeral is tomorrow," I said.

"I'll be glad when it's over," she said. "Maybe then his brother will quit hanging around and my family will leave. I need to try to make a life for my little guy and me." I smiled at her reassuringly.

"I'm sorry you have to go through this," I told her. I watched her for a minute as she struggled with her emotions. She wiped at her eyes with a napkin. "Alden and I weren't as close anymore as I wanted to be. It was like we were just going through the motions, but it still hurts."

"Of course. You were still married to him. It will probably take some time to heal. By the way, I will be at the funeral," I said.

She was surprised. "Why would you want to come?"

"To work," I said. Now she was puzzled. "I'm hoping his . . ." I paused. This was awkward.

But her eyes opened wide, and she lifted her eyebrows. "You think *she* will be there, don't you." It wasn't exactly a question, but it made the topic easier to discuss.

"I'm hoping so, and that I can talk to her."

"Or to them," she suggested.

"You think he might have had more than one girlfriend?" I asked. I hadn't even considered that thought.

"I have no idea," she said. "Maybe I'm just preparing for the worst at this point. I'm sure he had at least one."

"And I'm assuming you're right. I'm guessing that if she comes, she'll be alone and will stand out. I'll be watching for her, but I was hoping you would too."

Her face hardened, and she looked me in the eye. "I hope we find her." But then she suddenly looked guilty. "I can't hate her, though. Shanice doesn't hate me. So I have no right to hate whoever Alden was seeing. He's the one who hurt all of us."

"What about his brother?" I asked. "Do you think he'll know her?"

"I'm don't know. I barely know Chase."

"But he might know her, don't you think?"

"Possibly," she said thoughtfully.

"At any rate, will you pay particular attention to Chase while we are at the funeral, and again at the cemetery?" She nodded in understanding, and I added, "Even if he pretends not to notice, if she's there, he'll probably look at her. They'll probably send signals to each other that they won't think anyone else would notice. Assuming they know each other, that is."

"I'll do my best," she agreed.

Our lunch came, although it looked like breakfast—we had both ordered from the breakfast menu. The waitress placed a heaping plate of bacon, eggs, sausage, hotcakes, and grits in front of me, then placed

Pam's single egg and small stack of hotcakes in front of her. We thanked the waitress and began to eat. I felt guilty. Shanice had invited me to lunch, and I had declined. Now here I was having breakfast with another woman. *This is work,* I told myself, and tried to enjoy my meal.

We ate slowly and talked as we ate. Pam mentioned a call she'd received shortly before I came to her house.

"What did the caller say?" I asked.

"He said something about you ending up like Alden and . . . and he said some other name. I'm not sure what that was about."

I enlightened her, and her face went white. "Conrad," she said softly after I'd finished. "He works for Hal Rodgers. Or he did, at least. He's dead." I wasn't sure how she knew Conrad, but I didn't push her on the topic. She seemed to be trying to believe what I'd just told her. We began eating again.

"Chase was not there at the time. I suppose he'd gone out for a smoke because I won't allow smoking in my house. That was one habit Alden didn't have," she said. "I never would have dated him if he had."

She took a bite of egg and chewed slowly. I stirred some butter into my grits. "He came back after the call was over."

"How long afterwards?" I asked.

"Oh, maybe three or four minutes," she guessed. "I was in the kitchen telling Mom about it when he came in. The rest of the family was in the living room where you saw them. Chase came in and asked me what was going on. He said I looked upset. I told him I'd had a threatening call. He just shrugged it off. He didn't ask anything about it. Then my sister came in, and I told them I was going to go to my room and try to rest. I was going to call you, but I hadn't done it yet when Mom came and told me you were there."

"Did the caller say that I'd die just like Alden and Conrad did?" I asked, thinking about the previous threating calls and notes. *It's getting to the point that I should start a collection,* I thought.

"No. But now I remember," she said, her voice wavering. "He told me that if you didn't do what I told you to, you'd die in a most unexpected way and when you least expected it. He also said you wouldn't be the only one to die."

"That's cryptic," I said. I swallowed a spoonful of grits and tried to quell the fear that welled up inside me. *I have to find this guy soon or he just might succeed,* I thought. But I squared my shoulders and put on a brave face for Pam's sake. "People like this always talk big," I said.

"Rocky, this guy doesn't just talk," she reminded me. "You've got to let the cops take over."

"They're working on this too, now," I told her. "What we've got to do is find him and do it quickly."

Chapter Fourteen

I PULLED UP A FEW minutes later outside Pam's house. I got out, walked around my truck, and opened her door. She stepped out, looking around as she did so. "I wonder where Chase is—not that I care," she said.

"What does he drive?" I asked, assuming that his car was gone and that that was how Pam knew he wasn't here.

"A black convertible," she said. "He hasn't had it long. I think it's a Chrysler Sebring."

"Fancy wheels," I said. "What does he do?" I asked.

"He has a body shop in Ogden," she said.

"What is the name of the shop?" I asked, wondering if I'd passed it before.

"He calls it Chase's Auto Body."

"Hmm, haven't heard of it. Do you know anything about the business? Is it pretty profitable?

"I really couldn't say. I think he does okay. I think he works on some pretty nice cars. I hope he doesn't come back," she added bitterly.

"I'm going to want to talk to him," I said. "He might know something that would help the cops and me."

"If he does he wouldn't tell you," she replied.

"We'll see about that," I said. "I'll see you at the funeral in the morning."

She stepped close and gave me a hug, followed by a kiss on the cheek. The kiss caught me off guard, and I felt a flutter in my stomach. "Be careful, Rocky," she said tenderly.

As I walked back around my truck, I again wondered how in the world a creep like Alden Overton had managed to get two good women to fall in love with him. There must have been two completely different sides to him. I got in and pulled onto the street. Pam was watching me when I looked over. She waved at me with a sad smile. I waved back. I wondered if the woman I was going to be looking for tomorrow would be as kind and easy to be with as Pam and Shanice.

I left and drove to Ogden to Hal Rodger's office. I wanted to pick up the rest of the Gridley files. I just hoped Hal or someone else hadn't tampered with them. When I entered Hal's personal office, he came quickly to his feet. "I'm sorry about Conrad," he said. "I had no idea he tried to kill you. He never seemed like that kind of man at all." I looked at him sharply, wondering who had clued him in on Conrad's death threats. *I should be used to this by now, though,* I thought. No matter how tight a lid you tried to keep on information in an investigation, it seemed people always talked. I didn't respond, though. I had yet to determine if I believed Hal's sincerity or not. Right now, I was leaning heavily toward *not.*

"I need the Gridley files," I said shortly.

"They're not here," he said as he sat down heavily in his chair. He looked like he'd aged several years since I'd seen him last. I felt like I had, too, and if the files were in the wrong hands, I knew I'd feel like I was at least forty before the day was over.

"Where are they?" I asked suspiciously.

"A cop took them a few minutes ago," he said.

I was not sure what to think about that. If a cop had them, it had to be one of the sheriff's men, and I hadn't heard from them since the eventful meeting at the Box Elder County sheriff's office. "Who was the cop?" I asked. "Was it Detective Blaine Springer?"

"I don't think so, but I don't remember his name," Hal said nervously.

"Did he have a court order or authorization from Glenn Gridley?"

Hal shook his head. "He said he could get one if he needed to so I just let him have them. After what happened to Conrad, I wasn't about to not cooperate with the cops."

"Do you even know what department he was with?"

Some of the color returned to Hal's face. "He said he was from the Box Elder County Sheriff's office."

"Is that what it said on his ID when he showed it to you?" I asked.

That question chased the color away again. "He . . . he . . . didn't show me any. He just flashed his badge. It looked real enough."

"But you didn't ask for ID?"

"He was intimidating," he said defensively. "He had a badge. I'm sure he was a cop."

"And I'm sure he wasn't," I said, glaring at him. "Describe him to me."

Hal's hands were shaking. "He was probably under thirty, maybe twenty-six or twenty-seven. He was quite a bit shorter than me and not very heavy."

"You are six feet if you're an inch," I said sarcastically. "Some little guy intimidated you?"

"It wasn't his size," he said. "He just looked very official and his eyes, well, they could drill for oil. He was not the kind of cop you would want to cross."

"Hal, you need to understand something," I said angrily. "Whoever this guy was, he was not a cop. He was a fake and, I'm afraid, a lot of other things. Maybe even a killer."

For a moment, I thought Hal was going to pass out and bash his face on his desk. But he shook it off. "You mean I might have given the records to someone unofficial?" he stammered.

"That's exactly what I mean. Finish describing him," I ordered, trying to drill him with my eyes the way the thief had done. Apparently I didn't have the look down, because, even though he was squirming, he didn't appear to be afraid of me.

"He had a suit and tie, cowboy boots, and dark blond hair."

"His hair, was it short or long?"

"Short. Real short," he said.

"Eye color?"

He scrunched his face thoughtfully. "Not brown. Not blue."

"Green or hazel, maybe?" I suggested

"Yeah, greenish, I guess," he said.

"What color was his suit?" I asked.

"Dark," he said. "Blue or black, but I'm not sure which. It was Western cut."

Now we were getting somewhere. "What color were his boots?" I needed distinguishing details if he had any. But he couldn't remember the boot color. Nor could he think of anything else. I was actually surprised at how much he'd given me. I just hoped he wasn't making it all up. But somehow, I was starting to believe him. I was also searching my memory for anyone who could possibly fit the description he'd given. The size, age, hair color, and eyes could fit Chase Overton. But it couldn't have been him, I reasoned, not unless he'd cleaned up, cut his hair, shaved off his beard, and bought a suit and pair of boots. Stranger things had happened, but I dismissed him and kept thinking. I drew a blank.

"Mr. Revada, I'm sorry. I hope I haven't done something that will hurt the Gridleys," he said.

"I don't think Cindy will be very happy," I said rather unkindly.

The mere mention of her name caused him to blush. "I thought I was helping," he said. "I feel terrible. I would never hurt Cindy."

"Intentionally, you mean. Did you give him everything?" I asked.

"Everything in the hard files that I hadn't already given to you," he said. "But of course, a lot of the records are in the office in Tremonton."

I felt a surge of hope. "Are the hard files, by any chance, a backup to computer records?"

His eyes lit up. "Yeah, of course they are. Naturally, receipts and things like that aren't in the computer, but all of the spreadsheets, checkbook records, and that kind of thing are."

I looked at him, shaking my head. "Why didn't you mention this at first?"

"You had me worried," he said. "I wasn't thinking clearly. I'll print you a copy of everything. Will that help? I'll do anything I can to make it up to Glenn and his family."

"Thanks, Hal. That will help," I told him.

As he worked at his computer, I had a thought. He knew Alden well. I wondered if he also knew his brother. I asked, "What can you tell me about Chase Overton?"

"Who's that?" he asked, looking up from his computer.

"You should know him. You knew Alden."

"Yeah, that's true, but I don't know anyone by the name of Chase. Is he a cousin or something?"

"You honestly don't know?" I asked, very surprised.

"I've never heard of him. Alden and I were good friends at one time, but I don't remember ever meeting any of his family." He looked at me, clearly puzzled. "Does he look like Alden?" he asked.

"Not at all," I admitted. He shook his head, mumbled something, and went back to work at his computer.

Thirty minutes later I left with an armful of papers, including copies of what I already had stored in the hotel safe in Logan. I was back in business.

As soon as I was back at my truck, I unloaded my arms and called Sheriff Perkins. I told him what had happened, and asked him if he had anyone who could go over to Hal Rodgers' satellite office in Tremonton and get whatever Gridley records might be left there. "I'll go myself," he said.

There was nothing more I could do about the financial records for now, so I decided to check out Chase Overton's business. It was as trashy looking as he was. I drove slowly past, then turned and came back again, my camera in my hand. I snapped several pictures. Then I circled the block and parked my truck. I walked past a couple of buildings that fronted the street there. They looked like warehouses, and no one was in sight. A tall chain-link fence surrounded Chase's entire business. I took more pictures and looked into the yard. There were no dogs there as far as I could tell.

After getting back to my truck, I finally pulled through the gate of the auto body shop and parked in front of the garage itself. The place was open for business, but there was no black convertible parked in front. I went inside. The tiny lobby was filled with smoke, so it took me a moment to see the receptionist behind the front desk. "Can I help you?" asked an overweight girl with a cigarette hanging between her fingers.

"Is Chase in?"

"Nope. He won't be in today or tomorrow. You got a job you need done?" she asked.

"I do, but I wanted to talk to Chase about it personally," I said as I studied her. She must have picked up her grooming habits from her boss. Her oversized black T-shirt was ratty and frayed at the edges, and her dirty jeans had large holes in the legs. When she spoke, crooked yellow teeth showed in her mouth, and there were piercings in her lip, her nose, and along her right ear. Her hair was tied in a messy bun on top of her head. She was enough to drive good business away. It made me wonder what kind of clientele he had here.

"Sorry, mister, but his brother went and got himself killed. Chase won't be back for a few days," she said. "He's pretty broken up."

"I can imagine," I said as I noted the Marlboro package lying beside the overfilled ashtray where she flicked the ash from her cigarette. I tried to visualize her crossing the fence on the northern edge of the sprawling Gridley ranch. Awkward, but with help, it certainly wasn't impossible. She wasn't that big. She had her head down, but lifted it and took a long drag on her cigarette. She slowly let the smoke out, looking out the window to her right to watch a guy in tight, stained blue jeans dig around under the hood of a white Audi A8. She was more or less ignoring me.

Her lack of attention was to my advantage. I again looked for any sign that they had dogs, and I searched quickly but thoroughly for surveillance cameras. They had neither. In my search, I noticed two framed photos standing alone on a wall to my left. Stepping closer to one of the photos, I was face-to-face with a solid brown quarter horse. *What in the world*, I thought, placing my hand on the wall and leaning in to examine the photo more closely. The horse looked eerily like Badger and stood next to a familiar man with long, greasy, blond hair and a beard.

"When were these photos taken?" I asked the girl from across the room.

She looked over at me briefly, then down at the desk. "How should I know?" she said softly. It looked like I wasn't going to get much more information from her, and I couldn't find any indication of a date on the photo, so I continued my examination of the room.

I oriented myself to the section of the building where I was now standing and saw what I assumed was Chase's office. The door was closed, but judging by the size of the tightly drawn windows lining the office, I assumed the room was pretty good-sized. I walked casually to the office door and tried the handle. It was locked, but the lock appeared to be a simple mechanism. When I looked up, the receptionist was eyeing me, a scowl etched deeply on her face.

"I'll come back some other time," I said, smiling. "Tell Chase that Frank came in."

"Whatever you want," the girl said.

"I didn't catch your name," I said.

She finally looked at me, took a deep drag on her Marlboro and blew it out, right at me. As I stepped back to avoid the smoke, she said, "Perla."

"Thanks Perla. Say, that's a pretty pricey car he's working on there," I said, pointing to the guy she had been admiring. She followed my finger out the window. "Don't you guys have dogs or surveillance cameras here? "

"Nope, no dogs or cameras, but we got a good fence," Perla said, still looking out the window. "Nobody has ever got in here that wasn't supposed to."

"That's good, 'cause if I bring my car in, I want it protected. I've put a lot of money into it. My lawyer and I would not take lightly to damage, if you catch my meaning," I said, hoping to scare her a little bit. If she wasn't careful, she could end up on the wrong side of the law. I had an idea circulating through my head that dogs and cameras could make difficult—an idea I wouldn't want the cops to know about. My idea and I left—for now.

Back in the truck, I wondered what Shanice was up to and decided to find out. "Hey," I said when she answered, "why didn't you tell me about Chase?"

"Who are you talking about?" she asked. I could hear a whistling in the background.

"Where are you?" I said.

"Don't change the subject on me, mister," she said lightly. "If you must know, I'm on a horse helping the guys round up some cattle on the ranch." I smiled. Only Shanice would talk on the phone while she galloped around on a horse.

"Now answer my question," she said.

"I'm talking about Chase Overton, Alden's mangy little brother who smokes Camel cigarettes and has a sloppy receptionist that smokes Marlboros."

"Alden doesn't have a brother," she said defensively. Apparently she'd missed my dropped hints about the cigarette brands. "What makes you think he does?"

"I met him," I said, "but I thought he was a liar. That's why I called you. You told me what I need to know. Thanks."

"Rocky, what's going on?" she asked, her voice slightly strained. "You mentioned Camels and Marlboros." So she *had* caught those hints.

"Quite a lot is going on," I said. "I'm worried about you guys. Our killer called Pam again and threatened me, which is getting to be old news, but he also said that if I don't back off, others would die."

I could hear her gasp over the phone, and I could feel the fear in her voice when she spoke again. "Rocky, what are we going to do?" she asked.

"We're going to get whoever is responsible for all of this," I said. "In the meantime, I want you and your family to take extreme care."

"Rocky, let the sheriff and his deputies take it from here. I'll talk to Dad about it," she said with a plaintive note in her voice.

"Are you trying to fire me?" I asked with a forced chuckle.

"Of course not, Rocky. But I kinda like you, ya know. In fact, I need you. In my life. How can that be if you are left for dead in a ditch? Please, I can't stand it Rocky," she pleaded. I was surprised at the emotion in her voice, and it made my own breath catch. Could this be a sign that she wanted me as more than just a good friend?

"I know what you're saying, because I feel the same way," I said with conviction. "But I'm fine, Shanice. Really, I am. I can take care of myself—I have years of practice. More than anything, I'm worried about you. I can't always be there to protect you, not while I'm solving this case. Is there someplace you could go for a few days, just until we get this matter wrapped up?" I asked.

"*Please*, Rocky. We've got work to do here. We are shorthanded," she said. "I don't think we can spare anyone at the moment. Cindy's in the house on the computer, trying to figure out a way to take over the work Conrad was doing. Jena's in Logan getting a load of grain."

"And Tyra?"

"She's on her way home from school right now. Rocky, they wouldn't touch her, would they?" she asked abruptly, her voice full of terror. Her panic mirrored my own. Why hadn't I thought about that sooner?

"I don't know," I told her honestly. "I hope not."

"I'm taking her out of school," she suddenly said with resolution in her voice. "We'll keep her home."

"That's a good idea," I said.

"I can't stand the thought of anyone trying to hurt her," she said with a catch in her voice.

"She's probably safe," I said lamely, trying to reassure both of us. "I'll stop by sometime this evening and bring you guys up to date on what I've learned. If you must stay on the ranch, so be it, but promise me you'll be really careful."

"I promise. You too, Rocky," she said softly.

A few minutes later, Sheriff Perkins called. "I got some records," he said. "However, they are not complete, just what they could get me from the computer. A guy matching the description of Hal's unofficial visitor had been there ahead of me. I'm checking into it."

"I was afraid of that. Anyway, thanks, Sheriff. I'm on my way north. It might be helpful if you and I and Detective Springer could meet," I suggested. I was still wary of Blaine, but I was making an effort at giving him the benefit of the doubt.

The sheriff agreed and we set a time. I drove to Logan and pulled all the cameras from my office but one. Then I went to my house and took all but two of them from there. I left one in the front and one in the back, in the best spots I could find. Finally, I went to my hotel room. I took a shower, and then collapsed on my bed for a little rest. I wasn't sure how much sleep I'd get that night, so I decided to get what I could now. I was tired and fell to sleep quite easily. Two hours later, I got up, put on my gun, gathered up all of my things, including the files and the jump drive I'd put in the hotel safe, and headed for Tremonton. I didn't intend to return to the hotel that night, but I kept my room just in case I changed my mind.

I met with Sheriff Perkins and Detective Springer as arranged. A third man by the name of Patrick Dent was with them. The moment I saw him, I thought he matched Hal's description of his mysterious visitor and felt relieved. This had to have been the guy who grabbed the files. I asked the sheriff why he hadn't mentioned the man during our phone call. He said that it had been an honest miscommunication: he hadn't known until later that day, when Springer informed him of the situation. It turned out that Dent was a certified public accountant who worked for the county. The sheriff felt confident Dent could take over on the embezzlement part of the case. I turned everything I had over to him except the jump drive, which I had put in the bottom of my truck's jockey box. I took time to show the accountant what I'd found, and he agreed that I was onto something nefarious. He left with the financial records, appearing anxious to get started.

After he was gone, the sheriff, Blaine, and I went over our recent activities. Blaine had attended the autopsy of the bookkeeper. He'd taken the bullet removed from the body to the state lab, where he'd learned what we already thought: the bullet matched the one taken from Alden's body. Both were .38 caliber, like the casings I'd found at the spot the men had been killed.

I told them that I was quite sure the pistol, if we ever found it, would turn out to be the one Alden Overton usually kept in his gun cabinet. I also told them about Alden's brother, Chase Overton, and the fact that Shanice hadn't known he existed. I didn't mention my visit to his place of business earlier that day. I planned to go back there tonight, and I didn't want anyone to know about it.

We also went over the list of smokers Shanice had given me, and I explained that I was interested in anyone in any way connected to the family who smoked Camels or Marlboros. Throughout all this, Blaine seemed like a different man. I still detected an undertone of distrust and dislike for me, but he was civil, and I felt like he would be more efficient than he had been. When the sheriff asked me to divide the list of smokers between us, Blaine didn't argue. He didn't even complain when I gave him the ones I felt no need to talk to personally. I kept ones like Mace Healy, the banker, and Glenn's ranch hands, the two still employed, and Vance Winskey, the one who had lost his job due to the Gridley's financial difficulties.

In the back of my mind, I couldn't shake the feeling that I needed to speak with both of the current employees. I had no reason to suspect them of anything, but I was wishing that I'd talked to them both sooner. I told the officers what I planned to do the next day when I attended the funeral of Alden Overton.

"If you locate the woman, you'll let us know?" Sheriff Perkins asked.

I agreed that I would. After I left the sheriff's office, I drove to Tremonton and checked into a motel there. I carried my suitcase and equipment inside. Then I set up my monitoring devices, making sure the cameras I'd left in Logan worked okay and that those I was going to be putting elsewhere had fresh batteries in them. I had to use an expensive satellite connection, being this far away, but it worked very well. Everything at my office and house seemed to be normal.

I was getting quite hungry and thought about getting some dinner but decided to wait. I could eat later while I waited to begin my late-night investigation work at Chase's shop. I wanted to see the Gridleys first. I figured they would be through with their dinner by then so that I could give them a report, discuss the mystery of Chase Overton, or whoever he was, and set up some cameras around their barn and house. I had to provide for their safety the best I could.

By the time I got there, it was a little after eight and almost fully dark. I rang the doorbell, and Shanice met me at the door. Even though it had been shortly after noon when I'd seen her last, it seemed like forever. She hugged me—and I enjoyed it.

They had yet to eat dinner, since they had barely come in from their work. Rose was busy in the kitchen, Jena was in her room, and Cindy was still setting up a system for keeping their own financial records. "Cindy could use some help," Shanice suggested after I'd spent a moment with Tyra and told Glenn that I had quite a bit to go over with them before I headed back out again.

"Have you had dinner yet?" Cindy asked after I had given her a few pointers.

"I have some surveillance work I need to do later. I plan to eat before I get started." I didn't mention that I was going to do the surveillance up close and personal.

But Cindy didn't take no for an answer, and as soon as Shanice found out that I hadn't eaten, she invited me as well. She said with a pouty face, "I invited you for lunch and you turned me down. If you say no again, I'll be really hurt."

"Okay, you gals win," I said.

Jena had come into the room in time to hear Shanice make the invite. Cindy winked at Jena and then said, "I think Rocky is showing favoritism to our big sister. That's not fair." Then she laughed, and Shanice turned red. Glenn nodded at me, and I couldn't help but feel hopeful regarding the future.

Rose seated me between Shanice and Tyra at the table. Glenn called on Tyra to say a blessing on the food. She smiled shyly up at me and then proceeded to do a lot more than bless the food. She mentioned me and asked the Lord to keep me safe and help me come to dinner again. With all the threats and murder attempts going around, I felt a lot more secure after her sweet and faith-filled prayer.

After dinner, I brought the family up to date on my investigation and that of the sheriff and Blaine. When I mentioned Chase, I got several strange looks, but I didn't pause in my report except to say, "I'll talk a little more about him later."

"Shanice, you didn't mention that Alden has a brother. I don't remember him being at the reception," Jena said when I'd finished my report. Shanice just shook her head; she'd just spooned a bite of food into her mouth and couldn't talk.

"What's he like, Rocky?" Cindy asked, turning to me instead.

"Are you sure he's who he says he is?" Glenn asked.

"I'm not too sure he *isn't* an imposter," I agreed. "He's a slob, doesn't even faintly resemble Alden, and he's about half his size. His hair is long and greasy, and he has a huge beard. The thing that puzzles me is that Pam doesn't question who he is, but she did make it clear that she despises him and wishes he'd go away."

"If Alden had a brother, I'd have known it. I spent time with his family often, particularly when we were first married," Shanice finally said. "I wonder what this guy is up to."

"Hal Rodgers, when I was talking to him, said he'd never heard of the guy either, and of course, he and Alden were friends," I pointed out.

"They were?" Cindy asked.

"Yeah, I didn't know that," Jena chimed. "Did you, Dad?"

Shanice squirmed uncomfortably on the chairs next to me. "I'm sorry," she said. "I never mentioned it to anyone."

"Except me," Glenn said, not bothering to mention that he had barely learned it himself. "Alden worked for Hal for a while before he and Shanice were married. It's not important." His tone was clear— he wanted that subject dropped.

"Sorry," I said softly to Shanice.

"It's okay," she whispered back.

I got up and said, "My first concern is the security of this family. Glenn, I have some motion-detection cameras in my truck. They feed into a monitor that I keep by my bed. It has an alarm on it. I'd like to set them up around the house and barn."

"Do you really think that's necessary?" Glenn asked gruffly.

"I absolutely do," I said.

"Okay then, do it. Do they need power—extension cords or anything?"

"No, they are battery operated, and they have fresh batteries. It won't take me too long to set them up," I said.

"Does their signal carry clear to Logan?" Shanice asked.

"I have a satellite Internet connection from my monitor to them."

"They must be expensive," Cindy ventured.

"They are worth it," I said. "That's what kept me alive when Conrad decided to have his lackey blow me up."

"Are these the ones you had on your house and office?" Shanice asked. "We don't want to take away any equipment from your own property."

"I kept a couple of cameras there. We need them here more," I told her.

"You aren't going to sleep in your house again until this is over, are you?" she asked, wringing her hands.

"No, I have a motel room in Tremonton. My monitor is already set up there," I explained.

"Rocky, you are welcome to stay here. We have a lot of room in this big house," Glenn offered.

Shanice jumped on that. "Yes, please do," she begged.

"Thanks, but I'll be fine," I told them both. "Now I better get on it." I suddenly remembered that I needed to talk to the two ranch hands. "There is one more thing I need before I go outside," I said. "Could you give me the addresses of your former and current ranch employees?"

Glenn looked stunned at the mention of his ranch hands. He gave me a questioning look. "Surely you don't think . . ." he began. Then he shook his head. "Sorry, I've got to keep an open mind. Cindy, would you write down the names, phone numbers, and addresses for Rocky while I go out and help him with the cameras?" he asked.

"I don't necessarily have evidence against them, if that's any reassurance. I just don't want to leave any stone unturned. If you have it, Cindy, would you include Vance's address too?" I asked.

She nodded in agreement.

Shanice and Glenn followed me outside. While we were working, Cindy brought me a paper with the information I'd requested, lingered with us for a while, and then went back to the house. We finished up after about a half hour. I told them that I needed to be on my way then. Shanice followed me when I went to my truck. Her father had entered the house before she said, "Rocky, please, don't let anything happen to you."

I smiled at her. "You worry too much," I said, tapping her nose, then hugging her briefly. Then I was on my way again. Before the night was over, I would have tangled with the wrong side of the law, something I hadn't undertaken in my work for quite some time.

Chapter Fifteen

BACK AT MY MOTEL ROOM in Tremonton a few minutes later, I checked to see that the cameras were all working correctly. Then I set the monitor to forward signals to my cell phone, where I could access the pictures if I needed to. I wondered what PIs used to do without all the modern technology I had at my disposal.

The next thing I did was place a call to the hotel in Logan where I still had a room. I told the woman at the front desk that I might be very late getting in that night, if I made it back at all. But I also said that I was expecting a visitor whom I had been unable to get hold of to arrange a different time to meet him. I asked her to tell him or anyone who inquired that I wasn't in and then to call my cell phone so I could attempt again to reach the individual. I gave her my number, thanked her for her willingness to help me, and hung up. There was no way that I could be sure my enemies hadn't figured out that I was staying there. But if they had figured it out, I just wanted to know about it as soon as I could.

I rested again for a couple of hours and then, late at night, after making sure my gun was serviceable, I headed for Ogden. I drove past Chase's Auto Body. All was quiet and dark there except for a large light that lit up the front of the business. I would have preferred not to have that light. The large gate on the tall chain-link fence was locked with a padlock. That was not a problem except that I would have to be exposed to the light for a minute if I entered that way. I drove on past. It wasn't time yet.

I drove around for a while. I didn't know where Chase lived or I'd have checked there. Ogden has more than its share of bars, but

I decided that, to kill time, I might as well check as many of them as I could since he looked to me like someone who would spend his evenings at such places. I spent two hours looking, but the Sebring he drove didn't show up.

I drove past his business again and saw no activity there, which is what I expected and hoped for. But before I did my little breaking-and-entering routine, I decided to drive past one more location that was of interest to me. I had Mace Healy's home address, which I'd acquired through Sheriff Perkins. I'd intended to look him up after the funeral—either at the bank, if he was there, or at his home.

His house was in one of the more affluent suburbs of Ogden. As I rolled by, I did a double take. A black Sebring convertible was parked in the driveway. I honestly hadn't expected that. The house was totally dark as far as I could see. The doors to Mace's three-car garage were closed. I could only assume that Mace and his family were asleep at such a late hour. But that didn't ring true with Chase's car there.

I looked at my watch. It was two a.m. I drove back to Chase's Auto Body and parked my truck out of sight about a block away. Then I walked up the alley and approached the business from the rear. One look at the formidable roll of wicked-looking barbed wire that went all the way around the lot reaffirmed what I had thought earlier—climbing that fence would be detrimental to my pants, shirt, and skin.

I slipped to the corner of the fence, working my way through heaps of trash. When I reached the corner, I paused. I looked up and down the street. I detected no activity anywhere, so I hurried to the front gate, thin gloves on my hands, a small flashlight in my pocket, and my lock picking tools ready to go to work.

I was nervous with the light shining on me from above, but it I took me only a moment to open the lock. I slipped through the gate and put the lock back in place, unlocked but looking as if it were locked from a few feet away. I wanted to be able to make a hasty escape if necessary. I slipped around to a side door in an attempt to reduce my chances of being seen from the street. It only took a minute to pick the lock on the building door before I slipped inside. I stood still after closing the door, acquainting myself with the sounds inside the building. When I flipped my small flashlight on, I kept it that way for just long enough to locate the door to Chase's office. I then proceeded in that direction in the darkness.

As was the case earlier today, his private office was locked. So I picked yet a third lock. I shut the door, turned on my flashlight, and shined it around the office. It was cluttered and dirty, much like the man himself. I began with his desk, being very careful to put things back as close to how I'd found them as possible. I found nothing of interest on the desk, but in the bottom drawer on the right side, I found more than I could have hoped for.

There was a packet of photographs there. They were of a black horse and a dark brown one—the brown very similar in appearance to Badger and Switch One and the black very similar to Licorice Stick and Switch Two. These photos were labeled on the back with names I'd never heard before but which I hoped to get to know better. I was pretty sure the dark brown horse that I knew as Switch One was apparently registered as Beaver Dam. Similarly, Switch Two's real name was Nighttime Roper. I jotted down the names in my notebook. Before replacing the photos, I looked deeper in the drawer. I could see a bulging folder full of official-looking papers nestled along the side of the drawer. With a soft tug, I pulled the folder from the drawer and set it on the desk. Placing my flashlight in my mouth so both my hands were free, I riffled through the papers quickly. The papers appeared normal to me—just a series of sales invoices and inventory of car parts.

Halfway into the stack of papers—almost as though they'd been hidden—I found two registration documents, one for Beaver Dam and the other for Nighttime Roper. *Jackpot,* I thought triumphantly, pausing and admiring my find. The papers included names of ownership for the horses: Brent Swan for Beaver Dam and Jackson Thomas for Nighttime Roper. Neither of the names rang a bell. There was still a chance that Chase knew these men, but I now thought there was a real possibility that Switch One and Switch Two, or rather, Beaver and Nighttime, were stolen themselves.

I organized all the papers the way I'd found them, slid them back in the folder, and replaced both the folder and the packet of photos in the drawer. I turned off my light and peeked out of the office door to make sure I was still alone. Then I checked a file cabinet in a corner of the room. I once again checked to see if it was still safe to keep searching. Reassured, I thumbed through some dusty cardboard boxes that were stacked near the file cabinet. That was where I once again found something very interesting. One of the boxes was filled with miscellaneous blank papers. Among them was a writing pad. At the top of each page on the pad was the name Chase L. Hideman. I tore off one sheet of the paper, put it in my pocket, and put the pad back.

I spent another thirty minutes in Chase's messy office. In that time, I found no more items that furthered my investigation. But as I lifted the blinds and gazed out the back window, my heart started beating fast. From my viewpoint, I saw several vehicles in varying stages of dismantlement and what looked to be a bin of misshapen license plates next to one of the cars. I whistled softly as I took in the stripped vehicles. *The sucker's running a chop shop right under people's noses,* I thought in amazement. The white A8 that I saw in the shop earlier today flashed across my mind. That car might have been stolen, too. If I were to try to gather evidence of the illegal activity that was taking place there, it would just incriminate me and be unusable to the police as illegally obtained evidence. However, I did make a mental note of what I found and determined to make an anonymous call later that would hopefully inspire the authorities to look into the activities of Chase's Auto Body.

I had been there for nearly an hour and a half by the time I thought that I'd learned all I was going to, so I made sure everything was as close to the way I found it as possible. Locking the doors behind me, I left the building.

As I walked out the side door, I saw vehicle lights coming up the street, so I flattened against the wall, moved toward the back of the building, and hunched down behind a rusty fifty-five-gallon oil drum around the corner. I expected that the lights would pass and I'd be able to hurry to the gate and get away in a matter of seconds. But when the vehicle turned in and faced the gate, I knew I'd made a serious mistake. I should have locked the padlock. Whoever was in the vehicle, whose lights were shining into the yard on the other side of me, would soon know that someone had entered the compound and might still be there.

I hoped for a moment that the car would just turn and leave, but it was not to be. A second vehicle pulled in behind it. Even though I couldn't see either the gates or the cars from my hiding place, I could hear the throbbing of motors and see the light cast by the headlights. I held my breath, wondering what to do, when a man's voice carried to me. "Chase," the voice said, "this lock is open. I think someone's in here."

"You check inside. I'll take a look around the yard," Chase's unmistakable voice said urgently. "I'll lock the gate behind us so no one can get out."

The two cars drove in and then I heard the gate squeaking as it was closed. I also saw light flood through the dirty windows of the shop as lights were turned on inside. I felt about me for a weapon. I had my pistol, but that was a last resort—using it would incriminate me. I found a piece of wood. It was splintery and smaller than I would have liked, but it was the best I could find on such short notice.

I slipped behind the building and waited. I could see the occasional gleam of a flashlight as someone—Chase, I assumed—moved slowly toward me. I raised my stick when I thought he was getting close. When he stepped just beyond the edge of the building with a gun in one hand and a flashlight in the other, he failed to look my way. That error cost him the advantage of the gun. I brought the stick solidly down on his head. The stick broke, but Chase fell hard and lay still. I grabbed his flashlight just as I heard a crunch on the gravel behind me. I lunged to the side but not before something struck me with sickening force on my shoulder.

Pain shot through me, but I continued to move to the side, twisting, even as my attacker came at me again. I swung the flashlight with my right hand and felt it connect at the same moment that a hard object struck my ribs with brutal force. I felt at least one of them crack as I hit the ground, and pieces of Chase's flashlight scattered everywhere. With an adrenaline-powered rush, I jumped to my feet, bent my head, and lunged headlong into the shadowy figure who was staggering against the building.

The flashlight must have worked better than I thought, for when I hit him again, he went down like a rock. I turned back to the one I assumed was Chase. He was out cold but had a strong pulse. I pulled his wallet from his pocket and checked his ID with my flashlight. His driver's license had the name *Chase Overton* on it, but when I kept looking, I found a Visa card that read *Chase L. Hideman*. And he reeked of alcohol. That would explain why he let me get the drop on him. I used the flashlight to search for the gun he'd been carrying. It was lying just a few feet ahead of where he was sprawled. I picked it up, and since I knew instantly that it was not the right caliber for the murder weapon, I threw it onto the roof of the body shop.

I dropped his wallet and turned to the other attacker. He was stirring, and I didn't want him to see my face, but I had to know who he was. So I quickly searched for a wallet. There wasn't one. He groaned but didn't attempt to get up, so I took another moment and checked him for a gun, thinking he didn't have one or I would have had a bullet in my back. He didn't, but I took another moment to check his pulse. It was strong, but his left hand was badly damaged. I didn't think I had done that, but the junk piled against the back of the building—the junk that he'd fallen on—may have. Of course, I was responsible for him falling, so I guess I ought to take credit for his injured hand.

He stirred again and groaned. I decided it was time to get out of there. I headed around the building at a lope. My shoulder and ribs were killing me, but I ignored the pain the best I could. I rapidly picked the locked gate, opened it, glanced around, and had another thought—a dangerous and delaying thought. I acted on it anyway. Working as quickly as I could, I pulled the registrations from both cars. I rapidly jotted down the information, then took the keys, tossed them onto the roof of the shop where I'd thrown Chase's gun, and headed for my truck.

I was five miles away from Chase's Auto Body before I pulled into a convenience store and made a quick call on a pay phone to the Ogden Police. Without revealing my identity, I told the dispatcher that there was a stolen car sitting just inside the gate of Chase's Auto Body where, if they looked, they'd find evidence of a ton of illegal activity going on. When the dispatcher asked my name I said, "Believe me, I know what I'm talking about." I then told them the name of the registered owner of the potentially stolen car, a blue Crown Victoria, and told them to call the owner, if they didn't believe me. And I said if they hurried, they'd catch the thieves on the premises. Then I hung up, went back to my truck, and crawled in gingerly.

I sat there trying to breathe, something I was finding increasingly hard to do with my damaged ribs. I pulled off the gloves I'd been wearing, started my truck, and headed north. My phone began to vibrate, and I pulled it out and looked at the screen. I groaned and then answered it. It was the night manager of the hotel in Logan asking me to please come as soon as I could because my room had been broken into and thoroughly trashed.

I wasted my breath when I told them that they might want to call the police. They said they already had, and it was the cops who hoped I could come to see if I could tell them what had been taken; they said the room was pretty much empty, which was how I'd left it. I was told that even my suitcase was gone. I groaned for effect, which, in my present condition, was easy to do.

The bed in my Tremonton motel room was going to have to wait. Instead of going straight there, however, I turned off of I-15 at Brigham City and started up Sardine Canyon. More than anything else, I knew that I was in a ton of pain and that I couldn't let the cops in Logan know that. That meant that I had to get a rib belt of some kind on me before I went to the hotel. Thank goodness my house was closer than the hotel and the officers who were awaiting my appearance there didn't know how far I had to drive to meet them.

As I drove I thought about what I knew. For example, I knew who had *not* broken into my hotel room. It wasn't Chase Overton, aka Chase Hideman, nor was it the unidentified man who'd caved my ribs in and bruised my shoulder. I also knew that Chase was up to his ears in the matter of the horses and probably the murders, and I suspected that the other man was too.

When I arrived at the house, I stopped in the driveway and waved at my camera as I approached the door. I felt a sudden lurch in my stomach when no alarm registered on my phone. I gave a cursory look around my property, as dark as it was, to see if there might have been an intruder. A few seconds later, a ping indicating the camera alarm finally sounded on my phone, and I breathed a sigh of relief.

I walked inside the house and searched in my closet for where I thought I'd put my rib belt. I got lucky and found it on a high shelf blanketed by a thin coating of dust. After cleaning it off, I soon had it tightly in place. In no time at all, it provided some relief to my aching ribs. For the pain in my shoulder, there was only one thing I could do. I grabbed a bottle of ibuprofen and swallowed four capsules. Then I headed for the truck again.

By the time I reached the hotel, the painkiller had kicked in, and I was able to fake an absence of injury well enough to keep from raising suspicion. I knew all three of the officers who were there, and they all knew of the previous attempt on my life, so they were very sympathetic.

My hotel room had been turned upside down, but when they asked what was missing, I told them the truth: I'd taken everything to a different place miles from here since I was afraid that the guys who'd tried to have me killed before might have discovered where I was staying and try a second time. That made perfect sense to them. One of them made the assumption that I'd been at that other location sleeping when I got the call. I made no attempt to persuade them otherwise.

Thirty minutes later, I was on my way to Tremonton. I sincerely hoped that my alarm wouldn't go off again and thought it not too likely since at least three bad guys—Chase, his sidekick, and whoever had sacked my hotel room—had been quite busy at other locations that night. However, as I crawled gingerly between the clean, white sheets at five a.m. I had to admit to myself that I honestly had no idea of the size of the organization, if that's what it was, that I was up against. Three hours had passed since I'd made my very fruitful yet painful visit to the body shop. Despite the pain, I fell asleep almost instantly.

The alarm I'd set on my cell phone went off at eight. I got up slowly and carefully, swallowed another handful of ibuprofen, and took a shower. I put on my rib belt and my gun, took time for a quick breakfast at a fast food joint, and then headed for Brigham City for the funeral, which was scheduled for ten o'clock.

It was a quarter after nine when I got in my truck and headed south. My truck phone rang just as I hit the freeway. Seeing that it was Shanice, I felt instantly better.

"Hi, Rocky. Did you sleep well?" she asked in what sounded to me like a pseudo cheerful voice.

"Like a baby," I said, not bothering to mention that it was only for three hours. "Is everything okay there?"

"It was when we left," she said. "Dad and Tyra and I are on our way to Alden's funeral. Are you still planning on making an appearance?"

"Sure am. I just got on the freeway."

"Then we aren't far behind you," she said. "We'll be looking for you."

"I'll be there," I promised.

"So I guess you had a quiet night, without alarms," she said. "You didn't call us during the night, and everything seemed to be in order."

She'd guessed wrong, but she wasn't going to find that out, if I could help it, for some time. "I hope it's a quiet funeral too," I said in response to her statement.

I said hi to Tyra and told her I was looking forward to seeing her in a few minutes. Then we ended the call.

Chapter Sixteen

I WENT INTO THE CHURCH—without my gun—and entered the Relief Society room, where the viewing was being held. Pam looked drained, and her eyes were red, but when she saw me walk in, she favored me with a weak smile. I was relieved to see that the supposed brother wasn't in the line of well-wishers. It was a short line, and since the viewing was nearly over, it only took a minute to reach Pam. She hugged me tightly, making me wince despite myself, and kissed my cheek just as I, out of the corner of my eye, saw Shanice enter. Pam's mother shook my hand, murmuring something, and I glanced at the casket.

The murdered man looked as good as could be expected. I didn't let my eyes linger; instead, I whispered to Pam, "Where's the grieving brother?"

"I don't know. He was in and out last evening. And he finally left around ten for the last time. I haven't seen him since. And I hope I don't!" she said forcefully. "He'd been drinking."

"Does the name Hideman mean anything to you?" I asked.

She gave me a puzzled look but shook her head. "No, should it?" she asked.

"We'll talk about it later." There were a few people behind me, so I moved on. I waited for Shanice and her dad and daughter outside the door of the viewing room.

"What was that all about?" Shanice asked when they joined me after going through the line. "Pam looked puzzled over something you asked her."

"She did, didn't she," I said. "I'll ask you the same question I asked her. Does the name Hideman mean anything to either of you?" Glenn shook his head.

"Should it?" Shanice asked as Tyra stepped over and took hold of my hand.

I smiled down at her and then looked up at Shanice. "I just wondered if you recognized the name."

"I don't," she said. "Is it someone I should know?"

"Probably not," I said, flicking my eyes as I saw Mace Healy walk down the corridor toward us. "I'll tell you more later."

Shanice nodded and then waved at Mace, who walked right up to us. "Bad deal, here," he said. "Sorry about your daddy," he added, looking at Tyra, who moved tight against me as if she felt bad vibes from the banker. He ignored me completely, and that was fine with me. My attention had just been drawn in another direction, to a lone woman who was just stepping into the chapel.

The woman was pretty in a worldly way. She had too much paint on her face, and the rows of rings on her ears were beyond ridiculous. She also had a nose ring and one just below her lip. Her black dress was very short, both from the top and from the bottom, revealing tanned skin and curves that should have been concealed for modesty's sake. Blonde, wavy hair with streaks of pink cascaded down her back, and she walked with a pronounced wiggle in her shapely hips. I judged her to be in her early twenties.

I felt a jab in my ribs, and I winced with pain. I'd done a good job concealing my injuries that morning, but when Shanice poked me, it was all I could do to keep from crying out. I turned toward her. She was looking at me with a strange expression. Mace had disappeared into the viewing room. "What is the matter with you?" she asked. "I couldn't have hurt you."

I pasted a smile on my face and said, "No, you just caught me off guard."

Shanice knew better. "Yeah right," she said, threatening to poke me again. I shied away. "Well, I couldn't help but notice the once-over you were giving the half-dressed girl." As she spoke, she nodded toward the doors of the chapel, where a crowd was starting to gather. People were taking their seats. I could see the girl in question sitting on a bench just inside the doorway. She appeared to be sitting next to someone, but my view was blocked.

The pain in my ribs had subsided to a dull ache, so I smiled easily at Shanice. "Have you ever seen her before?"

"No. Why do you ask? She's not exactly the kind of person I'd hang around with."

"She must know Alden. If not, why would she be here?" I asked.

Understanding dawned in her eyes. "Oh, so you've pegged her for Alden's other woman?" she whispered in my ear so that Tyra couldn't hear her. "I'd say she isn't exactly Alden's type." I shrugged, but she had said exactly what I'd been thinking in that moment. The woman seemed a great deal different from Pam and Shanice, both of whom were very attractive but modest women.

"Maybe his tastes have changed over the years. It's worth checking out," I said. I realized suddenly that the woman hadn't gone into the viewing, a sign that maybe she didn't want to see the spurned widow. But it also meant her name would not appear on the guest register.

"Maybe we should go in and sit down," Glenn said and reached for Tyra's hand. She let go of me as he added, "We'll save you two a seat."

The two of them had barely entered the chapel when a second man I recognized came through the door, hurried past Shanice and me, and entered the viewing room. Chase's face was battered from where he'd struck the ground when I'd hit him over the head late last night. He had a bandage on his head, and he was clearly in pain, a fact that gave me some grim satisfaction. What *didn't* give me satisfaction was the fact that he was not in jail. Either the cops hadn't responded to my anonymous call or Chase and his friend had regained consciousness and left the premises before they arrived, despite my throwing their keys away. At any rate, Chase made it just in time for the end of the viewing, a lot worse for wear and with a look of anger on his face. He didn't give me a second glance nor did he show any recognition to Shanice.

"Who was that?" Shanice asked.

"You really don't know?" I inquired, meeting her eyes.

"I'm sorry. I'm not part of your club of know-it-alls. You can enlighten me, though," she said, aiming another playful elbow at my ribs. I caught her hand in time to stop her from making contact, wincing at the quick move it required of me.

"Rocky, are you hurt?" she asked with sudden concern.

"I'm okay," I said very softly. I took her hand and led her past the chapel door and closer to the main entrance of the building. "That man is Chase Overton, the supposed brother of your ex," I said when I was sure we wouldn't be overheard.

"There's no way," Shanice said, shaking her head and pulling a face.

"True. His real name is Chase Hideman," I revealed.

"How do you know that?" she asked after she'd taken a moment to digest what she'd just learned.

"I'd rather not say," I answered. "Just take my word for it."

"Well, I promise I've never seen him before in my life, nor did Alden ever mention him," she protested.

Chase stayed in the room with Pam and the family members when the funeral director closed the door to the Relief Society room for the family prayer. "What is that creepy little guy up to?" Shanice asked, as she took hold of my arm and started directing me toward the chapel.

"Whatever it is, it's not good," I told her. "You go on in. There's something I need to do. Are you coming to the cemetery?"

"Yes," she said. "What do you have to do?"

"I'll explain later," I said. "You go in, and do me a favor, if you will."

"What's that?" she asked.

"Kind of keep an eye on the "lady of the night." Just let me know how she acts in there."

She chuckled at the nickname. "I'll do that." She let go of my arm and started away, but then hesitated and turned back again when she was four or five steps away. "Rocky, you look really great today," she said, a serious look on her face, and then she hurried toward the chapel door before I had time to return the compliment. Her comment lifted my heart.

I went outside to my truck after watching Pam, with Chase holding her right elbow, enter the chapel behind Alden's casket. I drove off and found a payphone. This time, I made a call to the Brigham City Police Department. "Are you looking for a man by the name of Chase Overton?" I asked the dispatcher.

She didn't know, but she did inquire of an officer and, a minute later, she came back on the line and told me that they did have a warrant on Chase. She asked my name, but I said, "It doesn't matter, but Chase Overton is in Brigham City at a funeral service right now." I gave her the address.

She put me on hold for a minute or so. When she came back on she informed me that officers were on their way. I thanked her and quickly hung up. I killed some time before driving back to the church, but when I got there, I parked across the street and down a ways where I could see what happened without being too obvious.

I had expected a short funeral and was not disappointed. I recognized Detective Burke Christensen but made sure he didn't see me. He waited until an unmarked car with two other cops showed up. The three of them met, put their heads together for a moment, and then they stood a short distance from the hearse.

The church door opened, and the casket came through. Chase was one of the pallbearers, although he didn't look like he was carrying his share of the weight; the casket sagged a bit on his side. The cops waited until the body was in the hearse and the pallbearers dispersed, heading for their cars. Chase walked over to where Pam was waiting with her head bowed, looking very subdued in her flowing black dress. Chase didn't even see the cops coming until Burke took hold of his arm and said something. He jerked away violently and started to run. But Burke bolted after him, and the two other officers cut off his flight. Pam's eyes were wide as they rapidly cuffed him and pulled a gun from inside his jacket. I didn't expect it to be the one from the night before—it was probably still on the roof of the auto body. Alden's small .38 was somewhere—could it be that one?

After the cops left with Chase, I crossed the street and approached Pam. She saw me coming as she was being ushered into a car by one of the other pallbearers, a young man I remembered seeing at the house when Pam had introduced me to the group in her living room. She said something to the fellow, who looked like he could be her brother, and then hurried toward me.

"Who is he?" she asked as she rushed up to me.

"You mean Chase?" I asked.

"Yes. You know I've doubted all along that he was Alden's brother. I think he and Alden lied to me about that. Did Shanice see him?" she asked.

"She did, but she's never seen him before," I revealed.

"Ooh," she said with a grimace of anger.

Her mother came just then. "Hello, Rocky. Thanks for coming," she said. Then she addressed Pam. "Be glad he's gone. I just hope they keep him."

Pam turned to me again and said, "I wonder what they arrested him for."

"I'll find out," I promised.

She gave me a searching look and then she said, "You already know, don't you?"

I smiled at her. "I'll see you at the cemetery, Pam. You and your mother better get going."

She suddenly threw herself at me as tears erupted from her eyes. She wrapped her arms around me and squeezed so hard that I again had to bite my tongue to keep from crying out in pain. But she let go quickly, planted a kiss on my cheek, and said, "Thank you for whatever you did." In that moment, I saw Shanice, Glenn and Tyra coming my way and gently nudged Pam away. She took her mother's arm and started toward the car. But she stopped and looked back at me. "I think the other woman was there," she said with scorn in her eyes. "She stands out the way she's dressed. Watch and you'll see her."

"I already did," I said. "Now you two go."

"Is she okay?" Shanice asked a few moments later.

"I think she will be," I said with a frown.

"Rocky Revada, you are a good guy." Both the inflections in her voice and the look on her face when she said that left no doubt in my mind that she meant it.

"I try to be most of the time," I said, thinking of what I'd done not many hours ago that could land me in jail and cost me my investigator's license if it was ever discovered. I looked down at Tyra and said to her. "Your mother is very pretty today, don't you think?"

"My mom is gorgeous," Tyra said with a huge smile. "And I think you look very handsome, Rocky."

"I sometimes fool people that way," I said, winking at her. "And you are gorgeous, too."

"Thank you," she said as her face lit up.

"That other girl, the one who looks like a . . . you know who I mean," Shanice said as I looked at her again. We both nodded, and she went on. "She came out of the chapel with Mace Healy."

"There's something wrong with that man," Glenn growled. He'd been listening to our conversation while appearing to be deep in thought.

"You think?" I asked.

"Yeah, I think," he said. "I'm wondering if I should move my accounts to a different bank."

"Probably, but maybe not right away," I said. "The sheriff has a more in-depth audit taking place than what I was doing. It will include close scrutiny of your bank accounts."

"That's good, but I better not lose any more while that's being done," he said in a warning tone. Then he abruptly shifted his focus. "Shanice told me about that supposed brother of Alden's. I don't see him now. Did he leave?"

"Yeah, he did. He had a small team of cops waiting here to greet him when he came out of the church. They hauled him off to jail, I think."

"For what?" Shanice asked.

I shrugged. "Maybe for going into a church," I suggested face-tiously. "That alone has got to appear suspicious to the cops."

Shanice pulled a face as she said, "I'm serious. What did he do?"

"I suppose I could call and try to find out if you'd like me to," I said.

She was looking at me very suspiciously now, and then she asked, "How come they came here for him? That seems like very unlikely timing."

"Maybe they got a tip from someone," I suggested.

"But who . . ." She didn't bother to complete her question. The look of suspicion turned to one of understanding. "You," she said, tipping her head and smiling.

I shrugged again. But I neither denied nor admitted anything. Instead, I said, "I'm going to go to the cemetery. I'd like to see if the lady of the night shows up there. And then I hope to find a way to talk to her, see if she is who I suspect she is, and then find out, if I can, if she knows anything that might help me unravel this mess."

"Would you like some company?" she asked.

If she was suggesting herself, that would be hard to turn down, even though I knew it could mean that I was in for a grilling of sorts. I knew she knew I was injured, and she wasn't happy about it. "Sure," I said, willing to take the risk.

"Dad, would you mind taking Tyra with you?" she asked.

"Come on, Tyra," was his response, and he took his grand-daughter by the hand and led her toward his truck.

"I'm parked on the street," I told Shanice, and we headed around the chapel together.

I guided my truck to a position near the end of the procession. As we rode together, Shanice did exactly what I thought she was going to do. "Rocky, you are in a lot of pain," she said. "Would you like to tell me what happened?"

"Maybe sometime," I hedged. "I'm okay. It was just a busy night for me."

"Rocky, don't you trust me?" she asked, lowering her eyes and chewing on her lower lip when I looked over at her.

"Of course I do," I told her. "But for your own safety, it might be best if you don't know all the details of my investigation."

She looked hurt, but she nodded in understanding. "Okay, but can you at least tell me where you are hurt?"

I would have preferred that she not know, but since it was clear that she was going to persist, I finally said, "I do have some little bruises."

She raised an eyebrow. "Just little bruises?" she asked, clearly guessing that I was not being terribly forthcoming.

"Okay, maybe some big ones, and a cracked rib or two," I said. "But it's nothing that will keep me from doing the job your dad is paying me for."

"I knew it," she said. "I could see that you were hurting. But won't you at least tell me how it happened?"

"I got too close to a big stick," I said and held up one hand toward her, palm out, as she opened her mouth to speak. "That's all I'm going to say for now. And please don't repeat what I've told you. Not to anyone. It could cause me some serious problems. Now let's talk about something else." I then told her about the break-in at my hotel room in Logan during the night, making sure she understood that I was absent from that location at the time of the incident.

When we reached the cemetery, I parked where I could make a quick exit if I needed to. I explained to Shanice, "I don't want to be bottled in if I need to follow someone who leaves early. If that happens, and if I suddenly take off from here, you'll need to go with your family again."

We walked together toward the gravesite, taking a more round-about route than everyone else. I wanted to be able to observe people, and that was easier to do when I wasn't in the middle of the crowd. I applied the same principle when we got close to where everyone was gathering around the grave. I stood back, and Shanice stayed with me. I was able to see everyone who had gathered there. Mace and the other woman were standing side by side, trying to give the appearance, it seemed to me, that they were a couple. I wasn't buying it. They were too stiff and awkward around each other.

There was no one else there who was of interest to me. I touched Shanice's arm. When she turned toward me, she had tears in her eyes. I had to remind myself that she had once been married to the man whose body was about to be lowered into the cold ground, that she had once loved him. "I'm sorry, Shanice," I whispered, turning to her and brushing back a strand of hair that was stuck to the tears on her cheek. "I need to leave. Will you be okay here without me?"

"I'll walk over by Dad and Tyra," she whispered back. "Be careful, Rocky. *More* careful than you have been."

"I will," I said, meaning that I didn't have any more felonies planned for my foreseeable future.

"And find out what the pseudo brother of Alden got arrested for, if you can," she added softly.

"Will do," I agreed, and I really did plan to do that, because I didn't know what charges had been brought against him.

I'd planned to speak with Pam before leaving the cemetery, but I had something of higher priority on my mind now. I returned to my Silverado and drove a short distance from the cemetery. I was waiting for a shiny silver Lexus, the same one that had been parked in front of Pam Overton's house the first time I had spoken with her.

Chapter Seventeen

I FOLLOWED THE SILVER LEXUS to Ogden. The area of the city where Mace Healy dropped off Alden's girlfriend was not an area I'd ever want to pick up a woman for a date. The area was woeful to say the least, made up of run-down apartments and unkempt people. Nevertheless, after the sleek silver car had smoothly rolled out of the neighborhood, I parked my truck and pursued the woman. Perhaps I was being paranoid, but I took a moment to put on my bulletproof vest beneath my shirt.

I entered the building and followed her to the second floor, keeping a discreet distance. As I climbed up the stairs, I saw the woman enter an apartment down the hall, and I waited a moment before I followed, knocking lightly at the door. My trusty little digital recorder was on and recording in my pocket by the time the door opened. I encountered a problem: I had never seen the young woman who was standing there, looking at me in a way that made me very uncomfortable. Actually I had a second problem—I didn't know the name of the woman I needed to interview nor did I feel comfortable describing her.

Of course, I could abbreviate the description by saying something like, "I need to speak with the young woman who is dressed about like you are but has blond hair with pink streaks instead of black hair with blue streaks." But I didn't do that. Instead, I said, "I need to speak with the young woman who just returned from her boyfriend's funeral. It's very important."

That got me the result I needed. "Pixie, there's a guy here to see you," she shouted over her shoulder. "He says it's important."

"Not now, Moonbeam," came a muffled reply from somewhere out of sight in the apartment. "Tell him I just got back from my boyfriend's funeral. Send him away."

I got the answer to my first question without having to even ask it. Pixie was Alden's girlfriend. It was very important now that I speak with her. Experience had taught me that this was a vulnerable moment for people in her position and that it was the best time to get answers to the rest of my questions, especially those about the murder of the man she loved . . . or thought she loved . . . or whatever.

"Sorry, but you heard her, mister. She's grieving," Moonbeam said. "She can't talk to you now."

"Pixie is grieving over a murder," I said quite loudly as my eyes quickly scanned the area of the apartment within my view. I spotted something that I hoped was all I needed to ensure an interview. "I'm trying to catch Alden's killer. She needs my help, and I need hers," I went on as I pulled out my ID. "My name is Rocky Revada; I'm a private investigator, and I'm working with the Box Elder County sheriff. I don't take no for an answer. She can either talk to me now or I'll call and have the cops come themselves. And I don't think that you want that, what with that partly smoked joint of marijuana you have in that ashtray." I pointed as I spoke, and her face paled beneath the thick layers of makeup.

Pixie came into view then, wiping her eyes so hard that she was streaking mascara all over her face. It was really quite an awful mess she was making. "Okay, so I'll talk to you, Mr. Revada."

"Thank you, Pixie," I said. "We'll need to speak alone."

Pixie looked from me to Moonbeam, and she said, "You heard him. We need to be alone."

"Talk to you later, then," Moonbeam said. She grabbed a jacket from a small closet near the door, slinked into it, and left with a flounce.

As soon as she was gone, Pixie said, "You may sit down," waving long painted fingernails at a cluttered sofa.

I moved the clutter and sat while she dropped into an overstuffed chair at an angle to the right side of me. She made me very uncomfortable. She was not the kind of woman I liked to be alone with under any circumstances, and dressed the way she was only made it worse. I wanted to get this over with as quickly as I could.

"I know this is a hard time," I began, "but I've been looking for you for days, and it's important that we talk now. Whoever killed Alden Overton needs to be caught, and I don't want the trail to get cold."

"Why have you been looking for me?" Pixie asked, her eyes wide.

I cleared my throat and said, "Well, I was hoping you can help."

"But I don't know who it was," she said. "If I did I'd already have told the cops. I loved Alden. He was good to me."

I didn't bother to tell her that others had loved him as well and he'd betrayed them in the cruelest way. Instead, I said, "Some of the questions I am about to ask might seem like they couldn't possibly have anything to do with his death. But trust me, Pixie, everything I ask is relevant. Now, first, what is your name?"

"I'm Pixie," she said. Her eyes were still red, and she wasn't fooling around.

"Pixie who?" I pressed.

"Oh, yeah, you want my last name." She suddenly started to cry, and through her tears, she said, "It was going to be Overton."

"But he was already married," I reminded her.

She dried her tears while I waited for her to say something in response to my remark. She finally did. "He never told me he was married until just before he was murdered."

My dim respect for Alden found a new low. My heart went out to Pam, who had been fooled by Alden in the same manner. "Really?" I asked. "How does a man live a lie like that?"

Pixie sniffled, "I don't know. He was just so sweet to me. No one has ever treated me like he did."

I'd heard that before, but I hadn't yet heard a last name, so I asked again. "What is your last name, Pixie?"

"Jansen," she said. "My name is Pixie Jansen."

I wasn't so sure about the Pixie part of the name yet, but I didn't pursue it any further. Instead, I asked, "How did you become acquainted with Mace Healy?"

"He and Alden were friends," she responded. "Alden introduced us."

"I take it that you met him just shortly before Alden's murder," I said, doubting that was true but trying to draw her out.

"Oh, no, we met months ago," she said, as I'd expected. "And Mace has been really good to me since Alden was killed."

I didn't bother to acknowledge that statement. I asked, "So you consider him a good friend?"

"Yes, a very good friend," she agreed.

"He's the kind of friend who would warn you if he thought you were being deceived by Alden? And of course, you know that Alden did deceive you," I said bluntly.

"Yes, he would warn me, but he must not have known about Alden's wife," she said.

"And that, I suppose, would explain why he was at Pam Overton's house when I visited Pam shortly after Alden's body was found?" Her eyes registered surprise, as I'd suspected they would.

"Are you sure he was . . . he was there?" she asked.

"I couldn't be more sure. He claimed to be an old and trusted friend, and he tried to keep her from talking to me. He was very protective of her," I said.

"I don't believe you," she said defiantly.

"He also did not ever tell Pam about you, even though she suspected that Alden was being unfaithful to her. Mace is not much of a friend to either of you, I'd say. And you might say you don't believe me, but you know it's true, don't you, Pixie?"

Pixie began to wring her hands as she looked down, avoiding my eyes. I decided to see if I could catch her off guard with my next question. "What did Mace and Alden tell you about Shanice? You did know that she was Alden's first wife?"

The wringing of her hands ceased, and she tugged nervously at her short skirt, as if she could make it grow longer by doing so. "I don't know what you're talking about," she said without looking at me.

"It was on the ranch of Shanice Overton's father that Alden's body was found. It was found by Shanice," I said.

She finally looked up. "I guess I heard of her, but Alden never said he was married before." She didn't meet my gaze. I was quite certain she was lying.

"And Mace didn't tell you either?" I pressed.

"No. Why would he tell me?" She was defiant again.

"You were friends, remember?" I didn't expect an answer to that question, nor did I wait for one. Instead, I threw another curve at her. "Did Mace help Alden steal the horses?"

Her eyes popped, and her hands flew to her mascara-streaked face. "Alden didn't steal them," she said. "He tried to stop it."

I don't know if I was surprised or not that Pixie knew about the theft. I'd come here hoping she did, and she had just admitted as much. I pressed my advantage with another shot in the dark. "If Alden didn't help Mace, then who did?" I asked.

"I didn't say Mace stole them," she said as her face grew red and she again began to tug at her troublesome little skirt.

"We both know he was involved," I bluffed.

But Pixie shook her blonde-and-pink hair quite vigorously. "Alden told me that he tried to stop the guy who did it," she said angrily. "And I think that was why he was killed."

I had a hard time believing that, and yet I had to recognize that it would be a very strong motive for murder. "Who did he try to stop?" I asked.

"I don't know," she answered. "I don't know anything else. You'll need to go now. I've got a terrible headache, and I need to lie down."

"Pixie, when the sheriff talks to you, it won't be here in your apartment. It will be in his office, and he won't accept excuses," I said coldly. "And you also need to understand that just knowing about the theft makes you a party to it. That means you can also be charged with a crime. The same is true of murder. If you know who killed Alden, or even *think* you know and don't tell, you will be in trouble along with the killer."

Her face, beneath the layers of streaked paint, went pale. "Why don't you tell me everything you know," I said, thinking about the recorder in my pocket.

Failing to successfully stretch the skimpy skirt, she began wringing her hands again. Her eyes filled with tears, and she looked like she was hoping she'd find a way to escape my demand. But when she found no way, she finally met my eyes and said, "I honestly don't know who stole Mr. Gridley's horses. You've got to believe me."

"Let's just assume for a moment that I do choose to believe you. I would then expect you to tell me what Alden told you about the horses," I said, leaning slightly forward, my face grim. "So let's have it."

Pixie took a deep breath, pressed her hands together, and said, "He told me that someone stole a couple of horses from some people he knew and that he was worried about it."

"He did tell you what his relationship was with Glenn and Shanice, didn't he?" I pressed.

She slowly nodded her head. A pink strand of hair fell across her face. She brushed it back and slowly began to speak. "Okay, I admit, he told me that it was his ex-wife and her father whose horses were stolen." After a pause, which I chose to let go on as long as she needed for it to, she continued. "He said he didn't care about the ex-wife, but it was his daughter he cared about. He said that stealing from Shanice was like stealing from his little girl, and that made him angry. I never saw his daughter until today. That was her, wasn't it? She was standing beside Mr. Gridley."

"Yes, that was his daughter," I said.

"She's beautiful," she said softly. "So is her mother." She looked at me again and added, "But you've got to believe me, Mr. Revada. I knew about Shanice, but I didn't know about Pam until just a few days ago." She looked directly at me then without hesitating.

"You can call me Rocky, and I believe you this time," I said.

"You do?" She sounded surprised.

"Yes, now let's get back to the horses, Pixie. Alden was upset. What did he tell you about it? I need some specifics. He knew who took them, didn't he?"

"I think so, but he never told me who it was. He just said he had to fix it," she revealed.

"How did he plan to do that?"

"He said he was going to try to get them back for the Gridleys."

"Did he say how he was going to go about that?" I asked.

"He said he was going to make it happen, that's all," she said. "I told him to let the police handle it, but he wasn't willing to do that. It scared me, but he wouldn't listen to me."

"Tell me about Alden's brother," I said.

"I don't like Chase," she said with sudden fire in her eyes.

"Why?" I asked.

"He's just not a nice man, that's all." I felt like reminding her that Alden hadn't been so great himself, but I refrained. She added, "The whole thing seems kind of strange to me, anyway. They don't look like brothers."

"So you wonder if his claim of being Alden's brother is a lie?" I asked.

She looked at me with surprise in her eyes. She chewed on her lower lip for a moment as she thought about my question. Finally she said, "I sort of do. I've never admitted that to anyone."

"Could Chase have had anything to do with stealing the horses?"

She looked at me through wide eyes. "I never thought of that. I think he'd do things like that."

"Are he and Mace friends?" I asked.

"I guess so. At least, I think that he does his banking at the bank where Mace works."

"Who are some of Alden's other friends?"

"I never met many of his friends," she said. "Just Mace and, well, his brother."

"When was the last time you saw Alden?" I asked.

"The evening before he was found dead," she said. "We had dinner together."

"Where?" I asked.

"Here," she said. "I fixed it. He left right after dinner."

"Did he say where he was going?"

"No. He just said he was going to get the horse matter taken care of. He told me he'd see me the next day. He didn't seem to think he was in any danger," she said as her eyes again filled with tears. "I can't believe someone would do that to him."

I stood up. I'd gotten more than I'd dared hope for from Pixie. I needed to talk to others now. She also stood and followed me to the door. "Rocky," she said, and I turned and looked at her. She could have been a very pretty girl. But a lot of paint needed to be peeled away, rings and other pieces of metal needed to be removed from unconventional places, and a hard life needed to be recalled, something that couldn't be done. I actually felt sorry for her. She smeared more mascara around her eyes with the back of her hand and then said, "Please catch whoever did this to him."

I handed her my card. "Oh, I will," I said. "Believe me, I will. If you think of anything else, please call my cell phone."

She nodded her head, brushed the offending pink strand of hair back, and watched me as I left her apartment. Back in my truck, I kept my commitment to Sheriff Perkins by calling him. I reached him on his cell phone.

I explained what I had learned and then said, "I have her interview recorded. I'll give you a copy."

He thanked me and asked, "Do you believe this woman who calls herself Pixie?" he asked.

"Pretty much," I told him. "She may know more, and I believe that if she does, she'll eventually tell me."

"Who is your top suspect at this point?" he asked.

"For which crime—the murders or the switched horses?" I asked.

"Both," he said.

"I honestly don't know," I admitted. "But I can't get Mace Healy off my mind. That guy's guilty of something. I'm just not sure what."

The sheriff asked me what I was going to do next, and I told him that I was going to the Gridley ranch to speak with the two ranch hands.

"I appreciate you keeping me posted," Sheriff Perkins said. "We're working hard on our end as well."

After completing the call, I drove to the Gridley ranch where I inquired of Rose—the only one at the house—if she had any idea where the two ranch hands were working. She knew they had come to work that morning and pointed out one of their pickups parked near the barn. But she had no idea where they were or what they were doing. "Glenn probably knows, but he won't be home for a while," she said. "We could try his cell phone, but I think he forgot to charge it. He does that a lot."

"Maybe I'll just poke around a bit out on the ranch, if you don't mind. I'd really like to talk to the two of them. They might know something helpful," I said.

"If they do, I think they would have come forward with it," Rose said. "They are good men, both of them."

"At times people know something that they don't realize is helpful until someone like me points it out," I said.

"Oh, I see," she said. "They'll help if they can."

"I hope so. That, I suppose, brings me to another question. I'm trying to track down Vance Winskey to speak to him as well. What is his character, from your perspective?" At my question, I watched her facial expression change. Her brow furrowed, and her eyes narrowed.

"I never did like him."

Even though I wasn't completely surprised by the remark, Rose saying that seemed out of character, and so I followed up with another question. "Wasn't he let go because things were getting tight with the ranch finances?"

Rose shook her head very slowly. "I'm speaking out of turn, I suppose. But Glenn and the girls have done so much for me that I can't just sit by and watch them get hurt." She paused, and I waited patiently to hear what else she had to say. She finally went on. "The answer to your question is yes. Vance was let go because of the tight finances and because he was the one whom Glenn had most recently hired. But truth be told, I think Glenn was glad for an excuse to fire him."

"He hasn't mentioned that to me," I said, wondering why he hadn't.

Rose shrugged her shoulders. "Maybe it's just me," she said. "I shouldn't have said anything. One of the men might be in the barn. You might check there," she said. "If you find one of them, he'll know where the other one is."

Chapter Eighteen

I FOLLOWED HER ADVICE AND found that her guess had been right. I found one ranch hand in the barn, a lanky man of about forty. He was shoeing a horse when I walked into the barn. He let the horse's hind foot down and stood erect, brushing himself off. While surveying me with a friendly face, he wiped the sweat from his forehead with a rag. Then he extended a hand. "Ricky Snyder," he said. "You must be the PI Glenn talked to me about."

"Rocky Revada," I replied, wondering why at his age, he was still a Ricky rather than a Rick. Of course, I was still a Rocky and not a Rock.

"What can I help you with, Detective?" he asked. "I'd sure like to see you get to the bottom of this here situation before someone else gets hurt. I don't suppose I can help much, but I will if I can."

I asked several questions while watching his body language and facial expressions closely. I soon decided that Rose had been right. He didn't know anything that was of any help, and he seemed like a genuinely good guy. I asked him where the other ranch hand was working.

"Shawn's checking cows and calves down on the southwest corner of the ranch," he said. "He'll be there until five or so, I'd guess. Glenn has us keeping a close watch on the stock, counting cows and so on. I guess he's jumpy about losing something else. Not that I blame him."

I didn't blame him either. "Is Shawn in a pickup?" I asked.

"No, he's on a horse," he responded. "His truck is parked around back of the barn."

"Can I get to where he is okay in my pickup?" I asked.

"Not all the way," he said. "Do you ride?"

"Yes, I have horses," I said, wincing inwardly as I thought about my sore ribs and shoulder.

"Let's saddle one for you, and you can ride out unless you want to wait for him to get back," he said.

I didn't expect to learn anything new, but I had to try. So I said, "I guess I'll take a horse, if that's okay." I hoped I wasn't making a mistake.

"Sure thing," he said. "Let's go to the corral out back."

Ten minutes later, I was ready to get on a paint gelding who acted like he had a lot of energy to expend. The weather had turned cooler, and a wind had begun to blow in the past thirty minutes. This kind of weather usually makes horses more energetic than usual. I was looking forward to a good ride, telling myself sternly that my ribs and shoulder had better enjoy it along with the rest of me.

"Is there anything else?" Ricky asked as I prepared to mount the paint gelding.

"Yeah, as a matter of fact there is," I said as I remembered what Rose had told me. "Vance Winskey; what kind of guy is he?"

"He's okay," Ricky said. "Why do you ask?"

"Rose didn't seem to care much for him," I said.

Ricky grinned. "Yeah, I suppose that's true. He was a little rude to her at times. Seemed to me like he was just kidding with her, but she didn't take it that way. He told me she reminded him of an old aunt that he used to tease a lot. She's a good woman, but I wouldn't put much stock in her low opinion of Vance," he concluded.

"Thanks. I better get moving, see if I can find Shawn," I told him, and I mounted the horse, who started prancing and throwing his head the moment I was seated in the saddle. Before I left the barn, Ricky called Shawn on his cell phone to inform him that I wanted to speak to him and set a place to meet him in the next few minutes. While Ricky talked, I sat in the saddle regretting my decision to ride out.

After a few minutes, Ricky put the phone away and stepped over to me. "All set," he said, describing the meeting place. I nodded curtly, determined to see this through. Shawn was expecting me, so there was no turning back now.

"Are you okay?" Ricky asked in concern.

Ricky's concern told me I wasn't doing a very good job hiding my predicament. The gelding had a habit of throwing his head, which jerked the reins in my hands and sent shooting pain up my side. "I'll be fine," I said, grinding my teeth slightly. "I've got a couple of cracked ribs, but I can ride all right."

"You should have said so. I'll give you a ride in the truck if you can give me a few minutes to finish with my shoeing job," he said. "Shawn can ride out of the rough country and meet us."

"No, I'll be fine," I said. "But thanks anyway."

Ricky didn't ask how I'd hurt myself, and I didn't volunteer any information. He followed me around the barn and helped me through the first few gates so I wouldn't have to dismount, and then I let the horse have his head and we loped southeast. The paint had a smooth gait and my ribs, though a nuisance, were not unbearable, wrapped tightly as they were. In fact, my tight, bulletproof vest helped too, even though it added some weight.

The weather took a turn for the worse. The wind picked up, and dark clouds scooted rapidly my way from the western sky. I hadn't expected this. I really didn't want to get wet, and it was looking like it could storm. I hurried my horse along. When I got to the location where I was supposed to meet Shawn, several miles to the southwest of the ranch headquarters, he wasn't there. I rode around the area for a few minutes, thinking that he was probably just late for some reason. But after ten minutes, I called Ricky. I had neglected to get Shawn's number or I'd have called him directly.

Ricky answered almost immediately. "I just talked to Shawn," he said. "He found a dead cow a few minutes ago. The buzzards and coyotes have her messed up pretty good. He's having a little look around. I just gave him your number, so he'll be calling you in a minute. But just in case, let me give you his number."

He did that, and I entered it into my phone. I waited for a minute or two before Shawn finally called. He asked me to keep riding west, if I would. "I'd like you to see this cow," he added. He sounded stressed. My stomach gave an uncomfortable twist. Shawn gave me a couple of landmarks to look for and said he'd be watching for me. He was still a couple of miles from my location, so I urged the paint gelding into a gentle lope.

When I met Shawn, he looked very worried. "I'm Shawn Wheeler," he said when I rode up to where he was kneeling beside a big, black angus cow. "This is the second one I've found in the past little bit. The other one is back that way." He pointed farther west. "Take a look if you will."

"I'll do that. I'm Rocky Revada," I said as I painfully dismounted from my horse.

"Yeah, I know," he said.

I knelt beside him. The cow had been chewed on a lot and was starting to smell bad. "This makes no sense. Two dead cows but no sign of their calves," he said as a large drop of rain hit my hand.

Together, we examined what was left of the cow. Shawn carried a large knife in his saddle bags. With it, we dug and groped in the carcass. I took a turn after couple of minutes and a few hundred drops of cold rain. I found a bullet lodged against the inside of the cow's front right shoulder. I dug it out and showed it to Shawn.

His face was one of anger and shock. "Who's doing this?" he asked through tight lips. "I'll bet there's a bullet in the other one too."

"And maybe some more cows down," I said.

It began raining in earnest then. We were both soaked by the time the squall moved on and the sun broke out. We rode to the second cow and examined it briefly, and even though we didn't take time to dig through the rotting meat looking for a bullet, we both agreed that the cow had probably been shot. We then searched the area for the missing calves. After thirty minutes of searching, I asked him if they'd been branded.

"No," he said. "We do that a little later in the spring."

"Then they've been taken," I concluded with a tired sigh. "I better call the sheriff and Glenn."

"You call the sheriff, I'll call Glenn," he said. "Then I'll stay here while you go meet them," he volunteered. "I might scout around a little more and see if there are any I've missed."

He pulled out his cell phone and opened it up. Then he looked at me with a wry smile. "I guess you'll need to call," he said. "My battery seems to have gone dead. It was fine when I talked to you a little while ago. I'm always forgetting to charge it."

"That seems to be a common theme," I said. "I haven't been able to get a hold of Glenn today for the same reason. Hopefully he is back at the house now or someone knows where he is. I'll try calling them both as I ride back," I said. I swung up on my horse and took a minute to allow the pain to subside in my ribs before heading back to the east.

"I'll most likely be right around here when you get back," Shawn promised. "But for now, I'm going to check back farther that way," he said, pointing northwest. "I hope I don't find any more dead cows."

Shawn rode west, and I rode east. I called Glenn's number first, but after ringing several times, it went to voice mail. Next, I called the sheriff, but his phone also went to voice mail. *No one wants to make themselves available for me today,* I thought wryly. I tried the dispatcher but she told me that the sheriff was in a meeting with the county commissioners and would be for about another thirty minutes. I asked about Detective Blaine Springer. She told me that he was assisting some other officers on a bad accident on I-80 but that she'd have him call me as soon as he was free. I didn't want the news of the cow shooting to be put out on the police radio, so I politely declined to tell her what the problem was, only saying that I needed to meet with one of them as soon as possible.

The sun again disappeared, and once more the wind picked up. I'd gone probably two miles when it again began to rain. I still hadn't reached Glenn, and I thought about trying to call Shanice. But I didn't do that, knowing that she'd probably insist on coming out, and I didn't want her to have to come out in the storm. So I hunkered down on my horse and rode uncomfortably on, anxious to get back to the barn, out of the elements and off the horse.

The howling wind blew the rain hard against me, making it difficult to see. Thunder was pounding my eardrums, and the lightning was almost blinding. Suddenly, I felt a hard, painful thud on my back. I lurched forward and barely succeeded in getting my feet out of the stirrups before tumbling helplessly from the gelding. The impact with the ground added to my pain, and I felt myself going unconscious. The next thing I remembered was waking up, my face looking into a cold downpour and my body crying out in pain.

I tried to sort out what had happened. It took a few minutes for my brain to clear. I tried to move, but it hurt too much, so I just stayed where I was. Gradually, I remembered the hard thud against my back. I could only come to one conclusion—I'd been shot. I hadn't heard a gunfire, but with the thunder at the time, it was not surprising. Right then I thanked the Lord I put on that vest.

I felt my cell phone buzzing in my pocket, but when I tried to reach for it, I found it difficult. I finally got it out, but not before it quit vibrating. I tried to touch the right area of the screen so I could call back whoever had tried to call me. I assumed it was the sheriff or Detective Springer. But my hands were wet and muddy. The expensive cell phone slipped from my grip. I tried to recover it, but movement hurt too much. I finally gave up and lay there, hoping to soon recover enough strength to get up and get moving.

But then a thought occurred to me. If I had been shot, and I was afraid that was the case, I had reason to fear that whoever had done it might still be in the area. In fact, he might decide to make sure I was dead, and when he discovered that I wasn't, he might finish me off. That thought gave me strength, and despite excruciating pain, I forced myself to roll over and get to my knees. Once I'd succeeded in that, I looked around for my cell phone, only to discover that my efforts to get up had submerged it in the mud. I pulled it out and tried again to push the control on the front so I could make I call. As I did, it again began to vibrate. After unzipping my jacket and wiping my muddy hands on my shirt—the only mud-free area of my clothes—I finally succeeded in answering the call. I lifted the phone to my ear, but a wave of dizziness swept over me, and I toppled helplessly, face first, to the muddy ground. The cell phone once more escaped my weak grasp.

I was feeling helpless and vulnerable. I silently prayed for help. Then I lay still. It occurred to me after a few minutes that the rain had stopped and the sun was once more peeking through the clouds above me. I was shivering, but I also felt strength begin to seep back into my limbs.

After a minute or two, I struggled to my knees, but I could get no farther. The world was spinning around me, and I fought to keep from again plunging into the mud. A blurred figure rotated back and forth in front of me. I tried to reach for my pistol, which was tucked into my waistband at the back, but once again a wave of dizziness came over me, and I felt myself toppling to the side. I had no more than collided with the muddy ground once again before I saw the fuzzy figure appear above me.

That figure began to lean down toward me, and with all the

energy I could muster, I twisted away. "Rocky, let me help you! What are you doing?"

I stopped twisting when I recognized the voice. Shanice was on her knees beside me in a second, and she put her arms around me gently. "What happened to you?" she asked.

"I got a bump or two," I said in a shaky voice, even as I wondered how she had ever found me, or even why she might have been looking. "What are you doing here?" I managed to ask.

"I was looking for you," she said. "Ricky told me you'd gone out to meet Shawn. Rocky, you're hurt. I've been trying to call you, but you haven't been answering. I was getting very worried. Did the horse Ricky sent you out on buck you off?"

"No, I think someone shot me, and the force of the bullet against my vest knocked me from the horse," I gasped, trying to breathe normally despite the pain in my ribs. They hadn't appreciated the impact of the bullet nor my fall off the horse. "I'm a bit bruised, but I'll be okay in a little while." I looked up at her. Her face was streaked with mud.

Shanice's eyes were wide in alarm. "You've been shot?" she asked fearfully. "We've got to get you to a hospital."

"Shanice, I just took a hard punch and a fall," I said. "You told me to be careful." I tried to smile. "So I've been wearing my bullet-proof vest." To prove that I was okay, I tried to stand, but the effort was too much at the moment.

"Rocky, you can't even stand up," she said.

I tried again to stand and finally got to my feet—with her help, I admit, but nonetheless, I did it. With her support, I didn't fall again, but I was in a lot of pain. The way Shanice was looking at me, I guessed it showed on my face, despite my best effort to disguise it. "Are you sure something isn't broken?" she asked in concern.

"Other than a couple of ribs, which were already broken, I'm pretty sure I only have bruises. The worst is the one where the bullet hit me."

"Rocky, how did you break your ribs?" she asked as she peered behind me to examine my coat.

"Well, somehow that story doesn't seem very important at the moment," I said with a weak grin. She seemed unimpressed, but I said, "Don't worry. I'll tell you about it sometime. But right now I think that we need to get the sheriff out here. Someone just tried to kill me." As the words escaped my lips, the magnitude of the situation suddenly hit me. Someone had tried to kill me. And I hadn't even seen it coming. This seemed a step above any of the other close calls I'd had over the past few days. I started to shake, even as I tried to control my thoughts and keep myself calm.

I felt her finger fiddling with my coat. "Rocky, there's a hole here!" she exclaimed.

"Bullets do that," I said even as her discovery confirmed what I had already been pretty sure of. After several minutes, I was able to get a grip on myself, and the shaking subsided. I was gaining strength and with that improvement came sanity. I'd been shot, but I was alive. And my attacker could be hanging around somewhere in the trees. I wasn't about to let him get away. "I need my phone. It's here somewhere."

Shanice found it and wiped it off, handing it to me as it began to vibrate. I was grateful that it still worked, despite the mistreatment it had received. The sheriff was calling. I gave him a brief account of where I was and what was going on, and he said he was on his way, with several of his deputies in tow. "Someone has also been shooting cows out here," I said. "One of Glenn's men is waiting for us." At the mention of shot cattle, Shanice's mouth dropped open.

A terrible thought struck me then. Whoever had shot me might have gone after Shawn as well. I quietly shared my thought with the sheriff. Shanice, who was standing next to me listening to my side of the call, gripped my arm tightly. She looked faint when I said to the sheriff, "I hope he's okay."

"Rocky, we need to find Shawn now," Shanice said as she got a grip on her feelings of nervousness and fear. "Your horse has got to be close. He's trained to stay put when a rider gets off."

"Does that include when a rider falls off?" I asked with an attempt at a grin.

"Probably," she said. She was right about the horse, and with her help, I was soon back in the saddle, wet, muddy, cold, and in a great deal of pain, but not admitting it. I'd had a close call, but another person's life was in jeopardy. There was no time for me to be a wimp. She mounted her horse, and we rode west together.

Chapter Nineteen

WE FOUND SHAWN. HE'D FARED much better than I had. He too
had gotten wet and cold, but no bullets had been directed his way.
Like me, he hadn't heard the rifle shot that knocked me off my horse.
Unfortunately, he had located another dead cow whose calf was missing.

Someone had it in for the Gridleys. Or perhaps it was more than
one someone. I stood looking at the latest dead cow. Coyotes, or
cougars, or something had been gnawing on it, but that had been
evident at the first glance. Shanice and Shawn made a couple of
comments about the cow, but I barely heard them. My eyes were
blurry, and my mind had wandered by that point. I was focused on
how badly my body hurt, how numb my brain was, and how I would
love to be in bed in my own house getting some much-needed rest
and recovery. It was all I could do to keep standing. *Please,* I prayed
silently. *Please give me the strength to get through this. These people are
counting on me to keep them safe.*

Even in my stupor, a thought suddenly illuminated my tired
brain. It came so unexpectedly that it made me wince, and I inwardly
thanked God for such a blessing of insight. I might have just found a
reason for what was happening. Now I just needed evidence to back
it up. I felt a rush of strength flood my broken body for a moment,
and my blurry vision cleared. Once again, I saw the rotting carcass in
front of me and felt Shanice and Shawn standing next to me. I looked
up at them. They were both staring at me without speaking.

"Sorry, did I miss something?" I asked.

Shanice gave me a stunned look. "We were asking you questions
and throwing out ideas, and we realized after a few minutes that you

weren't paying attention. You just stood there staring at that bush," she said, pointing to the bush I must have been admiring without realizing it.

I had work to do, evidence to dig up, proof to establish—pain to suppress. I didn't say a word about what had just popped into my rattled brain. It might not even be right, but I was going to treat it as though it were until I learned differently.

"Well, I'm listening now," I said lightly. "Let's see if the bullet I was shot with is lodged in my vest." I pulled my thoughts back to the dead cows. "I'd like to know if the cows were shot with bullets from the same rifle. That will mean finding more slugs from the cows."

Shanice helped me dig the slug from my vest, and I put it in my pocket. We opted to let the unpleasant task of removing bullets from the other rotting cows fall to an officer. I hurt too much to be on my knees digging in a smelly carcass with a knife. I was starting to feel faint again. In fact, I was honestly afraid that the smell wafting around the carcass would render me unconscious. I really was in no condition to contribute much of anything to anyone—most particularly to the efforts of Sheriff Perkins and his men when they arrived. One look from the sheriff, and he seemed to agree.

So, after leaving the few jumbled thoughts I cared to share with the investigators, I excused myself. Shanice, bless her heart, accompanied me back to the ranch headquarters. She kept her horse uncharacteristically close to mine, presumably in case it started to fall off. When we arrived at the barn, I slid one leg over the saddle and eased myself off the horse, my legs almost buckling as the ground rushed up to meet me. It was clear I was in no condition to drive, but I refused to allow anyone else to take me somewhere for medical attention. I just needed a little time. After all, I hold the notion that time is the greatest healer.

Instead, I asked Shanice to drive me to my motel, where I could take a handful of painkillers and try to get some rest. I wanted to get out of this stupor quickly so I could follow up on the thought that had occurred to me in the presence of a dead cow. She refused, insisting that I stay with his family instead. She offered to be my nurse. I decided that was an offer I couldn't turn down. I gratefully accepted her invitation.

A hot shower, an excruciating rib taping, and a painful entrance into a pair of Glenn's slightly-too-small pajamas followed. Then, with the tender aid of Shanice and a cadre of helpful nurse assistants in the form of Cindy, Jena, Tyra, and Rose, I slid between a set of clean sheets in a soft bed and soon fell asleep.

I rested well, but I did awake often. It was hard not to do so whenever I moved significantly in my sleep. I was aware each time of a presence near my bed. I think it was Shanice, but I suppose it could, at times, have been one of her family members.

It was still light outside when I was awakened by something other than pain. When I first opened my eyes, I could see the fading light of dusk creeping around the edges of the window blinds. As I began to focus on my surroundings, I saw someone standing before me wearing a white coat. He had a stethoscope draped around his neck, and it only took a minute for me to realize that somebody had summoned a doctor. I didn't bother to complain, especially when he gave me something that put me out of my misery until early the next morning.

I felt like a human being when Shanice brought me a large plate of bacon, eggs, and hotcakes accompanied by a large glass of orange juice. What was really nice was having her stay to eat a similar breakfast beside my bed. When we'd finished, I said, "I feel wonderful now. All better, thanks to your specialized care," I smiled at her, and she smirked at me. "I need to get to work," I said finally. There was nothing more to it than that.

I tossed the sheet and covers out of the way and tried to slide my legs over the side of the bed, but a sharp pain shot up my side as I moved, making me pause. Shanice cocked an eyebrow. "Really. All better?" she said, mock disbelief in her voice. She handed me the orange juice abruptly, and I had to lean back into the bed to keep it from spilling all over me. "Honestly, Rocky, you're in no condition to move around just yet—especially considering the stunts you've been pulling the past few days. You have three broken ribs, for crying out loud. You can stay put for at least another day." I looked at her and let out a pitiful moan, trying hard to keep my mouth in a firm, neutral line. But I could feel a grin tugging at my lips.

She smacked me lightly on the shoulder, and said, "Oh, stop it, you baby. Another day in bed can't kill you!"

"You have no idea how much I have to do right now," I whined, taking a swig of the orange juice and handing it over to her waiting hand. "Honestly, I can manage. All I need is something to wear besides your dad's PJs."

"Well, it just so happens that someone washed your muddy clothes, but that same someone thinks you should stay in bed," Shanice said. Then she flashed me a smile that simply melted my heart.

It did not, however, melt my determination to get back on the job. She tried another tack. "There is a hole in your jacket and your shirt where the bullet went through," she said. "Someone will need to get you a shirt and a coat. You can at least stay in bed while I do that for you."

"I need to go now. I'll change later," I said firmly. "There is someone out there who has already killed twice, and but for the hand of God and a bulletproof vest, I would have been the third."

We bantered back and forth for a short while longer before I prevailed. I dressed and picked up my vest. When I left the bedroom and hobbled into the living room a few minutes later, Glenn Gridley greeted me. "Sorry about the injuries," he said.

"Don't worry about it," I said as nonchalantly as I could. Even though I was still hurting, I wasn't in so much pain that I couldn't go about my work. "I chose this profession. Occasionally things like this happen."

"Not on my dime," Glenn said gruffly. "At least not again," he amended. "I think you should forget the whole thing. The sheriff can take it from here."

I shook my head as I asked, "Are you firing me?"

"I wouldn't put it that way," he said. "I just don't want you getting killed. Those two horses and the cattle aren't worth your life—or anyone else's for that matter."

"There is more at work here than just horse theft," I said firmly. "And I believe I am close to figuring it all out. I'd prefer to continue until the matter is closed."

"In case you haven't noticed, my eldest daughter has taken a shine to you, Rocky. And I don't disapprove, but I don't want her hurt. If something happens to you—which I also want to avoid—she *will* be hurt. So I think it's best if we just conclude our arrangement now."

I was taken aback by his remark. Of all the obstacles in the case, I had expected this one the least, particularly now that I was so close to a solution. "I'm not the only one who is in danger," I argued. "You and your family are as well. And I've grown fond of all of you, and I want to keep you guys safe. I think I can wrap this thing up pretty soon and put the danger behind us. I have some ideas about who is behind all this."

"Then tell the sheriff and go home and get some more rest," Glenn said stiffly. "I can't have it on my conscience that anything else happens to you while you're working for me."

"Fine, I consider myself fired," I said, my temper flaring. "But I'm not someone who doesn't see things to their conclusion. Anyway, this case has become personal. No one tries to kill me and gets away with it. I'll finish up on my own time and my own dollar. I'll send you a bill for what I've done. It's been good working for you." With that I headed for the door, walking past him without another word.

"Rocky," he called out from behind me as I reached for the door handle. "Hold on a minute."

I stopped and faced him, not wanting to argue further. I supposed that my face must have shown my feelings. "Maybe we could work out something," he said.

"Thanks Glenn, but no. I know how you feel. That won't change, and I respect you for that. I do have one favor to ask, though. I'd like to keep my surveillance equipment operating on your house and barn until the matter is concluded and someone is behind bars," I said.

"Rocky, you are as stubborn as I am," he said roughly but with a catch in his voice. "I want you to keep working for me since you are—"

"You're off the hook," I interrupted sharply. Glenn's eyes widened.

"Then I'll hire you back," he said, the volume of his voice rising.

"No, I'm on my own now," I said firmly. "But I will leave my equipment here. I would appreciate it if you would let people know that I am no longer working for you. It might actually make it a little easier and safer for me." I wasn't sure if that was true, but it sounded logical.

"Rocky," Glenn said angrily. "I'm sorry I was so abrupt. I've changed my mind."

If I hadn't been so upset, I'd have relished in Glenn's apology—it was a rare occurrence. But as it was, I reached for the door handle again and opened it. "I haven't," I said, and I stepped through and shut the door behind me.

He opened it again and followed me out, shouting my name as I got in my truck and drove off. I ignored him, hoping I wouldn't come to regret it. I wondered, as I headed down his lane toward the county road, where Shanice had gone. It couldn't have taken me more than ten minutes to dress. She probably knew what he was going to do, and she must have approved. For a moment, that made me angry, but then I calmed myself down. Thinking about it, I could understand why she would want me off the case, but I feared that anything that might have developed between us would never be. That thought brought a sinking feeling deep in the pit of my stomach.

Chapter Twenty

I PARKED IN FRONT OF Pam's house a short while after leaving the Gridley ranch. I had a couple of questions for her that needed answers before I pursued my idea further. I hoped she'd be home. She was, and she invited me in warmly, hugged me briefly—and lightly when she saw my haggard face—and then asked the familiar question, "What can I do to help you today?"

"I just need to ask you a couple of questions," I said as I looked at her. She still appeared to be tired and red-eyed. She had a long, rough road ahead of her. "I won't take long. By the way, where is your mom?"

She said, "Please sit down, Rocky," waving me to a chair. "She's upstairs, but she'll be headed back to California soon."

"I'm sure it's been comforting to have her here."

"Yes," she said, sniffing softly. "This whole week has been simply awful, but I've been so lucky that Mom was already here when my world collapsed."

"Certainly," I said in response. "Where is Alden Junior? Will you be all right with him?"

She smiled. "Alden's napping now, so your visit was actually perfect timing. And yes, I think I'll manage just fine. I've gotten pretty used to being alone these past few months."

"What about living expenses and things?" I asked. Then I said quickly, "I don't mean to pry. I just want to be sure you'll be taken care of."

"Thank you, Rocky. That means so much to me. You've already become a dear friend—one of the few I can trust these days," she replied. "We had some good life insurance for Alden, so we can make do on that for a while until I can find a job. Alden will be going to preschool this fall anyway, so even if I can find something part-time, that should be good enough for a while." I was impressed by her faith and confidence in her ability to make the best of the situation.

The room grew quiet again, so I asked awkwardly, "So are you hanging in there?"

She didn't appear to hear my question. She asked instead, her eyes round, "What happened to your coat?"

Since I'd left the Gridley ranch, I hadn't given another thought to the state of my clothing. "It's nothing much," I said as I took the seat she'd indicated. "I need to get a new one."

"Rocky, are you all right?" she asked with concern in her eyes. "I don't mean to be rude, but you don't look very good."

I smiled at her before giving her a much condensed version of what had befallen me: "I involuntarily parted ways with a horse," I said. "I'm fine—just a little bruised up."

Pam didn't look convinced, but she let it drop and asked a question that was clearly painful to her. "So did you meet Alden's . . . uh . . . friend?"

"I did," I answered. "Her name is Pixie Jansen. I know this won't help much, but she was unaware that you existed until a few days ago. Alden told her he was not married."

Pam slowly nodded her head as she looked at her hands, which she was now holding folded on her lap. "He apparently liked to do that," she said softly.

Before Pam could ask about my conversation with Pixie, I asked her the questions I'd come there to ask. Her answers helped confirm the conclusion I'd reached so suddenly in the Gridley fields. I talked with her a little longer about things that really had nothing to do with theft or murder. She kept wringing her hands and fiddling with her hair. She seemed to have something on her mind because several times she started to speak, then didn't. Finally, I asked, "Pam, is there something you want to talk about?"

She teased a strand of hair for a moment. She looked down at the floor then she looked back up at me. "It's nothing," she said. "I just don't know what to do about Mace."

"What about Mace?" I asked. "He seemed pretty thick with Pixie at the funeral. I've decided that he must not have a family, or at least that he doesn't have one anymore. Why are you concerned about him? Has he called you or something?"

"He came over last evening," she said. "He just sort of hung around for a little while. Finally, he asked me if I'd like to go to dinner with him."

"Really," I said, caught off guard by her comment. I wondered if he'd taken a liking to Pam or if this was something more sinister. "What did you tell him?" I asked.

"Rocky, he creeps me out. It caught me by surprise. I don't really even know the guy. I know he was protective of me the first time you came, but I still don't know why. It didn't make any sense then, and it doesn't now." She paused, let go of her hair, and shifted in her chair. "I told him it was way too soon to go out with anyone. He pressed the matter, and I told him that I needed time to think about things and that I was having a hard time."

She didn't say anything else for a moment, and finally I asked, "I take it he didn't accept that answer either."

"He called me this morning," she said in response. "He said he was going to make reservations somewhere for dinner tonight. I told him that I wasn't really up to it, that I had barely buried my husband. It was like he didn't hear me. He said he'd call me later and let me know when he'd pick me up. Rocky, I don't like to be rude, but I don't want to go anywhere with him."

"Then don't," I said.

"But what do I tell him?"

"Maybe you can just say that you need to be with your son, that you don't have anyone to take care of him," I suggested.

"I thought about that, but he knows my mother is still here," she said. "She came into the room while I was talking to him. She said hello to him and then left the room. He said, 'Your mother will watch Alden while we go.' After Mace finally left, I asked Mom what I should do, and she didn't have any ideas other than just telling him no. That's what I thought I had already done. It didn't work. Rocky, I can't go with him anywhere. I just can't."

She was teasing that lock of hair into submission again. I came to its rescue by saying, "If I asked you to go to dinner with me, would you do it?"

She looked surprised, but she let go of the offending strand of hair. "Of course I would." She smiled a wan smile. "You aren't at all like Mace."

"You'd go even though it's been such a short time since Alden's death?" I asked.

Pam smiled shyly. "Do you mean like tonight?" she asked shrewdly.

"That's exactly what I mean."

"Are you asking me?"

I worried about what Shanice would think if she found out, but this was business. I could explain to Shanice later if I needed to. "Yes," I said firmly. "I am asking."

"Then I will," she said. "Thank you, Rocky."

"I'll pick you up at six," I said, wondering what an angry Mace would do, and not wanting to think about it. "And when Mace calls, you can just tell him that I insisted that you go with me." I was living dangerously. But what else was new. That seemed to be the way of my life the past few days.

A minute later I excused myself. She saw me to the door, and before shutting it, she said, "Thanks for all you're doing for me, Rocky, especially tonight." She blushed. "This thing has been really hard, but you've helped make it bearable. Thank you. I'll see you tonight."

"I'll be here," I promised. "But you probably won't get as good a meal as if you'd gone with Mace."

She gave me a weak smile. "Take care of yourself. I know you're not telling me the whole story about why you have so much pain in your eyes," she said, as she touched my arm briefly. She was a sweet woman. She didn't deserve what she'd gotten any more than Shanice did.

"Honest, all I have are some bruises and a couple of cracked ribs," I said. "But I will be careful." My phone began to vibrate. When I saw that the call was from Detective Blaine Springer, I said, "It looks like I've got to go. I'll see you later."

She was still watching me from the door when I answered the call. "Hello Detective," I said.

"How are you feeling?" he asked. His voice still held a slight cynical lilt, but I was surprised that he was capable of such a direct and almost concerned question.

"A lot better," I told him honestly. "A little rest and some pain pills helped a lot. I'll be fine." I hoped that was a true statement.

"Good. Glad to hear it," he said, sounding reasonably sincere. *What is going on,* I thought. "I just wanted to tell you about the ballistics tests on the bullet you took from your vest, the ones fired at you and the Sheriff, and the ones recovered from the dead cows. They were all fired from the same rifle." I was deep in thought, trying to figure out why Blaine would suddenly act so kind toward me, and I almost missed his information.

I replayed what he'd just said in my head to be sure I had it right. I wasn't surprised. "Now all we need to do is find that rifle and the person who's been using it," I said. "Was the lab able to determine the caliber?"

"It was a .30-06," he said. "You are lucky you had a good vest."

It wasn't luck. I'd chosen my vest carefully, but I didn't tell Blaine that. Might as well keep the civil feelings between us as long as possible, I thought. "I sure was," I said. He also told me something very annoying about Chase.

I was back in my truck by then. Pam was still standing in her doorway watching me. She was a strong woman. She'd get through all this. "I waved at her. She lifted her hand in return, and a sliver of a smile lit her face. She was still standing there when I drove away.

Blaine didn't have anything else to tell me, so our conversation was over quickly. I waited until I was out of Pam's sight before I pulled over to the side of the street and consulted my notebook. The next person I needed to speak to was Vance Winskey, Glenn's former ranch hand. The only address I had for him was his mother's home in Honeyville. According to the Gridleys, he was divorced and living with his mother. At least he had been when he'd worked for them. I put the address in my OnStar navigation system and started out again.

I knew that Vance was a man of medium height and about twenty-seven years old. I didn't really expect to find him at home, and I was not wrong, unfortunately. His mother had a small house, but it had a nice, big yard with two or three large buildings in the back. The front yard was neat and attractive. That's where Mrs. Winskey was working when I stopped out front and entered the yard through a gate. She was on her knees weeding a flower bed. A small woman who looked about sixty, she stood up as I approached her. I introduced myself, showing my ID, and she said, "I heard about the Overton fellow being killed. It's too bad."

"It is," I agreed. I wasn't certain how she'd heard about Alden, but I figured Vance must have heard it through the grapevine and informed her. She didn't mention if she'd heard about the death of Conrad Patel, and I didn't ask. "I'm trying to help the sheriff figure out who killed him. He asked me to talk to Vance. Is he around?"

"No," she said as she wiped her hands on her apron. "In fact, he left several days ago for Nevada." *Several days ago, huh?* I thought. *That's interesting.*

"Nevada, you say? Is he on vacation, or was this a permanent move?"

"Permanent, I guess you could say. He got a job on a ranch over there somewhere. He really needs the work."

"It's too bad that Glenn Gridley had to let him go," I said. "I guess you've talked to Vance on the phone since he left?" Mrs. Winskey didn't respond, so I continued. "If you wouldn't mind giving me his number, maybe I could just call him."

"Actually, I haven't got it on me," she said. "It's in the house. Would you like to come in? I'll get it for you."

I liked and she did. After I'd written it down, I asked, "What day did Vance leave for his new job?"

She named a date that preceded the theft of the horses by over a week. "I guess he's doing okay. If he wasn't he'd call," she said.

"I'm sure he would," I said, not being sure of anything. "Well, thanks for giving me his number. I'll try to reach him."

"I'm sure you can," Mrs. Winskey said. "But I'm also sure he can't help you. He hasn't had anything to do with the Gridleys since they laid him off."

"It was a difficult situation to be sure," I said. "Glenn Gridley's place is not doing too well. He hated to have to let your son go. But he said he had to cut back on his expenses."

"Vance thinks Mr. Gridley was wasting money on his horses, money that he needed to run the ranch," Mrs. Winskey revealed. "But he also said that being fired was probably lucky for him—that he'd make more money on the ranch in Nevada."

"I hope he does," I said, and I let myself out of the house.

I was troubled. Why hadn't someone told me earlier that Vance had left the area? I shook my head, got in my truck, and pulled into the street. I was determined to get to the bottom of this thing.

I thought about Pam and our date tonight. I knew that Mace was up to something; I doubted he would try so hard to get her to go out with him if he didn't have some sinister plan up his sleeve. He wouldn't take kindly to my interference. I decided that I would make it easier on Pam: I'd pay Mace a visit as soon as I could get back to the motel and change out of my bullet-riddled jacket and shirt. It was chilly out, and I didn't want to take time to go to Logan and get one from my house.

I stopped for lunch, since the breakfast Shanice had prepared that morning had pretty well worn itself out. I thought about her. I had hoped for, even expected, a call from her, but none had come.

At one sharp, I parked in the parking lot of Mace's bank and went in. I found him in his office. He clearly didn't want to see me. "I have work to do," he grumbled. "If you want to talk to me, come by the house tonight. I'll give you the address." He grabbed a pen and notepad from his desk and started scribbling.

"I can't do that," I said. Mace stopped his scribbling abruptly and looked up. "I'll be with Pam Overton. I'm taking her to dinner tonight."

If looks could kill, Mace's look would have finished the job that the .30-06 failed to do. I decided then and there that it would be most unwise to meet him at his home without backup of some sort. I did my best to return a look something like the one he'd given me. "Do you have a problem with that?" I asked.

"She's going out with me," he said.

"No she isn't," I said. "Anyway, I'm not here to talk about Pam. I have some questions for you."

"I have nothing to discuss with you," he said rudely.

"What kind of cigarettes do you smoke?" I asked.

"What kind of question is that?" His face was so dark with rage that I got the sudden desire to edge toward the door. *Don't be a coward,* I told myself and kept my feet firmly planted.

"It's a simple question. If you can answer that one, then I'll try some more difficult ones."

"Marlboros," he spat. And with that he stood up. "The more difficult questions will just have to go unanswered. I have nothing to discuss with you."

I had learned what I hoped to learn. I hadn't honestly expected him to tell me anything else. I was going to have to dig elsewhere to find the dirt that I knew regularly soiled Mace's laundry. "Good day, then," I said.

"Stay away from Pam Overton," he said. "She's too good for you." I almost laughed.

"That's funny," I countered. "I was about to say the same thing to you. Except that in *my* case it would have been true."

"Just you wait, Revada. You can't keep Pam away from me for good. One of these days I'll have what I want from her."

His comment ignited a fire in me so strong, I could almost feel it smoldering as it bubbled and boiled in my chest. My ears were ringing as I leaned over Mace's desk and stared into his small black eyes. "You don't know who you're tangling with," I said, barely able to control my anger. I had no use for this weasel of a man. "Don't ever try to call her again. So help me, if you do, I'll make your life miserable."

His black little eyes glowered. Sweat broke out on his face. I straightened up, stepped back, glared at him a moment longer, then turned and left his office. If he wasn't my enemy when I'd walked in, I had made him one now. *How stupid was I?* But I hadn't gone but a few steps before I turned and reentered his office. He had his phone to his ear. He slammed it down when he saw me. "That better not have been Pam Overton you were calling," I said, glowering at him again.

"And what if it was?"

"Was it?" I asked.

"No, and it's none of your business who I was calling. It was bank business. I have work to do. Get out of here," he ordered.

But I had come back for a reason. I again leaned over his desk, extending myself so far that I hovered directly over him. He had to tip his head back to look up at me. There was one thing I really wanted to learn from him. Not knowing if this would work or not, I said, "There is one more thing I meant to tell you. The next time Vance Winskey comes in, you tell him that you are closing his account. Have you got that? Close his account."

"I'm not doing that," he said in a less than forceful voice. "Who do you think you are, telling me to close a customer's account?"

"Just do it," I said. Then I left his office. In less than a minute, I had learned what would have taken me a lot of time in more conventional ways. Vance Winskey banked with Mace. It might not be helpful; but again, it had been on my list of things to ask Vance. Now it was off my list.

I called Pam as soon as I was back in the truck. I told her that I had just warned Mace off but to let me know if he called her again. She promised she would, thanked me three or four times, and said, "I will be looking forward to seeing you tonight." She was silent for a moment before going on. "Rocky, if you visited Mace, I doubt he will call me now. You don't have to take me to dinner."

"But I want to, just to make sure you're safe," I said. "Unless you don't want to go with me . . ." I let the question dangle. I didn't want to force Pam into anything she didn't want to do.

"I'll be ready at six," she said.

Throughout the day, I tried to call Vance Winskey several times, but each time his phone went to voice mail. It frustrated me. I really wanted to talk to him, especially since I had established a connection between him and my non-friend, Mace Healy.

I made several more visits that afternoon, including one to Hal Rodgers, the Gridley's accountant. He was nervous but seemed friendly enough and acted embarrassed about the trouble his now dead bookkeeper, Conrad Patel, had caused. He told me that Cindy Gridley was catching on fast and that he was quite sure she would do a good job with the books.

He blushed when I said, "And she's a lot nicer to work with than Conrad was."

The more I saw Hal, the clearer it became to me that he was in the dark about the things I was investigating. His behavior was too consistent, and he seemed to voice genuine respect for the Gridleys. It was difficult to picture him intentionally trying to do damage to them, but I was not about to write him off as a suspect. Hal had the Gridleys' trust and access to their livelihood in his hands, so he could be doing some serious damage if he were involved in any of the crimes.

I was in a lot of pain again, and so I went back to Tremonton and entered my motel room. I checked the monitor and made sure that everything was working properly with my surveillance cameras. After that was done, I took one of my prescription pills and collapsed on my bed fully clothed. I was out before I'd had a dozen coherent thoughts.

Chapter Twenty-One

I WAS SLEEPING SOUNDLY WHEN my cell phone began to ring. I had set the volume high just in case, knowing that I might be hard to awaken. I grabbed it too fast, causing a stab of pain in my ribs. I gasped for breath as I looked to see who was calling me. It was Shanice. I wasn't sure what to do. I entertained the thought of simply ignoring it and trying to go back to sleep.

I didn't entertain that thought for long. "Hi, Shanice," I said, trying to sound cheerful.

"Where are you?" she asked. "I've been worried about you. I thought you'd call."

"I'm in my motel room," I said.

"So you aren't working?" she asked.

"Not at the moment, but I have been most of the day. I'm just not feeling good, so I took a break," I explained.

"I thought as much. Rocky, you really hurt my dad's feelings," she said abruptly.

"I'm sorry. That was not my intention. He fired me, and when he tried to hire me back, I decided that I would be better working for myself right now. So that's what I'm doing."

"But why would you keep working the case if you aren't getting paid?" she asked.

"It's like I told your father: this is personal now. Somebody is trying to kill me. I intend to catch him," I said, praying that I could actually do that.

"Please, come back to work for us," she said.

"Shanice, answer one question for me," I said. "Did you and your dad talk about firing me?"

It was quiet on the phone for a long moment. Finally, she said, "Yes. We talked about it, but it was only because we both care about you, Rocky. We never had any idea that things would become so dangerous. We thought you would jump at the chance to just forget it and go home, to let the sheriff and his people handle it. But since you aren't, we want you back."

"Thanks, Shanice, but that's not going to happen. But I promise you, I will do my best on this thing."

"Rocky, can we meet and talk about this? Come out for dinner tonight. We'd all like to have you come."

"I can't," I said. "I have other plans."

"You're working?" she asked.

"Sort of, but not exactly," I said.

"You are stubborn," she said, and I could feel my cheek heat up against my phone. "Why can't you be reasonable? Please, come out tonight and we'll work this all out."

"Shanice, I have plans for tonight. Anyway, my mind is set."

"What kind of plans?" she asked, her anger increasing.

"Look, Shanice, I'm just trying to solve this thing. There are a bunch of people out there that I don't trust. One of them is harassing Pam. I'm trying to help her out," I said.

"So you will be with Pam tonight?" she asked, her voice hesitant.

"Well, yes, I'm taking her to dinner tonight, but as a favor," I admitted as my stomach tied up in knots. "I had to give her an excuse to keep Mace Healy off her back."

"What's Mace got to do with it?" she asked, tension back in her voice. "Oh, it doesn't matter. If you want to take Pam out that's your business. I gotta go now."

I tried to explain about Mace, but before I could get two words out, I heard the click of the phone as she hung up on me. I felt terrible. *That call didn't go well at all.* The last thing I wanted was for Shanice to be angry with me. And yet I honestly felt that all the Gridleys and I would be safer if it became known that I no longer worked for them. I hoped at some point that Shanice would see it that way. I groaned as I once again repositioned myself gingerly on the bed to see if I could get some more rest, but it was hopeless. I'd never be able to go back to sleep. I looked at my watch. It was almost four. I had time to go to Logan, check my house and office, and then go pick up Pam. I stepped into the shower and let the hot water run over me, soothing some of the pain.

Everything seemed fine at my house and office, which is as I'd expected since the cameras had shown no trespassing for some time. I picked up some fresh clothes at the house and a couple of items from my office. Then I drove down the canyon. I picked Pam up at her house a few minutes early. I left my vest and gun in the car, of course.

There was still grief in her eyes, but she had gone out of her way to spruce herself up for our dinner. Her mother smiled brightly at me as I helped Pam into her coat—Denise had high expectations, it seemed. That was not what I wanted, but there was nothing I could do about it.

I took Pam to a nice restaurant in Ogden. We ate a leisurely meal. As we ate, we talked. Pam told me a lot about herself, and I listened. She also asked questions, and I answered most of them. When she broached the subject of my broken ribs and numerous bruises, I hesitated. But when she pressed me, I admitted that I'd been shot, that the bullet had not penetrated my vest but that the force had knocked me off the horse and left me with some troublesome pain.

Her face went pale. She reached across the table, took my hand, and squeezed in a comforting way. "I'm so sorry, Rocky," she said. "I don't know how, but I'm sure that Alden somehow put all this evil in motion. When will it stop?"

"When we catch everyone involved and put them behind bars," I said. "And that's what I'm trying to do. So are the police."

"But it is so dangerous for you. You should let the police handle it now." *Not you too,* I thought. Her eyes were boring into mine, full of concern and fear. She wiped her mouth with her napkin.

I smiled at her, and she pulled her hand back. "The Gridleys said pretty much the same thing," I told her. "But I am in too deep now. I will see it to the end."

"But you *are* working for the Gridleys, aren't you?" she asked.

"I was. But I'm not anymore. I'm working for me now."

"Can I help?" she asked.

"Pam, Pam," I said gently. "You have suffered far too much already. And you have a son who needs you. Let me handle it."

She dropped her eyes to her plate, and we ate in silence for a few minutes. She took a sip of her water and then she looked at me. She wrinkled her brow thoughtfully, and a frown developed on her face. Then she chewed for a moment on her lower lip, ignoring her dinner. "Pam, what are you thinking about?" I asked after watching her for a moment.

She once again reached across the table, and I let her take my hand. She seemed to gain strength from me, and I didn't mind that. "I can help," she said. "And I want to."

That worried me a great deal. "Pam. No. I don't want you to be in danger. You've suffered too much already. Please, let me—"

She interrupted by squeezing my hand hard. "Help me think this through, Rocky. Why does Mace want to go out with me? He must know that I would never become romantically interested in him. So why is he being so persistent?"

She looked to me for my thoughts, so I shared one with her. "Perhaps he thinks you know something that could be dangerous to him, something Alden might have told you."

Her face brightened. "That's it, Rocky. He thinks I know something." Then her face fell. "But I don't think I know anything. It's like I explained to you earlier. Things were rough in my marriage toward the end. I spent very little time with Alden, and we didn't share much of anything. The romance was gone and so was the communication. We hardly talked at all."

"Mace probably doesn't know that," I pointed out.

"He knows the romance was gone. You saw him at the funeral. He was with that . . . that girl!" she said hotly. "He knows her, and he knew that Alden was seeing her. He must have."

"That's probably true," I agreed, watching her closely. She again chewed on her lower lip. Then suddenly she said, "Rocky, I want to talk to her, to . . . What did you say her name is?"

"Pixie," I said. "But why would you want to talk to her?"

"Maybe Alden told her something. And maybe she will tell me," she said. "After all, we're no longer rivals, with Alden dead."

"Pam, I talked to her. We need to leave it at that."

She was thoughtful for a little bit, absently eating. I took a few bites myself. Finally, she again put her fork down and caught my eye. "If I went to dinner with Mace, maybe when he tries to get me to tell him something that he thinks Alden told me, then I can make him think Alden actually *did* tell me something. If I'm successful, maybe I can give you the information you need to figure this whole thing out."

I had to admit that it was a good idea, but I wasn't overly enthused about putting her in that position with a man like Mace, a man I considered to be extremely dangerous. I expressed my reservations to her while acknowledging that she was thinking along the right lines.

"Hey, how about this idea, Rocky? Alden's death also hurt Pixie. You know that. If I could talk to her, maybe she would be willing to help." I was impressed that the Pam not only forgave Pixie for being with Alden but seemed unfazed at the idea of working with her.

"Are you thinking that he might try to press her like he is you?" I asked.

"That's exactly what I'm thinking. Will you help me get together with her?" Her face was almost glowing. I didn't have the heart to dampen her enthusiasm. I said, "How about the three of us meet together. Maybe I could get her to come with me, maybe to your house, for starters? And if we decide to let you, or maybe both of you, do something about Mace—if Pixie is willing—then I will provide security."

"How would you do that?" she asked. "Mace can't know that you are involved."

I smiled at her. "Pam, my dear," I said. "I do surveillance a lot in my job. I know what to do, and I can do it very discreetly."

She smiled, a nice thing to see. "Let's do it then," she said. "I can't wait. I want to help put that awful Mace away."

When we had finished our meal and were walking back to the truck, I said, "After I take you home, I'll see if I can locate Pixie and try to set something up for tomorrow. Is there a time that will work best for you?"

"Any time will be okay," she said. "But I don't want to go home yet. I'll stay in the truck if you'll let me go with you."

I looked over at her. I had to admit I enjoyed her company. We had reached my truck, and I turned to face her. The look she gave me melted my heart. "Sure, you can be my partner for a little while," I said.

She threw her arms around my neck and hugged me tenderly. "Thank you, Rocky," she said. I must have tensed slightly because she stepped back, and her face went red. "I'm sorry. I won't do that again."

It would be best if she didn't; I couldn't argue with that. Pam was a wonderful woman, and I'd be lucky to have her, but I knew who my heart truly belonged to. I felt suddenly guilty as my mind flashed to Shanice and our conversation earlier that afternoon. I didn't want to ruin any chance I had to be with her. I made a promise to myself that after the case was solved, I'd keep a reasonable distance from Pam. There was no question she had become a good friend, but it wasn't worth any doubt our friendship might leave in Shanice's mind.

Without another word, I opened the truck door for Pam and gave her my hand while she climbed in.

"We'll start at Pixie's apartment," I said. "Hopefully, we'll find her there."

When we arrived, I asked Pam to excuse my reach as I retrieved my gun from the jockey box. While Pam waited in the truck around the corner and across the street from Pixie's apartment, I walked to Pixie's building and knocked on her door. Moonbeam answered.

"She is with that Mace Healy guy tonight," she said after I'd asked for Pixie. "He took her to dinner."

"He doesn't seem like her type," I said quietly.

"She doesn't really like him, but he has been nice to her and she felt like she should go out with him," she said, wrinkling her nose in distaste. "Better her than me."

"Sorry I missed her," I said.

"Can I tell her what you want?" Moonbeam asked. "I'm not going anywhere tonight, so I'll be here when she gets home. If it's not too late, I could have her call you if she wants to."

"No, that's okay. I'll check with her later," I said.

Pam was squirming with nervousness when I got back. "Was she there?" she asked anxiously when I got in the truck with her.

"No, and you won't believe where she is," I said, unable to keep disgust from my voice. "But her roommate was there."

She looked at me across the truck, her face lit by the interior light. "I don't like the sound of that. Let me guess," she said. "She's out to dinner with Mace."

"You are right," I said. "You'd make a good detective."

She looked at me very soberly. "I was right earlier, wasn't I? He's pumping both of us for information."

"That could be," I agreed.

"So what now?" she asked.

"Surveillance," I said. "I want to be near when Mace brings her home. If he brings her home."

Pam shuddered. "You don't think he would do something to her, do you?"

"I don't know, Pam. Somebody is killing people. Somebody tried to kill *me*. I Just wish I knew where they were so we could follow them. It's like I said earlier. I wouldn't even think of letting you go with him without me being near."

"Thanks, Rocky. Maybe we should try to find them."

"I wouldn't know where to begin," I replied as I started the truck. "If you like, I'll take you home now. This could take a while."

"No, I want to stay with you," she said. "I'll call Mom and tell her that we are doing something together."

"And if she asks what exactly we are doing, what will you say?" I asked.

"That we are . . . that I'm helping you?" she said hesitantly as I pulled onto the street. "Are you looking for a better spot to watch Pixie's apartment?"

"That's right . . . if you're sure you don't want to go home now."

"We can't leave even if I did want to go," she said shrewdly. "You might miss her."

I found a suitable spot and sat back to wait. Pam made her call to her mother and then lapsed into silence. We spoke very little over the next hour. I couldn't help but wonder what she was thinking. And I kept hoping that Mace would return the woman soon. I was honestly worried about Mace losing his temper and doing something terrible to Pixie.

The silence in the truck was thick. I kept glancing over at Pam in the near darkness of the truck's interior. I was getting sleepy, and I was in pain. I needed another pain pill, but I was afraid it would make me even drowsier than I already was, so I didn't take one. Across the cab I heard Pam sniffling. "Are you all right?" I asked.

Her head turned in my direction, and she wiped her eyes and then her nose with a Kleenex she had pulled from her purse. "Not really," she said with a sob. "Rocky, I don't know what I'm going to do. I know that this sounds crazy, but I miss Alden."

"He was your husband," I said. "That's only natural."

"But he was not a good husband," she said.

"At the end, maybe. He was probably okay at first," I guessed.

"Better than okay," she said. "I guess that's the Alden that I miss." She sobbed again for a moment. "I'm sorry. I was trying to be strong."

"You were trying to pretend that you didn't care," I said. "We both knew better. Go ahead and cry, Pam. You need to grieve."

She took me at my word. She sobbed, and I watched Pixie's apartment. I let out a silent sigh of relief when I saw Mace's silver Lexus pull up in front of the apartment building. I didn't mention it to Pam until Pixie was inside her apartment and Mace and his Lexus were gone. I looked at my watch. It was almost nine.

"Pam, I'll be right back," I said. "Pixie is home."

Pam looked over at me and said, "I'm sorry. I'm falling apart."

"It's okay. I'll be just a minute. You hang in there, and I'll get you home shortly."

"Thanks," she said in an uncharacteristically meek voice.

Moonbeam answered the door. "Oh, it's you," she said. "Come on in. Pixie's back."

I didn't mention that I already knew. Instead I said, "I'm glad. I'll only need a minute or two of her time."

I was relieved to see that Pixie was dressed more modestly than the last time I'd been here. "Hi, Pixie," I said. "I have a favor to ask."

"What's that?" she asked.

"Is Mace a good friend of yours?"

"No! I don't like him. And I don't trust him," she said with a scowl.

"But you went out with him anyway?"

"Not that I wanted to. He creeps me out."

"Pixie, listen carefully to me," I said. "Mace Healy may be a dangerous man. I need help in making sure he doesn't do some very bad things. Can you tell me what kind of things you two talked about tonight?"

She cocked her head to one side and touched her finger to her cheek. After a moment, she said, "From what he was asking me tonight, I'd guess that he thinks I know something about those horses that were stolen from the Gridley ranch."

I was not surprised at this, particularly since she did know something. "Can you be specific about what he asked you?"

Again she thought it over for a minute. Then she said, "He talked about Alden wishing he could afford some expensive horses. He then said to me something like, 'He probably told you that?' Alden did talk about horses sometimes, and like I told you before, he was trying to get the Gridley horses back for them."

"Did you tell Mace that?" I asked.

"I only told him that Alden talked about horses. I didn't dare tell him the rest. He seems really hung up on Alden and the horses," she said, wrinkling her nose in disgust. "I wonder if he knows where they are or at least who took them, if it wasn't him."

"That's what I was wondering," I said. "This brings me to the favor I have to ask, and I know it's a big favor. Alden's widow, Pam Overton, wants to meet with you. She's helping me some in my investigation, and she thinks you can too."

"She must hate me. I didn't know—" she began.

"She knows that you thought Alden was an eligible bachelor, because he misled you. I'll pick you up here in the morning. You name the time, and I'll take you to Pam's house. The three of us will make some plans. We need your help."

Pixie squirmed uncomfortably. "I don't know," she said. "I don't see how I could help. And I wouldn't feel comfortable around her after all that's happened."

"I need your help. Alden was murdered. Will you do this for him, if not for Pam and me?"

She looked at me, then after another moment of thought, she nodded slowly, and finally she said, "For Alden. I guess I can. Is ten o'clock okay?"

"I'll be here. Thanks Pixie."

Back in the truck a minute later, I told Pam that Mace had indeed been squeezing Pixie for information. "Will she help us?" she asked.

"She says she will," I said. "Now, let's get you home."

Chapter Twenty-Two

IT WAS LATE AND I was tired and hurting when I pulled up at my motel in Tremonton. I got out of the truck and more or less stumbled to the door. I put the key in and turned the knob.

"Hi, Rocky."

I spun around, my heart racing. Shanice was walking through the parking area, her face grim. "We need to talk," she said firmly.

"I need to take a pain pill and sleep," I countered. I wondered why she was here and what she wanted to talk about.

"Please, Rocky," she begged.

"All right, come on in," I said with a sigh, and I held the door open while she stepped past me. "You look tired, Shanice. What are you doing here?"

"I came to apologize," she said as tears welled up in her eyes. "I feel like we need to clear some things up."

I agreed, but I wasn't sure how to go about it. "It's good to see you."

"Really?" she said quietly, her eyes searching mine.

"Yeah, really." It was truer than I thought it could be after the last few hours. I had enjoyed the evening with Pam, but not at all in the same way I enjoyed being with Shanice. As I stood there looking at her, I had to admit that there was something special about her. I wondered if that was why my heart was suddenly hammering in my chest. I needed to sit down.

I pulled out one of the two chairs that the room contained and offered it to her. She sat down wearily, and I sat on the edge of the bed near her. She looked me in the eye and said, "Rocky, I am so sorry."

"It's okay," I said.

"No, it's not okay. I had no right to hang up on you like that," she said. "It's just . . . I don't know how to say this, and I feel foolish." She looked down at her lap, where she was wringing her hands nervously. Finally she looked up again. "It's just that when I found out that you'd be having dinner with Pam, I was worried and upset. I had already lost Alden to her, and I don't want to lose—" She stopped, but the tortured look in her eyes told me the rest. My wildly beating heart did a flip as I realized there was hope again. I took a deep breath in an attempt to calm myself.

I took one of her hands in mine. "Shanice, it's not at all like you think. Let me explain what Pam and I did, and what we'll be doing," I said. "If you don't mind listening, that is."

"I don't mind, Rocky."

"Does your dad know you're here?" I asked.

"He knows I was going to try to find you. Of course, we didn't know if you'd be back here or not. I prayed that you would," she said. "It's been such a long, miserable day."

I swallowed, wondering if I had been the cause of her misery. "I'm sorry, what can I do to help?" I asked, thinking I probably sounded stupid asking that.

Shanice smiled and stood up, gesturing for me to do the same. I stood, and as she stepped closer, I wrapped my arms around her. She laid her head against my chest. "That's what you can do to help," she sighed. We stood that way for a long time, neither of us saying anything. I buried my lips in her hair and breathed in the wonderful scent of her. Finally, she gently pulled back and I let her go. She sat down again, her eyes shining.

"Thanks, Rocky. That helps more than you know," she said. "Now we can talk about what you are going to do, if you want to—but you don't have to. After all, you aren't working for us anymore."

"What I'm doing, I'm doing for me and for you, and for your family. We are in this together," I said. "Of course, this goes against the principles of good investigation."

"What does?" she asked.

"Becoming emotionally involved with clients. And I have done just that," I admitted.

"I—we are not your clients, remember?" she said, looking up at me with a tired smile. "Besides, I'd say you and my family have enough history that such a rule doesn't apply. Don't you agree?"

I nodded. "Well . . . I hope so." We sat there in silence until I spoke again. "Now, about Pam," I said. For the next few minutes, I told her about Mace and my suspicions regarding him. She agreed with what I had planned and how Pam and Pixie would be involved, but the worry on her face deepened as we talked.

"At least Chase is still in jail," she said.

"I'm sorry," I told her, and her eyes widened. "I understand that he bonded out. He's been charged with auto theft, but even though the bond was high, he found a way to meet it."

"Mace is a banker," Shanice said blandly. Her remark seemed random to me at first, but it took me only a few minutes to follow her connection.

"Yes, he could have gotten him out," I agreed. "At any rate, someone did, and so we still have Chase to worry about."

After a few more minutes, she said, "I guess I better get back home. You need your rest, and so do I." She hesitated. "I wish you were staying at our house again. Are you sure you don't want to come back with me?"

"Honestly, Shanice, yes, I do want to come back with you, but I better not. I'll let you know how things go after my little meeting with Pixie and Pam," I said.

We both stood up again, and without conscious thought, she once again was in my arms. As I held her, I silently prayed that somehow this wonderful woman and I could find a future together. That prayer addressed not only the relationship itself but the need for both of us to avoid bullets, knives, bombs, and other dangerous weapons.

I walked her to her pickup and watched as she drove off. I moved my truck from the parking area to a smaller area behind the motel. I didn't know who might be looking for me. With that finished, I returned to my room and got ready for bed. I put my gun within easy reach. My evening prayer expanded on the request I'd made of the Lord while holding Shanice in my arms. I hit the sheets with a sense of foreboding—a warning from the Lord that I needed to work hard and be diligent. I was determined to do that.

A good night's rest was not to be. My foreboding hit me like a thunderbolt when my surveillance alarm went off in the middle of the night. I sprang from my bed, to the detriment of my ribs and shoulder, and checked to see which camera had triggered the alarm. As I feared, it came from the Gridley ranch. I dialed the Gridley's home phone and then held my phone to my ear with my good shoulder as I began rapidly dressing.

It was Glenn who answered, and he was in a cranky mood. He'd obviously looked at his caller ID before answering. "What are you doing calling at this time of night, Rocky?" he barked.

I took no offense, knowing he probably wasn't even fully awake yet. "Glenn, listen to me," I said urgently. "Someone is prowling outside your house. My cameras are recording a shadowy figure right now."

Glenn was fully awake when he spoke again. "I'll get my shotgun and gather my family in the basement," he said decisively.

"I'll call the sheriff, and I'll come myself," I said, knowing that because of the distance from town, it would take the officers and me too long to be of assistance if the prowler meant the Gridleys immediate harm.

I dialed 911 and gave the dispatcher a short, urgent message. Then I proceeded to finish dressing. I had my Western shirt almost snapped up when I remembered my bulletproof vest. I was tempted out of haste to leave the vest, but I thought better and pulled the shirt off, added the vest to my attire, and then put the shirt on again. I had prayed for safety—I had to do my part if I hoped for God's intervention.

As I raced out of town, my phone vibrated. It was the sheriff himself. "I'm headed for Glenn's ranch," he said. "And so are a couple of my deputies. I take it that your cameras picked up someone?"

"That's right. The figure was actually within the fence around the yard of Glenn's house. I didn't see anyone else, but I didn't watch long in my hurry to call the Gridleys and get dressed," I explained as I skidded around a corner then stepped on the gas again, accelerating rapidly.

"What's your location?" the sheriff asked. I told him and then he said, "I'm behind you, but I have a man ahead of you. Be careful when you get there."

I understood the danger. After all, I was the one wearing a damaged bulletproof vest. "You too," I countered.

By the time the first deputy arrived at Glenn's place, the action was over. In fact, it had concluded just a few minutes after my call to Glenn. The intruder was gone. I questioned the rancher about what had happened, glancing up with gratitude at the full moon that illuminated the yard. There was just enough moonlight to see, and I was hoping Glenn had details that might shed some light on the case. He was quite certain he hadn't hit the trespasser with his shotgun, but he was sure that he'd hit his car. It was an older model car, possibly a Buick, with what he thought were out-of-state plates. He thought the car might have been either dark blue or dark green.

"What was he doing when you decided to fire at him?" the sheriff asked. "Besides alarming you and your family, I mean."

"He had something in his hand," Glenn said slowly, his brows scrunched in thought. "It was square and dark. When he saw me, he ran out of the yard and to his car. He threw whatever he was holding into those cedar bushes over there." He pointed to the thick decorative stand near the house. "It was about the size of a softball. Then he pulled a gun from his belt and fired a shot in my direction."

In the sheriff's eyes I saw the same alarm that I was feeling at the mention of the dark object. "Get everybody out of the house and away from here," I shouted.

The sheriff was already ordering one of his deputies to call for a bomb squad out of Ogden. The other deputy was instructed to assist me in getting the family out the back door of the house. When it dawned on him that the object might have been a bomb, Glenn also ran into the house. Between us, we had everyone out of the house and into the barn in a matter of moments. Then all we could do was keep our distance and wait for a bomb squad. As each minute passed, I became more hopeful. Of course, I knew that it could be on a timer or that it could be remotely controlled.

The missing car had not yet been spotted by the cops. Whoever had been here was gone, and it was not a happy thought because he was still free to strike again. I felt increasing pressure to find and put this man, whoever he was, behind bars. As I spoke briefly with the sheriff, I soon understood that he was also feeling the pressure. The danger level had been ratcheted up.

I joined Shanice and Tyra inside the barn, where the lights were burning brightly. Little Tyra was white-faced and looked up at me in confusion. "What's happening, Rocky?" she asked with a shaking voice.

I looked at Shanice for help. She understood my hesitation, and she took her daughter in her arms before she answered her question. "We don't know," she said gently. "But everything's going to be okay." I was impressed. I would have tried to explain about a possible bomb left by a dangerous criminal who wanted to hurt her family. Shanice's answer was sufficient. Tyra accepted that we didn't know what was happening but that we would be okay, and some of the color returned to her face.

"I want to go back to my room in town and review what the cameras recorded," I said to Shanice. "You guys wait here. I'll be back."

"Can we go with you?" she asked, her eyes pleading.

"I suppose that would be okay," I said, glad for the company. We told Glenn and the sheriff what we were doing, and the three of us got in my truck.

When we reached my room, Tyra curled up on my bed and was soon asleep. Shanice and I huddled in front of my monitor and began to play back the activity. The cameras were motion-activated, so most of the time, they were off. However, our mysterious intruder had managed to activate four of them in his wanderings around the barn and yard. He never actually entered the barn, but he did snoop around outside for several minutes. Then he walked back to his car, which was parked in the darkness about two hundred feet from the house. It was facing the direction that the driver would need to go to make his escape to the county road.

We watched the monitor and saw the invader, dressed in black with a hood pulled over his face, walking in the direction of the house, sticking close to the tall pine trees that lined the yard fence. He was moving slowly, slightly bent forward, his head turning back and forth, watching in all directions. One of his gloved hands held a square black object, and like Glenn said, it was about the size of a softball.

We watched him as he entered the yard and walked around to the back of the house. He kept going from one camera to the next unknowingly, never moving out of sight. "You placed the cameras well," Shanice commented while not taking her eyes from the monitor.

I split the screen when Glenn appeared at the back door with his shotgun. We watched as Glenn suddenly stiffened. He had just spotted the intruder, and he lowered himself and pressed his body to the house, just like the other man was doing.

Shanice put her hand over her eyes.

"What are you doing? You already know what happens," I teased, my eyes still on the monitor.

"I know, but I don't want to watch. That's my dad!"

I took her hand and pulled her over to me. She sat on my lap and I wrapped my arms around her. We turned our attention back to the video.

When the intruder went around the house to the east side, Glenn slipped from the porch and followed him. The large evergreen bushes at the front of the house forced the man in black to veer away from the walls. Glenn stopped and watched him from the corner, peeking around as the intruder stopped at the front porch.

"I think I see his gun," Shanice said. I stopped the footage and reversed it. Then I started it slowly forward. "Right there," she said, stabbing at the monitor with one finger.

I again reversed the image and then enlarged the view. "You're right," I told her, glancing at her face. She nodded at me. I started it again. The man turned and looked behind him.

That was when he spotted Glenn. He bolted and ran through the gate, which I noticed he'd left open when he entered the yard. It was there that he stopped momentarily and threw the black object across the lawn and into the shrubbery. Glenn ran straight for the fence, holding the shotgun with both hands. One camera showed the intruder draw a pistol and fire. I felt Shanice jump in my lap, and I held her tighter in my arms, despite the bit of pain it caused.

Another camera showed the foot long sheet of flame that spurted from Glenn's shotgun when he returned fire. Glenn ran forward until he was right at the fence. By then the intruder had reached the car and disappeared inside it. Glenn fired again, and then he stood and watched up the road, the direction the car had gone.

Once more I reversed the recording from the last camera to capture the image of the intruder before he was out of sight. I stopped it at the point where he fired the gun. Again I enlarged the picture. As I studied it, I said to Shanice, "I think it's a revolver. I wonder if it's Alden's."

She didn't reply. I looked at her, and she was holding her hands over her face. "Are you all right? Maybe I shouldn't have had you watch that with me," I said.

She slowly turned toward me, removing her hands and shaking her head. "He tried to kill Dad just like he tried to kill you," she said in a small, frightened voice.

"We don't know if it is even the same man," I said. "But whether it was or wasn't, one thing is for sure. We are dealing with deadly people."

She began to tremble. I pulled her closer to me. She leaned into my shoulder. "We'll get him . . . or them," I said with confidence. I didn't know how, but I was determined to bring this thing to a close before someone else got hurt or killed. A minute later I made a copy of the entire episode on a thumb drive. Then I thought better and made a second copy on a CD.

My cell phone rang as I was resetting the alarm on the surveillance unit. "Rocky," Sheriff Perkins began, "it was a bomb. It had a timer attached to it. It was set to go off at four a.m."

I looked at my watch. It was ten after four now. "What did the bomb squad do?" I asked.

"Those are some competent and brave people," he said. "They have a little robot that they had roll in and retrieve it, but not until after they'd cut a path through the bushes to the bomb. The robot carried it into the field south of the barn. When it detonated, it created a crater thirty feet wide and over two feet deep. It would have destroyed the house, and probably everyone inside would have been killed."

Shanice's head had been right against mine as the sheriff was speaking. She made a little whimpering sound when the sheriff mentioned the size of the crater. With the phone still to my ear, I lowered her to the floor. She had passed out completely. I told the sheriff what had happened and that I'd talk to him later, and then I disconnected the call.

For a moment, I simply knelt beside her, looking at her face, which was shrouded by her long dark hair. At that moment I felt a pain inside me. For once it wasn't my ribs or my shoulder—it burned from within my chest and expanded outward, engulfing me in a throbbing flame. I had thought I cared deeply for Shanice, but this feeling was more profound than any feeling I'd ever experienced. The very thought of losing her cut me deeper than anything I could imagine. I knew then that something had happened to me. I had truly fallen in love.

I gently brushed the hair from her face, leaned close, and whispered, "I love you, Shanice."

Chapter Twenty-Three

A MOMENT LATER, HER EYES flickered, and then they opened. She slowly focused on me. Then she said in a soft but clear voice, "What did you just say?"

"Are you okay?" I asked, embarrassed. I'd never said anything like that to a woman before. I'd never *felt* anything like that about a woman before.

"It depends on what you just said." She wouldn't be deflected.

I helped her to her feet. She clung to my hand after she was standing. She looked deep into my eyes. "You thought I was unconscious," she said with just a hint at a smile.

"Um, yeah I did," I confessed as I felt my cheeks redden.

"Rocky, I'm really, really scared. I can't believe someone would try to kill my family. Why would someone want to do that?" She leaned toward me, and I took her into my arms and pulled her tight.

"I don't know, but I intend to find out."

She laid her head against my chest. "This is the most horrible thing that's ever happened," she said, choking back a sob.

"We can get through it—together."

"Rocky," she said, her voice muffled by my shirt. "If you said what I think you did, then we can get through it together. I need you. I need your strength." She paused, and I didn't say anything. Finally, pleadingly, she added, "Mostly, I need your love."

"I think you heard me right," I said as I gently kissed her hair. "You have my love."

"And you have mine," she said, pulling back from me and looking up into my eyes. When she continued, the words seemed to spill from her. "The truth is, I have always cared for you, but I didn't know how much I needed you until now. Since you've returned, I kind of suspected as much, but I didn't really know. I thought I loved before, but it was nothing like what I feel at this moment. You are such a good man, Rocky. I feel safe with you. You make me laugh. I am totally rambling." She was talking fast, and as she spoke those last words, she laughed sheepishly. I smiled at her, shaking my head.

"I like to hear your ramblings," I said.

"Well, thank you," she said quietly. "I guess what I'm trying to say is, I really love you, Rocky."

"And I really love you," I said with a smile.

I reached up and cradled her face in my hands, then traced my finger along her jaw line. Very slowly, our heads moved together. When our lips met, it sent a feeling that I can only describe as an electric shock through me, to which I responded by pulling her closer as we shared a deep, passionate kiss. Even after it ended, we continued to hold each other.

Shanice was the first to speak. "Keep me safe," she said, her voice trembling. "Keep my little girl safe. And keep *you* safe." She poked me gently in the chest.

"I'll do that," I said. "Nobody is going to spoil something as good as what we have found."

Chapter Twenty-Four

THE PROMISE I MADE TO Shanice brought me back to the present world—the world of danger, greed, and evil. "Let's get back out to the ranch," I said.

"Will you stay with us the rest of the night?" she begged. "We need you. I do, Tyra does, and so do my father and sisters and aunt."

"If it's okay with your dad, I'd like to do that. But I'll bring this equipment with me." I pointed to the surveillance equipment. "I can set it up somewhere else later if I need to, but for now I'd like to have it in your house where I can keep a close eye on it. I won't be coming back to this motel. I don't think that would be safe. Let's get going." It went unsaid that I would wear my gun vest.

Twenty minutes later, we were in the truck. Tyra was belted into the back seat, but she was asleep. She'd never really come fully awake as I carried her from the hotel bed to the truck. Shanice was sitting as close to me as she could get. We talked about the men whom I suspected of committing the crimes and why I suspected them as we rode back to the ranch. I also told her something I hadn't intended to tell her. But having spoken to each other of our newly discovered love, I felt like I needed to be honest and open with her. "I committed a felony the other night. That's how I got my ribs cracked."

Her eyes grew wide, but she simply waited for further explanation. I gave her a very brief sketch of my break-in at Chase's Auto Body, and she gave a sigh of relief. "Tell me more about it," she encouraged me.

After I gave her the details, she reached over and patted my arm. "You have a lot of courage," she said. "I like that in a guy. But most importantly, you discovered Chase's lie. What I wonder now is why he was lying. What does he hope to gain from claiming to be Alden's brother?"

"Exactly," I agreed. "He's up to something, which puts him high on my list of suspects. Chase is up to no good."

"But he's not the only one," she said. "What is our banker up to? I never liked Mace, but I never had a reason not to trust him. But something is going on with him. Hopefully, Pam and Pixie can help you figure him out."

"Conrad was part of whatever this matter started out as, but for some reason, even though he tried to kill me, he himself was murdered. And I also can't help but think that Alden was somehow involved in the beginning as well. I'm also not so sure about Hal, your accountant. He's nice, a little soft, and is head over heels in love with your little sister. But I'm unconvinced that he's not involved in some way," I told her.

Shanice nodded. "I suppose you need to make sure of him. But he doesn't seem like the type to be involved in such terrible crimes. Of course, at first, despite the hurt he caused me, I wouldn't have thought Alden would stoop to stealing from Dad and me, either. Now I'm not so sure."

"What about the ranch hands?" I asked. "They seem like good guys, but I'm uneasy with them. They would certainly know their way around the ranch. I haven't met Vance, the one you let go. His mother says he's working on a ranch in Nevada now, but I still want to talk to him."

"But we know where Shawn and Ricky were when you were shot. It couldn't have been either one of them," she argued.

"You don't think so? Do we really know where they were when I was shot? Shanice, either one of them could have taken the shot and got back to where we thought they were without us knowing it, couldn't they?" I asked.

She was slow to answer, and when she did, I felt reluctance in her voice. "Yes, I guess so, but I don't think they would do it."

"But either one of them could have been prowling around your house too. As I watched the video of what happened here," I said as we parked in front of the house, "I could tell that whoever the man in black was, he knew his way around your place."

She nodded. "I guess you're right."

"Tell me, has Mace been to your home?"

"Several times," she said.

"What about Hal?"

"He's been out here a lot. Like you said, he likes Cindy. I think he was always making excuses to visit," she said, "just so he could see her."

"Chase. We know he's not who he claims to be. Could he have been at your ranch sometime?"

"I suppose so. I haven't ever seen him there, but then I'm not home all the time. And neither are the others. Aunt Rose is there more than anyone. We might ask her," Shanice suggested.

"That's a good idea. Tell me more about Vance. Is there any other reason that your father let him go?" I asked.

"He was the last hired; no other reason," she said. "I know Aunt Rose doesn't care for him, but he's a nice guy. We hated to lose him, but as you know, the finances have become tight—thanks to a thief or two."

"What about the car your dad saw, the one the guy was driving? We saw the car in the camera, but not very clearly. But your dad got a good look at it and gave us a pretty good description. Does that car ring any bells?" We were sitting in the truck. Without really thinking about it, I had taken her hand in mine.

"It doesn't," she said. "But I suppose whoever brought the bomb here could have stolen the car or borrowed it, or even bought it cheap."

"My thoughts exactly," I agreed as I watched the sheriff approach my truck.

We got out, and Shanice carried Tyra into the house. "I'll get a room ready for you," she said. "You can sleep where you did last night. Dad will be fine with it."

Sheriff Perkins was shaking his head. "This thing is way out of control," he said. "It just doesn't make sense why anyone would try to wipe out Glenn and his family."

He didn't have to persuade me to think it crazy, either. They were good people, hardworking and honest. But they *were* also perceived to be rich. I put my thoughts into words. "It was most likely over money, Sheriff."

"You're probably right. By the way, Conrad skimmed a lot of money, but my man has found some other problems. He thinks the banker was getting some of it as well," the sheriff said.

"Ah, yes," I said, not at all surprised at that. "It also wouldn't surprise me if a lot of other people have lost money to Mace Healy."

He nodded his head. "We have enough to call for a full audit of the bank. I'll call the police chief down there in a few hours," he said. "What else have you learned that might be helpful to me and my people?"

I told him what little I'd learned and what my plans were for the next day. "You don't look like you feel too well, Rocky," he said. "I gather that you are going to try to get some rest here." He nodded toward the house. "You better go do that."

"I need to set up my equipment here first," I said.

"You saved their lives, you know," he said. "Let me help you with that stuff."

But Glenn met us at the door, and he said, "I'll help Rocky. Thanks for all you did here tonight, Andy." Then he turned to me and said, his voice choking with emotion, "Rocky, we owe our lives to you. I'm sorry that I gave you a hard time. And I hope you will stay with me and my family until this matter is resolved."

The sheriff looked surprised, and by way of clarification, Glenn turned to him and said, "I tried to fire Rocky out of concern for his welfare. Actually, I guess I did fire him, and when I tried to hire him back, he refused."

"So you are not Rocky's client now?" the sheriff asked in surprise.

"I am working for myself on their behalf as well as mine," I said, jumping in. "And I will continue to do so until the job is finished."

"Rocky, please," Glenn begged. "I'd still like you to work for me again."

The sheriff added his two cents when he said, "Rocky, it would be much better from my point of view if you were working for Glenn. Please reconsider." He went on to reason that it would be easier for the sheriff's office to justify using my findings in their investigation if I was not without a client. Shanice joined us on the porch, and it was the begging in her eyes that changed my mind, albeit reluctantly. So once again, the Gridleys were my clients.

I didn't get much sleep during what remained of the night, but it was not because of further interruptions. It was strictly because I had to be up and working in time to keep my appointment that morning with Pixie and Pam. The two women, although from radically different backgrounds, were anxious to help catch the killer of Alden Overton.

I picked up Pixie from her apartment and then headed over to Pam's house. When we were settled on her living room couches, I explained that agreeing to help me by going out with Mace could be very dangerous. I added that if either of them didn't want to do it, I would understand.

Although clearly apprehensive, they both insisted that they wanted to proceed. "I will be watching," I promised. "And if you are willing, I'll have you wired so that I can hear you and Mace as well as anyone else who happens to come into your immediate vicinity. And if you feel threatened at any point, all you have to do is let me know by saying something to tip me off. If that happens, I'll be there right away."

Now I worried that Mace would not make contact with either woman again. But that worry soon vaporized. Even before I left Pam's house to take Pixie home, Mace called. Pam agreed to go to dinner with him that very night. She played it well, making Mace almost beg before she said yes. The time was set up, and the call ended.

Pam's face broke out with perspiration. "I'm scared," she admitted when I asked her if she was okay.

"That's a good thing," I told her. "This way you'll be really cautious. Now, let's talk about how you might encourage him to say more than he might mean to tell you."

After leaving Pixie at her apartment, I called the sheriff and told him what had been arranged. "I think I better have one of my men with you," he said. I groaned to myself. The groan almost got away from me when he said that he'd make arrangements for Detective Blaine Springer to accompany me.

An hour later, I got a call from Pixie. "I have a lunch date with Mace," she said. "He just called me. He's picking me up at one." I hadn't expected Mace to set up a date with Pixie so soon.

"I'll be right there," I said as I looked at my watch. It was after twelve already. I called the sheriff back, and he said that he would have Blaine head my way but acknowledged that Blaine might not be able to meet me in time.

"I can't wait for him," I said. "I have to get over to Pixie's place and get a wire on her."

"He'll contact you when he gets to Ogden," he said. "You go ahead and get started."

I was sitting out of sight near Pixie's house when Mace arrived. From that point, nothing went as planned. As Mace stepped into her apartment, I heard him explain to Pixie how much he enjoyed being with her and how he thought a nice private lunch at his home would be fun for both of them. From the tone of Pixie's voice, I could tell she worried about that, but she proved game and agreed.

Blaine joined me in the truck as Mace was leading Pixie outside. "Sorry I couldn't get here sooner," he said.

"That's okay," I replied, thinking that it would have been even more okay it he hadn't been able to come at all. But I kept my negative thoughts to myself.

He was actually behaving admirably, and I had to swallow my pride and tolerate his company given his newfound professionalism. He expressed concern over the danger that I had been in and the terrible events of the previous evening.

I explained what was happening, and when Mace helped Pixie into his silver Lexus, I said, "We need to follow them. Do you want to ride with me?"

Blaine hesitated, but then he said, "Sure. I'll pick up my car later."

As we listened, Mace and Pixie talked very little on the ride to Mace's home. But once inside Mace's house, Mace brought up Alden's name. "I'll bet you really miss Alden," he said. "What kind of things did you guys do?"

"We talked a lot," Pixie said. I had instructed her to say that if the opportunity arose. I was glad that it had come so soon.

"Really, what did you talk about?" Mace asked. "I mean, you know, he obviously didn't talk about Pam or his little boy."

"He never even told me about them," Pixie said. "If he had, I would have refused to see him from then on."

"Of course you would, my dear," he said. "I'm not like Alden in that respect. I am a one-woman man, and I assure you that I am no longer married. I'm not even dating anyone now—except you, that is. I guess you could say we're dating."

I held my breath. He was pushing Pixie very hard. I hoped she didn't mention Pam. I'd instructed her not to, but if she got mad, who knew what she might say. She didn't say anything in response for at least a full minute, and I worried that Mace's forward remarks would make her defensive. When she said sweetly, "I guess I'm game with that," I let my breath out. *Good work, Pixie,* I thought. *Way to keep it under control.*

"Great. I knew you would be. I think we're perfect for each other. You know why?"

"Why?"

"I love to talk, just like Alden did. I know women love a man who can hold a decent conversation." I heard a high-pitched giggle.

"Oh, Mace," she said. "You are such a sweet talker."

He seemed to take her comment as a compliment, because he continued, "So what did you guys talk about? You and Alden. I mean, you know, what kinds of things interested you both?"

"Lots of things," she said. "I'd never been very interested in horses before Alden and I met, but he was passionate about them, so we talked a lot about that. He taught me quite a bit about them."

I nodded at Blaine when he whispered, "More of your coaching?"

In the meantime, Mace asked, "What kind of horses did Alden like?"

"Good ones," she said. "I think he mentioned quarter horses a lot. That's a breed of horses, isn't it?"

"It sure is, honey," he said, the sweetness in his voice as thick as syrup. "Of course, there are good quarter horses and there are poor ones, like in every breed. Did he say anything about what kind of quarter horses he liked?"

"Well, he did mention roping horses. In fact, he told me that he wanted to get himself a good roping horse but that they were very expensive," Pixie said.

"Your lunch is on the table in the dining room, Mr. Mace," said a female voice I hadn't heard before. Apparently, Mace wasn't doing his own cooking.

"Pixie, my dear, why don't you come this way," Mace said.

For a moment the conversation stopped, but shortly after they began eating, Mace returned to the subject they'd been talking about. "So was Alden planning to buy a roping horse?" Mace asked.

"He was going to get one, I know that. He also said he had located a horse that was pretty good but that he was going to try to trade it for one that had some roping experience," Pixie said smoothly.

"Did he now?" Mace said.

"Yeah, but he also said that he was going to talk to you about borrowing the difference from your bank," she said. Pixie was following my script very well. Of course, Blaine didn't know that some of what she was telling Mace was my fabrication, not what she and Alden actually discussed. However, she *had* told me, and I was beginning to believe her, that Alden had hoped to return the stolen horses. I chose not to enlighten Blaine at this point.

"We did talk about a loan," Mace acknowledged. "But despite our being such good friends, I had to turn him down. His credit just wasn't good enough."

"Yes, he told me that," Pixie acknowledged. I found myself holding my breath in what was about to come—if she continued to follow the format we had discussed. "He also said that you were going to help him get a really good horse without having to come up with any money. I guess he meant some kind of straight trade instead of what he'd planned."

"Did he say where we were going to get our horses?" he asked.

For a moment, Pixie didn't answer. She was probably surprised, as I was, when Mace inferred that they were *both* going to get a new horse. Blaine and I looked at each other. Now we were getting somewhere.

"He didn't say for sure, but he did say that his former father-in-law had a couple of really good horses that you both thought you could get," she said smoothly.

Now it was Mace's turn to pause. I wished I could have seen his face. "Did he say how we were going to get them?" he finally asked. I didn't like the tone of his voice.

"Of course he did," she responded. But then she changed the subject by saying, "We also talked a lot about cars. He liked cars, too."

But Mace didn't make the shift with her. "Have you told anyone what he said about the Gridley horses?" he asked, his voice low and dangerous now.

"It's time for her to get out of there," I said to Blaine. "We learned what we needed to."

"No, I'm not like that," she protested. "He told me in confidence. I'm only telling you because he was your best friend and I figured you already knew. I don't want to talk about that anymore."

"Pixie, you *will* talk about it more," Mace said. "Come, let's you and I go for a ride. There's something we need to do."

"He wants to shut her up," Blaine said in alarm.

I was feeling the same alarm. It was time to communicate with her. She had a small receiver deep in one ear, hidden beneath her hair. I had told her I would use it only in an emergency. This looked very much like an emergency. I turned on my small radio and spoke into it so she could hear me in her receiver, "Pixie, don't go with him. Tell him you want to go home because you're not feeling well."

"This has been great," she said, "but I'm not feeling very well. I'm sorry. I think I need to go home now."

"Very well," he said. "We'll do that."

"Don't let him get you in his car, Pixie," I said. "Tell him you'll call a cab, that you wouldn't want to throw up in his Lexus."

She ad-libbed very well, but he wasn't giving in. "My car will clean up," he said. "I'll take you home. If you are that sick, why don't you use my bathroom now. You'll feel better, then we can finish our evening."

"We've got to intervene," I said to Blaine.

"Maybe I'll call him and tell him that I'm in Ogden and would like to speak with him again," Blaine suggested. "That might get him to let her call for a taxi." I nodded and then turned my attention back to Pixie and Mace.

The conversation between the two of them stopped. I assumed she was in the bathroom. A moment later, I knew she was because she whispered, "Rocky, I'm in the bathroom. You should see his face. I don't dare go anywhere with him."

"Lock the door and stay where you are until I tell you otherwise," I told her. "We are working on a diversion. Don't move from there until I tell you to."

Chapter Twenty-Five

I DIDN'T LIKE THE FEEL of the situation. We had to act quickly to keep Mace from doing something to Pixie. It seemed to me, and Blaine agreed, that Mace thought she knew something that could put him at risk if she told anyone.

Blaine quickly called Mace's home. I leaned close to his phone and listened. A woman answered. It sounded like the one who had announced that lunch was ready. When Blaine asked her to get Mace, she refused. So he told her who he was and that he would like to meet Mace in person. That got Mace to the phone. While Blaine was explaining that he needed to speak with him as part of an ongoing investigation, I stepped away from the truck and called Pixie a taxi.

As quickly as Blaine had finished his call, he said, "He tried to stall, so I told him I was near his home and that I'd be arriving in a few minutes."

"That's good. I'll see if I can get Pixie to come out while you go to the door." He nodded, got out of my truck, and headed for Mace's house. I again spoke to Pixie. "I have a taxi coming for you. Wait a bit, then tell Mace that you had the number in your phone and that you called one. Then simply head out the door. An officer by the name of Detective Blaine Springer is coming to talk to Mace. He'll see that you get away from the house safely."

A few minutes later, I could hear the click of the lock as she unlocked the bathroom door. Mace was clearly agitated, and his voice was low and angry when he asked, "You okay now?"

"I'll be okay, but I'm really quite sick," she said. "I'm sorry."

"Wait in the dining room. I have someone coming to see me. I'll take you home as soon as I'm finished with him."

"No, I've got to go now," she said. "I called a taxi on my cell phone. It should be here any minute now." In fact, the taxi had just arrived.

"You are not going in a taxi, Pixie. You came with me, and you will go with me when I say. Now sit down and wait," he ordered.

"Detective Springer is at the door," I said to Pixie through her earpiece. "You head for the door. If Mace tries to stop you, Blaine and I will both come in. Hurry."

She must have done what I instructed, because I heard Mace shout, "Get back here!"

"Run!" I said in her earpiece.

Blaine was at the front door when it opened. He was just in time to witness Mace grab Pixie by the back of her blouse. "Let go of me!" she shouted.

He did as he was told. "I'll talk to you later," he said to her. "I'm sorry you don't feel well."

"Get in the taxi and have it take you around the block, out of sight of Mace's house," I said to her through her little earpiece. "I'll meet you there."

I picked up a very frightened Pixie a couple of minutes later. I paid the taxi driver and told Pixie to get in my truck. I then returned to the spot where Blaine and I had been parked. He soon rejoined us.

"How did that go?" I asked Blaine.

He chuckled, a sound I hadn't heard from him before. "He wouldn't talk to me," he said. "I tried to ask him some questions, but he just sulked. He was angry, even though he tried to make me believe that he was just concerned for Pixie's health."

"I'm sure he is," I said facetiously.

"As soon as she ran for the taxi," Blaine said, "Mace told me that Pixie wasn't feeling well. He claimed that he was trying to get her to stay while he called a doctor, but she was afraid she'd throw up on his carpet, so she took off. He said he only grabbed her out of concern. He said that his carpet didn't matter, that he just wanted to get her some medical attention."

"I need to go home," Pixie said from the back seat.

"I don't think that would be a good idea," I said. "Mace is a dangerous man. I'm sorry I put you in such a perilous position."

"I think he killed Alden," she said and began to sob. "Don't let Pam go with him tonight."

"I won't," I promised. "You did great, by the way. We learned some very important things, thanks to you."

We returned to her apartment. "We will get you a hotel room," I told her. "You go pack, and don't tell anyone where you are going, not even Moonbeam. We don't want Mace to find where you are." I got no argument from Pixie on that. We left Pixie to her packing so I could give Blaine a lift to his car.

On the way back to Blaine's car, he suddenly turned to me and said, "Look, Rocky. I know what you did." I had no idea what he was talking about, but I was worried he was referring to my rude remark a few years ago. I opened my mouth to speak, but no words came out. He continued. "I don't know how he got his information, but one of the deputies who I work with was under the impression that the sheriff was interested in firing me the day that I took you into my office. He said you were the one who convinced him to keep me on." I was totally shocked by this comment, and by his reaction—he was pretty choked up. He continued gruffly, "I just wanted to thank you."

"Well," I said, "you're very welcome."

The conversation had happened so randomly that I had to sit there for several moments to process what it meant. This explained Blaine's sudden kindness toward me over the past couple of days. I concluded that I still didn't have a lot of respect for the man, but I was glad I could do something to somehow make up for offending him. We'd been sitting for quite a while in silence when I reached a hand out toward Blaine. He smiled weakly at me, took my hand, and shook it firmly. Then he nodded and opened his door.

Blaine went back to his car, saying that he'd check in with the sheriff and let him know what happened. He said they'd try to determine what the next step would be. Pixie was ready to leave in a matter of minutes. When I got back to her apartment, I took her to a hotel, gave her some money, and told her to keep a very low profile.

Then I called Pam and told her what had happened with Pixie. She was instantly frightened. "I don't know if I dare go through with having dinner tonight with him."

"Oh, no, I wouldn't let you even if you insisted at this point," I said quickly. I told her that Pixie shared our concerns, and then I suggested that we also get her someplace safe.

"Little Alden and I will go stay with my mother," she said. "She's about ready to leave. I can get us seats on her flight tonight."

"Where in California does she live?" I asked, hesitant about it.

"She lives in San Diego," she said.

"Have either of you mentioned to Mace where she lives?" I asked.

"No, I'm sure we didn't. In fact, the only thing he might have heard was how I was raised in Salt Lake. Mace probably thinks that she still lives there."

"That's great," I said. "The sooner you can be on your way, the better. Even if you have to spend a few hours at the airport, it would be better than waiting at home."

"What about Mace? Unless I call him, he'll come to pick me up," she said with concern.

"He'll find an empty house. Do you need for me to make sure you get safely to the airport?" I asked. When she hesitated, I decided for her.

An hour later, Pam's flight had been arranged, and I personally followed Pam, Alden Junior, and Denise to the airport. After seeing them make it safely through security, I headed back for Tremonton. As I drove, I thought about the case. Mace was involved, but who was he in league with? There was no way he could have made the horse switches by himself. I wondered where Chase was. That was something I needed to find out. Vance Winskey was also on my list, and I still hadn't been able to get a hold of him. I was also concerned about the ranch hands and the accountant. And I wondered if some unknown person or persons who I hadn't even heard about or considered might be involved too. I called Shanice to make sure she and her family was being vigilant. She assured me that they were but wished aloud that I was with them. I wished the same.

On my way back from Salt Lake, I decided to stop once more in Ogden. I drove by the bank. Mace's silver Lexus was not there. I drove by his house. His garage was shut. There was no way to know if he was home. On an impulse, I drove toward Pixie's apartment and decided to knock on her door to see if her roommate, Moonbeam, was home.

There was no response when I knocked. I tried several times. Finally, I decided to talk to some of the neighbors. An elderly woman lived next door to the girls. When I told her that I needed to talk to the two young women next door, she looked at me with a cocked eyebrow. "Who are you trying to fool, young man?" she asked. "I saw the one with pink hair, the one who calls herself Pixie, leave with you early this afternoon. Do you think I'm blind? You look like a fine young man. What are you doing spending time with girls like these two? You should be ashamed."

I couldn't help but smile at her. "It's not like that," I said as I pulled out my ID. "I'm a private investigator. They are helping me on a case I'm working on."

"Oh, I see," she said with a sheepish look on her face. "I'm Mrs. James. You must be working for the wife of the man with the silver car, the expensive looking one," she said with a knowing look in her eyes. *I'm sure his wife, if he has one, would have need of a private investigator,* I thought. Mace seemed to have his hand in all the wrong cookie jars.

"Has he been here?" I asked.

"Not since noon, when she left and then came home with you," she said. *This woman must have a lot of time on her hands,* I thought.

"What about the girl with the long black hair?" I asked. "When did you see her last?"

"About an hour ago," Mrs. James said. "These girls are always with someone different. I tell you, they are not very nice girls. Moonbeam left with a guy who was driving an older car, not an expensive one like the guy Pixie went with this afternoon."

"Can you describe the car in a little more detail?" I asked.

"It was older, like I said. It was dark blue. I noticed it had out-of-state license plates."

"Could you tell what state? I know it's a bit far to the street, but if you could tell it was not a Utah plate, I was wondering if you could tell what state it might have been."

She grinned mischievously and invited me in. Then she picked up a pair of binoculars that were lying on a small table next to the window. My face must have registered my surprise because she said, "This isn't a very safe neighborhood. I like to know as much as I can about who comes and goes." She put the binoculars up to her eyes and peeked through her thick curtains as though she were going through the motions from this afternoon. "I checked the plates through these," she said, her voice muffled by the curtains. Then she turned around to face me, setting the binoculars back on the small table. "They were Nevada plates."

"Did you happen to get the plate number?"

"No, I don't ever write numbers down."

"Understandable. Did you also happen to check out the make of the car?" I asked.

"I'm pretty sure it was a Buick," she said.

"Can you describe the man Moonbeam left with?" I asked.

She could and she did, and I felt like I'd been punched in the gut. Mrs. James squinted her eyes and shook her head. "I don't think Moonbeam wanted to go with this man," she said.

"Oh, why do you say that?" I asked in sudden concern.

"She just didn't look happy like she usually does. If anything, she looked scared. Would she have had anything to be scared about?"

"I'm afraid so. Let me give you my card," I said. I pointed out that the phone number was to my cell phone. "If you see either woman here, or if anyone comes to their apartment, please call me. I don't care what time of the day or night it is. Will you do that?"

She squared her thin shoulders and looked me right in the eye, craning her neck upward as she did. "I will do that," she said very seriously. "And I hope those girls are okay."

As I turned to leave, I thought of one more thing. "Oh, Mrs. James?" I said, turning back to face the old woman. "You're welcome to keep track of any license plate numbers in association with the two girls. It may be useful to me." She nodded, a determined smile on her face.

Upon leaving Mrs. James, I called Pixie and asked her if she knew anything about a blue Buick with Nevada plates. She didn't, but she was very concerned that Moonbeam had gone with whoever the driver of that car was. She wasn't aware of Moonbeam having plans to go with anyone that day. I next called the sheriff and explained what I had just learned.

"This is not good. I'm afraid that girl could be in deep trouble," he said. "I'll put the description of Moonbeam and the car on the air. Maybe we'll get lucky and someone will spot it."

Someone did spot a similar car, and I got a call from the Salt Lake City Police. I was told that an off-duty police officer had gone to meet his wife, who worked at a large industrial complex in Salt Lake City. Her car wouldn't start, and he was jumpstarting it when he noticed an older Buick just three spaces away from hers. He remembered the Attempt to Locate call that had been broadcast shortly before the end of his shift. This car was a close enough match that he called it in on his cell phone. Sheriff Perkins of Box Elder County had just been notified. Under Sheriff Perkin's authority, I called the Salt Lake police and got a report on the car.

It was getting late, I was tired, and unfortunately I was still hurting. But despite all that, I made another trip to Salt Lake. The Buick was still in the parking lot, but after one look, I suspected it wasn't the one. The Buick I was looking for, even though Mrs. James had not said so, would probably have holes in it where Glenn Gridley had shot it with his shotgun. Of course, I couldn't be sure the one that Moonbeam left in and the one that the bomber had driven away from Glenn's place were the same car. Within a few minutes, my suspicions were confirmed when the owner of the car appeared. He and his car checked out okay—it was not the man or the car Mrs. James had seen. I headed north, uncomfortable and very worried.

About eight that night, I arrived back at the Gridley ranch. I was sitting on a couch filling Shanice in on the latest when Pixie called me. She was so upset she could hardly talk. "Calm down," I suggested, "and then tell me what you are upset about."

"I just got a phone call," she said. "The guy said that he had Moonbeam and that if I didn't want her blood on my hands, I should tell him where I was at so that he could come and talk to me."

"Did it sound like Mace?" I asked.

"No. Well, I don't think so. It sounded muffled, like the guy was trying not to allow me to recognize his voice," she said. "Whether it was Mace or someone else, he sounded like he meant it. He said not to tell anyone or I would regret it. But I *had* to call you. Moonbeam is my best friend. She doesn't have anything to do with any of this mess. She didn't even like Alden. What should I do? He gave me thirty minutes to think about it, and then he's calling me back."

Shanice was watching me with wide, frightened eyes. I signaled for her to sit closer to me. She did so, took hold of my arm with both of hers, and rested her head against my shoulder.

"Stay where you are," I said to Pixie. "I'll have someone there shortly to protect you and help get Moonbeam back."

"Do you promise?" she asked, sobbing.

"Have I let you down yet?" I asked.

"No."

"Then do as I say. Trust me, Pixie. I'll keep you safe." I prayed that I wasn't lying.

Sheriff Perkins sounded at least as tired as I was when I again interrupted his evening. His voice filled with concern, he said, "I'll call the police chief in Ogden. He's a friend of mine, and he'll have his people discreetly go to the hotel. Hopefully, we can get Pixie to tell the caller, whoever he is, where she's at and when the guy shows up, we'll nab him." Knowing the kind of criminals we were dealing with, I wasn't so sure about the safety of that plan, but I didn't say so.

"What about Mace?" I asked. "Do you have enough to pick him up yet?"

"I think so, but we can't find him," the sheriff revealed. "I had him under surveillance, but the officer lost sight of him. We haven't been able to find him again."

I groaned. Lives were in danger. And I honestly didn't know what more I could do. I explained that to Shanice. "You can stay here and keep us safe," she said. "Dad won't admit it, but I know he's scared. And the girls and I are beside ourselves with worry. Even Aunt Rose is so upset she can hardly stop crying, and she never cries. She keeps begging Dad to stay in the house and watch the monitors. But he insists there is work to do."

There was something I could do. I thought of it as I listened to Shanice. "Your father is here in the house now," I said. "Despite all the work he has to do, it is dark outside. Surely he can stay in the house until morning. Will you attempt to convince him to stay here? I need to go talk to your ranch hands. But I want your father to keep a close eye on the monitors while I'm doing that. And I'd like him to keep his shotgun close by."

"Rocky, please, you can't leave," she begged, gripping my arm tightly.

"Let's talk to your dad," I said. I stood up, pretty much dragging her with me.

Glenn promised that he'd keep his family safe. "We have a house full of guns," he said gravely. "And the girls and Rose all know how to use them. With these cameras of yours, we'll be able to keep an eye on things." I didn't miss the fear in his eyes, but I admired his ability to put on a brave face for his family. Shanice seemed to relax a bit after hearing his confidence.

"Good," I said. "Then I'll be on my way again. Call me if you see or hear anything suspicious."

I then called the sheriff back and explained what I was going to do. He suggested that I take one of his deputies with me. Actually, he more than suggested—he insisted. Poor Blaine Springer had to once again endure my company. But he was okay about it. We left my truck and went in his unmarked police car. Frankly, as we drove up to the home of Ricky Snyder, I found myself feeling glad to have Blaine's help. I was also glad to have my gun with me.

Unfortunately, Ricky wasn't home. His wife said that he'd gone to see the other ranch hand, Shawn Wheeler. Blaine and I looked at each other. I suspected that my face displayed as much suspicion as his did.

Chapter Twenty-Six

RICKY'S PICKUP WAS PARKED IN front of Shawn's house. Detective Springer and I approached the door. Ricky's wife answered it. I introduced myself and Blaine, and then said, "We need to speak with Ricky and Shawn."

Her face looked drawn and tired, but she invited us in and offered us seats in a small, cluttered living room before disappearing down a hallway. Neither of us sat. It couldn't have been much over a minute before the two men entered the room. Like Ricky's wife, they both looked drawn, tired, and stressed.

All four of us had to clear stuff out of the way before we sat down. "We need some information," I said after a few moments of small talk. I nodded in Blaine's direction. "How well do the two of you know Mace Healy?"

They looked at each other. "The name sounds familiar, but I don't know him," Ricky said. Shawn agreed with him.

"He's the banker who has worked closely with Glenn for quite a number of years," I said.

They both shook their heads. "We just work for Glenn," Shawn said. "We don't have anything to do with his finances. We've been told that he's in financial trouble, which is why he had to let Vance go. But that's all we know."

I looked at Blaine to see if he wanted to say anything, but he gave just the briefest shake of his head, so I asked, "Did you know Conrad Patel, the second murder victim?"

It was Ricky who spoke up first. "He was an accountant, wasn't he?"

I shook my head. "He worked *for* their accountant, Hal Rodgers, but he was only a bookkeeper. I take it that you both knew Hal."

"It was hard not to," Shawn said with a wry grin. "He came to the ranch all the time."

"What kind of guy was he?" I asked.

"Are you expecting us to tell you if we think he would have stolen the horses?" Ricky asked.

"Do you?"

"Not really," Ricky answered. Shawn nodded in agreement.

"Would he have stolen money from your employer?" I asked.

They looked at each other. Shawn answered for them both. "We didn't know him all that well, but I don't think so."

"So you think he was honest?" I asked.

"I wouldn't have thought otherwise," Shawn said.

"Other than on the ranch, did either of you have anything to do with Conrad? You know, did you socialize with him, drink with him, that kind of thing?"

"Not at all," Ricky said.

"So would you both be surprised if I told you that he has been skimming money from the ranch accounts?"

Their faces answered my question. They looked genuinely shocked. They both made it clear that they would have a hard time believing such a thing. I pressed them again about Hal Rodgers. They claimed they didn't really know Hal, even though they had both met him and seen him around the ranch house more than a few times.

"You both knew the other victim, Alden Overton," I said. "What can you tell us about him?"

"Shanice was too good for him," Ricky answered with a touch of fire in his eyes. "I never did like him or trust him, quite frankly."

I looked at Shawn. "I couldn't have said it better myself." He and Ricky both expanded a little on their dislike of the former family member.

"Could he have been involved at any point in the theft of the horses?" I asked.

There was no hesitation as they answered in the affirmative. For the first time, Blaine asked a question of the two cowboys. "Who do you men think might have killed Alden?"

They both shook their heads to that question, but a look passed between them that made me hesitate. Apparently Blaine noticed because, like me, he sat silent, his eyes flicking from one of the ranch hands to the other. Finally I said, "Hey, if you guys have any suspicions at all, tell us. Two men are dead, and attempts have been made on the lives of others, including your employer and his family. We want to find out who is doing all this before more lives are lost."

They both hesitated further. Leaning toward them and adding a touch of anger to my voice, I said sternly, "An innocent girl has been kidnapped. She too could die. Tell us what you suspect. And tell us now."

The two men looked at each other for a moment or two. Finally, Ricky nodded, and Shawn rocked me with his response. "Glenn and Shanice certainly had reason enough to kill Alden. I like them both. Glenn is a great boss, but he was awfully angry when Alden did what he did to his daughter. And Shanice was also angry. They both seemed to be over it, but when the horses went missing, the first person Glenn mentioned was Alden. And Shanice didn't disagree with him."

Ricky spoke up then. "I know you don't want to hear this, Rocky," he said. "But that was what we were talking about when you came. We can't imagine who else would have a better reason for killing Alden than the two of them."

"Thanks for reminding us that we can't afford to overlook anyone in an investigation as serious as this one," Blaine said, looking at me with just a touch of guilt on his face.

I wanted to shout and scream at them for suggesting such a horrible thing. But I didn't. I couldn't. What they had just said went against everything I felt about my employers, especially Shanice. But what they said also made a certain amount of sense. My skin felt cold, and my tongue felt like it was swelling, but I forced myself to speak, trying to keep the feelings that were raging inside me under control. "You are all three right," I managed to admit. "But why would either one of them try to kill me? And why would either of them get someone to bomb their own house?"

They had obviously considered this question. Ricky was the spokesman this time. "Alden had violent friends," he said. "One of them could have been trying to get even with the boss. And they might have thought that you were in the way by protecting Glenn and Shanice."

I considered that a very weak explanation, but I had to admit that it couldn't be ruled out just yet. "Okay, we'll consider them as possible suspects," I said, looking at Blaine for confirmation and receiving it. I didn't for a minute believe it, especially regarding Shanice. But I kept those feelings to myself.

"Don't get us wrong," Shawn said. "We don't think they had anything to do with it. But as we've talked about it, we couldn't shake the idea, as much as we hate it."

Ricky nodded in agreement and then said, "I'm sure it's not them. We probably shouldn't have brought it up."

I made no comment about that, but I then asked, "What can you men tell me about Chase Overton?"

"Who?" Ricky asked. "If you're talking about some relative of Alden's, I don't know him. I don't know any relatives of his."

"Nor do I," Shawn said.

"What if I told you that he only *claims* to be Alden's brother. What thoughts would that give you?" I asked.

"I suppose that he might be someone who would want to get revenge for Alden's murder," Shawn said. "Could that be who has been trying to kill you and the Gridleys?"

"It does make sense, doesn't it?" Blaine interjected.

"What about the name Chase Hideman?" I asked.

"That sounds familiar," Shawn said. "I've heard the name somewhere. Could he and Chase Overton be the same person?"

"You tell me," I said.

Ricky's brow was furrowed. He spoke slowly, deliberately. "I think that Alden mentioned that name. But he never said it was his brother." He turned to Shawn. "Do you remember Alden saying something about him?"

Both men were thoughtful. Blaine and I waited. Finally Shawn said, "Yeah, now that I think of it, I do remember Alden saying something about a friend of his by that name. Vance mentioned it too. I mean, one day Vance said something about 'Alden's friend Chase.' I know neither of them said Chase Overton, but they could have said Hideman. Or they might not have even mentioned a last name."

"Speaking of Vance, have either of you talked to him lately?" I asked.

"Not recently," Shawn said. "Right after Glenn fired him, he came to me and asked me to try to get Glenn to hire him back."

"Did you?" I asked.

"No. He wanted me to tell Glenn that we couldn't get along without him. But I wouldn't do that. Glenn's girls picked up the slack, and we've been making it okay," he said. "I felt bad about him getting the sack, but I didn't feel like I had the right to intervene."

"He asked me the same thing," Ricky agreed. "Shawn and I talked about it. Vance was a pretty decent worker. I also felt bad when he was let go, but I couldn't blame Glenn if he was in fact short on money. And if he was being pilfered, I suppose he *really* could have been having a hard time financially." He pursed his lips for a moment, and then he asked, "Was the bookkeeper really stealing from Glenn?"

"It looks that way," I said.

"Have you thought about the fact that if Glenn knew that Conrad was stealing from him, it would give Glenn a reason to murder him?" Ricky asked, his eyes avoiding mine as he spoke.

"Not until today," I admitted. And frankly, I didn't believe it. Why would Glenn hire me if he was a killer himself? I knew that his ranch hands were trying to appear totally objective, but I didn't think either of them believed what they were suggesting any more than I did. Rather than make me suspect Glenn or anyone in his family, it moved the two of them much higher on my list of possible suspects.

"It makes sense, doesn't it?" Shawn added. "But I can't see it happening."

I nodded, not believing that it was possible. But I didn't tell them that. "Do you know where we could find Vance?" I asked. "He might be able to help us. You men have certainly been a big help."

"He's working in Nevada," Shawn said. "When Ricky and I didn't help him get his job back, he found a job over there. I haven't seen him for a long time. I don't even know exactly where the ranch is that he's working on. Do you, Ricky?"

"No, but I'm sure his mother could tell you," Ricky suggested.

We didn't gain much more information over the next few minutes. However, both men made it clear to us that even though they had talked about what they had just told us, they didn't really believe it. They claimed to be very fond of their employer and his family. But these two cowboys had suggested a solution that I hadn't even considered, nor did I seriously consider it now. When we were back outside, Blaine echoed my sentiments, saying, "I wonder about these two. Seems to me like they are grasping at straws." I was glad he was thinking the same thing, as disturbing as the possibility was.

"Let's go have a talk with Vance Winskey's mother," I suggested. "If we can find Vance, maybe he can tell us more about Ricky and Shawn. We may have been overlooking them just because they were right under our noses."

"However," Blaine reminded me, "if it was them, then who has taken Moonbeam and why? Or are a whole bunch of people in this together, including Mace, Conrad, Chase, and maybe others?" He had, I admitted to myself, summed up my thoughts pretty well.

When we got back to Detective Springer's car, I received a call on my cell phone. It was the sheriff, who reported that Pixie had received another call from the man who claimed to have taken Moonbeam. He hadn't even asked Pixie where she was. Instead, he told her that she was to meet him alone on a dirt road about three miles off Highway 30 several miles southwest of Snowville, a city in the far northwest corner of the state. She was told to drive there and meet him at two in the morning. I was not very happy about this turn of events. I just hoped the sheriff realized the kind of danger he was putting Pixie in.

"The man told her that all he wanted to do was talk to her but that if she didn't come alone, or if she didn't come at all, she would never see Moonbeam again," the sheriff said. "As you can imagine, Pixie is petrified. She doesn't know what to do, but she's sure that if she shows up way out there by herself, the guy will kill her."

Well, yeah, I thought emphatically. "I can't argue with her reasoning," I said as my mind raced ahead. "Does she even have a car?"

"Yes, she drives a little Ford Escort," the sheriff said. "I thought it would all take place down in Ogden, but this throws an entirely different light on things. The chief was all set to help us down there, but I don't know how we can handle this. That's open country out there, with rolling hills—not a lot of trees. Of course I don't know what it's like at the exact location he specified, but I don't see how we can get people there without this guy knowing it."

"Maybe there's a way around the situation entirely. Let me think on it for a few minutes," I said. "We are on our way over to speak with Mrs. Winskey. When we get through, we'll come in to your office and see what we can figure out."

"Don't be long," he said, the worry in his voice spilling out of my phone.

After I hung up, Blaine and I took the short drive to Mrs. Winskey's home. She was in her robe when she came to the door. It was almost ten p.m., not a good time of day to visit people—but then, we weren't home teaching or selling vacuum cleaners; we were conducting a murder investigation. Of course, we'd rung the bell three times and knocked loudly at least that many more times, and she looked more than a little annoyed. Her anger didn't bother me, but something in her eyes did, something more than their redness.

After a brief moment, she tried to close the door, and Blaine stuck his foot in the way. "I don't want to see you. I want you to get off my property right now," she said, her voice shaky. I had no intention of leaving without learning where Vance was living now. More than ever, after our meeting with the men he used to work with, I felt it imperative that we speak with him.

She never did actually invite us in, but Blaine used his badge and a lot of cop talk to force our way into the living room. I shut the door behind us. "What do you men want from me?" she asked with a voice that was filled with something besides anger. Was it fear?

"We need to talk to Vance," I said evenly.

She began to tremble. Something was not right here. I exchanged glances with Blaine. The look in his eyes told me that he was also suspicious about the way this woman was acting. "He's not here. You already know that," she said with a fierce shake of her head. "He had to move because that rich rancher fired him."

She said *rich* like it was a dirty word. I wondered if her bitterness mirrored that of her son. "We need for you to tell us where he is. We think he can help us in our investigation," Blaine said.

"I don't know where he is," she repeated.

"We are not asking you where he is right at this moment. All we want is the address where he's living now. You said it was a ranch in Nevada," I said, my eyes taking in the room behind her.

The TV was on, but it was muted. There was an old movie playing in black and white. There was a glass of something amber in color on a small table beside a comfortable-looking but well-worn chair. Judging from the smell of her breath, I suspected that the glass contained scotch.

"Yes, he's on a ranch," she said, her hands wearing each other out with fierce wringing.

"All I need to know is where that ranch is," I said. "I'll contact him there."

"I gave you his number," she said, pointing a finger weakly at me.

"Yes, and you also said he would answer it. I've called several times, and he's never picked up. I've left several voice messages, and he's never returned my calls."

"I don't have an address," she said.

"Does the ranch have a name?" I asked.

"If it does, I don't know it. Now you need to go. I don't know anything more." She was swaying on her feet now. I was pretty sure she was drunk. That could account for the way she was acting. Then again, it might not be all of it.

"Approximately where in the state of Nevada is this ranch where he works?" I asked. "It's very important that I talk to him."

"I've never been there, and he hasn't said," she answered, her words beginning to slur.

I could see that we were getting nowhere. Blaine was looking impatient. So I said, "Sorry to have bothered you."

She said nothing, but she staggered to her chair and sat down. The last glimpse I got of her as I shut the door was the glass of scotch making its way to her lips, the amber liquid sloshing out of the glass as her hands shook like she had just had a terrible fright.

"I think we scared her," I said to Blaine after we had reached his car. "Something is wrong with that woman."

"But what could it be?" he asked.

I was surprised that he didn't have any idea. I had a nagging feeling that I knew, but I wasn't sure I wanted to share my idea with him just then. What I had to do now had to be done alone—like my little foray into Chase's Auto Body.

"Let's get back to the office," he said. "The sheriff is probably chomping at the bit."

"I don't blame him if he is. Why don't you take me back to my truck at the ranch, and I'll meet you guys there in a few minutes," I said.

Blaine dropped me off at my truck. I waited until he was out of sight before heading back toward the Winskey home. I left quickly so that no one at the ranch would delay me. I didn't drive all the way there, however. Instead, I parked around the block from the small house. There was something I wanted to check out, but I knew that Detective Springer would never have allowed me to do things my way, seeing as how my way was illegal. I was glad to be alone again.

It was a cloudy night, which made everything seem darker, even with the full moon. I donned my bulletproof vest, checked my pistol, pulled on a jacket, put on a black ball cap, and slipped into the yard of the house directly behind Mrs. Winskey's. I stole my way to the back of that yard, where I had to scale an old wooden fence. When I dropped to the ground on the other side, I winced from the pain. I took a minute to let the pain ease, and then I moved to my left and crouched down behind one of the small sheds. A dog began barking from a yard to the west, and I thought I was done for, but the dog quit after a few minutes. I breathed a sigh of relief and peered around the shed. It was hard to see clearly because the only light was from a couple of windows in Mrs. Winskey's house, but it allowed me to get some idea of what was back there.

It was a large backyard. The yard held several outbuildings, one of them large enough to be a garage or shop of some kind. A couple of rusty pickups stood abandoned on blocks. I also saw an old two-horse trailer near the largest outbuilding, and I made a mental note to check up on it later, but I didn't see a working vehicle, not even a car like I would have expected Mrs. Winskey to drive. It was a mess back there. It appeared that Mrs. Winskey exercised her green thumb skills only on her front yard. Waist-high weeds littered the fence line, surrounded the outbuildings, and grew beneath several large trees. Piles of trash littered the area.

I wanted to peek inside the largest outbuilding. It looked large enough to contain three or four cars. I surveyed the house for a moment before slipping out of my position of obscurity and rushing to the back of the large building. I worked my way along the back of it, again out of sight of the house. Then I started up the east side. Near the front, the weeds were not as thick, and a small door appeared. I examined it but did not attempt to open it until I had searched the building perimeter. I peeked around the front of the building and noticed two large overhead garage doors. They were closed. I returned to the small door, and with a gloved hand, I tried the knob. It was locked. I worked my magic with the small set of picks I had in my pocket. In less than a minute, the door opened, and I stepped inside.

Chapter Twenty-Seven

As I WALKED INTO THE pitch-black building, strong smells of grease, gasoline, and oil hit my nostrils. As I stepped farther into the building and scoured the area around me for signs of the building's contents, my phone began to vibrate. The vibration sounded like thunder in the silence, and my heart started to race. I pulled out the phone. It was the sheriff calling. Until I was certain that the building I was standing in was empty, I didn't want to make a noise. It was bad enough that I allowed the cell phone to create light around me. I rejected the call and put the phone back in my pocket. The sheriff would just have to wait for a few minutes.

In those few seconds that the cell phone had created some light, I had noticed that I was standing very close to a vehicle. I reached out now and touched it. Then I worked my way up the side, soon determining that it was a medium-sized sedan of some sort. I discovered another vehicle right in front of it. But as I began to feel my way along the side of it, I heard a muffled sound coming from the far side of the garage. I froze and listened intently.

The sound faded, but after a moment, it started again. It sounded like something was moaning. It could have been an injured animal of some type. Then there was a slight squeaking sound and a couple of small thumps. I abandoned my exploratory trip alongside the second vehicle and instead passed slowly between the front of the sedan and the back of what I soon figured out was a pickup. I stopped again. The thumping grew slightly more pronounced, as did the other sounds. I felt for and discovered another vehicle parked to the west of the sedan. I felt a slight movement of the vehicle under my palm.

The squeaking came from beneath the vehicle—shocks or springs, I assumed. Something, or someone, was inside the vehicle. I crouched beside that third vehicle, listening intently. The vehicle moved slightly from time to time. And the moaning inside was interspersed with muffled sobs.

Finally, after hearing no other sounds in the garage except those near me, I slowly stood up, lifted my small flashlight, then, peeking over the top of the back door, I turned on the light. I caught a glimpse of black-and-blue hair and a bundled body before ducking back down and shutting off the light. I had found Moonbeam. She was bound, gagged, and blindfolded.

The car began to rock as the young woman inside moved with more force than before. The sobs became louder. Moonbeam was alive, and I intended her to stay that way. But I didn't want anyone, including Moonbeam, to be able testify that I was in that garage illegally. So I did not free her at that moment. I did, however, slowly let the air out of one tire. No one would be driving this car to Snowville or any points beyond in the near future. I quickly but silently left the garage.

I returned rapidly to my truck and drove around the block to where I could see the front of Mrs. Winskey's house. I got out of the truck and walked closer. There was no movement in front of her house and no sign of anyone trying to leave the backyard. Finally, I returned the sheriff's phone call.

When he answered, he said, "Are you going to be here shortly? We need to get a plan in place."

"Sheriff," I began, speaking softly but urgently. "I am on the street near Vance Winskey's mother's house. I have a feeling about something. Get someone here to help me as fast as you can. Blaine knows where it is."

There was silence for a moment. Then the sheriff said, "But we have to get on our way toward Snowville. And we have to have a plan in place before we do."

"Forget Snowville," I said urgently. "Get up here now, please. Come around back to the big garage."

There was no further argument from the sheriff. "I'll be there, and so will Blaine."

I closed the phone and stood there for a moment, trying to decide what to do. Moonbeam was undoubtedly scared to death. I could free her, but I wanted to do so in a way that would not land me in jail and jeopardize catching Vance Winskey; at this point, I was convinced that he was the man who had taken her and done a lot more besides. I also suspected that he was in the house, waiting to drive to the location he had set up for the rendezvous with Pixie.

Not sure what was happening in back of the house, I decided that I needed to get to where I could see the garage and make sure no one took Moonbeam away before my backup arrived. A minute later I was in position. It was none too soon. The lights in the house went out, plunging the backyard into almost total blackness. Then I heard the back door open, and someone carrying a flashlight walked briskly to the garage.

The flashlight lit up the side door. The shadowy figure inserted a key and unlocked the door. Then he stepped inside, closing the door behind him. I made a dash for my truck, and without turning on the lights, I drove it past the house and parked it in the driveway that led to the back of the house. There was no way anyone could leave the yard now. I got out and returned to my former position near the northeast corner of the house. From there I was facing the bay doors of the garage in which Moonbeam was being held. Lights were now on in the garage, and the vehicle that contained Moonbeam was backing out of the open bay door on the left. But it stopped just as the front end cleared the exit.

The driver, cursing audibly, got out and circled the vehicle, a black, older model sedan. He spotted the flat tire, cursed again, and kicked the fender. I decided that I couldn't wait any longer for police backup. Moonbeam was in danger. The killer, for that is how I now thought of him, was angry, and anything could happen.

The killer moved around the car and stepped into the open bay doorway, where he was bathed in light. He turned and looked back at the house as if trying to decide what to do. I had never seen Vance Winskey, but the man whose face I now saw was clearly someone I had seen before. Chase Hideman, aka Chase Overton, was scowling. Then he pulled out a cell phone and made a call, vanishing into the garage as he did so. I had not expected to see him here, although I probably shouldn't have been surprised. I'd learned earlier from Sheriff Perkins that he had made bond and gotten out of jail down in Ogden.

I didn't wait any longer. I pulled my pistol, left my place of concealment, and rushed to the southeast corner of the garage. From there I slid slowly to my right with my back against the closed bay door until I was beside the open one. I listened for a moment and could soon hear Chase's voice inside. Taking a chance, I walked at a crouch as silently as I could across the open space and around the black sedan, squatting on the left side, farthest from the tire I had flattened.

Then I waited, my right side pressed against the car. My intent was to surprise and overpower Chase if he attempted to change the tire. A moment later, I caught a glimpse of Chase coming through the open door, his phone in one hand and a tire iron in the other. At that moment, my bulletproof vest again saved my life. The bullet that struck me in the middle of my left side didn't have the force of the rifle bullet that had knocked me from my horse. But it still slammed me against the car, causing me to lose my balance and fall on my back. The second bullet struck the car just above me.

I flipped onto my stomach, saw a figure running toward me with a pistol in his hand, and fired a quick shot at him. He went down and I rolled away from the car, stopping on my back and firing this time at Chase, who had appeared near my feet. His tire iron had vanished, and he was also holding a pistol, but he never got a shot off before my bullet sent him reeling into the garage. I didn't wait to see if he went down before turning my attention to the first gunman. He was slowly getting to his knees. He had dropped his pistol but was groping for it with his right hand. His left hand was heavily bandaged.

In that next brief instant, I pictured that hand as I had last seen it, partly mangled by the small pile of rubble I had knocked him onto behind Chase's Auto Body. "Let it lie," I said when his fingertips touched the pistol. When he didn't pay any attention, I fired again, and his right hand became as useless as his left. He screamed in pain, and I turned the other way, looking for Chase.

But before I spotted him, I heard someone call out, "You beside the car, drop your gun."

With relief, I recognized the sheriff's voice. I let my gun slip from my fingers and then said, "It's Rocky. Chase is in the garage, and he's armed."

"Then pick up your gun again," the sheriff said as he and Blaine both approached cautiously from opposite directions. The sheriff used the black sedan to shield him from the open bay door while Blaine slipped to the side of the yard and worked his way toward me from the east, keeping out of the light as much as he could.

All the caution turned out to be unnecessary. Chase was alive, but he was in no condition to fire a weapon. He was lying on his back about ten feet inside the garage. The man with the bandaged left hand and mangled right one was lying still, saying, "Don't shoot," over and over again.

The door of the house opened, and I saw Mrs. Winskey come out. She was unarmed, but she ran toward the man on the ground, calling out his name in alarm, confirming my suspicions that it was Vance Winskey. I picked up the pistol he had shot me with just before she reached him. A quick look told me that it was like the one Pam had told me belonged to Alden. I shoved it in my pocket and turned away.

A moment later, I opened the back door of the sedan and freed Moonbeam from the ropes that held her bound. She sobbed and hugged me, and then she hugged the sheriff.

I made the call to Pixie while the sheriff and others secured the injured men in an ambulance. Later, the sheriff said that they would conduct interrogations as soon as the men were in stable enough condition to do so. "It looks like we can wrap this thing up," he told me. "You've done a great job. I'm just glad you weren't shot again."

I smiled, and when I did, he looked at me suspiciously. "You were?" he asked. I pointed out the hole in my jacket and he said, "You must be wearing your vest."

"I am," I said. "But I feel like a fool. I let Vance get the drop on me." I pulled the man's pistol from my pocket and held it out to the sheriff. "There's a very good chance you'll find that this matches the bullets taken from the bodies of Alden and Conrad. I'll need to give you the lead that's stuck in my vest, too."

"You should have waited for us," he said with a frown as he slipped the gun into his own pocket.

"I'd fully intended to, but then Chase backed out of the garage, discovered a flat tire, and got very angry. It scared me for Moonbeam. I had a feeling she was in that car, and I just couldn't take any chances. Unfortunately, I don't think things are quite finished yet. These aren't the only ones involved—of that I'm sure. Mace is a part of this, and as long as he's running around free, we still have danger."

The sheriff agreed and said, "I'll have someone pick up Mace as quickly as we can find him. We are also going to take Mrs. Winskey in tonight. She lied to Blaine and to you, and that hindered the investigation. She won't be happy to hear that."

"If she'd been honest with me initially," I said with a nod of my head, "we might have caught Vance sooner and saved us some trouble and pain."

"What about the attempted bombing at Glenn's house?" he asked. "I'm guessing it was Vance Winskey."

I thought about that for a minute. "I don't think so," I said. "You saw his bandaged left hand. That was not in the video at Glenn's. The guy there that night was using both hands."

"Maybe his injury happened after he left there," he suggested.

I knew it hadn't, but I couldn't tell the sheriff that or I would have to explain that I had done it to Vance after a break-in. That was not going to happen, so I just said, "Good point, but I don't think we should assume that."

The sheriff agreed, but he didn't seem very enthusiastic about it. He shifted his focus and said, "I wonder if the rifle you were shot with happens to be in Mrs. Winskey's house."

"I would guess that is a distinct possibility," I agreed. "But you also will want to search Chase's home and his body shop."

"Don't forget the other ranch hands," Blaine said. "As I was telling you a little while ago, Sheriff, I'm not sure they aren't involved with these two."

We talked a little longer. As other officers arrived, the sheriff began to bark out orders. I began to feel like I was on the sidelines. But I had an idea that would keep me busy while the cops did their work. "Sheriff, I said, "we still have two very expensive horses missing. While you and your deputies work on the murders, maybe I should work on finding the horses. After all, that was what Glenn Gridley originally hired me to do. I would probably just be in your way now as you finish things up. Unless you feel otherwise, I would be willing to concentrate on that for a while." I figured that if I could find the horses, I might find the other killers, unless the cops beat me to it. I was still thinking about Mace, but I was also thinking about Shawn and Ricky, as Blaine had mentioned.

"That would be good," he said. "We can take it from here. But keep me advised if you learn anything."

I nodded toward the house. "Sheriff, to begin with, I think it would be helpful if I were allowed to talk to Vance's mother. Do you mind if I go in and visit with her before you arrest her?"

"Go ahead, if you think she can help," he said.

"I think she can help, I'm just not sure she will," I admitted as I headed for the house.

Mrs. Winskey wasn't thrilled about me bothering her again. "Haven't you caused enough trouble already?" she demanded angrily.

"Ma'am," I said, trying to keep my voice devoid of the anger I was feeling, "your son and his friend kidnapped a woman. She was being held against her will, bound and gagged in the backseat of a car in your garage. And that's not all. Your son tried to kill me. Had I not been wearing a bulletproof vest, he probably would have succeeded. And you want to blame *me* for your troubles?"

The color in her face faded away. "That's only the beginning of the problems your son is facing. For all I know, he might be guilty of murder. The sheriff intends to find that out. What I want of you right now is to tell me where your son has been the past few days."

I stopped and watched her steadily. She squirmed uncomfortably. "I told you that he was working on a ranch in Nevada," she finally said without meeting my gaze.

"Yes, you did, and yet here he was, right here in your house when you last told me that. You lied. The lies are going to end or I'll do what I can to see to it that you spend the rest of your life in prison," I threatened. I didn't bother to tell her that the sheriff was already working on something that could result in prison time. "I expect an answer now. Where is the ranch he worked on? Or is there one? Did you lie about his having a job?"

"No, he has a job," she insisted, finally lifting her eyes to meet mine. A cloud of anger blanketed her face. "He wouldn't have needed to go there if it weren't for that selfish man, Glenn Gridley. He had no cause to fire my son."

"You don't know that," I said. "Someone was stealing money, lots of money, from Mr. Gridley. It made it impossible for him to continue to pay Vance."

"My son is not a thief," she said defensively.

"I didn't say he'd stolen the money," I countered. I did not say what I was thinking: that he had to have at least had knowledge of what Mace, Conrad, and possibly others were doing. I suspected it was more than just knowledge, but I didn't know that. "Where is the ranch?" I insisted.

She finally broke down and told me. I grabbed a nearby notepad and pen and scribbled down the address as she spoke. "But if you are thinking he stole that man's horses, he didn't. He's not a thief," she repeated.

"Are you trying to make me believe he didn't steal those two roping horses of the Gridleys?" I asked.

"He didn't steal them." She paused. "He traded for them. They are legally his."

"Where are they?" I asked, carefully masking my surprise.

"What does it matter?" she asked, a stubborn look on her face. "Like I just told you, they are his."

She had unwittingly told me what I had hoped to hear. I decided to let the sheriff deal with her from this point. I thanked her for her time and rejoined the law enforcement folks in the backyard. To the sheriff, I said, "We should hold that little horse trailer." I nodded in its direction. "Glenn's horses' DNA is on file at the association. If we need to, we might want to take some hair samples from the trailer, if we can find any. In the meantime, is there any way you could impound it?"

"Consider it done," he said. "How did your interview with Mrs. Winskey go? Did she admit anything to you?"

"Very little, except to claim that Vance made a legal trade for the missing horses. Let's just say that she believes her son can do no wrong. My task now is to find what he did with them."

I stayed at the Gridley ranch that night. We all slept easier knowing that two men were in custody. However, I worried about Mace. He seemed to have disappeared despite an extensive effort by the cops to find him. I couldn't help but wonder what he was up to. The two ranch hands were located, and before the night was over, they had been cleared by Blaine and the sheriff. They both begged Blaine, he told me later, to not repeat what they'd said about Glenn and Shanice. They were both ashamed that they'd even mentioned it, Blaine told me. I promised him that I would certainly never say a word about it.

Chapter Twenty-Eight

EVEN THOUGH IT WAS A very short night, I was up and on my way before anyone else stirred in the Gridley house. I was planning to spend the day doing what I had originally been hired to do—and, incidentally, what I had told the sheriff I would do. I was hunting for two very valuable roping horses. By eleven that morning, I pulled into the yard of a very large Nevada cattle ranch. I was startled to see, parked in front of a large and sprawling house, a silver Lexus with Utah plates.

I wasn't nearly as startled as Mace Healy was a minute later. He stepped out of the front door as I stepped up to it on the long veranda that ran the entire length of the front of the house. When Mace looked at my face, his jaw dropped, and he attempted to back into the house, but I nabbed him by the collar of his shirt and dragged him away from the door. He kicked, struggled, and did his best to hurt me. I admit my ribs and shoulder didn't appreciate it.

I pulled out a pair of PlastiCuffs that I carried for emergencies such as this. As I wrestled with him, I cinched them on his wrists while watching the door for anyone who might come to Mace's aid. I had him restrained before a large man with a big cowboy hat on his head came running through the open front door. My pistol was in my hand before he got close to me, and he skidded to a stop, his hands extended in front of him, palms out.

"Whoa there, mister," he said. "Don't be shooting anybody."

"Just stay put while I make sure this man doesn't cause me any more trouble."

"What's he done?"

"A lot," I said.

"This man is a killer, a robber, and a thief," Mace blurted. "Don't believe him."

"I am Rocky Revada, a private investigator," I said, speaking over the blubbering Mace. "I am working for the former employer of Vance Winskey. I'm looking for a pair of stolen roping horses that belong to Glenn Gridley and his daughter. I've also been working with Sheriff Andy Perkins from Box Elder County, Utah, who has a warrant for Mace here on charges of embezzlement."

The big man's eyes narrowed, and I worried about what he would do next. I really didn't want to have to shoot him, but considering my injures and his size, fighting him physically didn't seem like a winning proposition.

But I read his anger wrong. It was not directed at me but rather at Mace. "I thought there was something fishy," he said, turning his bright-red face toward Mace. "I wondered if those horses were worth a lot more money than you could have afforded. And I know Vance didn't have enough money to buy them."

He turned to me and held out his hand. "I'm Bryant Sherman," he said. "You won't need that gun. I own this place." I holstered my gun. He nodded at Mace, who was now sitting on the steps with his hands behind his back, his expensive pants dirty and scuffed and his shirt wrinkled and torn. "This man was introduced to me shortly after I hired Vance Winskey. The two of them brought a couple of nice horses here a few days ago. They claim they bought them in Wyoming. They have papers on them, but after I saw Vance riding them, I wondered where he got the money to buy horses of such high quality and extensive training. I don't suppose they could be the horses you're looking for?"

"I'm here to find that out," I said as I stuffed my gun back into the holster. "They are top roping horses and belong to Glenn Gridley and Shanice Overton, a rancher and his daughter from Box Elder County, Utah."

"Mace and I were just discussing moving them from here. But he didn't have a good explanation for why Vance wasn't here to move them himself. Vance works for me, and he's a pretty good hand," Bryant said. "But I haven't seen him for several days. He asked for some time off, saying that his mother was ill and he needed to make arrangements for her and then he'd be back."

"His mother is fine, physically. Vance is in custody. Well, actually, he's in the hospital under close guard, but he'll be going to jail as soon as a doctor declares him well enough. By now, his mother may be in jail too," I said, glancing at Mace, amused at the alarm in his eyes.

"What's Vance being charged with?" the big rancher asked.

"Oh, he'll face a number of charges. So far, the only ones I know of for sure are attempted murder and kidnapping," I said, turning my eyes again to Mace. "He shot me last night, but I was wearing a bulletproof vest." Mace's eyes continued to bulge, and he looked very ill. The color had completely drained from his face. For his benefit, I added, "I shot him and your friend Chase Overton, or should I say Chase Hideman? They will both recover and have a lot to say to the authorities about you."

"I didn't kill anybody," Mace said defensively.

"That may or may not be," I said. "Would you care to tell Mr. Sherman and me who *did* shoot someone?"

"It was Vance and Chase. They did the killing," he blurted.

The big rancher looked increasingly amazed, but he didn't say a word. I did. "Why did they kill Alden?" I asked.

To say that his answer was a surprise would not be the truth. Remembering what Pixie had told me, I was not shocked to hear him say, "Alden found out Vance and Chase had taken the horses," he said. "They killed him when he said he was going to make sure Glenn got them back."

I frowned at him and asked, "Why did they kill the bookkeeper, Conrad Patel?"

"Same reason," he said. I knew that was a lie. There was no way that Conrad had hired someone to kill me if it was his intent to see that the horses were returned.

I shook my head. "And also because he was going to rat on you for embezzling from the Gridley ranch," I said, doubting that was true, since Conrad was as guilty as Mace himself. "Or perhaps it was because Conrad took matters into his own hands and tried to have me blown up." Mace's guilt showed in his face. "They may have pulled the trigger, but you are just as guilty of murder as they are," I said coldly. "You encouraged them. And you also encouraged them to try to kill me."

He spluttered, but I turned away. "Mr. Sherman, we need the local sheriff out here."

While we waited for officers to come, I secured Mace in the back seat of my truck and then gave the rancher a brief account of what had happened over in Utah. He shook his head as I finished.

"Would you like to see the horses?" he asked.

"I can wait until the cops get here," I said. "And just in case you wonder, both horses have their DNA on file. Proving they are the ones I am after will be easy enough."

I then called Sheriff Andy Perkins and told him what I had been up to. He promised to head for Nevada with Detective Springer. A few minutes later, I got my first look at the horses. Then I made another call.

"Hello," Glenn's gruff voice sounded in my ear.

"I have your horses," I said flatly. "They are in Nevada. And I also have Mace Healy in custody. I think you and your family are truly safe now."

"Thank goodness," Glenn said breathlessly, and I heard a huge shout of joy from his family in the background.

That night, I found myself in the arms of the prettiest girl I've ever known. We spent some time in the barn, getting Switch One and Switch Two—I preferred my nicknames to their real names—ready to move the next day. Shanice was overjoyed that I'd found Licorice Stick, and I was rewarded with several kisses as we worked. It was hard to leave her at the ranch, even though she was safe now.

The drive back to my modest home in Logan was the loneliest I've ever experienced. That night, it was not just my aches and pains that kept me awake. Thoughts of Shanice and a possible future with her made sleep impossible.

It took a couple of days, but everything eventually became clear. The theft of the horses had been Vance's idea. He'd conjured up the switch as a way of getting back at Glenn Gridley. But he made a mistake when he enlisted the aid of his friend Chase Hideman. Chase was a friend of Mace who was up to his ears in embezzlement, something Vance claimed he knew nothing about. Alden had aided Mace, Conrad, and Chase in the embezzlement until he'd learned that Shanice and her family were among the host of victims. He was a crook, but he had never intended to hurt his daughter or her family. All of the men were involved in the illegal activities at the auto body, including Alden and Vance.

Mace had not originally been involved in the theft of the horses, but he could see the opportunity for a fast buck when the fine horses would sell quickly, so he wormed his way in. At that point, Alden had put his foot down about stealing the horses from the Gridleys just like he had about stealing money from them. Despite his many faults, he had apparently insisted that Shanice had never done anything to him, and he would not let his friends hurt her or her family anymore. His resistance cost him his life.

Conrad Patel had been recruited by Mace to assist in the embezzlement. He died because he knew too much and because he'd overstepped his bounds with the others. Mace eventually admitted that Conrad had become paranoid over the progress that I was making. He'd told Mace how nervous I was making him, but Mace had scoffed at it. It was after that when Conrad had decided, on his own, that I had to die. Hal Rodgers was totally innocent. He probably should have caught on to the embezzlement, but Mace and Conrad were both too smart for him.

Vance was the triggerman in both murders, assisted by Chase. Vance was again the triggerman when I was shot out on the ranch, but he was acting alone that time; Chase had not yet bonded out of jail. Ballistics done on a rifle found in Vance's bedroom at his mother's house proved that Vance was also the one who had killed the cows, though it never became clear why he'd done it. Not surprisingly, it was also he who had taken a couple of shots at the sheriff, Shanice, and me in the dark. The night vision scope he'd used was found in his mother's house with the rifle. Much of the truth was only discovered because the three men frantically pointed fingers at each other in an attempt to get a better deal from themselves. Unfortunately for them, despite their willingness to blame each other, good deals were not plentiful.

I had been right about the gun Vance used to try to kill me at his mother's place, the one I had handed to the sheriff. It was a .38-caliber pistol, and ballistics showed that it was the one Vance used against me. It had originally belonged to Alden Overton, as proven by the serial number. The sleeping bag that Vance and Chase had used to make it easier to drag their two victims was found, of all places, in Vance's little two-horse trailer. The lab had no trouble matching it with the small fragments of cloth that I had found along the route between the murder site and the ditch that the bodies had been dumped in. Finally, it was determined that it was Chase, fresh out of jail, who had gone out to the Gridley ranch with the intent of blowing up the house. The old car, which was in fact a Buick, was found at Chase's Auto Body, full of small holes made by Glenn's shotgun.

I never did find out for sure why Chase Hideman had posed as Alden's brother. I supposed that it had to do with some other criminal venture that none of us knew about. I guess it really didn't matter once the killings were solved. Chase would probably spend the rest of his life in prison, and no one cared what he called himself.

With the jailing of the killers and the return of the roping horses, my professional relationship with Glenn Gridley and his family came to an end. My personal relationship with Shanice, however, did not. We began to date almost immediately, and I found that my love for her was very real. One evening, about a month after the case had concluded, I was sitting in the Gridleys' family room, simply holding Shanice's hand and talking quietly with her, when Tyra came in.

She and I had formed quite a friendship, but I wasn't expecting what she said that evening. She stood with her hands on her hips and looked at us quite sternly. Then she said, "Mom, is Rocky going to be my new daddy or not?"

I grinned at Shanice, who looked quite taken aback. She glanced back and forth between me and her daughter for a moment before she said, "I don't know, Tyra. He hasn't asked me to marry him, and that has to happen for him to become your daddy."

Tyra turned her eyes on me, but before she could say anything more, I said, "Tyra, maybe it's time I do that."

I turned to Shanice and asked her to marry me. I admit it wasn't the most conventional way to propose, but Shanice and I aren't exactly a conventional couple. Shanice threw her arms around me and said, "I'd love to, Rocky." We made a date to go ring shopping the next afternoon.

Later that week, Shanice had a small but sparkling diamond on her ring finger, and Tyra helped us announce the engagement to the rest of the family. Glenn smiled and said, "You took my advice very well, Rocky. I know I was a bit rough on you at first, but I'm so grateful that you did what you did for me—for all of us. I will be proud to call you my son-in-law."

"And I'll be proud to call you my dad," Tyra chipped in.

It turns out I had been right all along. Shanice really was the most wonderful woman I ever could have hoped for. I still can't imagine anyone letting someone as special as Shanice get away. As for me, I consider myself the luckiest private investigator in the whole country. Never could I have imagined that the search for two switched horses would result in finding love with the woman of my dreams.

ABOUT THE AUTHOR

CLAIR M. POULSON RETIRED AFTER twenty years in law enforcement. During his career he seved in the U.S Army Military Police, the Utah Highway Patrol, and the Duchesne County Sheriff's Department, first as a deputy, then as the Duchesne County Sheriff. He currently serves as a justice court judge for Duchesne County, a postion he has held for about 20 years. His forty-year career working in the criminal justice system has provided a wealth of information from which he draws in writing his books.

Clair has served on numerous boards and committees over the years. Among them are the Utah Judicial Council, an FBI advisory board, the Peace Officer Standards and Training Council, the Utah Justice Court Board of Directors, and the Utah Commission on Criminal and Juvenile Justice.

Other interests include activity in the LDS church, assisting his son in the operation of their grocery store, ranching with his oldest son and other family members, and raising registered Missouri Fox Trotter horses and other farm animals.

With *Switchback,* Clair has published twenty novels, many of them bestsellers.

Clair lives in Duchesne, Utah, with his wife, Ruth, and are the parents five children. They have twenty-two grandchildren.